Praise for *A Slip in Time:*

ALSO BY KATHLEEN KIRKWOOD

A Slip in Time

SHADES
of the
PAST

Kathleen Kirkwood

A SIGNET BOOK

SIGNET
Published by New American Library, a division of
Penguin Putnam Inc., 375 Hudson Street,
New York, New York 10014, U.S.A.
Penguin Books Ltd, 27 Wrights Lane,
London W8 5TZ, England
Penguin Books Australia Ltd, Ringwood,
Victoria, Australia
Penguin Books Canada Ltd, 10 Alcorn Avenue,
Toronto, Ontario, Canada M4V 3B2
Penguin Books (N.Z.) Ltd, 182–190 Wairau Road,
Auckland 10, New Zealand

Penguin Books Ltd, Registered Offices:
Harmondsworth, Middlesex, England

First published by Signet, an imprint of New American Library,
a division of Penguin Putnam Inc.

First Printing, October 1999
10 9 8 7 6 5 4 3 2 1

To Josephine S. Williams, Dean of Arts & Letters, Charles County Community College, Maryland, my English 101 professor an eon ago. You lit a fire in my mind and heart for the art and craft of fiction and for its boundless possibilities. To you, my endless thanks.

Chapter 1

September 17, 1882
Royal Sherringham, ancient seat of the
   Viscounts Marrable
Herefordshire, England

Vanessa fought back a fresh rush of tears as she
slipped the small, cloth-covered Bible into Lady
Gwendolyn's still hands.

"Rest, dear friend. You are home at last at your
beloved Sherringham."

Bending, Vanessa placed a kiss to her late employer's
snowy head, then withdrew, lips trembling.

Lawrence Marrable, the younger of Lady Gwendolyn's twin nephews, quickly stepped forward.
Steadying Vanessa by the arm, he gently drew her back
into the small, black-clad circle of the Marrable family
where they stood at the fore of Knights Chapel.

Vanessa's gaze lingered a moment longer on Lady
Gwen's quiet form, lying pale in the open casket. But
then her control slipped, and hot tears spilled over her
cheeks and dampened the bodice of her dress.

"There now. Just a little longer," Lawrence heartened.
"When all is done you can seek the privacy of your
room and have it out." Producing a crisp handkerchief

from his coat pocket, he offered it in place of her sodden one. "Poor Vanessa. How crushingly hard this must be for you. I daresay you were closer to Aunt Gwen than any of us these past few years."

Vanessa blotted her cheeks with the large square of monogrammed linen, ignoring his intimate use of her given name since he had been so good to her otherwise. Ignoring, too, his disregard for what she'd made clear earlier. She would depart Sherringham directly after the interment and funeral feast.

Majel, the elder of Lawrence's two younger sisters, turned from her husband's side, her gaze flicking to Vanessa then to her brother. "It's not as though Auntie couldn't return. Had she wanted to, that is." Her gaze cut to Vanessa once more.

Vanessa froze in place, stunned by the inference. Did Majel believe *she* had prevented Lady Gwendolyn's return to her childhood home these past two and a half years? Vanessa started to assure Majel it was her aunt's dearest wish to make the journey back to Sherringham, but it had always been Lady Gwen's decision to put off returning home in favor of some other unexplored locale.

Before Vanessa could voice her thoughts, Majel turned toward her husband, Sir Nigel Pendergast, at the same time looking once again to her brother and encompassing him with her hazel gaze.

"We've delayed long enough, Lawrence. Mourners from the village have been gathering all morning at the mausoleum, and the children and our guests are waiting outside in the carriages for the procession to commence. We simply must begin the services."

"Oh, no, but we can't!" Cissy, the youngest of the Marrable siblings protested, sweeping forward from her own husband's side. "Adrian has yet to arrive. We cannot conduct the service without him."

"And precisely how long do you suggest we wait?" Majel's nostrils flared delicately. "It's deplorable he's not seen fit to join us already."

"Why do you assume the fault is his?" Cissy's voice rose defensively.

"And why do you assume it is not?"

At that, the two sisters dissolved into a peppery discussion, with their brother and spouses attempting to inject their own opinions and a measure of calm rationale.

Vanessa stepped apart of the animated clan, rubbing the space between her brows. It was not the first time the high-spirited family had disagreed over some aspect of the funeral arrangements. Poor Mr. Marrable—or rather "Lawrence," as he insisted she call him. He'd overseen every detail, doing his utmost to ensure the very finest provisions be made for his aunt and that all proceeded smoothly.

As the voices continued to rumble in her ears, Vanessa drew a breath and sought to regain hold of her own emotions. Slowly, she allowed her gaze to wander over the chapel and its rich Gothic interior.

Knights Chapel was exquisite, centuries old but carefully maintained, filled with a profusion of oak and stained glass. A huge clerestory window rose behind the altar while other, narrower ones, filled with bearded saints, lined the side walls. Before the railing of the sanctuary, bronze candelabras flanked Lady Gwendolyn's casket, while flowers overflowed the steps and stands, their heavy floral scent underlined by a slight mustiness of ancient wood and stone.

Sherringham, Vanessa had discovered, held many

treasures such as Knights Chapel. In truth, she'd seen only a small portion of the entire complex, but she could easily understand Lady Gwendolyn's longing to return.

And yet she hadn't.

Vanessa shifted her stance along with her thoughts as she walked toward a row of splendidly canopied stalls, intricately carved, the seats lined with cushions of crimson velvet.

Lady Gwen *had* intended to return, one day. Certainly, there had been opportunity. And yet, from the moment Vanessa first entered Lady Gwendolyn's employ as her companion, the two of them were ever bolting off in diverse directions throughout the Isles and the Continent.

These past years had been grand, exciting, breathless. But the choices of their destinations had all been Lady Gwen's. She'd meant to visit Sherringham, truly. But time suddenly ran dry. Lady Gwen died this week past of a massive apoplectic attack in their Paris apartments.

Vanessa glanced to where Lawrence stood with his sisters and brothers-in-law, the top of his bright head visible above theirs. She didn't know what she would have done without him. She'd known nowhere else to wire the sorrowful news but Sherringham, or rather "Royal" Sherringham, as it was properly called. Fortunately, Lawrence was in residence when her telegram arrived. He came at once to Paris and took charge of preparations to see herself and his late aunt home to England.

Vanessa's gaze drifted to the row of banners overhanging the family stalls and fastened on one in particular. It carried the distinctive coat-of-arms of the Marrables—a black panther with gold spots, rising from an equally black helm, surmounted by a viscount's coronet. The beast reared up in fight, its claws extended and painted blood red.

"No, no! We *cannot* begin without him," Cissy's cry snapped Vanessa's attention back to the group. "Adrian is Viscount after all, the family patriarch. Oh, Henry, convince them," she pleaded with her husband, Lord Norland. "It would be unseemly to inter Aunt Gwendolyn without him present. She was like a second mother to us all."

The remark elicited a sharp retort from Majel which, in turn, brought further debate over the "inexcusably absent" viscount.

Vanessa tried to envision an identical copy of Lawrence—hair full of sunshine, sky-blue eyes, a pronounced dimple in one cheek which gave him a boyish look. Patriarchs should be grayed or balding, she mused. But Adrian Marrable, like his twin brother, was but one and thirty years.

"My dear Cissy, we might delay a very long time indeed and never see poor Auntie laid to rest if we wait on our brother," Lawrence reasoned, as though he were solacing an hysterical child. "You know he hasn't returned since . . . well, since the accident."

Silence descended abruptly over the group like a pall. It was as though Lawrence had just uttered the unspeakable, something forbidden, taboo. As the foursome stood momentarily mute, Vanessa's mind scrambled for what little she knew of Lady Gwen's eldest nephew, the viscount.

"Notable but ill-fated," she'd once called him. Despite his age—midway through his twenty-eighth year when Vanessa first met Lady Gwendolyn—he had already been twice wed, and twice widowed, with each of his wives having died after brief marriages and each quite tragically.

Vanessa knew nothing of the specific circumstances surrounding the women's untimely deaths. Lady Gwen did not share them. Still, it was evident she ached for her nephew and his great misfortune.

Instinctively, Vanessa felt her gaze drawn once more to the banner where the fierce panther of the Viscounts Marrable seemed to rage against life itself.

"Then, it's settled," Lawrence declared. "For whatever reason Adrian has chosen not to appear, or to communicate his wishes or regrets with us at this sad time, it is our duty to continue in his stead."

Consulting his watch, he signaled to Mr. Brown, the undertaker, and his assistants to attend to the casket.

"The mourners have now waited an additional quarter-hour thanks to our indecisiveness. We shan't leave them a moment longer." Returning his timepiece to his pocket, he turned and started toward Vanessa.

As Lawrence moved to her side, Vanessa stole a parting glance of the banners overhead.

"Are you ready?" He encircled her shoulders with his arm and gave her a gentle squeeze.

Vanessa stiffened, surprised by his familiarity. But before she could object and step from his embrace, the Marrable banner, with its angry panther, stirred to life. The folds rippled conspicuously, as if caught on a sharp and sudden breeze. Yet there was none. None that she could perceive.

"Is something the matter?"

Too late Vanessa realized she had released a soft but audible gasp. "There. Do you see that?" She gestured to the fabric still swaying above them as it settled back into its original position.

"A draft, no doubt." Lawrence shrugged, releasing her shoulder. "Bound to have a good many of them in a place like Knights Chapel."

"But the other banners were not affected," she observed, drawing his attention to their dormant forms.

Again he shrugged. "Just an oddity. Sherringham has an abundance of those. Come along now. It's time."

Drawing her gaze downward, Vanessa glanced toward the coffin, glimpsing Lady Gwen's narrow hands and the volume they clasped as the lid closed over her.

Tears sprang to her eyes once more. Death was not unfamiliar to her, but that did not take away the awful finality of each passing.

"May you rest ever in peace, dear lady," Vanessa whispered softly. "You are home at last."

Slipping her hand through Lawrence's arm, she braced herself for the coming hour and allowed him to lead her out.

Despite the chill that clung to the morning air, the sun shone strong enough to warm Vanessa's cheeks as she stepped into its brilliant light.

A long row of carriages lined the drive, at their lead the windowless hearse, adorned with black ostrich feathers. Its four midnight horses bore the same inky plumes upon their heads, plus black leather trappings studded with silver and black velvet coverings on their backs.

Behind the hearse, in place of honor, stood the Marrable carriage which Majel and Cissy now mounted. They were assisted by the two official "mutes," the undertaker's solemn-faced staff, cloaked and sashed in lusterless black, with long crape weepers flowing from their tall hats.

Next came the Pendergast and Norland carriages containing the children—girls, all—who sat straight and silent, awaiting their lordly fathers to join them. Additionally, the fourth conveyance held two more of the Norland children, Beatrice, the youngest, and Geoffrey, the eldest and the only boy between both broods. Accompanying them were the only nonfamily members—Nurse Ridgely who attended Baby Bea, and Nanny Pringle who, as Vanessa understood it, had raised all four of the Marrable siblings and now lived in permanent retirement at Sherringham.

The remaining carriages were filled with an assortment of family friends and acquaintances, though positioned at the very rear were a number of empty equipages, sent by those unable to be in attendance.

Vanessa started to withdraw her hand from the crook of Lawrence's arm, thinking to seek a place in the latter vehicles. At the same moment, he paused before the fourth carriage and turned to assist her up.

Young Geoffrey, Cissy's eleven-year-old-son, smiled broadly and scooted close to Nanny, freeing a place beside him on the cushioned seat. Realizing Lawrence's intent and Master Geoffrey's expectations, Vanessa took a polite step back.

"Thank you, you are most kind. But my place is properly in the back carriages."

"We won't hear of it, will we, Geoffrey?" Lawrence shared a conspiratorial glance with his nephew who promptly shook his head. "Aunt Gwendolyn certainly would wish it. From her letters, we—that is, the family—know you brought her immeasurable happiness."

A deep-felt pleasure stole through Vanessa at his words. "I do hope that's true, still it would be inappropriate for me to—"

"As a personal favor then," Lawrence interrupted, leaning close for her alone to hear. "The lad could use a bit of help with Nanny despite what my sister thinks."

Vanessa glanced past his shoulder to where Nanny sat beside Geoffrey, fumbling with the ribbons that dangled from her bonnet. Suddenly the boy's presence in the carriage became clear. Nanny tended to be a "bit fuddled" these days, according to Cissy. Lawrence, she knew, deemed Nanny's condition more serious, her lapses in memory progressively worsening, though she could recall the past with astonishing clarity.

From what Vanessa had observed during her brief stay at Sherringham, she tended to agree with Lawrence. Still it was both thoughtful and perceptive of Cissy to arrange a companion for Nanny, even one so young as Geoffrey.

Vanessa looked to the boy and smiled. "I would be honored to ride with you," she agreed, though in truth she felt completely out of place to be included within the family circle.

At that, Lawrence handed her up, then touching the brim of his hat, withdrew to join his brothers-in-law. The three waited respectfully for the coffin to be borne to the hearse before climbing into their own respective carriages. Moments later the somber procession pulled away from the portals of Sherringham.

Geoffrey continued to smile at Vanessa. He was a bright, cheerful lad who'd been her second shadow since her arrival. Just now, he looked as though he wished to make conversation but hadn't a hint of what to say.

With a jolt and a sway, the carriage left the main road, entering a narrow track that stretched across luxuriant open fields. Nanny's hands quieted, and she gazed out over the expanse to lofty but distant trees. Meanwhile, Baby Bea nestled in her nurse's plump arms, and despite the jolting, fell asleep.

"Is this the customary way to the mausoleum?" Vanessa pulled her gaze from the scene and turned to Geoffrey.

He nodded, still smiling. "It lies past the follies. Well, two of them anyway—the Abbey Ruin and the Orangery."

"Ah, follies, how delightful." It did not surprise her that Sherringham possessed those picturesque and ofttimes fanciful edifices aristocrats were so fond of raising in their landscape gardens.

"Do you like them? Some of Sherringham's are quite old and authentic too," Geoffrey continued, enthused by her interest. "Others are only made to look that way. Uncle calls those 'sham ruins.' They are scattered all over the estate. Uncle says the idea is for each folly to be hidden from sight of the others so when one happens upon them it seems as if they've stepped back into another time."

"What a lovely thought," Vanessa commented, thinking it supremely romantic. "And what else does he say?"

Geoffrey straightened. "That it is the duty of each of the Marrable men who inherit the estate to improve it in some way so that future Marrables might enjoy Royal Sherringham for generations to come."

"How very noble." Vanessa felt a warm glow in her heart for this man and his high ideals. "I think your Uncle Lawrence is quite right."

"Oh, not Uncle Lawrence. Uncle Adrian."

Vanessa's heart dropped from its place. She wished to snatch back her bit of flattery. Though she'd kept her sentiments concealed, it rankled sorely that Viscount Marrable had not the civility to appear for his aunt's funeral, a woman who, if Cissy had the right of it, had been "as a mother" to him.

Geoffrey's eyes suddenly brightened. "Oh, look, there is my favorite folly now."

As they passed a wooded copse of towering oaks, the skeletal remains of an ancient abbey came into view. Its haunting silhouette leaned against the sky, conjuring ages past.

"The south side is real, part of a thirteenth-century cloister that was moved stone-by-stone from Wales after King Henry destroyed it," Geoffrey explained. "The rest is a sham. Mama used to let us play there but Uncle won't allow it anymore."

Nanny, who had been listening intently, suddenly leaned forward and pinned Vanessa with her small round eyes.

"I told the boys not to dally there. Portions of the ruins are crumbling, you know. The viscount was very angry when they disobeyed me."

Vanessa leveled Geoffrey a surprised look. "You and your companions directly disobeyed Nanny?"

Geoffrey's brows shot upward. "I? Er, no . . ."

Nanny studied the boy, confusion clouding her eyes, then the look cleared.

"Not Master Geoffrey. Dear, no. He's a good boy. Always listens. I was speaking of Masters Adrian and Lawrence. Now, they are a handful, I can tell you."

She stopped again, her brows knitting.

"I mean, they *were*. Indeed yes, they were." She patted Geoffrey on the hand. "Your Uncle Lawrence is right. The ruins are dangerous. You must stay away from them, child."

Vanessa tilted her head. Surely, Nanny had confused Lawrence's name with Adrian's, the viscount. Not that it mattered which brother forbade the children to play here, as long as one did.

The procession trundled on, the ruins disappearing from view. In short order, they came upon a second building, this one so exquisite it stole her breath. The creamy, fairy-tale confection sat amid a glade at the end of a long reflection pool. The shape, she could scarcely define. Two octagonals joined by a narrow central hall, she would say. The whole of it rose two stories high while a smaller, central tower crowned this, adding a third story.

Despite the plentiful use of Gothic embellishments, the pavilion was an airy, lyrical creation, its surface seemingly faceted. This was due to a multitude of large, gracefully arched windows, each filled with a dozen hexagonal panes. Vanessa studied them closer, realizing the windows on ground level were not glazed at all but completely open, the hexagonal partitions empty.

"That is the Orangery." Geoffrey pointed to the won-drous construction. "It was to be Uncle Adrian's addi-tion to Sherringham. He began it for his last wife, Mama says. But he stopped work on it after she died."

"How sad. It's far too beautiful to leave abandoned."

"Oh, don't worry. Uncle Lawrence convinced Uncle Adrian to allow him to finish it. When it's complete, Uncle Lawrence promises it will house all kinds of ex-otic trees and plants. Maybe even some tropical birds. He calls it Sherringham's most special treasure box."

"If it is unfinished, as you suggest, might I assume your uncle doesn't permit you to play here either?"

"No, but there are other follies we are allowed to play around, if we have adults with us." His smile widened.

Vanessa returned the smile, suddenly wishing she had more time to linger at Sherringham and seek out its many fascinating and varied secrets. As it was, her train would leave Hereford late this afternoon.

"Geoffrey, you said the mausoleum lies past the second folly. Are we near to it then?"

"It's just over the rise. Uncle considers it one of Sherringham's finest works of architecture."

"Truly now?" She eased back in her seat, not asking to which uncle he referred or what could be so enamoring about a house of the dead.

Minutes later the path dipped downward, and the funeral cortege entered a small forested dell. At the heart of the hollow dwelled a circular temple of classical design, elevated on a high podium and colonnaded all around. A large dome dominated the structure, floating above a band of windows. Vanessa deemed the edifice neither Greek nor Roman, precisely, but certainly evocative of those ancient times. Truly, as Geoffrey said, it seemed they had just passed into yet another world.

Single file, the carriages progressed around the mausoleum to the far side. There, wide marble steps marked it as the building's front and ascended to massive bronze doors adorned with black wreaths. Before the building, the open green stretched several hundred yards then abruptly dropped away, exposing a view of the River Wye rushing at a far distance below.

Here, too, before the steps, gathered a substantial crowd, waiting to pay their last respects to a grand lady and lay her to rest.

Vanessa helped Geoffrey aid Nanny Pringle and Mrs. Ridgely from the carriage, then accompanied them to join the family and Canon Greeley. As they came to stand with the other children behind Lawrence and their parents, Majel turned and swept a cool look over Vanessa, arching a brow at her presence.

Seeing this, Cissy instantly reached back and gave a squeeze to Vanessa's hand. "We are all so glad you are here," she heartened, then darted a reproving look at her sister.

As the pallbearers bore the coffin from the hearse to the funeral bier, erected before the steps, the three women faced forward again and looked on with silent respect.

Periodically, Cissy glanced over her shoulder as if in search of someone. No doubt she sought her brother, the viscount, Vanessa reasoned, for despite his failings this day, his sister remained steadfast in her faith of him. Oddly, in that moment, Vanessa saw herself reflected in Cissy, reminding her of her own unswayable faith in a man, a man once pledged and joined to her, but perpetually absent from her life.

As the canon intoned the Prayers of the Dead, Cissy relinquished her vigil, as did Vanessa her thoughts of the man she had buried three years past.

The clergyman continued his recitation, his melodious voice soon fading to a singsong chant in her ears. Vanessa fought her wandering mind but with no great success. Death had altered the course of her life once more. Still, she would not soon forget this exceptional time in her life.

Vanessa glanced over the crowd, again struck by the number in attendance and by their genuine outpouring of love. Lady Gwen had touched so many lives. How her family and friends must have missed her these last years. But of course, the loss was hers as well.

Majel's words came needling back to prick at

Vanessa's thoughts. Why *hadn't* Lady Gwen returned when, seemingly, she had every reason to do so?

Vanessa's eyes shifted to the polished, elm coffin with its spray of white lilies. Only Lady Gwen held that answer, and she took it now with her to the tomb.

The canon closed his prayer book. Lowering it before him, he folded his hands over the volume and addressed the gathering. Nanny sniffled into her black-edged hanky as he began to share his own recollections of the ever vibrant and generous Lady Gwendolyn Marrable.

Vanessa found herself fighting back her own tears once more but fortified herself, hoping the services were near to completion.

Officially, the funeral observances began two days earlier when Sherringham opened its doors for the customary public viewing. Last night, Lady Gwen was moved to Knights Chapel for a formal and extended prayer service, at which time Lawrence delivered the eulogy in his brother's stead. This morning the coffin was opened for a final viewing for the immediate family, preceded only by a brief photographic session in order to catch the morning light.

For Vanessa, the custom of photographing the deceased seemed a rather morbid practice, but wishing to please the family, she did as they asked. Lady Gwen, an expert and accomplished photographer in her own right, had personally tutored Vanessa in the art. Apparently, Lady Gwen had written the family glowing reports of her progress. Thus, confident of Vanessa's abilities, they made their request.

Cissy especially asked that Vanessa assemble a "mourning album" in her aunt's memory and include individual portraits of the family. After all, she pointed out, Aunt Gwendolyn's death had been the catalyst for drawing the family back together at Sherringham. They had not been so for a very long time. Not since the last funeral, that of the most recent Viscountess Marrable.

Vanessa held the sittings yesterday afternoon. The viscount's portrait, naturally, was not among those taken. Nor did she intend to substitute another in the album. Let the volume speak for itself, honestly reflecting this occasion.

She felt her ire rising once more. One should not judge another, still she found the viscount's absence indefensible. Oh, had she but two solid minutes with the man, face-to-face, wouldn't she furnish him with a few sharp opinions of her own on the matter of such negligence?

Before she could draw a breath, the thud of hooves and heavy rumble of wheels reverberated in her ears. Turning, Vanessa spied a shiny black coach rounding the drive. As it rolled to a halt before the mausoleum, she saw it bore a distinctive coat-of-arms on its door— that of a fierce, growling panther, its claws spread and ready for battle.

Vanessa took a deep swallow, not needing to ask who rode inside. Dear Lord, had she conjured the man by mere thought?

Murmurs rippled through the crowd and she heard the viscount's name gasped from many a pair of lips. In front of her, several paces away, Lawrence stilled, his features turning to granite.

"Well, well, if it isn't Viscount Marrable," he uttered as if to himself. "So Adrian's made the funeral after all."

The coldness of his tone startled Vanessa. It was not at all sympathetic as earlier in the chapel when he defended his brother's absence. To the contrary, his voice now held a purely derisive note.

Vanessa returned her gaze to the coach where the footman hastened to open the door. Her pulses quickened. What had Lawrence said? His brother hadn't returned since the "accident"? Presumably, he referred to the death of the last viscountess.

Her thoughts deserted her as the door opened and a man began to emerge. She waited, breath pent, anticipating the familiar golden features that would perfectly duplicate Lawrence's own.

Instead, a dark and powerful figure appeared, his broad shoulders momentarily filling the carriage door as he stepped out and descended. He wore a long, black frock coat and a mourning band on his arm. His tall silk hat shadowed his face, yet his eyes burned beneath its brim, their color as dark as his sable hair.

Vanessa fought to keep her chin from dropping to her chest. Why had she presumed the brothers to be identical? No one actually ever suggested as much, not even Lady Gwen. Obviously, Adrian and Lawrence Marrable were fraternal twins. In looks at least, the two were as different as night from day.

As the viscount started forward, the crowd parted, opening a wide path before him. Looking neither right nor left, he proceeded toward the mausoleum, his lips a tight, unsmiling line set above a hard, square-cut jaw. As he neared the place where the Marrable family stood, his eyes sheered to Lawrence, scalding him with his look.

Shivers skimmed along Vanessa's neck and spine. She could not fathom the man's behavior. Was it so aversive to him to return to Sherringham?

Severing his gaze from his brother, the viscount continued on, advancing to where the coffin reposed upon the bier and the canon stood with prayer book in hand, his fingers trembling noticeably.

But the master of Sherringham ignored the cleric and afforded him not a second's glance. Reaching into his coat, he withdrew a single white rose and placed it atop his aunt's coffin. Then, sinking to one knee, he laid a gloved hand upon the elmwood and bowed his head. After a prolonged moment of silent meditation, he rose again to his feet, but not before he leaned toward the casket and pressed a light kiss to its side.

What criticisms Vanessa held of Adrian Marrable dissolved in her heart. Those around her appeared equally astounded as she.

Turning on his heel, the viscount headed toward the Marrable clan, swiftly closing the distance between them. Fire kindled in his eyes once more while tension spread along his jaw, sharpening its line.

As he came to stand before them, he swept his gaze over his brother, his sisters, and their husbands, then glanced past them to the children and Nanny Pringle. His dark eyes next fell upon Vanessa and he paused, his brows drawing together.

Heat flushed through her, straight from her scalp to her toes. He continued to study her, obviously having not the slightest notion as to her identity or why she, a stranger, stood among his relatives. Oh, why did she agree to Lawrence's request and allow herself to be included where she did not belong?

Something flickered in the depths of his eyes just then, but in the next instant, he broke away his gaze and directed it to Lawrence.

"We will speak later, brother." His fine rich voice carried back to Vanessa. "For now, I would know what arrangements remain concerning the interment."

The viscount's expression darkened as Lawrence apprised him of the final provisions for the funeral rites.

"You mean to say, *all* the pallbearers are supplied by Mr. Brown's establishment? Is there not one relation or friend among them to see our aunt to her crypt?"

"Brother"—Lawrence's voice softened to a conciliating tone—"surely you realize, the closest of her acquaintances are older than she. I did arrange for a number of them to be honorary pallbearers, with Mr. Brown providing alternates to act in their place."

"And are *we* in our dotage?" the viscount challenged, bringing a look of surprise to Lawrence's face.

"It was unclear you would arrive in time, and more, the grieving family is not expected to—"

Adrian stepped toe-to-toe with his brother, standing a full six inches above him and glaring down hard at him.

"Some things should not be given over to others. And sometimes it's best to do the unexpected. Aunt Gwendolyn deserves our hearts *and* our hands this day. By God, she shall have mine."

At that, he motioned over the undertaker, and announced the he, himself, would replace one of the pallbearers.

"Adrian, you *cannot*." Majel bristled. "It is unbefitting your station as viscount to labor at what others are employed to do. Think of propriety, brother."

At that he spun on her. "Propriety be damned! I shall have my will in this, with or without your approval, or anyone else's."

He tugged at his gloves, at the same time eyeing Lawrence and Lords Norland and Pendergast.

"Join me or not, as you will, but my mind is firm. I shall carry Aunt Gwendolyn in death, as she carried me in life, when I could not bear myself."

With that he stalked toward the coffin and Canon Greeley who stood gaping, his mouth dropped wide.

"I will help you, Uncle!" Geoffrey blurted, breaking from Vanessa's side and slipping between his mother and Uncle Lawrence. He rushed to join the viscount, crooking back his head to look up at him. "Please, Uncle, may I help?"

Vanessa watched amazed as the boy waited expectantly, displaying not a whit of fear of his lordly uncle. Others, much older, positively quaked before the man, she noted, their perceptions obviously far different. Still, as she watched Adrian Marrable give an approving pat to Geoffrey's shoulder, she could only wonder if the boy's perceptions might be the more trustworthy.

A step away, Cissy smiled proudly at her son, tears rimming her eyes. She turned her watery gaze to her husband who appeared equally moved.

"I shall lend my strength as well," Lord Norland volunteered, stepping forward.

Lawrence remained stock-still, coloring to a deep, ruddy red. A hard, bright anger flashed in his eyes.

If the brothers shared any similarities, perhaps it was a choleric temperament, Vanessa thought fleetingly. Yet Lawrence's aspect transfixed her, jarring her back to an incident in Paris, shortly after he arrived.

It had been a trivial matter over a bit of spilled wine. In truth, Lawrence was the one who caused the mishap. To her mortification, he exploded in a fit of rage, berating the waiter and making a rude scene in the hotel dining room to the embarrassment of all. Now as she looked on his mien, so like that night, she wondered that she'd forgotten it.

Lord Pendergast's voice drew Vanessa's attention as he argued a point with his wife. He then spoke briefly with Lawrence. Though a muscle continued to twitch in his jaw, Lawrence acquiesced and, together, they strode toward the others and relieved two more of the pall-bearers. Majel watched, fury in her face.

Reopening his prayer book, Canon Greeley began reading the Twenty-third Psalm as he led the small procession up the mausoleum steps. Cissy and Majel now also followed, leaving the children to their nurses' care. Accompanied by Mr. Brown, they trailed at a respectful distance behind the coffin and its bearers.

"We must wait now," Nanny informed Vanessa, nodding as the others disappeared inside the mausoleum. "It is Marrable custom for only the family and necessary attendants to enter the crypt during interments. It is a most private time, of course."

"Of course," Vanessa echoed, noting the mourners remained essentially where they stood, breaking into clusters and murmuring quietly among themselves.

Nanny, meanwhile, moved off to gather the wildflowers sprinkled over the lawn, white corn-daisies and purple heartsease. Vanessa strolled close behind, lest Nanny wander too near the promontory's edge.

Twenty minutes lapsed before anyone issued from the mausoleum. The Pendergasts first appeared, followed by the Norlands with young Geoffrey at his mother's side.

Descending to the bottom steps, Majel, who had presided as Sherringham's official hostess these past days, addressed the crowd, extending her gratitude for their presence. With that she instructed the servants to distribute the family's gifts of mourning gloves and scarves to those who had come up from the village and not yet received them.

Ensconced in their carriage once more, the Pendergasts led the entourage back to the mansion while the villagers disbursed across the green and down the road.

Happily, Geoffrey quickly rejoined Vanessa for it took considerable effort to persuade Nanny to abandon the unpicked flowers and return to their carriage. At last, bouquet in hand, Nanny climbed heavily into her seat, situating herself across from Nurse Ridgely and Baby Bea. Without pause, Geoffrey and Vanessa followed.

As the driver snapped the reins and the horses pulled away, Adrian and Lawrence Marrable emerged from the mausoleum's great bronze doors. Lawrence stilled his step and looked straight toward her, but in so doing, drew his brother's gaze. Adrian followed Lawrence's line of sight, finding Vanessa at its end.

In the crisp autumn air, she went inexplicably warm as the viscount's dark eyes fastened on hers. Instincts deep within knelled their cautioning bells. But of what they warned remained unclear.

Vanessa shook away her sudden unease. There was nothing of which to be concerned, she chided herself, aware of her racing heart. In roughly four hours' time, she would board her train and depart Sherringham and this man forever.

Chapter 2

Vanessa revisited her bedroom long enough to re-move her cloak and bonnet, secure her trunks, and refresh herself.

She splashed her face with cool water, smoothed her hair into place, then stepped before the full-length mirror to assess her appearance.

She grimaced. The dull black bombazine of her mourning dress siphoned all color from her face, leaving her a pallid-looking creature. Even her aqua-gray eyes appeared drained of their normal blue and green hues, turning them to slate.

Her hair improved matters little, the honeyed mass being swept back from her features and coiled into a heavy chignon at the nape of her neck. Only the fringe of soft curls framing her face added any color.

Very little color, Vanessa decided as she regarded the image that stared back at her. Stepping closer to the glass, she pinched color to her cheeks and bit her lips. It wouldn't last, but there was little more she could do.

With a sigh she drew back, trying to ignore the translucent quality of her skin and the tiny blue veins visible beneath her eyes, trying to ignore how her face had thinned in a single week's time. Lord, it was a wonder someone hadn't attempted to carry her off to the crypt this day, mistaking her for one of the departed.

Vanessa shut her mind to her looks and transferred her attention to her attire, a tailored, three-piece combination comprised of a pleated underskirt, bustled overskirt, and a fitted bodice with jet buttons running down its front. A large intaglio brooch fastened the high collar, the piece as coal black as everything else she wore.

As Vanessa made an adjustment to her skirts and the soft bustle gathered at the back, a knock sounded at the door. The maid, Mary Ethel, entered in the next breath, her hands clasped before her.

"You wished to see me, madam?"

"Yes, Mary Ethel." Vanessa smiled, pleased the girl had come so promptly. "I must leave for Hereford Station no later than two o'clock. Mr. Marrable has arranged for a carriage, but my trunks will need to be carried down and loaded before then."

Vanessa crossed the room to where her luggage stood to the left of the door. "As you see, there are three pieces. The men will need to take particular care with the two marked Breakables. Those contain my photographic equipment and chemicals."

Mary Ethel nodded attentively. "And what of the box, there by the bed? Should the men take that as well?"

Vanessa looked to the sizable square box sitting on the floor, V. G. WYNTERS stenciled on the sides.

"No. It holds my undeveloped plates. I'll return later to carry it down personally." She smiled. "That way, should anything break, I can only blame myself."

Mary Ethel again nodded her understanding and turned to leave. With a start, Vanessa remembered Lawrence's handkerchief and called to the maid. Producing the linen from a hidden pocket in her skirt, she gave it over.

"Please see this is laundered and returned to Mr. Marrable."

"Yes, madam." Mary Ethel eyed the embroidered initials adorning the handkerchief then, with a courteous bob of her head, withdrew.

Vanessa skimmed a glance over the room once more, wishing she could have visited under happier circumstances. The guest bedchamber, like so much at Sherringham, was a gem. Decorated in the Gothic Revival style, it possessed several centuries-old pieces plus the most charming of windows—a six-lobed rosette, filled with mullioned glass and bearing a heraldic device.

She wished she would have had the opportunity to photograph it, and so much more at Royal Sherringham. The preparations surrounding the funeral had left little time. Then, too, there were the arrangements she had to make pertaining to her own immediate future.

Her future. *What lay there*, she wondered, then put the thought aside. For now, she must attend to the present and see through the funeral feast before taking her leave. The future would be upon her all too quickly, wherever it led.

Quitting the chamber, she made her way along the vaulted passageway of what was called the Upper Cloisters. Here the vaulted, ribbed ceiling soared overhead while beautiful Gothic windows arched along the right wall, overlooking an enclosed courtyard. Classical busts, mounted on pedestals, stood between each window. Despite the mix of styles, the ecclesiastical tone prevailed. She'd not be surprised if a long-robed monk appeared any moment from an adjoining corridor.

Vanessa smiled at that thought as she came to a flight

of stairs and turned onto them. They reminded her of the turreted stairs of centuries past, the stone steps twining narrowly downward. Presumably, this section of Sherringham owned a great age. How old, she could not begin to guess, though Geoffrey told her Sherringham had its beginnings as a border castle on the Welsh Marches. Before that, he divulged, wide-eyed, the place had been the site of ancient Druid worship and ritual.

That thought sent a decided chill sledding through her. Gratefully, she reached a landing at that moment. Though the stone steps continued to spiral downward, she abandoned them, passing through an arched portal and entering a long, broad gallery.

Here the decor changed dramatically, dispatching all thoughts of robed monks, border lords, and Druid priests. Though Gothic inspired, the opulent gallery was far different from anything the medievals ever experienced. Crimson-colored damask covered the walls, rising above milky-white paneling, trimmed with gold. Overhead, ornate plasterwork embellished the ceiling, festooning it with gilded circles, trefoils, and medallions.

Midway down, the gallery opened onto one of Sherringham's two grand staircases leading to the ground level and entrance hall. Vanessa began her descent, pleasuring in the journey as ever she did. The elegant staircase turned back on itself time and again, offering intriguing vistas through additional landings and corridors. Tapestries and paintings graced the walls, while a huge glass lantern hung suspended in the stairwell on a heavy bronzed chain, all of uncertain age.

However far back Sherringham's history truly reached, Vanessa was aware that, early in the last century, its owners had enthusiastically embraced the Gothic Revival movement. For more than a hundred and fifty years, the viscounts had restored, refurbished, transformed, and added to Sherringham with a zealous passion. She imagined it cost them a staggering fortune. Perhaps, several.

The stairs brought her to a large chamber at the front of the manor house, adjacent to the entrance hall. A second grand staircase flanked the opposite side, in a similar chamber. In truth, the rooms and doors along the front of the manse aligned in such a way as to provide an extended perspective in either direction.

Vanessa glanced into the entrance hall and observed the activity there where a number of the guests mingled and conversed. Recognizing none of them, she began to withdraw her gaze. Just then, the heavy front door opened wide and Adrian and Lawrence Marrable appeared.

Vanessa's limbs momentarily froze as they entered, and she found she could do no more than stare. The others stared too, pausing in their conversations. One-by-one, they offered reserved, though polite, acknowledgment of the viscount's presence.

He acknowledged them as well, with equal restraint, his bearing aristocratically remote, unapproachable. A near tangible tension crackled about him, and she thought of a panther caged.

Vanessa continued to watch, fascinated, as he removed his overcoat and hat and gave them over to one of the servants. She saw now that Adrian Marrable possessed a wondrously thick mane of hair. Saw, too, how his profile was perfectly straight and his eyes deep-set, bordered with long black lashes.

She transferred her gaze to Lawrence as he, too, divested himself of his outer garments. Curiously, he neither looked nor spoke to his lordly brother, nor anyone else in the hall. Instead, he strode unsmiling from view.

Before Vanessa could dwell on it further, a movement caught her eye. A stout man with balding pate left his place by the portal and approached the viscount, causing him to turn in her direction.

Recovering herself, Vanessa quickly moved off before he could catch sight of her or entrap her once more with his dark, possessive gaze.

She headed toward the Grand Saloon, expecting the preponderance of the funeral guests to be gathered there. Entering, she found herself more than correct. A crush of people filled the magnificent room, overflowing the furniture and standing about in small clutches.

She scanned the room for a familiar face, realizing it likely to be a futile gesture. She knew scarcely a soul. Most of the guests had arrived only yesterday and were primarily distant relatives and acquaintances of Lady Gwendolyn from years past. Most of her more recent friends, those whom they'd visited during their extensive travels, were wide flung and naturally unable to attend.

Vanessa did glimpse Cissy and Majel moving through the room, speaking individually with the guests and receiving their condolences. Recognizing no one else, Vanessa threaded her way slowly through the body of people, making her way toward the immense bay window on the opposite side.

Of all the rooms she'd been privileged to see at Sherringham, the Grand Saloon was her favorite. More than any other, she wished she might have photographed it, for words simply could not capture its breathtaking beauty as adequately as a lens.

What most won her heart and awed her to speechlessness was the extravagant, lacelike plasterwork that erupted over the ceiling, encrusting it with a profusion of decorative webbing and motifs. Even the towering bay, with its double row of traceried windows, rose beneath a canopy of the riotous, petrified lace.

Vanessa came to stand there now and look out on the formal gardens, in the last of their bloom. Surely, there was an enchantment cast over Sherringham, for even in the short space of a week she'd felt its unmistakable pull. Indeed, not for the first time this day, she must wonder how Lady Gwen could have borne to leave the place, not once to return.

She tried to refocus her thoughts and concentrate on the shrubbery without, clipped to interesting shapes. But instead of greenery, her mind's eye beheld the image of dark, magnetic eyes.

"My dear, there you are!" a high, familiar voice trilled. Just to her left, a round little couple rose from the settee and hastened to join her at the window. Vanessa had overlooked Mr. and Mrs. Billingsworth, though she'd been informed of their arrival early this morning.

"Dear Vanessa, how are you bearing up, poor girl?" The woman patted Vanessa's hand, her eyes filled with compassion. She chattered on without drawing a breath. "Such tragic news, and we all dined together just last month in Yorkshire."

"Just last month," Mr. Billingsworth echoed, shaking his head gravely.

"Gwendolyn seemed in the bloom of health, positively robust. Didn't I say so that very night, Mr. Billingsworth?"

"Indeed, sweeting, that very night."

"And now she's gone and all so quickly," the woman wailed dramatically. She stopped abruptly and darted a look around. "Why, my dear, you appear quite alone. But of course you are, with our Gwendolyn gone. How foolish of me. You simply must lunch with us. We insist. Don't we Mr. Billingsworth?"

"Actually, I'd hoped Miss Wynters would grant me the honor and dine with me," a deep, rich voice sounded directly behind Vanessa.

She spun on her heel, gasping her breath as her eyes collided with those of Adrian Marrable. She felt instantly swallowed by his ebony gaze. A cautioning alarm warned once more from deep within, but now it clanged like a deafening bell.

"You *are* Vanessa Wynters are you not? My aunt's companion?"

Vanessa nodded, unable to coax a single word from her throat, afraid it would come out a miserable squeak if she did. The man positively towered over her, a dark impressive figure. Again she sensed the tension enveloping him, palpable and barely leashed.

He studied her closely. "Forgive me. We have not been introduced. I am—"

"The panther," she murmured, the words slipping past her lips before she could stop them. Heat shot to her cheeks as she stood in utter shock of herself. She cleared her throat. "I—I mean, I recognized the coat-of-arms on your carriage, the black panther. You are Viscount Marrable."

Maybe God would be kind and open a wide crack in the floor for her to jump in, she thought wildly. She was about to die from acute mortification anyway.

The viscount tilted his head and gave her a quizzical look. Vanessa felt herself shrink under his penetrating stare, causing him to loom even larger before her eyes.

The side of his mouth twitched. "I've only arrived this

hour, as you are obviously aware. My brother's wire was rather terse, as those things tend to be. I regret I know almost nothing of my aunt's passing. I am told you were with her at the time."

"Y-Yes," Vanessa managed. "She died in my arms."

At that, a servant appeared at the door and announced the luncheon was served.

The viscount proffered his arm. "I shall be interested in learning all you can tell me of my aunt's last hours, and anything else you might offer."

Vanessa found she could not decline. Had he not exhibited a fine devotion to Lady Gwendolyn, despite his lateness to the service? Surely, she could answer his questions before she departed Sherringham.

Laying her hand atop his arm, Vanessa allowed the viscount to escort her from the room.

It startled looks followed their withdrawal, she remained wholly unaware of them, for Adrian Marrable had trapped her in his midnight gaze once more, and she found she could look upon no other.

As Lord Marrable conducted Vanessa through the great double doors of the banqueting hall, she pulled her gaze from his and transferred it to the immense, medieval-style chamber, wholly dissimilar to the saloon.

The ceiling arced two stories high over a space seventy, perhaps eighty, feet in length. Enormous triple windows filled one wall, glowing with stained glass, as did a row of smaller trefoil windows above them. Oak paneling warmed the remaining walls while elaborate, carved woodwork crowned the doors. Pennants, antlers, and huge bronze chandeliers further enhanced the decor, lending it a masculine air.

As the viscount guided Vanessa left of the banqueting table, she felt a muscle tense in his arm, beneath her fingers.

"The hall dates to Elizabeth's reign," he offered abruptly, unexpectedly, as they proceeded toward the chamber's far end.

Warmth spread through Vanessa as she realized he'd been watching her.

"It served as an entrance for many years but fell into disuse over time," he added informatively. "My great-grandfather remodeled it, preserving many period elements while satisfying his own tastes. Does it meet with your approval?"

Surprised he would ask her opinion, Vanessa kept her eyes studiously fixed on the opposite end of the room. There a massive crenellated chimneypiece scaled the wall.

"Very much so. I find all at Sherringham enthralling, though I confess to know little of architectural styles."

She moistened her lips, pleased she'd been able to complete two coherent sentences without faltering. Emboldened, she pressed on.

"In my travels with Lady Gwendolyn, I encountered nothing to compare to Royal Sherringham, though I understand some say it rivals its neighbor, Eastnor Castle."

"And some say it surpasses it."

His clipped words took her aback. Naturally, he would be proud and defensive of his own estate. But, had he mistaken her meaning? Or was it the reminder of his aunt's long absence that sharpened his voice? Yet, somehow, she'd detected no censure in his tone.

Vanessa stole a sideways glance of him, mindful of his own architectural accomplishment—the lyrical pavilion in the glade. It struck her as incongruous that this forbidding man should create something infused with such passion, light, and grace. And certainly with love.

If he'd built the Orangery for his last viscountess, as Geoffrey had claimed, then surely he'd loved her to excess. Perhaps that explained the barrier she sensed surrounding him, shielding a heart cleaved with pain.

"I've not had occasion to visit Eastnor and own no opinion of it," she said at last, attempting to repair any misunderstanding she'd wrought.

As he brought her to the chair, right of his own at the table's head, she mastered her nerves enough to look directly at him and hold his gaze with her own.

"In truth, I cannot imagine a place lovelier than Sherringham. I would explore every nook had I the time or opportunity. And your permission, of course, Lord Marrable."

As the words left her lips, a frigid draft of air swept over her. Vanessa tried to suppress the shiver that ran through her, hoping it went unnoticed as she withdrew her hand from the viscount's arm.

Seeing his brows deepen, she assumed her seat and gave her attention to the table, gleaming with a plentitude of silver, crystal, and china. Along its extensive length, arrangements of white lilies, Lady Gwen's favorite, alternated with fruit laden epergnes and porcelain baskets, all beribboned with black. Meanwhile, as etiquette decreed, Lord Marrable remained standing as the others found their places.

Majel, acting as hostess, entered last on the arm of the aged Earl Silverbrooke, the highest ranking man present, after the host. She took her seat at the table's far end in the hostess' place of honor. Vanessa observed Lawrence moving to join Majel there and was mindful of his own expectations this day. Had it not been for the viscount's arrival, Lawrence would now be presiding over the funeral feast.

Cissy and Sir Henry dew Vanessa's attention as they settled directly across from her. Meanwhile, servants helped Sir Fotheringgay, the Marrable's octogenarian cousin, many times removed, into the chair to Vanessa's immediate right. He gave her a genial nod, then bent to inspect the array of silver flanking his plate and began counting it.

As Lord Marrable seated himself Cissy leaned toward him, wearing a slightly crooked smile. "I see you're still defying convention, brother." She spoke in a low, mischievous tone, sending a glance to Majel and Earl Silverbrooke at the table's opposite end. "Fortunate for you, the earl has no wife, though I'm not sure Countess Hove will soon forgive you."

Vanessa's stomach did a somersault. She realized, as a matter of precedence, the countess should have been the viscount's dining partner, being the lady of highest rank attending. Once more, Vanessa found herself where she did not belong. And though the viscount, himself, had bid her join him, she'd usurped a privileged place. Vanessa pressed her lashes shut. True, she was born to the gentry, but she was likely the least ranking guest in the hall.

"Vanessa, dear, don't be alarmed," Cissy heartened as if reading her thoughts. "Adrian will enjoy your company far more than Countess Hove's."

Startled by the comment, Vanessa quickly glanced up at Cissy, but found she'd already turned to her brother, eyes twinkling.

"Oh course, you might have allowed Henry or me to properly present Vanessa to you before capturing her away to yourself. Naughty man, you best not have smutched her reputation. Auntie would never forgive, nor shall I. Vanessa is an absolute gem."

Vanessa's cheeks flamed with embarrassment. She had quickly grown supremely fond of Lady Gwen's convivial niece and was flattered by her words, but what was she about at the moment?

Cissy opened her mouth to speak again but Lord Marrable leveled her a quelling look. Cissy instantly quieted, but in the next instant, broke into a wide, irrepressible grin.

In keeping with the formality of the occasion, a retinue of servants attended the guests, stationed several paces behind their chairs. The butler maintained his position directly behind the viscount, coordinating the entire affair—ringing in each course with timed precision, ensuring his staff's smooth efficiency, and seeing to the viscount's personal needs.

Polite conversation and niceties flowed along the table as the courses arrived, beginning with the soup and fish dishes—a consommé and poached salmon. Majel received praise for the selection of dishes, and Lawrence for the wines, all drawn from a list of Lady Gwendolyn's favorites and served in her memory.

Lord Marrable remained silent as Cissy took it upon herself to spur conversation and keep alive an active exchange. They made their way through the meat dishes—beef, leg of mutton, and pheasant pies. Mostly, conversation centered around fond memories of Lady Gwendolyn and humorous incidents from the Marrables' childhood years. Much was made of how Lady Gwen would mercilessly dress them in costumes and pose them for hours for her "allegorical" photographs.

As the servants cleared the soiled dishes and refreshed the wine, Cissy aimed a number of comments directly at Lord Marrable, in an obvious effort to coax him from his silence.

"If you don't know it, brother, Vanessa was great friends with Auntie as well as her companion. She was also Auntie's personal protégée."

The viscount's gaze slipped to Vanessa then back to his sister. "Few escaped Aunt Gwen's camera or her enthusiasm for photography," he commented, breaking his silence at last. "I'm not surprised she made a convert of Miss Wynters."

"It's *Mrs.* Wynters, actually," Vanessa clarified. "And she didn't have to make a convert of me. I truly love the medium."

The viscount's eyes swung to hers, but she continued, trying to ignore the sudden intensity of his gaze. Trying to master the sudden tremor in her hands.

"I've not a jot of artistic ability, you see. Photography is more a matter of technical knowledge and applied skill, as opposed to the sort of talent required for sketching and oils."

"Vanessa, you are too modest!" Cissy exclaimed, leaning forward and nearly tipping over the footed glass of lemon ice the servant was attempting to set before her. "Aunt Gwen wrote you are truly gifted—'intuitive,' she said. And photography is most certainly an art, and one at which you excel."

Cissy sat back in her chair as the servants offered an assortment of jellies, blancmange, and small iced cakes. When they withdrew, she leaned forward once more.

"Aunt Gwen's words were not mere flattery. She sent along bundles of photographs to Sherringham—both hers and yours, Vanessa—from all your travels. She instructed they be held in storage here."

Vanessa acknowledged Cissy's statements with a nod. Lady Gwen had graciously made the offer, knowing Vanessa had no home of her own at which to keep them, and no relations closer than her cousins.

"I've seen your work for myself." Cissy chattered on. "Your photographs are superb. You should see them too, Adrian." Cissy lay a hand to his arm. "They are stored in the west study. In fact, the last package was posted from Brussels, before Aunt Gwen and Vanessa departed for France."

Lord Henry, who had been listening attentively, wiped his mouth with his napkin and set it aside. "That arrived rather swiftly, wouldn't you say? Lady Gwendolyn died shortly after arriving in Paris. Isn't that so?"

Multiple pairs of eyes turned toward Vanessa and she found herself the center of attention.

"Yes, we'd arrived only three days before. I feel I should have recognized the oncoming signs. But then, they were unremarkable. Even Lady Gwen discounted their importance. She always enjoyed excellent health and assumed she was simply fatigued."

The viscount eased back in his chair, contemplating Vanessa. "I'd like to hear the details if you are up to it."

"Adrian, you cannot be serious," Cissy objected. "We are still in the midst of the sweets course."

"I don't mind," Vanessa offered. "And really, there's no better time. I'll be leaving Sherringham presently."

Instantly, an icy thread of air spiraled about her, causing the fine hairs to raise along her arm and the back of her neck. Once again Vanessa suppressed the shiver sleeting through her. Sherringham, she decided, was plagued by a distinct problem with drafts.

"What of these signs?" Lord Henry's voice drew her

back to the moment. "Had Lady Gwen been ill during the weeks previous to the attacks?"

"Not noticeably so. She experienced a few minor headaches, nothing more. Then, during an outing on our second day in Paris, we were photographing on the Champs-Élysées. Lady Gwen had finished adjusting her camera to her satisfaction and was peering through the lens when her vision blurred in that eye. Her right eye." Vanessa tapped a finger to her cheekbone beneath her own. "I took the photograph for her and we returned to our suite directly.

"Lady Gwen slept for a time. When she awakened, she seemed quite well, her vision and energy restored. So much so, that same evening we attended a small dinner party. At one point, she experienced some difficulty understanding what was being said. She waved it away as one of the nuisances of advancing age. I realize now, the headaches and vision and hearing problems were all indications of an oncoming attack."

The viscount's gaze remained fastened on Vanessa and, if possible, intensified as she began to describe Lady Gwen's passing. The images loomed to life once more as she relived each tragic moment.

"The first attack came during the night," Vanessa said in a near whisper. "Evidently, Lady Gwen had risen from her bed some time before. I awoke to the sound of her footsteps, pacing the floor."

In truth, Lady Gwen paced the floor most nights. A more restless soul, Vanessa had never encountered. She had suspected Lady Gwen experienced some physical ailment that prevented her from lying abed prone for any extended length of time. Vanessa encouraged her to see the doctor, but Lady Gwen refused, jesting she was working out the troubles of the world when she walked the nights, and the world certainly needed that, she assured.

On this particular night, Vanessa rose to check on her, as was her custom.

"I was approaching the door to the front room, when I heard Lady Gwen fall. The attack incapacitated her, leaving her paralyzed along her right side and her speech badly slurred. I managed to lift her and assist her into bed, then sent immediately for the physician."

The side of her face had sagged most distressingly, the muscles having given way, and her right arm and leg were utterly useless. Vanessa recalled her own anguish in that moment and her utter powerlessness. The dear lady deserved nothing so wretched to befall her.

"Lady Gwendolyn rested, comfortably I believe, as we awaited the doctor."

Comfortably, yes, until she remembered her small Bible. Vanessa could not explain what happened next.

Lady Gwen became greatly agitated and through her thick speech, implored Vanessa to find the book. When Vanessa brought it to her bedside, Lady Gwen struggled to voice two words and did so again and again. "Burn it! Burn it!" she demanded urgently. Lady Gwen would not be calmed until Vanessa promised she would do as she requested.

"The doctor had only just arrived, when Lady Gwen suffered a second, massive attack. I was holding her, helping her take a sip of water when the fit seized her."

"And you say the second stroke took her?" Lord Henry queried. "Swiftly, I hope."

Vanessa nodded. "She suffered little. I wired Sherringham at once. Fortunately, Lawrence was in residence to receive it and came at once."

Lord Marrable retracted his dark gaze from her and

leveled it down the length of the table at his brother. Vanessa was unsure what she saw in his eyes, only that he look unpleased.

"Thank heaven Lawrence came to your aid so promptly," Lord Henry declared.

Vanessa avoided Lord Marrable's eyes which she sensed had returned to her. Instead, she concentrated on those last moments in Paris.

The small Bible lay forgotten until Vanessa was vacating the Paris suite to return to England with Lawrence and Lady Gwen's coffin. At the last moment, she tucked the volume in her own case. She was glad now she hadn't fulfilled Lady Gwen's strange request, but thought to inter it with her instead.

She looked up to find that the family solicitor, Mr. Whitmore, had come to stand by the viscount's side and was saying something to his ear.

Cissy waited for him to finish before taking up the conversation and steering it into a new vein.

"Vanessa is compiling a mourning album for the family, Adrian. Isn't that splendid of her? She held the sittings yesterday afternoon."

"Are the portraits ready to be viewed?" Lord Henry asked with marked enthusiasm. His interest in photography, or at least the finished product, was almost as keen as young Geoffrey's.

"Actually, I intend to develop the plates at my cousin's home in Hampshire, where they can provide me with space for a temporary darkroom."

"I didn't know it was possible to travel with exposed plates." Surprisingly, the question came from Lord Marrable.

Vanessa studied her hands, avoiding his eyes. "If one uses the 'dry' process, then yes. The gelatin plates are fitted into a specially designed box which protects them. I will personally carry it on the train."

Cissy's eyes grew suddenly wide. "Vanessa, what of my brother? He must be included in the album. You could pose him now and take the plate with you."

Vanessa's heart skipped a beat. "I fear there is not nearly time enough. I've a train to catch in Hereford."

An arctic coolness pooled over her, causing Vanessa to stiffen. Perhaps it was good she was leaving, she decided, before she caught her death of cold.

She consulted the watch attached to her bodice. "Actually, I see I should gather my things now. It's drawing near time for me to leave."

In all honesty, there was a wide margin of time to spare, but after discussing Lady Gwen's demise, she suddenly craved the privacy of her room. And a warm jacket.

"If you will excuse me . . ." Vanessa started to rise but suddenly felt the weight of a hand upon her right shoulder, pressing her firmly back down into her chair.

With a gasp, she plopped ungracefully onto her seat, crushing her bustle as she did. Shocked by the rudeness of the gesture, she looked to Sir Fotheringgay to her right. But his hands were occupied with his spoon and fork as he sampled the jellies and cakes.

"Leave?" Mr. Whitmore, who still stood by the viscount's side, blustered aloud, his shrubby brows shooting heavenward. "You cannot leave, Mrs. Wynters. Not yet. You are among those named in Lady Gwendolyn's will."

Surprise lit the eyes of all who turned to her, excepting at the table's far end where Majel's narrowed to slits.

Chapter 3

Whether she was relieved or disappointed that Mr. Whitmore delayed the viscount in the banqueting hall, Vanessa had yet to resolve.

But then Cissy and Lord Henry allowed her not a moment to ponder it. They quickly took her under wing and swept her along with them, the solicitor having promised an immediate reading of the will to accommodate Vanessa's pressing schedule.

Lawrence joined them now as they quit the hall and headed for the family's private "sitting library." He chatted easily, seeming much more the man she'd known this week past. *Seeming* so. Admittedly, she wasn't paying close attention. Her mind still spun as they approached the library doors.

Lady Gwen had included her in her will, likely to bequeath her some small memento. That would have been most kind of her, and Vanessa felt deeply appreciative. At the same time, she dearly hoped she would not miss her train.

It wasn't so much the cost of her ticket which would be forfeit that concerned her. Once she arrived at her cousins' in Hampshire, she must promptly begin advertising for a new position. She could not afford to delay. Though her late husband had not left her totally bereft, he had not left her financially secure either. She hoped to find a new position soon, though she'd be fortunate to find one half as satisfying or fulfilling as the one she enjoyed with Lady Gwendolyn.

The future that awaited her promised to be lonely, isolating. Whether she served as a companion or governess, she would be a genteel woman caught in that restricted, nebulous realm, existing above the household's hired servants but below the family, neither belonging nor associating with either beyond her duties.

No, she could not hope for such a close association with her next employer as that which she'd experienced with Lady Gwen. They shared a true friendship, special, irreplaceable. Indeed, they had very much been companions to each other. Vanessa confessed, she'd not known a moment's loneliness since entering Lady Gwen's employ.

Following Cissy and Lord Henry, Vanessa crossed the library threshold on Lawrence's arm.

She found the room spacious, though smaller in scale than most she'd visited at Sherringham. Its pale apricot-and-cream decor was cultivated yet informal, touched with Gothic overtones. Recessed bookcases reached along the walls, appearing part of the architecture. There, books tooled in gold and busts of philosophers crowded the shelves. Slender cluster columns fronted the cases, running to the ceiling and flaring into lacy fans and roundels, fanciful yet not as opulent as that of the Grand Saloon.

Numerous overstuffed sofas surrounded the wide fireplace, its detailed chimneypiece reminiscent of medieval choir screens. Above the mantel, a lion and a unicorn supported the Marrable Achievement of Arms, the spotted panther rearing from its crest. Inscribed on the riband beneath the shield appeared the motto "Fierce when roused."

Vanessa smiled inwardly, remembering the viscount's look when he first arrived at the funeral.

At the room's far end loomed a great hexagonal bay, its multiple windows soaring to an extravagant height with jewel-tone coats-of-arms painted into the upper lights. Situated in the bay's alcove stood a great double library desk of mahogany and a deep leather chair behind it. Additional chairs, also leather, had been drawn forward and positioned in semicircular fashion, facing the desk and bay.

Feeling somewhat out-of-place, Vanessa indicated to Lawrence that she preferred to take the chair on the far left, thinking this would allow the family to be seated together. He graciously led her there then assumed the seat beside her. Cissy and Lord Henry took the chairs to the right, and Majel and her husband, trailing into the library behind them, installed themselves on the far-most right.

Mindful of the passing time, Vanessa slipped a glance to her watch and wondered how long they would wait before the viscount and Mr. Whitmore appeared. Several moments later, they strode into the room.

Lord Marrable, his features once more an unreadable mask, seated himself behind the great desk. He did so in order to observe the others, or so it seemed to Vanessa.

Mr. Whitmore, a sober, heavy-jawed man with untamed brows and hair, stood to the left of the desk. He waited a moment as the others finished settling themselves, then removed an envelope from his jacket. Adjusting his spectacles, he cleared his throat.

"My Lord Marrable," he began in a gritty voice that oddly suited his gruff looks. "Lord and Lady Pendergast, Lord and Lady Norland, Mr. Marrable, Mrs. Wynters, as you know by your requested presence here, Lady Gwendolyn has named you in the disposition of her personal holdings. In keeping with my promise to Mrs. Wynters to expedite matters, let us begin."

The milky-white paper crackled beneath his fingers as he removed it from the envelope and unfolded its creases.

"The document is dated May 9, 1882, four months prior to Lady Gwendolyn's death. To my knowledge it is her most recent and last statement of her wishes." He peered over the tops of his glasses at those seated before him. "Unless anyone present is otherwise aware."

Majel eyed Vanessa with a hooded look. "Mrs. Wynters would know better than any of *us*. She rarely left Auntie's side and helped her conduct all her activities. Or so I'm told." Her lips slanted into a razor-thin smile.

Vanessa's stomach tightened into a thick knot, just as it had this morning in Knights Chapel. Then, Majel had the audacity to imply that she'd personally prevented Lady Gwen from returning to Sherringham. Did she now suggest something more sinister? Did Majel actually imagine she'd persuaded Lady Gwen to alter her will to benefit herself?

Vanessa raised her chin. "I know of no other will. I didn't know of this one."

Majel lifted a brow of disbelief at that. "You did accompany her to the solicitor's office on the date mentioned did you not?"

Vanessa met her gaze levelly, piqued by Majel's innuendos. "Yes, of course, but I was not present in her meeting with Mr. Engle, nor was I aware of her purpose for seeing him that day. She did not reveal it to me, nor did I expect her to do so."

Mr. Whitmore cleared the roughness noisily from his throat, gaining everyone's attention. "Mrs. Wynters, did Lady Gwendolyn have occasion to seek legal consul again after May ninth?"

"To my knowledge, no."

"Then, unless proven otherwise, this document stands as her last will. Now, let us begin." He adjusted his spectacles once more then commenced reading.

" 'I, Gwendolyn Alicen Marrable of Royal Sherringham in Herefordshire, England, daughter of the late Right Honorable Talbot Marrable, sister to the late Right Honorable Lionel Marrable, and aunt to the right Honorable Adrian Marrable, current and fifteenth viscount of that line, being of sound and disposing mind and memory do hereby declare this to be my Final Will and Testament.

" 'Being a woman born to privilege, but having remained a maiden lady throughout my life, I own no great private wealth. That is to say, I hold no lands or properties of which to dispose, my person having ever relied upon the munificence of the Marrable men for my support, first, upon that of my father, next my brother, and finally, my nephew, all viscounts of the House of Marrable. I am compelled to add in regard to all three, their generosity rose high above duty and for that I am endlessly grateful.' "

The corners of Vanessa's mouth lifted in a smile. She'd encountered many a grand lady too stingy of heart to offer even a modicum of gratitude when due. Lady Gwendolyn, however, had always been unsparing in her appreciation and praise. It was but one of her endearing qualities.

Mr. Whitmore continued, his growly voice providing

a curious contrast to the feminine tone of the words he read from the page.

"'I do leave a number of personal possessions of value and herein set forth my wishes for their disbursements. First, to my nephews and nieces, Adrian, Lawrence, Majel, and Cecilia, fondly known as Cissy, I leave you first and foremost my love which you ever enjoyed in life—during your growing years, and those more mature, and of late, during my prolonged absence and travels. Be assured my love continues to flow to you, for I believe such things are possible. Death is no barrier to strong felt emotions such as love."

Lady Gwen's sentiments did not surprise Vanessa. She knew Lady Gwen believed unfalteringly in life in the Hereafter. She also believed that the earthly and spiritual planes coexisted, and that souls could easily transcend them should passions or purpose move them to such.

Mr. Whitmore rumbled on. "'Of a more tangible nature, there is the matter of my personal apparel including my garments and varied accessories that include shoes, hats, purses, gloves, fans, muffs, parasols, and the like. I do exclude, however, my jewelry from this particular bequest. Still, these habiliments are of significant value, and I have considered their disbursal at some length.

"'I am mindful that both my nephews are well situated but without wives, and that both my nieces are also well situated with husbands who can amply afford for them.

"'Therefore, recognizing that my relations have no recognizable need for my personal apparel, I do instruct that my garments, those for indoors and outdoors wear, and all my accessories, exclusive of my jewelry, be sold in their entirety and that the proceeds be distributed to the fund established by my nephew, Adrian, Lord Marrable, to provide for the widows and orphans of the coalminers working the Marrable mines. Sustaining them in their need is the least we Marrables can do as the mines have been the basis of our family's wealth for the past century.' "

Vanessa glanced to the viscount, surprised a second time this day by the man. In the same instant, Majel thrust to her feet.

"But there are furs!" she cried. "Full-length mantles and coats of sable and chinchilla. And there are gowns by Worth and costly trimmings—pearls, lace, feathers, and beading. Surely she does not mean to include the furs, or for the clothes to be sold with their embellishments.' "

Mr. Whitmore pursed his lips as he stared at Majel. "Lady Gwendolyn specifies the garments, 'those for indoors *and* outdoors wear,' are to be 'sold in their entirety.' "

"But there are edgings of marten and fox, rain fringe of jet. And what of the silk shawls from Egypt and their embroideries? They could all be reworked."

Mr. Whitmore removed his spectacles, his eyes fired with impatience. "The sale will be open to all. Might I suggest your ladyship purchase what pieces interest you at that time and thus make a generous contribution to the widows and orphans fund?"

At Mr. Whitmore's suggestion, Majel went rigid but behind the desk Adrian Marrable broke into a wide grin. The sight of that dazzling smile, slashing his features, nearly caused Vanessa's heart to stop.

"Whitmore, you've earned your entire year's retainer this day." The viscount chuckled.

Vanessa blinked at that. The man actually chuckled. The others stared at him too, as if it were a singular event. Excepting Majel, who glared hard at her brother.

He settled back into the leather chair, his smile settling into a pleasant line. "I concur and intend to hearten all attending the sale to be most liberal in their purchases and offer top coin."

As his smile lingered, Vanessa felt something inexplicable stir deep inside her. She strove to ignore it, not wishing to place a name to it.

All seriousness, Mr. Whitmore replaced his glasses and straightened his papers. "Where were we?" He scanned the page for his place.

"'As to the disbursal of my jewelry, I have ever considered myself fortunate to possess a fine collection. For the most part, the pieces were inherited through my mother and through her maternal line. My collection also contains a number of prime items that I confess, somewhat blushingly, were gifts from admirers over the years.'"

A soft, rumble of laughter rolled through the group.

"'In contemplating the dispersal of my jewels, I am again reminded of my nephews' marital status and of my nieces' positions.'"

Majel shot to her feet once more. "She cannot mean to leave her jewels to the orphans too! Or to the *widows*." She swiveled in place, shooting a white-hot look at Vanessa.

From the corner of her eyes, Vanessa glimpsed the viscount's dark eyes boring into her. Lord help her. Lady Gwen couldn't have left *her* all her jewels. At least, she hoped not. It would then most certainly appear she'd manipulated her elderly employer and taken complete advantage of her.

Vanessa sought to calm herself. Perhaps it was merely the mention of her widowed status that netted the viscount's interest. She doubted it, yet her marital status had not been specified during the luncheon, only that she was a Mrs. rather than a Miss. The conversation had then veered to another topic, as she remembered.

Could Lord Marrable have assumed her to be still married, abandoning a husband for some outrageous reason to trail over Britain and the Continent with his aunt? She dismissed the thought as preposterous, her reasoning strained.

Mr. Whitmore again cleared his throat. "Lady Pendergast, if I might continue—"

"Do sit down, sister," Cissy pleaded, turning to Majel. "We must finish or Vanessa will miss her train."

"And what a pity that would be," Majel snipped, reseating herself.

Whitmore skimmed the page, then leafed to the next. "Ah, yes. Here, Lady Gwendolyn becomes personal in her address once more. It reads as follows:

"'Adrian, you are heir to the family's famed jewels, bestowed upon the Viscounts Marrable through our famous, and rather infamous, ancestral relation, Leonine Marrable, mistress to Charles II. It is my hope you will recover them in time to come, if you have not done so in fact already. Their loss is a loss to all Marrables as it has ever been the special treasure about which we Marrables are most fond of boasting, however scandalously they were acquired.'"

Famed jewels? Charles II's mistress? Vanessa found this a fascinating revelation. But they had slipped from the viscount's possession somehow. She saw now that his smile had vanished, his look darkening once more.

"'But I digress'"—Mr. Whitmore read on—"'Adrian,

your personal wealth allows you to purchase whatever gems you wish, should you have the inclination or again take a wife. You have no need for my trifles. Therefore, I leave you but one item from my own collection, one by which to remember me.

" 'Knowing your love of history and antiquities, I have chosen a seal ring, once belonging to one of the minor maharajahs of Jaipur a hundred years ago. You will see it is set with an oval sapphire which has been carved in a flowing script with the maharajah's name. When you look on it, remember the woman who enjoyed a zest and passion for life. I would that your own passions be re-born.

" 'Presumably, if this paper is open to your eyes, then I am dead, so I will be perfectly frank and say what needs to be said. Let go the pains of the past, Adrian. Before your great-grandfather changed the Marrable motto, the older one read *Virescit vulnere virtus.* Courage grows strong at a wound. So does love.' "

Mr. Whitmore fell silent as Lord Marrable rose and moved to the window. Vanessa could sense the barriers thickening about him as he gave his back to all in the room and stood looking out onto the gardens and lawn. Lady Gwen had touched upon an unspeakable topic, the same one hinted at earlier in Knights Chapel. It was obviously bound up with Lord Marrable's wives, either one or both.

Vanessa suddenly wished she were already on her train, headed for Hampshire. She was an outsider here and shouldn't be privy to such personal matters.

Mr. Whitmore reached into his jacket and withdrew a small, velvet-covered box. He pondered Lord Marrable's back, obviously uncertain whether to disturb him. Cissy, owning no such reticence, sprang to her feet and accepted the box for her brother. As she opened it, Vanessa spied a flash of bright gold and the deep blue of the sapphire.

"How marvelously thoughtful of Aunt Gwen." Cissy's voice sparkled as she moved to the viscount's side. "Look, Adrian. Have you ever seen a ring so fine?"

Lord Marrable took the box and for a moment he and Cissy spoke in low tones. A moment later, he turned and retook his seat, his features shuttered. Once Cissy settled herself, he gestured for Mr. Whitmore to continue.

"Y-Yes." Mr. Whitmore fumbled his spectacles back in place on the bridge of his nose. "The next passage is directed to Mr. Lawrence Marrable. It reads as follows:

"'Lawrence, I am mindful of your own wide interests. In particular, I am mindful of your love of beauty, extravagance, and also, shall we say, of your unbridled generosity toward the ladies.'"

Lawrence shifted self-consciously in his seat.

"'These words are intended with your best interest at heart, so again I will be frank. I encourage you to employ restraint in your life, to rule over your impulses. It is precisely because of those impulses, sometimes given to excessive and, in certain cases, undeserved magnanimity, I fear you might allow portions of my small though precious collection to trickle to others outside the family.

"'Thus, Lawrence, knowing you are well able to provide for any lady who draws your interest, I leave you also with a single, but carefully chosen memento by which to remember me. In this case, a cameo, its profile carved of my own likeness at the workshops outside the ruins of Pompeii.'"

Vanessa recalled the trip, recalled stumbling onto the place after visiting the ancient city and the cameo being carved.

" 'I have had it fashioned into a stickpin of purest gold and set with a small diamond. When you look on it, remember a woman whose own impulses led to varying consequences, but who loved greatly in this life, loved you most dearly, and would see you set your world aright.' "

Aware Lawrence might feel some embarrassment at the moment, Vanessa kept her gaze from him as he received the velvet-boxed gift from Mr. Whitmore. Evidently, Lawrence's proclivities had met with Lady Gwen's disapproval. He was an attractive man who doubtless had many lady admirers and who appreciated their beauty as well. She conceded to not having been wholly unaffected herself when she first met him. He was an engaging man with golden good looks. And yet...

Dare she admit it? Lawrence paled from thought when his brother, Adrian, appeared. It seemed unfair, congenial Lawrence overshadowed by his dark, unapproachable brother.

Mr. Whitmore returned to the desk and, after taking a sip of water from a glass on a small silver tray there, he took up the will once more.

"The message now turns to the ladies," he announced.

Majel shifted forward in her chair, sending a confident glance to Cissy.

" 'Majel and Cissy, again I will be plain. You both enjoy coffers heaped with jewelry. Majel, you wait with your husband for an expected inheritance. When the time of your father-in-law's passing occurs, you will rise in status higher than your own brother, being elevated to the rank of countess. Though you do not wish your father-in-law ill, I am sure, I know you look forward with great anticipation to that day. At that time, you will have access to the Pendergast jewels and though not to compare with the Marrable jewels, I understand they would leave most women breathless.' "

Majel held her head high, sliding a superior look to her brother Adrian.

" 'My dear Cissy, your husband spoils you with countless baubles. It is plain to see he adores you, though personally I encourage him, like Lawrence, to exercise more restraint least he soon exhaust his fortune on your account. You know I say this with love, for to enjoy a husband's devotion and generosity is in itself a priceless gift.

" 'Therefore, carefully considering all this, and also respecting that many of the jewels in my collection are family heirlooms, owning sentimental as well as actual value, it is my wish for them to be passed down through the female line, ensuring they stay within the family. I hereby bequeath them to you, my nieces, Majel and Cissy, to be divided equally and equitably between you. I encourage you to continue this tradition and pass the pieces on through your own daughters and your daughter's daughters, keeping them within the bloodline.' "

Majel expelled a breath, obviously relieved. As her gaze sliced to Cissy, Vanessa felt sorry for the younger woman. The disposition of Lady Gwendolyn's jewels was far from settled.

Mr. Whitmore informed the sisters the jewelry was being kept in Lord Marrable's safe and asked that they wait until after the reading before taking possession of if.

"Lady Gwendolyn's will now turns to Mrs. Wynters," Mr. Whitmore informed.

Vanessa dropped her gaze to her lap as the others directed their attention her way.

" 'As you are all well aware, for over twenty-five years

I have experimented with photography. It is a passion and a pursuit that I have enjoyed immensely and for which I have spared little expense. To date, there are literally hundreds, if not a thousand or more, of my photographs stored at Sherringham. These I leave to my nephews and nieces jointly and appoint Adrian to oversee any and all final decisions concerning their fate. Divide them as you please, or keep them together in a single collection, as you will, but do enjoy them.

"As regards my photographic equipment and supplies, however, these, in their entireties, I bequeath with great joy and satisfaction to my dear friend and companion, Mrs. Vanessa Wynters."

Vanessa's jaw dropped, her gaze flying to the solicitor. "In their entireties?"

"Why?" Majel leaned forward of her chair to better view Vanessa. "Is any of it valuable?"

"Majel, do shut up!" Lawrence clipped out, his tone sharp with impatience. "Mr. Whitmore, proceed."

"Yes, here we are. Oh, and yes to you Mrs. Wynters. All photographic equipment and supplies 'in their entireties' are bequeathed to you. Now, I'll begin where I left off.

"'My dear Vanessa, you possess an innate talent, which in only two years' time is already impressive and still reaching toward its full potential. I realize that my death will consequently result in your lack of employment. As you are widowed and have little family on which to rely, you will necessarily feel forced to seek a new position elsewhere.'"

Vanessa kept her gaze fastened on the solicitor, aware of the other's directed at her. Oddly, she felt the weight of the viscount's gaze most of all.

"'Vanessa, do not. Do not seek another position, I

pray you. Instead, I encourage you to be daring, to take a chance—on life and on yourself. You are a first-rate photographer with an excellent eye, as they say. Pursue your gift, my dear. Develop your skills to your fullest potential.

" 'To help you to that end, I have written letters of introduction to some of the leading studios in London. Their owners are long acquaintances of mine. Hopefully, you will gain entrance there, if that is your wish. Another possibility you might consider is to assemble your photographs from our journeys and collect them into a book for publication. Picture travelogues are all the passion these days and should bring you a tidy sum.

" 'You must find your own way, Vanessa, create your own special niche in the field. This will not be easy. It is difficult for a woman to support herself, even in these enlightened times. Still, I encourage you to attempt to establish yourself in photography. With that in mind, I call upon my nephew, Adrian, to lend his assistance.' "

Vanessa's eyes leaped to Lord Marrable's and found surprise equal to her own in their depths.

" 'Adrian, it is my wish for you to be in fact, Mrs. Wynters' benefactor, temporarily at least, by assigning to her whatever remains in my accounts of my personal annual allowance.

" 'In closing, I encourage you, my dear nephews and nieces, to watch over one another. Marrable blood is strong and constant and binds you together always.

" 'And now I do close, content in the knowledge that as you read these words I will have taken up my long rest and sleep at Royal Sherringham.' "

Everyone sat silent as Mr. Whitmore placed Lady Gwendolyn's will on the desk, open for all to review. He then delivered into Vanessa's hands a neat stack of letters tied with a blue satin ribbon.

One by one, those in the room began to rise from their chairs. Lord Marrable remained seated, however, giving his attention to a slim ledger he'd withdrawn from a drawer. At the same time, he bid the solicitor to his side.

"So, Vanessa, what will you do?" Lawrence smiled, offering her a hand as she rose to her feet.

"I'm not sure. There is so much to think on. I imagine I'll have time enough to sort it out in Hampshire."

She glanced to Mr. Whitmore who bent to examine something in the viscount's book and then straightened and offered some comment.

Vanessa turned back to Lawrence. "Excuse me. I should arrange for the equipment and supplies to be sent on. I really must hurry if I am to catch my train."

Vanessa moved to stand before the wide desk and waited for Mr. Whitmore to conclude his conversation with the viscount. When he did, the viscount made a notation in his book that caused the solicitor's brows to rise. The men's eyes then turned to her in unison. She took a self-conscious swallow, but before she could open her mouth to make her request, Mr. Whitmore began to speak.

"Mrs. Wynters, on reviewing Lady Gwendolyn's account, Lord Marrable has noted that, it now being September, only one-fifth of the funds allotted his aunt annually now remain. They are deposited the first of each December, you see, which coincides with the anniversary of the late viscount's death and the establishment of the fund."

"Yes, of course. I understand." Vanessa's heart sank a little. Not that she hoped for a great sum, but establishing herself in the field of photography would take time and be costly. There was, also, no guarantee she would find entrance into the London studios to help sustain her.

For one brief moment she'd dared entertain the thought of following Lady Gwen's advice. But she didn't see how it would be remotely possible to do so.

"However"—Mr. Whitmore continued—"Lord Marrable, in assuming you wish to pursue your photographic endeavors, desires you have funds enough to carry you for an entire year. Therefore, he proposes to provide you the *full* annual amount, if you decide to follow that course, that is."

"What?" Majel shrieked from where she now stood, several yards away.

Vanessa ignored the woman's protests, turning huge eyes on Adrian Marrable. She couldn't seem to get her voice to leave her throat.

"I—I don't understand," she managed at last.

"Lord Marrable means to quintuple this figure." The solicitor scribbled numbers on a slip of paper and laid it on the desk before her.

Vanessa gasped aloud at the sum staring back. "Oh, but he can't!"

"No, surely he can't!" Majel rushed forward, intent on viewing the figure for herself. But Lord Marrable stayed her with a hard, layered look.

Slowly he rose from his chair and stood to full height.

"I believe I can do as I please," he said without the trace of a smile, pinning his sister with an icy gaze. "I am, after all, viscount and Master of Sherringham."

Majel took a step back.

"B-But this amount, Your Lordship." Vanessa's words tumbled over one another. "It's far too excessive. And

Lady Gwen had much to say of excess in her will, if you remember. I doubt she'd approve."

Lord Marrable turned toward her, instantly trapping her in his midnight eyes.

"She'd more than approve, Mrs. Wynters. We both know what a generous person she was."

Generosity surely runs in the Marrable family, Vanessa thought to herself.

"But why would you make such an offer? You've seen nothing of my work."

A light appeared in his eyes. It was like a small glowing window suddenly illumined from somewhere deep inside.

"I trust in my aunt's faith in your abilities and only wish to honor her request. I would also remind you that my sister, Cissy, has seen your work and spent a good portion of the luncheon praising your skills. The offer stands, Mrs. Wynters. The decision is yours."

Vanessa glanced to the paper again, still stunned by the sudden shift of events. "I—I don't know quite what to say."

"Say yes," Cissy urged as she came to Vanessa's side. "Why, I have a sensational idea. You can stay here and begin your new career, photographing Royal Sherringham. It would be a marvelous project for a picture book."

Lawrence moved to Vanessa's other side. "What a splendid idea. Sherringham is a masterpiece of Gothic Revival architecture and has a long and fascinating history to tell."

"What Lawrence says is true," Cissy quickly added. "We could all help you with the text."

Lawrence pressed closer. "And don't forget the photographs you took on your travels. Aunt Gwen's too.

You could publish them in association with her estate. The public is always eager for exotic photographs. Indeed, you *must* stay at Sherringham." A note of eagerness grew in his voice, and he looked to his brother, smiling. "What do you say to that, Adrian?"

An indefinable look entered Lord Marrable's eyes as his gaze passed from Lawrence to Vanessa and back.

"You are welcome to stay at Royal Sherringham for as long as you please, Mrs. Wynters," he said stiffly but graciously, his dark eyes returning to her.

Cissy grabbed Vanessa's hands at once and turned her toward her. "Do say you will stay. It's a wonderful idea and the books will be wonderful too. Henry and I plan to remain a while longer. Think of the fun it will be."

Vanessa still felt quite overcome, but the plan seemed sound and not even Majel voiced further objection. Of course, that had much to do with the silencing hand Lord Pendergast had placed to her shoulder. In truth, Majel appeared ready to burst with emotion.

Vanessa's eyes drew once more to Lord Marrable. "How can I refuse so generous and kind an offer? Yes, I accept and I will happily stay at Sherringham."

Vanessa smiled widely, the first time she'd done so in a week. But no sooner than she made the pronouncement, a deathly cold sliced straight through her, stealing her breath away.

Chapter 4

Adrian rode out, his exchange with Lawrence still burning in his brain.

Perhaps he'd been too harsh with his brother yesterday. Perhaps their wires *had* passed one another, as Lawrence insisted.

Adrian pressed on, feeling the power of the stallion beneath him as the steed's hooves ate up the road. He passed rapidly along the lane, leaving Sherringham, with its brooding towers and pinnacles watching from behind.

His anger remained, unabated, boiling in his veins. Word of Aunt Gwen's death had not reached him for nearly a week. A week! Thank God for Cameron Kincaid. His friend had appeared on his doorstep late at night, bearing Lawrence's telegram which Cameron's uncle had forwarded from the moors of Scotland.

"Did I do wrong to dispatch the wire to Glengyle?" Lawrence had challenged when Adrian took him to task over the matter. "Last we spoke, you were to be salmon fishing with the brother of that runner with whom you've become chums."

"I was with his *uncle*, and Cameron Kincaid is not a 'runner' as you put it, but an inspector with Scotland Yard."

Lawrence waved away his words. "Whatever his post with the police, how the devil should I have known you left Glengyle for London?"

"By the telegram I sent you when I learned of Kincaid's discovery." Adrian moved around his desk. "I expected you to meet me."

"Well, when I didn't appear, you might have assumed *I* didn't receive *your* telegram," Lawrence countered, then rested back in the deep, cushioned chair, lacing his fingers. "Presumably, my man Wilfred forwarded your wire to Hadleigh Hall where I was grouse shooting. As luck would have it , I left prematurely. Word came from Sherringham that the tiles had arrived from Italy—the ones that are to line the upper fireplace in the Orangery. I departed straightway to inspect the shipment, never having received your missive."

Lawrence rose then and began to pace.

"As it happened, I was but a day at Sherringham when a lad from Hereford appeared, delivering Mrs. Wynters's telegram. I needn't tell you, Auntie's death came as quite a shock. I drafted messages to you and our sisters and instructed your butler, Timmons, to wire them on. I then set off for Paris to assist Mrs. Wynters in the bitter task of transporting Auntie home."

He stopped his pacing and faced Adrian.

"I suppose I should have waited for you, brother. I was stricken and not thinking rightly. You were so blasted far away. I simply dashed off to the rescue, as it were. That is what family does in a crisis, after all, especially when one of their own has fallen on foreign ground."

That and, in your case, rush to succor beautiful young women in distress, Adrian added hotly to himself.

Instantly, he upbraided himself. The accusation was undeserved. How did the thought even burrow into his head? True, Lawrence had a weakness for a pretty face, but he had no way of knowing Mrs. Wynters was so exceedingly comely.

Adrian frowned at his own admittance, again wondering from whence it sprang. He expelled a breath, then fixed Lawrence with his gaze.

"Fortunaely, Laird Kincaid sent your wire on to his nephew at the Yard and, in turn, Cameron delivered the news to me personally."

And barely in time, Adrian thought to himself as he spurred his horse on. Despite his brother's explanations, he still felt somehow dissatisfied with his meeting with Lawrence.

Leaning into the great black, he welcomed the wind in his face.

He would have never forgiven himself had he missed Aunt Gwendolyn's funeral altogether. It was damnable enough that he hadn't been the one to secure her remains or to arrange or even attend the services for her. He keenly felt the need to have overseen every detail. It mattered. Deeply.

It wasn't just that he loved that dear woman, or that it was his place as head of the Marrable family to have done so. But more, he was the reason she'd lived in self-imposed exile these past years. It remaincd an open wound in his heart. He knew Aunt Gwen had stayed away from Sherringham specifically to keep her distance from him.

Passing through the twin gatehouses that marked the entrance to Sherringham, Adrian headed along the road that led through the Herefordshire's rolling hillside and stretched toward the city. In the far distance to the west loomed the Black Mountains of Wales. The sight of their rugged outline jerked his thoughts back to Scotland and to Glengyle.

Cameron Kincaid was to have joined the fishing party in the Highlands but was delayed at the Yard. The delay proved providential, however. For a third time since their disappearance, one of the Marrable jewels had surfaced. This time the piece appeared not far from the Yard itself, in the posh section of Kennsington High Street. On receiving Cameron's news in Glengyle, Adrian had wired immediately to Lawrence and departed for London.

So many wires, he thought grimly—his, Lawrence's, Cameron's, Mrs. Wynters's. It was not surprising they'd crossed, that he'd not received word of his aunt's death for so many days. He had to accept Lawrence owned no fault in the matter, though a devil in him wished to find a place to lay the blame.

Adrian hardened his jaw. Guilt rode him. That was at the root of his anger, he knew. Though he'd tried, he had never gotten a chance to see his aunt again after those fateful days surrounding Olivia's death.

At the time, Aunt Gwen had been overcome by the tragedy. She was doubly stricken when he was accused of his viscountess's death, of tampering with her carriage which led to the fiery accident.

Had Aunt Gwen heard their violent argument earlier that night? Did she believe the accusations even for an instant? But soon, it wasn't Olivia's death alone that shadowed him. The accusations triggered suspicions about the death of his first wife, Clairissa.

People liked to believe what they wished, he reflected bitterly, slowing the horse as the road began to wind downward.

After Olivia's accident and the subsequent investigation surrounding him, Aunt Gwen decided to travel awhile, saying she needed a change after so much distress. Privately, the doctor agreed. It would be therapeutic for her to get away from Sherringham where both the viscountesses' tragedies had taken place.

Adrian gave in to her wishes and increased her personal allowance so she might experience not a moment's worry in that regard. A maiden lady, thirty some odd years old and seemingly stable, served as her companion. But, to his understanding, the woman proved shockingly unreliable when she eloped across the Scots border with one of his aunt's poet friends.

He learned through his sister that their aunt had found another lady to accompany her, this one younger than her last companion but quite acceptable. That was Mrs. Vanessa Wynters. Somehow, he was sure Cissy failed to mention the "Mrs." part.

Neither he, nor his siblings, expected their aunt to stay away from Sherringham entirely. But then, hadn't he stayed away as well? Perhaps they were both fleeing, unable to bear the memories.

If anything, Sherringham clung to her memories, of that he was sure. Even last night, as he lay abed in his room for the first time in years, he could still hear Olivia's voice, haranguing him, Clairissa's too. Would he never cease to hear her screams?

Closing upon a sharp bend in the road, Adrian reined in the stallion.

Dismounting, he walked with the horse to the road's edge, halting at the place where Olivia's carriage had hurtled off the side, tumbling down the ravine and bursting into flames from the lamps and coal heaters.

He stood unmoving for a long moment, scanning the rocky landscape below. Then slowly, he reached into his coat and withdrew an ornate piece of jewelry from an inner pocket.

He contemplated it, rubbing his thumb over the baroque pearl that formed the body of the gem-studded dolphin brooch—Leonine Marrable's brooch, once presented to her by her kingly lover but lost two-and-a-half years ago when Olivia escaped into the night with her lady's maid, taking with her the Marrable jewels.

Adrian closed his fingers over the brooch. He'd returned to Sherringham to lay more than his aunt to rest, but also his last viscountess and the mysteries haunting her death. He wanted answers. Once and for all, he wanted to know exactly what happened that fatal night after he'd left Sherringham, and who now possessed the Marrable jewels.

Slipping the brooch back into his pocket, Adrian began to pace the ground, picturing the sequence of events in his mind's eye. At the time, Lawrence had been able to provide the most complete and reliable details. Not only had he been the first to arrive at the scene, but prior to that, he'd actually seen Olivia and her maid make their hurried departure.

Lawrence had been working in the study in the west tower at the time. It overlooked the stables and carriage house and owned a superior view of the grounds and surrounding countryside as well.

Voices drew him to the window that night where he observed two women rushing toward the outbuildings, baggage in hand. Both were easily identifiable—

Olivia in her satins and velvet cloak and her maid, Bonnie Beckford. Soon they reappeared in a small carriage, Olivia driving and whipping the horse to a swift pace.

Lawrence continued to watch the dim light of their carriage lanterns as they moved along the road and passed out of Sherringham's gates. Being in the tower, he could still see the lights for a time. Just when he expected them to disappear altogether, at a point the family called the Devil's Hairpin, he saw the light seemingly bounce to the left, flaring bright, then tumbling down the embankment. Fearing the worst, Lawrence raced from the tower, secured a horse, and quickly rode out.

Brave Lawrence. He had scrambled down the hill somehow, to try to pull the women from the burning wreckage. The palm of his right hand bore a wicked scar for that effort. But his attempts proved hopeless from the start. He found Olivia's body engulfed in flames, burned beyond recognition. Later, only the ring she wore could identify her. Bonnie Beckford, however, was not to be found.

It was not until the following day that the jewels were discovered missing from Sherringham's vault. Only Olivia could have procured them. It was assumed the jewels had spilled out during the accident, or leastwise came to the maid's notice. Discovering the fabulous fortune, she evidently seized the moment and the jewels and fled.

Six months to the day after the tragedy, one of the pieces reappeared in an exclusive shop in Highbury. Twelve months after that, Countess Hazelden attended a charity ball wearing a pair of Leonine Marrable's earrings. She'd acquired them from a jew-

eler with an elite clientele in Brompton. It cost Adrian
a significant sum to reclaim them.

Now, after another year's lapse, the dolphin brooch
came into the possession of a jeweler on Kennsington
High Street. This time, the store owner supplied a detailed description of the seller, which proved as startling as it was beneficial. The woman, he recalled,
possessed an abundance of flame-red hair, large
golden-brown eyes, and stood to a height of, approximately, five feet, five inches. It wasn't Bonnie Beckford
he described, but Olivia!

Cameron Kincaid, with whom Adrian had worked
from the outset on the case, pointed out that the
woman had likely worn a wig, and that Bonnie Beckford stood near in height to that of Lady Marrable.
Though no one could remember the precise color of
the maid's eyes, brown—even golden brown—was
fairly common. That she'd chosen to pose as his late
viscountess, Cameron deemed tasteless, if not sick-
minded. Still, he found no reason to doubt the woman
selling the brooch was, in fact, Bonnie Beckford.

But was it?

The question plagued Adrian no end, as did another
matter—the ring that had identified the body as
Olivia's. It was a simple cluster design, set with rubies,
not one he'd personally given her, but one that she'd
worn on numerous occasions. Yet, he couldn't recall
her wearing the ring that night when they argued no
more than two hours before her death. She had, however, been wearing her wedding band.

What became of it? Had Olivia removed it after their
angry words and tossed it into her case along with the
other jewels? That would explain why the band remained missing to this day.

But could there be another possibility? Could the body have been mistakenly identified? What if Bonnie Beckford now lay entombed in the family mausoleum, and Olivia yet lived, richly provided for by the Marrable jewels?

Adrian shook his head at the strain of his logic. It created more questions than it answered. Why, for instance, would the maid have been wearing Olivia's ring? It was improbable, though not impossible, that his wife had gifted it to her. If Olivia was anything, she was lavish in her generosity, much like Lawrence.

Lawrence. He must speak with his brother and sift through the details of his account once more. The servants too, those who'd remained in service since the time of the accident, would need to be re-questioned. Adrian vowed to have his answers and to trap the thief who was selling off the Marrable jewels.

Remounting his steed, he touched his heels to the stallions flanks and turned back for Sherringham. Minutes later, he passed through the gates and headed for the sprawling manse which, in reality, was part castle, part manor house. When it appeared in sight, he thought it presented a rather forbidding aspect this day, the layers of centuries clinging to its stone, shrouding it with a melancholy air.

Arriving before the porticoed entrance, Adrian leaped down, tossing the reins to the stable boy who rushed forward to greet him. On entering the manse, he immediately encountered his butler, a short, spindly man of about sixty with thinning, white hair.

"Do you know the whereabouts of my brother, Timmons?" He handed him his hat and gloves.

"I believe he is with Mrs. Wynters, your lordship."

"Indeed?" Adrian tried to mask his surprise, or was it irritation that he felt?

"Yes, your lordship. He offered to open the Photo House for Mrs. Wynters and help her transfer her photographic equipment there."

"I see." Adrian's brows pulled together as he imagined the nature of help Lawrence might wish to offer her in Aunt Gwen's darkroom.

He loved his brother but was not blind to his shortcomings, in particular those regarding women. That Lawrence now closeted himself with the beautiful widow, irked Adrian. Considerably.

"I sent James and Woodrow to assist in the task," Timmons added. "And Master Geoffrey wished to lend a hand too."

"Good! Then Mrs. Wynters has plenty of chaperons," Adrian blurted without thinking, his mood instantly lifting.

"Your lordship?" Timmons canted his head.

Adrian felt his heat rise, realizing what he'd just said."

"*Assistants*. I meant to say, Mrs. Wynters has plenty of assistants to help her with her cameras and chemicals and the like."

"Yes, your lordship. And happy they are to do so, I am sure," Timmons replied perfectly straight-faced. "Assist her, that is."

"Indeed." The word came out a near growl. Adrian tried not to glare at his butler. "Thank you, Timmons. Tell my brother to join me as soon as he is able. I'll be in the west tower."

Without looking back, he started to make his way through the enfilade of doors that stretched along the front of the house and led to the tower stairs on the far end. Changing his mind, he retraced his steps and climbed the grand staircase, heading for Olivia's former room.

Arriving there, Adrian paused at the cream-and-gilt double doors. On his instructions, the bedchamber had remained untouched since his wife's death, excepting for an occasional airing and dusting.

He eased open the right door then stood on the threshold, unmoving, gazing into the darkened interior. The air assaulted him at once, stale and cloying. Even now, it carried a trace of roses, Olivia's favorite scent.

Though heavy curtains shut out most of the light, the open door allowed in enough to illuminate the furniture and trappings which glowed of pale embroidered satins, the room decorated in the French rococo mode. It was the only chamber of its kind in Sherringham. Olivia had claimed the style reflected her own nature, calling it "sensually erotic."

He hated the room, her sanctuary, where once she'd made grand love to him, then later prohibited him. But not so others, as he had learned.

Adrian stalked to the center of the room. He would order it searched, inch-by-inch, for the missing gold band. Then he'd have all the furnishings and trappings removed and burned.

As he passed his gaze over the chamber, he could feel Olivia's suffocating presence. It was near tangible. Somehow, he must rid himself of her, for she continued to linger in his veins like a contaminant, poisoning his every waking day.

The scent of roses suddenly filled his nostrils once more. Unable to bear it, he strode to the wall of curtains and yanked them back, then threw the center window wide. He inhaled deeply, imagining the memories, along with the odors, escaping their prison.

"Oh, hello," a feminine voice called from below.

Adrian glanced down to the courtyard which the room overlooked. There stood Vanessa Wynters, holding a box and smiling up at him. As his eyes met hers, her smile widened. It was like a brilliant flash of sunshine beaming up at him, illumining the darkness that held him, slipping past the chinks in his carefully maintained armor. His knees nearly buckled as he felt it reach into his heart.

"Hi, Uncle." Geoffrey came into view, carrying a bundle, long in length and wrapped in cloth. "Mrs. Wynters said I can be her special assistant. She's going to teach me all about photography."

Adrian looked to Mrs. Wynters whose smile now shined on his eager-faced nephew. He found his voice but only after he'd cleared it twice.

"Then you must pay close attention and do all she says."

"Oh, yes, sir." Geoffrey grinned.

At that moment, Lawrence appeared in the door of the Photo House, then stepped aside briefly to let James and Woodrow pass through and out. Seeing Adrian, Lawrence paused a moment, obviously noting the room in which he stood. He shuttered the surprise in his eyes, though it was not lost to Adrian.

"Timmons informs me you wish to see me." Lawrence moved to the pretty widow's side causing Adrian to frown.

"When you are finished. You'll find me in the west tower study."

Lawrence nodded, then relieved Mrs. Wynters of the box she carried and waited for her to precede him into the Photo House. Casting up a parting glance, Lawrence smiled.

"I'll see you later, brother," he called out as he disappeared into the house, Geoffrey trailing behind.

Adrian balled his hands to fists as he stepped back a pace from the window. It did not improve his mood when he discovered his heart thudding heavily. He could not explain the force of his emotions just now, or the sudden spike of jealousy he'd felt—still felt—knowing his brother basked in Vanessa Wynters's sunny smile.

He clamped down on his feelings, shutting them off. He'd vowed two-and-a-half years ago to allow no other woman near his heart.

It disconcerted him that his emotions had near struck him prostrate. He'd been too long without a woman, he told himself. Any attraction he felt for Vanessa Wynters was wholly physical. After all, she was fair and shapely and could heat any man's blood.

But he wanted no entanglements with that tender sex. None of a serious or lasting nature. Had he not endured two ghastly marriages? If he wasn't cursed in matters of love then, certainly, he was a supremely poor judge of women. Clairissa and Olivia tormented him still.

No, he'd not risk his heart again. Better for him if he didn't become involved. Better for her. Then too, what would Vanessa Wynters think of a man suspected of both his wives' murders?

His eyes drew to the courtyard once more. Just then she reemerged from the Photo House, a vision of loveliness and light.

Adrian cast up a wall against his feelings. But in the next instant, a fierce anger welled up inside him afresh. He was a man shackled by his past, a past that refused to release him.

Again the scent of roses teased at his nostrils. It served only to heighten his ire. Images of Olivia flashed in his mind's eye. It was she who bound him, more so than Clairissa. She'd promised that last night that he'd never be free of her, that she'd ruined him for all others.

A sudden fury took hold of him. Crossing to the great bed, he lay his hands to the silk hangings and began ripping them down.

"Witch! You have no power over me," he shouted aloud. "I'll not allow it."

Trampling the silk underfoot, he swung his angry gaze over the room, then stood heaving for breath. Still, her suffocating presence surrounded him, the scent of roses intensifying.

It was only an illusion, a trick of mind, he told himself. The chamber, itself, with all its tangible reminders, preyed mercilessly on his mind.

But then the dark truth assailed him, as it had for months. He was far from free of his second viscountess.

Mad with frustration, he fisted his hands and shouted out once more.

"Damn it, Olivia! Are you even dead?"

Chapter 5

Adrian Marrable possessed Vanessa's thoughts as she reentered the Photo House.

When first she'd spied him in the window overlooking the courtyard, he'd worn a deep scowl. But it quickly changed to a look of surprise when she sent him her smile. Or was it shock she'd seen register in his features? Even now she was unsure what she'd read there. Could the man find a simple, heartfelt smile so unsettling? Did others so rarely give him theirs?

"Where would you like the chest, madam?"

Vanessa glanced to James where he waited on the door's threshold, gripping Lady Gwen's weighty oak chemical chest by its side handles. *Her* chemical chest now.

"Against the far wall will do," she directed, feeling a sting of guilt that she should gain from her employer's death.

Vanessa stepped aside for James to pass then swept her gaze over the spacious, square room with its dust laden tables, benches, and shelves.

"We will need cleaning supplies—brooms, buckets, soap . . .," she commented, half to herself, as she ordered her thoughts. "Everything will need a thorough scrubbing."

She plucked a filmy glass beaker from a nearby shelf and held it to the light.

Geoffrey left his Uncle Lawrence's side where they were in the course of opening the shuttered windows and hurried over to her.

"Can we unpack the boxes first, Mrs. Wynters? Mama says I'm capital at unpacking, and I'd very much like to see all your equipment."

Vanessa smiled at the boy's eagerness. She replaced the container then lay her hand on his shoulder.

"One of the first lessons a photographer must learn is that *cleanliness* is vital to our craft."

Geoffrey's smile visibly drooped along with his enthusiasm. Resolute, she pressed her point.

"Dirt can ruin a camera's mechanisms and contaminate the solutions and sensitive papers we use to produce our photographs." She gave a heartening squeeze to his shoulder. "Why don't you scare up some buckets and brushes and the like? There will be time aplenty for unpacking and perhaps even for some picture taking today."

Geoffrey's grin sprang back into place at that prospect. With a bob of his head, he scurried out.

"I'll help him find what you need, mum." Woodrow tipped his soft cap and, having finished relocating a tall cupboard at her request, followed after the boy.

Moments later, James likewise withdrew, saying there was yet another crate to fetch.

Vanessa found herself suddenly alone with Lawrence. As his blue gaze settled on her from across the room, she realized he was equally aware of their circumstance.

Self-conscious, Vanessa crossed to the long work-table that lined the wall, left of the room's entrance. She began to inspect the worktable's row of deep drawers, suspecting Lady Gwen had once used them for drying and storing her glass negatives.

The fine hairs raised along the back of her neck as she felt Lawrence's presence as he moved directly behind her. Vanessa stilled and was next aware of him leaning forward. His body brushed hers as he reached past her side and drew his finger through the table's thick dust.

"Two-and-a-half years' worth of dirt will take hours to remove," he said at her ear in a low, liquid voice. "Perhaps, I should send for a battery of maids and free your day."

Vanessa stiffened, as much from his closeness as from his warm breath teasing her neck. Obviously, he held his own plans for her day.

Taking a sideways step along the worktable, she managed to free herself enough to turn and face him. She forced a smile then felt it wobble.

"I am sure Geoffrey and I are up to the task here. But thank you," she said firmly.

Lawrence straightened his stance, then flicked a glance past her shoulder to where she knew a large basin stood with double spigots projecting from the wall. His gaze returned to her then began to drift over her face and hair.

"At least the water need not be hauled. It's one of the advantages of converting a wash house into a photographer's laboratory." His eyes strayed down her bodice to her hands. Closing the space between them, he captured her fingers in his own. "I do hate to think of your lovely hands shriveled and red. Scrubbing is not a lady's chore, Vanessa dear."

"But it is a *photographer's* chore." She tugged her hands free and moved apart of Lawrence, crossing to the center of the room. She tried to not appear as nervous as she felt. When would the others return?

"You say this was a wash house?" Vanessa could only hope to distract him and engage his thoughts with something other than herself. "Of course, this is not really a house, is it? Not a separate, freestanding building, I mean."

Lawrence slowly strode toward her. At the same time, he ran his gaze casually over the room.

"The entire wing that stretches along this side of the courtyard once functioned as a service area. Those quarters were relocated long ago, during one of Sherringham's many renovations."

"I see." She fell back a pace as he neared.

"My father converted the old laundry to a Photo House for Aunt Gwen on the occasion of her thirty-fifth birthday."

"That was certainly generous of him," Vanessa replied, finding herself nearly backed to the cupboard.

Lawrence smiled. "Father feared his sister might not see another birthday, if he didn't. Auntie had acquired a host of ailments from inhaling fumes from those blasted chemicals she was using. She even fainted several times while heating her mercury."

"How frightening."

He shrugged. "Yes, but not surprising. She'd insisted on working in a cramped cell of a room with poor ventilation."

Vanessa found she could retreat no more. Thankfully, Lawrence stayed his own step.

She felt suddenly silly as they stood there, staring at each other, she fearing he was about to pounce on her. Lawrence was a well-bred gentleman, after all. Though he seemed to enjoy flaunting conventions at times, and his advances were certainly bold, surely he would never compromise a lady or her reputation.

"Father deemed the old laundry at the end of this wing perfect for Auntie's needs," he was saying. "I think you'll find it most functional. He incorporated many clever details to suit a photographer's special requirements. Here, let me show you."

Vanessa forced herself to relax a degree—but only a degree—as he led her to the window at the back of the room. Like its twin on the opposing wall, the window was bracketed with solid-paneled shutters.

"See how these are edged with felt strips so that they completely seal out the light?" Lawrence pointed out, then purposely closed the shutters, casting them in instant shadow.

He turned back to her, a gleam appearing in his eyes. Catching her by both arms, he drew her against him. Vanessa gasped at his audacity and tried to wrest free, but he held her fast.

"Vanessa, you must know how I—"

"This is the last box, madam," James's voice rang out from the portal, startling them both. "Shall I put it with the others?"

Lawrence glared at the servant but released Vanessa. She quickly threw open the shutters, her pulse drumming in her veins, her temper burning.

"Yes, James. Over here." She left Lawrence at the window and conducted the manservant to the exact spot where she wished him to place the box. When he wouldn't meet her eyes, she feared he would seek to leave as quick as he could. She had to delay him.

"James, I made a dreadful mistake when I instructed Woodrow to move the cupboard," she improvised. "Could you move it back to where it was before?"

James did not look pleased when he eyed the bulky piece of furniture which, in actuality, was an old, oversized armoire. Nevertheless, he set to work without a word.

Lawrence likewise looked displeased—displeased that she'd detained the man. Just as she was about to suggest he leave, he dusted off the end of a table with his handkerchief and perched there, apparently accepting his temporary setback while he waited for James to finish.

Vanessa glanced out the door for Geoffrey and Woodrow. Finding no sign of them, she sent up a prayer they would hurry back, then thought to engage Lawrence in conversation once more to end the awkward silence.

"Your father and aunt must have been exceptionally close," she remarked. "Majel mentioned that Lady Gwen was 'as a second mother' to you and your brother and sisters. Did your own mother die early in life?"

Something moved in the depth's of Lawrence's eyes. When he did not immediately answer, she wondered if she'd tread upon a painful subject.

"No," he said at last. "But Mother kept very busy being the Viscountess Marrable and impressing London society and the Country House set. She died only six years ago, and most fashionably, I would add."

Vanessa detected a trace of bitterness in his tone.

"Aunt Gwen, on the other hand, rarely left Sherringham and was as much a part of our lives as Nanny. Of course, as we grew older, Adrian and I were sent away to school, and Mother drew the girls more and more to London to acquaint them with society and 'finish' them. Fortunately, Aunt Gwen's photographic endeavors filled her time."

Lawrence pushed off the table, causing Vanessa to tense. But he only shoved his hands in his pockets and paced back and forth, watching James reposition the cupboard. Moments later, he turned back to Vanessa. Thrusting his fingers through his hair, he came to stand before her.

"See here, I'm sorry if I seemed a bit rough or frightened you just now. I can be an impetuous cad at times, but I'd not have you think ill of me. You quite intoxicate a man, Vanessa Wynters. Forgive me?"

His sudden contrition took Vanessa by surprise, as did his professed attraction to her. Lawrence was an impulsive man, she was fast learning, his emotions ever near the surface and only lightly reined. She never knew quite what to expect. At the moment, he looked like a repentant overgrown child, a lock of golden hair tumbled over his forehead, his dimples appearing as he flashed her a tentative smile.

"Say, I have an idea." His eyes brightened with his thought. "Not all of Aunt Gwen's photos are stored in boxes. Those of the family are kept in albums, a sort of visual history one could say. You might enjoy seeing the Marrable siblings when wc were wee mites. Perhaps you'd allow me to show them to you later on, or tomorrow if that's more preferable."

Vanessa tried to gauge his sincerity as he held her eyes with his. Reasonably satisfied, she allowed him her smile at last.

"Perhaps. Though, in truth, I find it hard to imagine you four as being young. You and Cissy, I can, but not Majel or your brother, Adrian."

Lawrence raised an amused brow. "You'd be surprised. Between Auntie and Nanny, we were thoroughly spoiled and carefree." Just as quickly his brow smoothed, weighted with some thought. "Time does change a person, of course. As does marriage. Or, in my brother's case, should I say *marriages*?"

Vanessa tilted her head at the comment, wondering at his meaning or that he should have voiced it at all.

At that moment Geoffrey and Woodrow materialized in the doorway, laughing at some banter they'd shared, each burdened with a host of mops, brooms, and cleaning supplies.

"Ah, the troops return," Lawrence murmured lightly, though his smile dimmed at the further invasion. "I suppose it's best I take my leave and see why my distinguished brother has summoned me."

He sketched a brief but charming bow to Vanessa and headed across the room. At the portal, he paused and turned back.

"I believe tea will be served on the east terrace at five. I look forward to seeing you then, fair lady."

Vanessa felt herself flush at Lawrence's unconcealed flattery.

As she glanced to the others, their gazes darted away. They'd been watching. What they'd not seen, they'd certainly heard, she realized. Especially James. Marching to where Geoffrey propped the mops and brooms, she snatched one of the latter and attacked the dirt.

*   *   *

Hours later, she and Geoffrey stood side-by-side, surveying their sparkling domain. James and Woodrow had departed long before, when other duties pressed. Still, the work had proceeded rapidly.

Smiling, Vanessa draped an arm over Geoffrey's shoulder.

"Now we unpack," she announced and laughed when her young assistant gave a whoop of joy.

They spent the next hours opening boxes and crates and finding homes for their contents. Even Vanessa found herself stunned by the photographic arsenal she'd inherited.

The array of cameras alone astonished her. Aside from the faithful Meagher "tailboard" model that Lady Gwen had relied upon during their travels, there was a collection of early cameras dating back to the 1850s and several specialty cameras.

The oak, sliding-box camera was by far the oldest and possessed an even earlier Petzval portrait lens. Another, a folding camera of Austrian make, possessed *parallel*, rather than *taper*-sided bellows. They were the only bellows she'd seen that were not red.

Geoffrey's favorite was a binocular stereoscopic camera. Vanessa could only wonder what or who Lady Gwen had photographed with the double-lensed camera. She hoped the prints and a stereoscope for viewing them were stored at Sherringham. She would need to ask someone. Her thoughts went to Lawrence, skipped to the viscount, and finally settled on Cissy.

Perhaps the greatest prize of the collection was a fine field camera for photographing large, outdoor scenes such as landscapes and architecture. She even found a unique swiveling lens to fit it, making it possible to record panoramic scenes. With some practice, she should be able to capture breathtaking views of Sherringham and the surrounding countryside.

In addition to the marvelous assortment of cameras, there were reams of paper, all of high-quality, and a store of glass plates for negatives, their sharp edges already sanded smooth and ready to be sensitized. There were also quantities of powdered chemicals, sealed and preserved in glass jars.

Together, Vanessa and Geoffrey labored steadily throughout the afternoon. She handled the more delicate and dangerous materials, and assigned her young assistant to less risky tasks. He busied himself setting out washing trays, porcelain pans and dishes, and an army of glassware—bottles, funnels, dippers, syringes, and more. When he'd finished with those, he filled buckets with water and stationed them at designated places around the room.

As they worked, Vanessa took the opportunity to explain some basic principles to Geoffrey, including her darkroom rules, as she termed them.

Shelving the last of the chemicals and solutions, Vanessa instructed Geoffrey to touch nothing there. "Most are highly poisonous and they can blister your skin right up," she explained. "They can blind you, as well, should any get in your eyes."

She pointed to the buckets. "That is one reason we always keep clean water on hand—for emergencies of various kinds. We also wash our hands a *lot*." She smiled, then surveyed their work.

"Do you remember why we set up a 'wet' and 'dry' side in the room?"

Geoffrey nodded, eager to show he'd paid attention. "The 'wet' side is for developing and printing and it's always located near a source of water."

"That's right. We'll be using a great deal of water for all our processes. And, what of the 'dry' side? What is it used for?"

"To expose the negatives," he said brightly.

"Very good! Geoffrey, you are remarkable. I do believe you are ready for your first photography lesson."

"Really? You mean with the camera?"

She chuckled at that. "Yes, with the camera. We are finished here. I thought we'd set up on the east lawn and photograph your relatives taking their tea on the terrace. You will be my assistant."

"Capital!" He grinned, using his favorite word.

Vanessa glanced down at her soiled work dress, then at his clothes and tousled hair. "Of course, we need to freshen up. A photographer must always be presentable while publicly employed at his craft."

She consulted her pocket watch.

"Let us meet back here in the Photo House in thirty minutes. That will give us ample time to transfer our equipment to the east lawn. Have you a watch, Geoffrey?"

He shook his head. "No, Mrs. Wynters, but I won't be late. I promise!"

He dashed from the room on a wave of excitement.

Vanessa followed at a slower pace, smiling at his energy and passion.

For her photographing session, Vanessa chose to wear a walking ensemble of dark blue serge. Its ample skirt would not hobble her step, and its short jacket, while close-fitting, was designed with enough ease to allow her the freedom of movement she required. She added to this comfortable, low-heeled boots.

As Vanessa repinned her hair, she felt supremely

happy and equally terrified. Since Reginald's death, she'd been forced to be self-reliant. She'd been fortunate in her employment of Lady Gwen. Now startlingly, overnight, she'd essentially become her own employer.

Her natural impulses cried out that she follow a more conventional, secure course than to pursue photography professionally. Perhaps, it would not seem so risky a venture were she a man, for then the entire world would be open to her. As a woman, most doors were firmly shut.

Thanks to the generosity of Adrian Marrable, she would be free of financial concerns for a full year and more as she sought to establish herself. It was crucial she succeed. She did not wish him to feel his confidence or money to be misplaced in her, of course. But even more important, she needed a dependable means of supporting herself for the years to come.

Wile many a widowed lady of her age might hope to make another marriage, she could not. It was not that she was opposed to the thought of remarrying, should she find a man whom she could love and respect. The truth of the matter was, she feared she was barren.

Vanessa gave forth a resigned sigh, her hand slipping downward to rest over her abdomen. How could she ask a man to commit himself to her for a lifetime when she very likely could bear him no children? How could she hope he'd wish to do so? Despite her own heartache over the matter, she knew she must face the future knowing she would need to make her own way and provide for herself until the end of her days.

Unwilling to dwell further on her unhappy circumstance, she caught up her bonnet from the bed, then tossed it down again, deciding not to wear it.

Vanessa glanced over the splendid Gothicized room with its wonderful rosette window and century-old furnishings. Her spirits lifted. She would have the opportunity to photograph it after all, along with Sherringham's other treasures.

As her gaze drew to the French crédence—an intricately carved storage cabinet that stood on high legs—she spied a clean handkerchief lying folded neatly atop it.

Crossing to the crédence, she retrieved the linen and saw that it bore the monogram "L. M." Despite her instructions to the maid, the handkerchief had been mistakenly returned to the guest chamber rather than delivered to Lawrence. She slipped the handkerchief into the pocket in her skirt, deciding she could attend to the matter easily enough herself.

Departing the room, Vanessa quickened along the vaulted corridor of the Upper Cloisters, her thoughts reaching ahead to the Photo House and the equipment she would need for the group portrait of the Marrables at tea.

Chapter 6

Vanessa and Geoffrey arrived at the east terrace before the others, save for the servants who were busily setting out the table and arranging it with fine linen and china.

Seeing that a flight of low, broad steps fronted the terrace with no balustrade obstructing her view, Vanessa chose to set up her equipment on the lawn.

She first walked the ground, assessing where to position her camera for the best perspective and the proper distance she would need from her subject.

"It is important to envision the finished photograph in your mind before you begin working with the camera itself," she explained to Geoffrey, who trailed behind her with the leggy tripod in his arms.

Stopping slightly left of the terrace, she held up her hands before her, the tips of her thumbs touching and her forefingers extended skyward, framing the terrace and the activity there. She took two measured paces backward.

"Yes, this will be good."

After situating the tripod, Vanessa and Geoffrey began transferring the other equipment from where they'd left it resting on the green.

Geoffrey watched fascinated as Vanessa unlatched a

plain oaken box and folded back its hinged panels, revealing the camera compacted within. Firmly but gently she pulled the front lens panel forward, extending the attached maroon-colored bellows.

"Smashing!" Geoffrey exclaimed.

Vanessa smiled as she affixed the camera onto the tripod.

"A camera is no more than a box, really," she informed Geoffrey. "It supports a lens at the front and a plate holder at the back. The leather bellows form the main body, but the whole affair is 'light-tight,' as we say."

Geoffrey scrunched his face as he eyed the shilling-sized hole in the front panel. "I don't see a lens."

"Patience." She chuckled, turning to the small chest they'd brought with them and opening its lid. From a box nested inside, she lifted out a costly lens and fitted its brass barrel in place.

Vanessa next draped the black focusing cloth over the back of the camera then ducked underneath to inspect the image on the ground-glass viewing screen. Emerging for a brief moment, she made adjustments to the lens and bellow extension then checked the glass again.

"Light passes through the lens and reflects the image onto the back screen," she continued to lesson Geoffrey as she brought the image into focus. "Here, have a look for yourself."

The lad happily took her place, disappearing under the cloth.

"It's upside down!" He sounded roundly disappointed.

"True, but you will find that actually helps us compose better photographs," she assured.

"Oh, look, there's Mama and Papa. They're walking on their heads! And, they've brought our new puppy.

He doesn't have a name yet, but Mama wants to call him Crumpet."

Geoffrey popped out from beneath the cloth and waved madly toward the terrace.

"Why don't you take a moment to visit them?" Vanessa suggested, seeing the boy's excitement as he tried to catch the pup's attention.

While Geoffrey dashed to join his family, Vanessa continued to work, thankful the day was favorable enough to take tea out-of-doors. "September blows soft," she recalled the saying. All too soon the days would shorten and grow cold.

Pondering the composition that appeared on the viewing plate, she decided to move the camera another foot to the left and increase its angle. In so doing, not only would she be able to capture the central portion of the terrace with its rugged stone facade and huge windows of plate glass, but also the wonderful tower to the right of it, occupying the corner where the east and south wings met.

Vanessa made further adjustments to see how much of the tower she could include. A scarlet creeper scaled its face, encompassing a row of diamond-paned windows on the second story. The creeper climbed higher still, to where arrow slits punctured the wall, ringing the tower beneath its crenellated crown.

Vanessa knew it would be impossible to capture the upper half of the tower, but she succeeded in including the picturesque windows within the picture's frame.

Emerging from the cloth, Vanessa took up her notebook and pencil and began to make notations as to the brightness of the day, angle of the sun, and the steepness of the shadows. Geoffrey rejoined her just as she dipped under the cloth again.

She began to scan the focused image for distortions around the margins, then paused as Majel and her husband appeared on the glass. Even though the figures reflected from the terrace were inverted, Vanessa observed a marked coolness between the two sisters. She remembered then Majel and Cissy were to have begun dividing Lady Gwen's jewels between themselves this afternoon.

Leaving the camera, Vanessa moved to locate the box containing her brass Waterhouse stops. As she straightened, she noticed Lawrence emerging from the door onto the terrace. His eyes drew to her immediately. With a smile and nod of his head, he acknowledged her presence without hint that anything improper had passed between them earlier in the Photo House. She sincerely hoped the man would comport himself fittingly throughout tea.

Vanessa redirected her attention to Geoffrey, who was amusing himself with the images on the viewing glass. As she approached, he came out from the focusing cloth.

"Can we take the photograph now?" Hopeful expectancy stamped his features.

"Not quite yet, Geoffrey. We have focused the image but we must now decide on the correct exposure." She opened the velvet-lined box containing a dozen brass discs. "These are called stops, and they slip into a slot on the front of the lens. They help control the amount of light entering the camera. The shutter controls the amount of time the light is allowed in."

She cast another brief glance to the terrace to see if Lord Marrable had yet arrived, and felt a flash of disappointment that he had not.

"But, how do you know which stops to use?" Geoffrey's brows pulled together as he peered into the box.

"By experience and instinct." She winked and added, "And by keeping excellent notes."

Timmons drew her gaze as he and his assistant arrived on the terrace with trays of sandwiches and cakes and an elaborate silver tea service. Majel seated herself behind the cups and shiny pot, prepared to preside as hostess. Meanwhile, the puppy took notice of the stuffed bird atop Majel's hat and broke into a rash of yapping. Pasha, the blue-gray Persian cat, which had been lazing on a step, darted for higher ground and found security on a nearby ledge.

Vanessa's mood dipped as the others began to engage in the rituals of afternoon tea and partake of the table fare. Had Lord Marrable sent word he would not be attending?

Ignoring a fresh and inexplicable wave of disappointment, Vanessa turned back to Geoffrey. Taking up her notebook, she opened it to the back.

"Lady Gwen and I worked out a table to determine the proper exposure under different conditions," she began, showing him the page. "There is much to consider—the brightness or dullness of the day, the differing intensities of light reflected from the objects and surfaces in the picture, the details contained in the shadows.

"You will hear me say often the camera records light and form," she continued. "Look at the terrace—the people, the stone, and paned windows behind them. Think of it all in terms of light, shapes, and textures. Now, look at the vines on the tower."

She lifted her arm and pointed to the creeper surrounding the upper windows.

"See how those lay in deep shadow? We won't want to lose any of their definition nor that of the leaded glass."

A fleck of movement caught the corner of her eye. Skimming a glance to the terrace, Vanessa found Adrian Marrable standing there, his midnight eyes fixed upon her.

Vanessa froze in place as their eyes locked, her arm still lifted high. His gaze swept down over her and back again, so swiftly she questioned in the next instance whether he'd done so at all. Yet, her breasts and thighs tingled—and everything else in between—as though he'd just caressed her with more than the dark heat of his eyes.

Vanessa broke away her gaze and lowered her arm, diverting her attention to the box of discs. She fumbled for the desired piece, feeling as though she'd just sprouted ten thumbs.

"Here, Geoffrey. Why don't you insert the stop? Look for the slot on top of the lens barrel."

"Oh, may I?" He exclaimed, taking the disc and hastening to do so.

Vanessa flicked a glance back to the terrace and discovered that Lawrence had moved to Adrian's side and engaged him in conversation.

Adrian? Had she truly just mentally referred to Viscount Marrable so personally? Vanessa reprimanded herself for the slip. It would not do to think of the unfathomable master of Sherringham in familiar terms. Indeed, judging by the clamorous warning sounding in her heart, she suspected it would be supremely hazardous to do so.

Daring another glance, she watched as he took a chair at the table's left end and answered a question Lord Norland, Cissy's husband, posed. Vanessa took a small swallow at the powerful figure the viscount cut, so potently virile even while seated and seemingly relaxed.

"I don't understand, Mrs. Wynters." Geoffrey's young voice broke through her thoughts. "How is the picture made? Is it etched onto the viewing glass?"

"What? Oh, no. It's not etched at all," she replied distractedly. Drawing her attention from the terrace scene, she turned to the lad. "Once we complete our adjustments to the camera, we will carefully remove the screen and replace it with a specially sensitized glass plate which will become the negative."

She felt the pull of Lord Marrable's dark eyes, reaching across the green to her. She resisted the temptation to meet his gaze though found, by tilting her head, she could see him in her peripheral vision, staring intently in her direction.

She cleared her throat. "What was I saying? Oh, yes. The plate is coated with an emulsion containing silver nitrate. The crystals of silver are what record the image. They are highly sensitive to light and turn black when exposed to it."

Vanessa's resistance wavered. Hesitantly, she lifted her eyes toward the terrace and instantly met Adrian Marrable's magnetic gaze. Her mouth turned desert dry.

"I'm not sure I understand." Geoffrey cocked his head to one side.

"Neither am I," she said softly, wondering why the viscount should be staring at her so. She moistened her lips. "I mean, that's quite all right, Geoffrey. There's much to learn and you'll understand better as we go through the various steps of photographing and developing and printing out."

With that, Vanessa took refuge under the focusing cloth, claiming the need to examine the viewing glass once more. Her heart beat steady and rapid as she observed Lord Marrable there. Even upside down and in reverse, his was a surpassing figure.

She inclined her head to one side to better view him. The cloth dragged at her hair, causing pins to slip free.

Adrian Marrable had the most magnificent brows, she decided. They arched wide, bracketing his large, ebony eyes.

There was something guarded in the depths of those eyes. It was a look that was ever present. Yet, just now, she beheld something more there, something intense, burning.

Vanessa slanted her head the opposite direction, aware more pins fell from her hair. As she viewed the four Marrable siblings, it struck her how different were their looks, most especially Lord Marrable. While Lawrence's head shone of bright gold, Majel possessed gingery hair. Cissy's tended to the brown tones, though nowhere nearly as dark as her brother Adrian's. None of the younger Marrables bore the viscount's midnight eyes.

"Mrs. Wynters. May I have another look?" Geoffrey tugged at her skirt. "Mrs. Wynters?"

With a start, she realized she'd been under the cloth for a prolonged time. "Yes, of course you may."

Vanessa emerged from beneath the fabric thoroughly heated, sure she glowed red. She started to smooth her hair but at the touch of her hand, with so many pins having dropped from place, her hair began to slide down from atop her head. She grabbed for the mass and what pins she could salvage, the others lost to the grass.

Vanessa attempted to re-pin her hair into a high, soft bun, but again and again its weight pulled it downward, sending more pins into the grass. Discovering Lord Marrable's eyes resting on her once more, a light smile playing at the corner of his lips, Vanessa abandoned her attempts. Quickly, twisting her hair, she draped the coil over one shoulder and left it at that.

Her pulse pounded foolishly as she made an additional check of the shutter, though it needed none.

"Mama is waving us over for tea, Mrs. Wynters."

Looking up, Vanessa saw Cissy bidding them to join the others.

"Run ahead, Geoffrey. I'll be right behind you."

Vanessa closed the chest containing her supplies, then followed. As she crossed the green, Lord Marrable watched her approach. Beneath his consuming gaze, she felt positively naked.

Adrian battled against elemental instincts and an array of emotions he'd long buried and denied. They'd leaped jarringly to life the moment he first set eyes on Vanessa Wynters. And now, with each new encounter, they grew stronger and more mutinous against his will.

He watched her graceful movements as she worked with her camera and wondered what about the woman affected him so.

He preferred to believe the feelings she aroused in him were purely physical, that and no more. Yet he recognized what first began as a craving was fast growing into an acute and sizable hunger, a hunger filled with need.

That need pulled at both heart and soul, reminding him of the emptiness there.

He continued to observe the young widow and his nephew. She had an easy way with the lad, which pleased him. Geoffrey's interest shifted toward the terrace. As he left her side and headed in that direction, she bent to close one of her equipment chests.

His gaze glanced over her delicately refined features, the sweep of brow and the slim nose, her cheek bones high and flushed with color just now, her mouth full and ripe.

She rose, standing to a medium height. Her slender but shapely build made her appear taller at this distance than he knew she truly was. Adrian allowed his gaze to trace over her high round breasts, then move lower to a waist he could easily span with his hands, and then to her softly rounded hips.

When her hair first tumbled from place, he'd found himself transfixed. Now, he felt equally so as she started toward the terrace, moving with a natural grace, completely unaffected, her hair flowing like a river of honey over her shoulder.

Adrian found he could not pull his gaze from her lovely form as an unwelcome surge of desire built in his loins.

"What is your pleasure, Adrian?"

Vanessa Wynters lifted liquid eyes to his as she progressed toward him, crossing the green.

"Pleasure?" He mumbled, feeling the heat in his veins rise. With a start, Adrian straightened in his chair, his gaze skipping to Majel as he realized it was she who had spoken. He stared at her blankly. "What about pleasure?"

"Sugar or cream, brother? How do you prefer your tea?" Majel asked, her tone slightly impatient.

Cissy, however, smiled wide, her gaze drawing to Vanessa Wynters and back again. An unmistakable beam sparkled in her eyes.

"Black," he said irritably to his one sister and strove to ignore the other.

In typical fashion, Cissy refused to be dismissed and slipped into the chair beside him.

"Adrian, you must be sure to pose for Vanessa." Her smile remained fixed in place.

Adrian leveled her his most forbearing look then next grimaced at his first swallow of tea. He handed the cup back to Majel for two lumps of sugar.

"Have you forgotten the mourning album?" Cissy pressed. "As I told you, it's a keepsake, in memory of Auntie. Really, Adrian, you must let Vanessa take your portrait for it." She reached over and patted the back of his hand with teasing reassurance. "Do not fear. I'm sure you will find the experience most pleasant."

Cissy's grin disappeared behind her cup as she lifted it and sipped its contents.

Adrian gave her a noncommittal grunt. Feeling a weight press on the toe of his boot, he looked down to find the puppy had plopped his furry little rump there as he fixed his attention on Cissy. Excitedly, the pup watched as she lifted a sandwich from a nearby tray.

Spying the anxious fellow, Cissy laughed and broke off a piece which was filled with anchovies. "There you are, Crumpet."

She proffered the treat and laughed again as the puppy sprang forward to gobble it down, then plopped on Adrian's boot once more.

"Perhaps I should call you Anchovy." She broke off another piece and held it out.

Cissy's husband appeared behind her, then leaned slightly forward, over her shoulder, to watch the animal's antics.

"Darling, it's silly to name a dog after food. A fine fellow like him needs a more sensible name. Rutherford, for example."

Cissy wrinkled her nose. "I think a better name would be 'Henry,' Henry." She sent him a mischievous smile.

Geoffrey mounted the steps, greeting Adrian and his parents with a smile as he approached the table and scanned the fare. Passing over the spreads and delicate sandwiches, he eyed the scones and custard cakes.

Majel paused in her conversation with Lawrence and her husband and arched a thin brow, her eyes half-lidded. "Shouldn't you be taking tea with your sisters in the nursery, dear?"

Geoffrey's hand froze, poised over a scone, his smile falling from his lips. He looked to his parents as if to ask whether he should leave.

Adrian started to censure Majel, realizing she bedeviled the boy only to annoy his mother. Cissy, he knew, had successfully thwarted Majel's manipulations earlier regarding the division of their aunt's jewels. Predictably, Majel now wished to draw a little blood. But before he or anyone else could open their mouths, Mrs. Wynters came to stand behind Geoffrey and laid a reassuring hand on his shoulder.

"Geoffrey is my assistant and utterly indispensable to me. Does his presence pose a difficulty?"

Majel's eyes narrowed over her new prey. "You surprise me, Mrs. Wynters. I would expect you to know in well-bred circles it is inappropriate for children to attend the adults' tea."

The widow's own eyes constricted.

"And which children do you mean? I see only a fine young man," she returned evenly, completely unruffled and budging not one inch.

"As do I," Adrian quickly added before Majel unsheathed her claws fully.

He rose from his chair, silently castigating himself for

not having done so immediately, when Mrs. Wynters first stepped onto the terrace.

Her cool handling of his overbearing sister impressed him no end, as did the very fact that she stood her ground where his nephew, Geoffrey, was concerned. Majel made an art of dissecting others when it suited or amused her. It was an art which had often discomposed his former wives, sending Clairissa into hystereics, Olivia into rages, all to the delight of Majel. But neither had dared challenge Majel as did this young woman.

Adrian glanced to Cissy, who wore a look of gratefulness, and Henry, wearing one of admiration, for Vanessa Wynters. Vanessa.

"I, for one, am delighted you could join us, Geoffrey." Adrian stepped toward his nephew, smiling. In truth, he was not one for strict formalities himself. "I believe you've grown a foot since last I saw you."

This elicited a smile from the lad.

"I see you have an eye for the sweets. Here, you must try a Fat Rascal." He lifted the dish of soft currant cookies. "They're my own favorite and intolerably good."

"Thank you, Uncle." Geoffrey claimed the top cookie, his spirits returning.

Adrian glanced over his head to Vanessa and saw that she too wore a smile. A smile that lit a small flame in the recesses of his heart.

As Geoffrey bit into the cookie it broke, half of it falling to the stone terrace. The puppy instantly sprang forward and gulped it down, then licking its mouth, looked pleadingly to Geoffrey for more.

"Rascal! We can call him Rascal." Geoffrey grinned at his parents for his cleverness.

"He's definitely that!" His father chuckled. "Rascal it is then, but in reference to a scamp, not a cookie."

Lawrence moved to Vanessa's side. Adrian did not miss the glow in his eyes as he settled his gaze on her.

"Do pour Vanessa a cup of tea, sister dear." Lawrence directed his comment past his shoulder to Majel. "We mustn't let her think you are wholly without manners."

Adrian lifted a brow at his brother's use of Vanessa's first name. Were the two on more familiar terms than he'd realized?

Lawrence relieved Majel of the steaming cup of tea and, in turn, offered it to Vanessa. As her fingers closed on the saucer, he deliberately brushed her fingertips with his own. Startled, Vanessa jumped back a step, jarring the cup on the saucer and spilling the tea.

"How clumsy of me," she blurted apologetically, a stain of pink growing in her cheeks.

Cissy quickly came to her aid with a napkin and helped her blot the wetness from her dress.

"Are you burned?" she asked anxiously, at the same time shooting Lawrence a hard look.

"I'm all right," Vanessa assured. "The tea caught my skirt mainly. No harm done."

Lawrence appeared entirely uncontrite to Adrian's eyes. Indeed, he seemed to relish the sight of Vanessa wiping at a small irregular blotch just below her breast. Adrian considered tossing his brother down the steps.

Vanessa suddenly became conscious of Lawrence's interest as well. She turned aside a moment, then, seeming to remember something, she fumbled in her skirt pocket and withdrew a folded, linen handkerchief.

"I—I almost forgot." She turned back to Lawrence. "I had this cleaned for you but it found its way back to my room by mistake. Thank you for its use."

Vanessa held forth the handkerchief to Lawrence, the

initials "L.M." clearly visible on the corner. Adrian felt his stomach knot.

As Lawrence reached to accept the linen, he covered Vanessa's hands with his own. "No thanks is necessary, fair lady."

Adrian bit down on his annoyance with Lawrence. Or was it jealousy that stabbed at his gut? Regardless, his brother's manners and forwardness were deplorable.

Vanessa repossessed herself of her hands and stepped back several steps.

"If you will excuse me, I best take the picture before the light begins to dim. I do hope you are all ready to be photographed. A portrait of the Marrable clan gathered for tea will make a nice frontispiece for the book on Sherringham, I should think. Geoffrey, if you would like to be included in the picture, then stay. You might sit on the top step there with Rascal."

Geoffrey nodded he would remain, his mouth filled with cookie.

Adrian's gaze followed Vanessa as she descended the steps and started across the green. There was a stiffness in her spine and a briskness to her step that caused a most captivating sway to her bustled hips and skirts.

"She's an absolute vision isn't she?" Lawrence commented, moving to his side.

Adrian glanced to his brother and saw that his gaze was hotly devouring Vanessa.

"I can tell you one thing, brother Adrian. She fits in a man's arms just right."

Lawrence tossed Adrian a knowing look, his lips lifting in a smug smile. The smile remained as he transferred his gaze back to Vanessa, all too obviously undressing her with his eyes.

Adrian restrained himself from putting his fist across Lawrence's jaw.

"I'm going to ride out," he growled. "Tell Cook not to hold dinner for me."

Adrian stalked down the steps and headed for the stables.

Vanessa watched as Lord Marrable strode from the terrace, a storm of emotion darkening his face. Cissy called after him to no avail. Lawrence, in turn, sent Vanessa a mystified look, shrugging as if to convey his brother's actions were wholly inexplicable.

Perplexed, Vanessa thought back over the moments that had transpired on the terrace but could think of nothing to have provoked Lord Marrable.

Thinking it best to proceed with the portrait, she asked the others to gather around the table. Lawrence preferred to stand, while Cissy, Majel, and their husbands remained seated. When Timmons appeared with a fresh tray of sandwiches she asked him to join the grouping. Geoffrey sat on the top step, center front of the table, but the playful puppy refused to settle down and join him.

Vanessa made a final check of the image on the viewing screen. Satisfied, she called to everyone to hold their pose then worked quickly to remove the screen, insert the plate holder containing the negative, and pull the slide.

As she worked, Adrian Marrable continued to embroil her thoughts. Did his moods always veer so sharply, so dramatically? Would she ever fathom the man?

"Look at the camera and smile!" she called with forced brightness.

Just as Vanessa released the shutter, the puppy erupted in a fit of yapping and the cat let loose a strident yowl.

Vanessa checked her watch by the dim glow of the ruby lamp. She would allow the plate four minutes more in the metol, a total of twelve, which would hopefully produce the degree of contrast she desired on the glass negative.

Vanessa leaned her hip against the work table as she waited, watching the seconds tick off.

Her thoughts wandered back to the previous hours. She'd left the others directly after dinner and came to the Photo House to develop the exposure she'd made during tea. She found herself as anxious as Geoffrey to see the results of their efforts. Regrettably, she could not allow the lad to assist her in the developing process. It required she handle a host of toxic chemicals and work in total darkness most of the time.

In any event, it was far too late for him to assist her, the hour being well on its way to midnight. She did promise he could be present when she printed the negative tomorrow. Though she'd still employ many of the same chemicals, the printing would be carried out by gaslight, minimizing the risk of an accident. Then Geoffrey could witness photography's "magic" when the finished picture appeared on the sensitized paper.

Vanessa focused on her watch again. Two minutes remained.

She swept a wayward strand of hair back from her face then rubbed her forehead. What a disaster dinner had been. Lord Marrable had not appeared at all. Majel was scarcely civil to Cissy owing to their latest argument over Lady Gwen's jewels. This, in turn, put their husbands at odds. Lawrence tried his best to lighten the evening but with poor results. He then centered his full and untiring attention on Vanessa.

When dinner came, at last, to a blessed end, Vanessa escaped to the Photo House. Fortunately, to her relief, just before she left, Timmons appeared, informing Lawrence his brother requested his presence in his private study. Still, she feared Lawrence might appear unannounced at the Photo House while she worked alone, late at night. She'd locked the door on her arrival and stood prepared to send away anyone who sought to interrupt her.

Seeing the last seconds tick off on her watch, Vanessa extinguished the lamp and moved to the developing tray.

Removing its lid, she set it aside and felt for the edges of the glass plate with her fingertips. Lifting the plate, she drained the solution from its surface then rinsed it in a bath of acetic acid and warmed water. This halted the negative's development, though it did not remove the undeveloped silver salts which remained light sensitive.

Moving another pace down the work table, she transferred the plate to the fixer to remove the remaining salts. She then quickly washed her hands as she counted off the prescribed time beneath her breath. Removing the plate, she placed it in the final tray containing the wash, then relit the ruby lamp once more.

Her excitement climbed as she viewed the reverse image of the scene on the glass negative. This was always the most magical and rewarding moment for herself.

Carefully, she lifted the plate from the wash, draining off the liquid. She then examined the image for negative contrast and density which, when printed, would render the range of gray tones. First, she studied the shadow areas for detail, then the highlighted ones. The people appeared in focus and well defined, the elements surrounding them sharp and clear.

Pleased with the results, she made a notation of the developing time in her notebook. Her first photographic endeavor at Sherringham appeared to be a success.

No sooner than the mental thought formed in her mind, Vanessa spied the puppy's image on the negative plate. Rascal stood on his hind legs to one side of the table, barking furiously. Nearby, Pasha arched her back in a perfect U, her fur bristling, as if she feared the crazed pup was about to attack.

Vanessa smiled, remembering the furor that had erupted at the very moment she'd released the camera's shutter. Despite Rascal's agitation, he appeared in focus.

Her brow dipped as she realized the pup's attention was not fixed on the cat, as she anticipated it would be. Instead, Rascal stared at something high above the terrace. Vanessa followed the puppy's line of sight to the tower's second-story row of leaded windows. There, she discovered a soft blur in the leftmost panes—the right panes, when printed out.

Disappointment stung Vanessa straight through. Light must have somehow crept into the camera. A pinhole in the bellows would be enough to cause the aberration.

As she continued to scrutinize the muted blur, she realized with a start that it was continuing to darken. Assuming silver salts remained on the plate, Vanessa quickly returned the glass negative back to the acid bath and doused the lamp. She agitated the pan, attempting to completely rinse off the crystals, then repeated the fixing and washing steps. She could only hope she wasn't damaging the quality of the rest of the negative. She'd never repeated the process on the same plate before.

Relighting the ruby lamp, she checked the negative. Relievedly, its quality had not deteriorated, and the area in question appeared to have ceased darkening. When the image printed out, it would appear a whitish mist.

Perhaps, it was a reflection of the sun off the panes, she reasoned, and not the camera's bellows that were at fault. And yet, she surely would have noticed the problem at the time.

In truth, the area in question didn't appear intensely brilliant, as one might expect from a flash of the sun's rays. "Luminous" was the word she would choose. It was as if light glowed from within the tower itself, its source on the other side of the leaded panes.

Curiously, despite the seeming diffusion of light, the area now appeared to contain significantly more detail than she'd first noticed.

As Vanessa bent close to the lamp and continued to study the plate, the temperature plummeted all around her. It was as if she were suddenly standing in an icehouse in the dead of winter.

Opening one of the worktable drawers, she placed the negative inside to dry and to keep it free of dust. She then breathed warmth on her hands, lit one of two oil lamps, and set about cleaning the worktable as swiftly as she could.

The room's temperature did not improve. With shaky fingers, she poured the solutions back into their containers, washed the pans, beakers, and utensils and stored everything in its place. By the time she finished cleaning, she was sure she'd turned blue.

Shivering, Vanessa removed her apron and slipped into her jacket, then hastened to unlock the door. She returned long enough to turn down the lamps, then hurried outside into the courtyard.

Instantly, the warmer night air greeted her. Vanessa fitted the key into the door's mechanism, scarcely able to manage it, her fingers still trembling with cold. Hearing the click of the lock, she turned and made her way along the courtyard, blanched by moonlight.

In the distance, at the far end of the complex that comprised Sherringham, rose a thick tower, silhouetted against the indigo sky, looming high over all—the west tower.

Vanessa stayed her step as she saw a movement in the topmost window there. Yet, no light shined from within. She told herself it was no more than a reflection of the night skies, of a shadow passing over the moon.

She glanced up and found a cloudless sky. Before she could form another explanation, the biting chill returned, flowing over and around her.

Vanessa clutched her jacket tight about her and dashed for the nearest door, escaping into the manse and fleeing to her bedchamber.

Chapter 7

Vanessa lit the ruby lamp. Lifting the print from the tray of fixer, she drained off the excess solution, then immersed the sheet in the wash.

"You can come over now," she called to Geoffrey who waited patiently on a stool across the room.

The boy had obeyed her directions so faithfully throughout the morning, she'd permitted him to remain in the room during the final steps of the printing-out process when she worked with chemicals once more in the dark.

"Has the picture appeared yet?" He joined her at the worktable.

"Yes, and the tones and values are excellent. See, for yourself. There you are sitting on the step, sharp and clear."

Geoffrey had been fascinated when they'd readied a sheet of silver bromide paper and, placing the glass negative atop it, exposed it by gaslight. But disappointment followed when he discovered the latent image it created remained invisible. Vanessa explained to the impatient boy the chemical process that was needed to bring out the picture itself.

"Would you like to take over agitating the pan,

Geoffrey? Just move it gently, like so, and rap it a bit on the sides."

Vanessa stepped to one side as he eagerly assumed her place and continued the motion. Together, they gazed at the print through the wavering water, Vanessa's eyes drawing immediately to the diamond-paned windows on the tower. She expelled a disappointed breath as she located the whitish mist in the right portion. It was the only thing marring an otherwise excellent photograph.

"That should be enough rinsing, Geoffrey. Why don't you lift the print out by the edges and tilt it so the water runs off. I'll open the shutters."

As Vanessa crossed to the back of the room, she heard the boy gasp.

"Mrs. Wynters!" His voice came out a high-pitched squawk. "There's a ghost in the window!"

Vanessa smiled as she moved to open the last of the shutters. "I'm sorry to disappoint you, but the blur you see is nothing more than light that somehow leaked into the camera and onto the negative. I'll need to check the bellows before I make another exposure."

Geoffrey's eyebrows butted together as he continued to scrutinize the picture. "But look, Mrs. Wynters. You can see the outline of a person. It has an arm and a hand lifted to the glass."

Vanessa returned to the worktable and looked over his shoulder. Cold trickled down her spine as she discovered what appeared to be a glowing human shape in the upper window, looking down on the terrace and the people there. The figure appeared to be dressed in flowing garments—a robe or a dress. Although nothing could be made out for a face, as Geoffrey said, the shape appeared to have an arm upraised, the hand resting against the paned window.

"I wonder which ghost it is?" Geoffrey said in a voice filled with awe, his excitement climbing.

"Whatever do you mean, *which* ghost?" Vanessa's gaze veered to the boy.

"Mama says Royal Sherringham is haunted, that many ghosts inhabit the grounds and manse. She says the shadows of Sherringham are filled with shades of the past."

"Shades of the past?"

"Yes." He nodded gravely, lifting eyes round and wide. "Spirits and bogies." He shifted his gaze back to the photograph. "Do you think this is the ghost of someone who died a gruesome death at Sherringham? Someone who is now bound here and must walk its halls and grounds for eternity?"

Vanessa lifted a brow at that. "What I think is you have an extraordinary and most active imagination, young man. I assure you, what you see on the photograph is no more than a trick of light."

But despite her words, Vanessa couldn't dismiss the distinctly human shape.

While Geoffrey took his lunch, Vanessa remained in the Photo House to inspect her camera. Opening it out and extending the bellows, she next mounted the lens in place and closed the shutter attachment. She verified the construction's overall sturdiness and examined the pleated leather for signs of wear.

Working with deft fingers, Vanessa removed the glass viewing screen at the back. Setting it aside, she then crossed to the window and held the camera to the light. Meticulously, she scanned the inside of the bellows for evidence of tiny cracks or pinholes that might allow in even the most minute amount of light. She discovered nothing. In every way, the camera proved light-tight.

Vanessa decided to test the camera further. When Geoffrey reappeared, to the boy's delight, she suggested they gather the equipment and photograph some exterior views of the manse.

Several hours later, upon their return, Vanessa set about developing the freshly exposed negatives. When none displayed irregularities or unusual inclusions of light, she had to accept her camera was sound.

As a last thought, Vanessa reinspected the negative of the terrace scene from yesterday, wondering if the plate itself might have been improperly prepared, the silver nitrate solution spread unevenly over its surface. She found nothing to suggest that it had.

Vanessa worked continuously late into the day, foregoing joining the others at tea but having some of the hot beverage and scones sent to the Photo House for herself and Geoffrey. The boy proved most helpful, and his carefulness around the chemicals allayed her initial worries. Still, she required him to perch on the stool whenever she found it necessary to work in absolute dark.

Several times more, she examined the finished print of the terrace scene. She wholly discounted that the lucent area in question was a reflection of the sky or sun. yet, she was at a loss to explain what might account for the effect or how its source appeared to emanate from the other side of the glass.

On completing the printing-out process, Vanessa secured the wet prints to the edges of the shelves with brass pins, leaving them to dry. She and Geoffrey then cleaned away the trays and implements.

Locking the Photo House, Vanessa and Geoffrey made their way across the courtyard and into the heart of the manse. She thanked him for his generous help and bid him a good evening, then proceeded to her bedchamber to dress for dinner.

Vanessa decided to remain silent on the subject of the terrace photograph. Perhaps, no one would inquire about it just yet.

"Geoffrey told me the most remarkable tale." Cissy's twinkling gaze alighted on Vanessa from across the table. "He said there is a ghost in the photograph you took of us at tea yesterday."

Vanessa choked on the morsel of beef she was in the midst of chewing and had to take a swallow of wine to clear her throat.

"He's a rather imaginative young fellow." She smiled and darted a self-conscious look along the table. Momentarily, she held everyone's attention.

Vanessa took another swallow of wine. Geoffrey, with his youthful enthusiasm, had likely spread the word from one end of Sherringham to the other by now.

"Light corrupted a portion of the negative some-how," she offered by way of explanation, unable to provide any other, though she held certain her camera was not at fault. "It's most embarrassing to have that occur with my first official photograph of Sherring-ham. Geoffrey fancies it's a figure glowing in the tower."

"Well, don't keep us tantalized," Cissy pressed.

"You must bring the photograph to the saloon after dinner."

"Yes, you must," Lawrence encouraged from his place a little farther down the table. "It should make for fascinating conversation this evening."

Vanessa glanced to Lord Marrable who sat near, at the table's head. As they took their evening meal in a small but exquisite dining room, no one sat at a great distance from anyone else.

Lawrence dropped his napkin on the table and leaned back in his chair, his gaze going to his brother. "Tell me, Adrian, how was your ride into Hereford today?"

"Productive," Lord Marrable commented in his rich voice, then fell silent once more.

Vanessa had not seen the viscount since yesterday's tea when he'd left so abruptly. As she'd taken none of her meals with the family today, she'd not realized he'd been absent from Sherringham. But then, the fact they'd not encountered one another was, in itself, unremarkable. The mansion complex and its grounds were extensive.

The side of Lawrence's mouth slid upward into a half smile, his eyes still fixed on his brother. "I understand you rode that black devil, Samson. I thought you were going to sell the beast."

"His fire suits me," Lord Marrable replied dryly. "He's settled down a bit since when last you encountered him."

"I'm glad to hear it, though I doubt he tolerates anyone near him save you. I certainly don't intend to attempt it." Lawrence turned his pale blue gaze on Vanessa. "Do you ride, Vanessa?"

Apprehension rose in Vanessa's breast. She suspected an invitation lurked behind Lawrence's question and that he would insist she ride out with him on the morrow should she answer yes. She held no wish to be alone with the man. He was entirely too presumptuous and forward in his attentions. After Lawrence's display in the presence of his family yesterday, she decided not to trust his judgment as to what constituted proper behavior.

"I haven't ridden for years, I'm afraid. I did so while growing up but not since my marriage or while traveling with your aunt."

Lawrence started to speak but Majel seized on Vanessa's comment and asked of hers and Lady Gwen's excursions abroad, particularly those to Paris and the Mediterranean.

"And how long did you say you were married?" Majel's husband suddenly interjected with little tact.

"I didn't say, Lord Pendergast." Vanessa grew aware of the viscount's eyes drawing to her. "But if you would know, Reginald and I enjoyed a full year-and-a-half of marriage."

The actual time they'd lived together was far less, but she saw no reason to disclose it.

"And did you and your husband travel?" Lord Pendergast prodded further, then paused. "Sorry, I suppose I should ask if he was a man of leisure. Or was it that he was obliged to engage in a profession?"

Vanessa detected a note of disdain in his voice at the mention of a profession. Really, the man surely needed to be lessoned in social graces. She raised her chin knowing it carried a measure of defiance and pride, the same as contained in her heart.

"Reginald was the fourth son of a baronet. And yes, he did pursue an occupation. He and a friend formed a private firm, actually. They engineered bridges. Reginald's last project was for the Home Office which took him to Raijapur. I was to join him, but before I could . . ." Her voice caught, going suddenly dry. She moistened her lips as she recalled the telegram bearing the devastating news. "The bridge collapsed. Reginald was among those who died."

"My condolences, Mrs. Wynters," Lord Marrable offered at once. "It must have been most tragic for you."

Vanessa lifted her eyes to his and found empathy there. "Yes, most tragic," she said quietly, realizing this was a man who understood such loss. "Please, call me Vanessa."

A light entered his eyes, warming their darkness. He inclined his head toward her, ever so briefly, accepting her request. She'd pleased him, she realized, and found that pleased her as well.

Henry Norland leaned forward at his place, curiosity etching his brow. "Am I correct to assume your husband's share in the firm fell to you upon his death? That you are engaged, even indirectly, in bridge construction?"

"No." She shook her head, feeling a familiar pain mixed with anger rise in her heart. "According to an agreement which predated our marriage, the firm became the sole holding of Reginald's partner at his death, a Mr. George Newland."

It had been a piece of slick business. When she'd spurned Mr. Newland's unwanted advances—made before her husband's body had even been returned from India—he seized the business and profits. Reginald had drawn up legal documents, provisions for her in the event of his death. Or so he'd vowed to her on their wedding day. But Mr. Newland claimed the two had a verbal agreement that, should one of them die, the surviving partner would inherit all. No papers were ever found in the firm's vault to back Reginald's claim to Vanessa. She assumed George Newland had burned them to ashes.

"But your husband did make arrangements for your care, did he not?" Lord Marrable's voice drew her attention. She found his brows deeply furrowed.

"He thought he had." She spoke past a lump that had arisen in her throat.

Whatever his faults, Reginald had been a good and thoughtful man. He'd been keenly aware of the dangers of his profession. But he'd utterly misjudged his partner.

Vanessa lay her napkin beside her plate. "If you will excuse me, I'll retrieve the picture from the Photo House. Geoffrey and I took several more exposures today. Perhaps you'd like to see them also."

The men stood as she rose from her place.

"Perhaps, I should accompany you," Lawrence offered.

"Thank you, but I would much prefer to walk alone just now."

At that she fell to silence and withdrew.

As Adrian entered the drawing room, the warmth of its decor and glowing golden oak instantly welcomed him.

He cast a swift glance to the others who had preceded him there and noted Vanessa's absence. As he'd already sent Timmons to locate her and inform her the family had adjourned here, rather than the saloon, he tempered his concern. Consulting his watch, he marked the time.

Adrian looked to where Cissy and Majel were in the course of seating themselves on adjacent couches, and to where Lawrence, Henry, and Nigel clustered before the great leaded window, debating some point on grouse shooting.

Holding no wish to join that particular exchange, Adrian lingered in place a moment and ran an eye over the fine furnishings, woodwork and ornamentation that graced the room. It seemed an age since last he stood here. Still, the Gothic drawing room remained one of his favorite retreats at Sherringham.

Blues and greens dominated the space—rising from the patterned Persian carpet, covering the sofas in solid jewel tones, and spreading overhead like a verdant canopy, the vaulted ceiling richly painted and its ribbing, pendants, and leaflike molding all gilded gold.

Adrian's eyes drew to the fireplace. There, above the mantelpiece, Leonine Marrable looked out from an ornate frame, her dark eyes flashing as she watched over all who entered her domain.

Adrian slowly crossed to the fireplace, his gaze still fixed on the portrait of his distant, and rather scandalous, relative.

Leonine smiled through the layers of paints and oils as she lounged unblushingly in flowing robes of damask and silk. Her loosely parted garments revealed a creamy expanse of neck and shoulder and one perfect breast, its rose-tipped nipple enticingly exposed.

Leonine's left arm rested on a red silken pillow, a small spaniel filling her lap. The symbolism was not lost to Adrian—the animal, representing fidelity, conspicuously placed over the cloaked prize awaiting her lover. Her long, black ringlets of hair spilled bewitchingly to her waist, and her open gaze offered invitation.

Adrian perused the costly rings gleaming upon Leonine's fingers, and the jewels sparkling at her ears. Upon her wrist she wore a bracelet of braided gold. A locket, faced with a porcelain miniature, dangled from its precious threads, the likeness it bore being that of King Charles II.

Adrian knew the monarch had commissioned the portrait of his much beloved mistress, meant for his royal eyes alone. But upon Leonine's untimely death, the king presented it to the family, being unable to bear to look upon her image, his grief so great.

The jewels Leonine wore in the painting, Adrian had held in his own hands, for they formed part of the Marrable treasure. Gazing on Leonine, he almost felt he should apologize that they should now be lost.

Adrian slipped his hand into his coat pocket and felt the square of paper folded there—a copy of his wire to Cameron Kincaid. He'd dispatched the message from Hereford earlier today, refining his latest theories about Olivia and the disappearance of the jewels.

Disappointingly, he'd found nothing of importance in his search of Olivia's room and subsequently had it cleared of all its contents. Her wedding ring remained missing, its fate as much a mystery as that of the Marrable jewels.

Adrian had also spoken at length with Lawrence, painstakingly reviewing the night of the accident and his brother's testimony to Hereford's constable. Again, Adrian discovered nothing new, or previously overlooked, concerning the events surrounding his wife's presumed death.

For his own peace of mind and satisfaction, he'd gone so far as to reenact his brother's account, to see if there was any detail Lawrence could have missed. Late last night, he'd sent Timmons out in the carriage with the lanterns lit. He then watched from the west tower as Timmons traveled as far as Devil's Hairpin. But all he saw in the dark distance was the carriage light moving farther and farther away. Adrian closed his thoughts to what his brother must have seen the night the carriage burst into flames.

Returning his attention to Leonine's portrait, he allowed his mind to wander, as he did his eyes over the painting's details. His gaze traced Leonine's smiling lips then trailed lower, over her pale flesh. As his eyes alighted on her tender breast, he heard Cissy greet Vanessa across the room.

Adrian turned and was instantly struck anew by how ravishing Vanessa appeared tonight. She wore an evening dress of garnet-red silk. Creamy lace spilled from its low, rounded neckline, which, at his height, offered a tantalizing view of cleavage. The bodice molded her figure past the waist and over the top of her hips, while below, the gown's silk faille was softly draped and trained.

Her open neckline and upswept hair bared a long column of neck. Throughout dinner he'd wondered if a name could be given to the true color of her tresses— a color which appeared a golden honey across the room, but he knew to be composed of many differing shades.

Vanessa's large aqua eyes were wondrously changeable, he'd discovered, sometimes more blue than green and, at others, the converse. Tonight, in the drawing room, their hues were perfectly balanced. As he drank in the sight of her, in her garnet gown that perfectly complimented the room, it struck him she seemed fashioned expressly to belong here, in this setting, that of his ancestral home.

Adrian's gaze traveled over her features then skimmed downward over her throat, coming to rest on the round fullness of her breasts. Perhaps he'd gazed on Leonine's attributes overlong, but he could easily envision Vanessa's sweet mounds of flesh and their taut, pink crests, awaiting beneath the layers of lace and silk.

Adrian shut his eyes tight and clamped down on his treasonous strain of thought and rising desire. Involvement with a woman would only lead to heartache, he told himself. Besides, Lawrence and Vanessa had apparently formed an attachment already.

When Adrian opened his eyes, again, he saw Lawrence crossing the room toward Vanessa. He could not fault his brother for the admiration shining in his eyes. Obviously, some bond of affection lay between the two.

Adrian started to turn away, then paused as Vanessa moved to the sofa and took a place beside Cissy. Did he imagine it, or had she just purposely evaded Lawrence?

As Adrian gazed on her, he wondered if Vanessa's feelings toward his brother matched Lawrence's enthusiasm for her, or even came near. What was their relationship after all?

Lord Marrable stood before the fireplace, staring up at the painting of a beautiful, dark-haired woman. Vanessa recognized instantly the woman depicted there possessed the same sable hair and midnight eyes as he.

As the viscount turned, she looked aside, aware of his gaze drawing to her. Her grip tensed on the photographs she held in her hand. Was she always to become so discomposed in his presence?

Vanessa became suddenly aware of Lawrence, midway across the room and heading toward her, a fire banked in his eyes. She dreaded what attentions he might attempt to press upon her. Glancing to Cissy, she met with her inviting smile, and decided to join her. Vanessa moved with as much haste as possible without being obvious, intent on surrounding herself with others. Given the circumstance, it was the best she could think to do.

As Vanessa lowered herself onto the sofa, Cissy spied the photographs in her hand.

"May I?" she asked, reaching for the prints.

Vanessa readily gave them over, at the same time mindful of Lawrence circling the sofa grouping and drawing behind herself and Cissy.

Not wishing to be wholly ill-mannered, Vanessa acknowledged his presence with a brief, cordial smile. He returned her smile with a warm one of his own, then allowed his gaze to drop to her shoulders and lower still, settling on the neckline of her gown.

Vanessa's temper flared as she realized what he was about. Self-consciously, she lifted a hand to her chest, barring any visual excursions he might attempt.

"Oh, my. Geoffrey was right," Cissy muttered beside her, lifting the topmost photograph and studying it closely. "There appears to be a figure glowing in the tower window."

"The devil you say." Disbelief colored Lawrence's

voice as he leaned forward and relieved his sister of the picture.

Cissy's husband, Henry, left Lord Pendergast at the window and started toward them. "Darling, you can't be serious. You aren't going to start that ghost nonsense again, are you?"

"Henry Norland, it's no nonsense at all!" Cissy thrust to her feet. Snatching the photograph from Lawrence's fingers, she shoved it toward him. "You did not grow up at Sherringham as did we four. There have always been strange happenings here. It's something we've all come to accept."

Vanessa's heart did a small somersault as the image of the Marrable banner, stirring to life in Knights Chapel, sprang to mind.

"*Just an oddity.*" Lawrence had shrugged at the time. "*Sherringham has an abundance of those.*"

She was mindful, too, of the icy airs that constantly plagued her.

Nigel Pendergast moved to Henry's side and eyed the photograph in his hands. "That *is* rather curious, is it not?"

"Am I to see it, or do you intend to keep the picture entirely to yourselves?" Majel complained, rising to her feet and stretching forth her hand, her interest plainly piqued.

Receiving the print from Henry, she took up her lorgnette and peered through the lens. Her brows lifted high as she inspected the image.

"'Curious' is hardly the word." She lowered the lorgnette as she looked to the others. "You do realize, whatever this is—if anything at all—it is occupying the Tudor gallery?"

"Majel's right." Cissy's voice carried a note of awe.

She turned wide eyes to Vanessa. "The Tudor gallery is one of the oldest and most haunted part of Sherringham."

Vanessa raised her own brows at that, incredulous at the bent of the conversation. Lord Marrable, she noted, listened attentively from the fireplace but, thus far, offered no comment.

"I do hope you're jesting." Vanessa forced a smile to her lips. Cissy's and Majel's faces, even Lawrence's, told her they were not. "I mean, this is no 'spirit photograph,' if that is what you imagine. What you see in the picture is simply an aberration of light, that is all."

Cissy picked up the other prints from where they rested on the sofa and sifted through them. "These contain no 'aberrations.' When did you photograph these?"

"This morning." Vanessa could guess the direction of her thoughts.

"Using the same camera as you did yesterday?"

"Yes. The equipment seems sound enough." Vanessa bit her lip. "I really have no explanation for how the negative became corrupted. But I am also reluctant to owe it to some resident phantom of Sherringham."

Majel's gray-green eyes swept to her brother across the room. "Adrian, you are exceptionally quiet." She started toward him with the blemished photograph in hand. "Here, you must see for yourself and tell us what you think of it."

Vanessa allowed her gaze to follow Majel then drift to Lord Marrable. Their eyes touched for the briefest of moments.

"Do you not believe in ghosts?" Cissy asked, pulling her attention back.

"I—I am not sure actually. I've never given it a great deal of thought."

That wasn't quite true, Vanessa mentally corrected. Lady Gwen had held distinct beliefs on the topic which they would discuss from time to time. Then too, whenever they traveled north to Edinburgh, they would gather with a particular group of Lady Gwen's philosophical friends. Evening's end would find them invariably steeped in discussions on life-beyond-death and the spirit dimension.

Lady Gwen firmly believed that the spirits of the departed remained on the material plane, coexisting with the living and capable of communicating if they strongly desired. A surprising number of her friends concurred, though usually only to a degree. They would argue that souls that lingered on the earthly plane were trapped. They further conjectured that tragic circumstance, or wrongs not righted, prevented them from proceeding to a "higher place of Light." Others felt all spirits who had progressed retained the power to return to warn loved ones and friends of impending dangers.

"Do you wish to know what I think?" Cissy asked, glancing to her brothers and sister but not waiting for their response. "Our return for Auntie's funeral has aroused the ghosts of Sherringham. For whatever reasons, it has stirred the shades out from the shadows."

"Surely not all of them," Lawrence tossed back, a light appearing in his eyes, his lips curving. "Only one figure is visible in the photograph, after all. Or were there others I overlooked?"

"I am serious, Lawrence," Cissy scolded. "Of anyone, you and Adrian should not dismiss the possibilities." She transferred her attention to Vanessa. "I should tell you, both my brothers have actually seen the ghosts of Sherringham, and a great many of them at that."

Cissy's words stole Vanessa's breath. She did not miss the quick exchange of glances between Lawrence and the viscount.

Lawrence cleared his throat. "Actually, we witnessed only *one* incident, or thought we did—a phantom army battling on the northwest grounds."

Cissy's eyes flashed with impatience. "But Adrian encountered another ghost from a different century—a Cavalier looking for his head." She furrowed her brows. "Or was it the monk who roams the Upper Cloisters?"

"Upper Cloisters?" Vanessa's heart skipped a beat, thinking of the numerous times she'd traveled its corridors, to and from her bedchamber. She decided not to ask where the Cavalier made his search.

Vanessa shifted her glance between Cissy and Adrian Marrable. "Just how many specters frequent Sherringham? Do you really consider them to be authentic?"

The viscount came away from the fireplace, leaving Majel's side. Crossing the distance, he came to stand before Vanessa. As he returned the photograph to her possession, the corners of his mouth drew into a pensive smile.

"As with most castles and manor houses of great age, Sherringham owns a wealth of legends and tales, passed down through the centuries. Each individual must decide for himself and herself what to believe."

Lord Marrable's rich voice leant a dramatic air to his words, sending shivers along Vanessa's spine. She glanced to the misted image in the photograph. She was struck again by how eerily the figure—if it could be deemed that—stood, with a filmy hand lifted to the window and, seemingly, contemplated those gathered on the terrace below.

Moistening her lips, Vanessa lifted her eyes to Lord Marrable. "If it is not too much to ask, I would very much like to hear of Sherringham's past and of those who once peopled its halls."

"What a splendid idea," Cissy enthused with a clap of her hands. "It will make for a most entertaining evening. Besides, Vanessa can use the historical information for the text in her book. And who knows, maybe a few legends too?"

Lord Marrable's midnight eyes skimmed over the others, then returned to Vanessa. "Then I suggest a bit of sherry and a fire are in order. If anyone has noticed, a chill has settled over the room."

Though Vanessa assumed it was Lord Marrable's nearness and words that had caused her to shudder, she realized now, the room's temperature had noticeably dropped.

"Perhaps, I could also request a shawl," she commented, wondering from her own recent experience, just how cold the evening might yet become.

Once summoned, the servants quickly laid in a fire and brought glasses and a decanter of sherry.

Wrapped in a heavy shawl, Vanessa took a place on the end of the sofa with Cissy and Henry beside her. Lord Marrable assumed a chair adjacent to the couch, to her immediate left. Majel and her husband occupied the sofa opposite, while Lawrence poised on its arm, at the farthest end. Surprisingly, it was Majel who first spoke.

"As you might imagine, we Marrables were bred on

Sherringham's history," she informed Vanessa proudly, elevating her chin. "Our brother, Adrian, has actually read the estate's documents in their original versions. He's even updated them with modern translations of his own."

"You may consult them for yourself, if you wish," Lord Marrable offered, catching Vanessa's gaze. "The ancient documents, being fragile with age, are stored in a vault. However, my own transcripts are readily available in the library."

"Thank you, I am sure I will find them most interesting." Vanessa paused as his dark eyes grazed hers. She suddenly felt more warm than cold and had to grope for a coherent thought. "Your nephew, Geoffrey, said Druids once worshiped on this land."

Lord Marrable nodded. "So it is believed. Standing stones exist nearby. It is thought they were once used by the high priests as sacrificial altars."

Vanessa drew the shawl more tightly about her. "What a gruesome thought. Please do not tell me the high priests are among those who haunt Sherringham."

A smile touched Lord Marrable's lips, then faded.

"As to Sherringham's history, it really began in the eighth century when defense castles were being raised along the border against the marauding Welsh. Sherringham was one of those. Fierce battles ensued for centuries. Sherringham was burned to the ground and rebuilt numerous times, the earliest fortifications being of wood.

"With the arrival of the Normans, Sherringham was enlarged and rebuilt in stone, becoming a true baronial castle. The warring continued, of course, and did so sporadically until the time of the Union with England in the sixteenth century. An inestimable number of men fought and died on these lands."

Vanessa swallowed. "Then the ghostly battle you and Lawrence thought to see, did it appear to be an encounter between the castle defenders and the Welsh?"

Again a smile played over his lips. Before he could answer, Cissy sat forward to the edge of the sofa.

"Not all the clashes were with the Welsh," she supplied. "England had other enemies such as the Norsemen, and, at times, she also warred against herself. Many famed battles raged over Sherringham's landscape or nearby."

"That is true," Lawrence spoke up. "You've heard of the famed battle of Brunnanburgh where King Athelstan triumphed against the Danes? And Mortimer's Cross, where the Yorkists and Lancastrian's engaged one another? Those actions occurred near to here."

Nigel turned to Majel. "Did you not once tell me, there are accounts of wounded soldiers from various battles being brought to Sherringham to convalesce? Presumably, some among them died and were buried on the grounds hereabout."

What a thoroughly dismal thought, Vanessa mused, but saw Cissy agreeing with a nod.

"That is most probable. The family has often speculated that the spirits of those soldiers also linger at Sherringham." She turned her gaze to Vanessa, the corners of her mouth tipping upward. "At least, those of us who believe in such possibilities do."

Vanessa found herself smiling too. "It must be crowded for them—with so many souls lost on these grounds, that is." She glanced to the photograph, laying on the sofa beside her, and to its glowing figure.

She lifted her eyes to Lord Marrable. "Do I understand correctly, the gallery dates to Tudor times?"

"Yes, the south wing and tower were raised during the reign of the first Tudor monarch, Henry the Seventh."

A curious look came into his dark eyes as some thought traversed his mind.

"One of the most fascinating tales connected with Sherringham dates from the next monarch's reign, that of Henry the Eighth," he continued. "It was also the time when the Lords of Sherringham first fell from power."

Lord Marrable leaned back deeper into his chair, resting his elbows on its arms and tenting his fingers as he gathered his thoughts.

"At the time of the Dissolution, after King Henry broke with Rome and seized the wealth of the Church, he sent his troops about, pulling down monasteries and destroying all who opposed him. Among those places marked for destruction was the Cistercian monastery in Wales known as Strata Florida."

Warmth flowed through Vanessa as Lord Marrable turned his intense dark eyes to her as he related the story.

"A legend persists that the monastery's most sacred treasure was that of the Nanteos Chalice, said to have been carved from the cross of Christ and to possess healing powers. Many believed, and still believe, it to be the Grail cup sought by Arthur's knights."

"The *Holy Grail*?" Vanessa's brows flew upward. "How incredible. But, what does the cup have to do with Sherringham?"

Lord Marrable smiled, as did his brother and sisters.

"When word of Henry's approaching troops reached

the monks of Strata Florida, they fled with their treasures. As the tale goes, two of the monks arrived at Sherringham's gates, seeking protection as they carried the miraculous relic to safety. The Lord of Sherringham, it was no secret, opposed Henry's divorce from Queen Catherine and his break with Rome.

"We know at least one of the monks died while in hiding here and, after that time, the Nanteos Chalice disappeared. There is no record of his companion's departure, only much speculation as to the cup's whereabouts and whether it ever left Sherringham's grounds."

"How utterly enthralling." Vanessa gave him her smile. "And what of Sherringham's lord? Did he escape Henry's wrath for opposing him?"

"Hardly. The king sent him to London's Tower on inflated charges of treason. It is said his wife paced the gallery continuously for three years, waiting her husband's return. When he did, he was in a wooden coffin."

Vanessa shook her head. "How desperately sad." Taking up the photograph, she studied the tower and illuminated area more closely. "Was it the Tudor gallery she paced for so very long?"

The viscount nodded. "At the time, it overlooked Sherringham's main approach, the opposite wing having yet to be built."

Vanessa raised her gaze once more to his, empathizing with the woman's loss and pain. "And what became of the widow?"

"Lady Jane did not live long after she received her husband's remains. Whether she died naturally or by intrigue, as some would have it, King Henry promptly seized the castle and lands for himself."

"Since that time, a Gray Lady has been sighted pacing the gallery," Cissy added. "She wears a pearl-gray gown and gabled headdress, similar to those worn by aristocratic ladies during the reigns of the Tudor monarchs."

Vanessa sincerely hoped the Gray Lady was a docile spirit, if a spirit at all.

"Was it during this period that Sherringham acquired its added name of Royal?"

"No, that came much later." Lord Marrable ran his thumb across his lower lip. "The lands first came back into the family when Queen Elizabeth's eye fell upon one of her couriers, the dashing and personable Christopher Marrable. Being a bright fellow, he had worked his way into the queen's presence and favor.

"The old disputes had long been forgotten, at least on the queen's part, who, herself, was quite aged. Elizabeth was also susceptible to flatteries and Christopher, apparently, was most skilled in their use. Not only were the family titles and lands restored, but, before she died, the queen found for him a wealthy heiress to wed."

"The Lords of Sherringham remained steadfastly loyal to the Crown, particularly through the civil wars," he went on. "That loyalty cost them dearly when the king was beheaded. Sherringham was seized during the interregnum, but not before Cromwell's men 'slighted' it, destroying the roof of the great hall and blowing up the courtyard."

Vanessa stared at him. "I confess, I am stunned to hear it. I never guessed . . . I mean, the hall is so magnificent and the grounds, works of art."

This evoked a warm smile from the viscount. "The

Marrable lords made vast improvements to Sherringham after it came again into their possession."

Vanessa tilted her head. "As I recall, with few exceptions, kings sat upon the throne. How was Sherringham regained? I assume there were no Christopher Marrables to influence the monarch."

"Ah, but there was Leonine." Lord Marrable's gaze shifted to the portrait over the fireplace, as did every other pair of eyes in the room.

"When the Cavaliers helped Charles regain his throne, they expected him to restore their lands and titles out of gratitude. He did not. When the Marrable lands were not returned, the vivacious younger sister of the current, and dispossessed, viscount became a maid of honor to Queen Catherine. She soon caught the king's eye and subsequently filled his bed."

"It is said King Charles loved her greatly." Cissy picked up the story. "Leonine asked nothing for herself, and so impressed was Charles he soon restored the family titles and lands."

"Not only that"—Majel pointed out—"Charles lavished Leonine with fabulous jewels and exquisite gowns and a mansion in London which remains to this day in Marrable hands."

The viscount rose and strode to the portrait. "Tragically, Leonine died prematurely of consumption, still much beloved by the king." He brought his gaze from the painting and looked to Vanessa. "It was he who commissioned his famed architect, Wren, to design and build the Marrable mausoleum. He considered it his last gift to Leonine, that she might rest eternally in peace."

The room fell silent. Several long moments passed

before Lawrence took it upon himself to refresh everyone's glass with a touch more of sherry.

Lawrence sent a smile to Vanessa as he topped off Henry Norland's glass. "So you see, Sherringham owns a rich past, one with infinite possibilities for such things as hauntings, if you wish to believe the accounts. I hope it does not disturb you in the least, for there are other souls and sightings of which we've yet to speak."

"Lawrence is right." Cissy's eyes widened. "There are tales of ill-starred lovers, deadly sword fights in the Tudor gallery, and the headless Cavalier."

Lord Pendergast rose and began to move about, stretching his legs. "If the photograph has recorded one of these specters that purportedly lurks at Sherringham, then I wonder which it might be?"

Vanessa watched as the others exchanged glances and considered his remark in earnest. She supposed it was vastly more diverting than simply accepting the mar on the print to be an accident of light.

"Why don't we each put forth our best guess?" Lawrence proposed. "Sort of a game, you know."

"I rather like the idea of the monk looking for the Grail cup, myself," Henry submitted.

Cissy turned to him. "I don't believe he's ever been seen beyond the Cloisters, Henry dear. The Gray Lady is a more logical choice."

Majel vented a short laugh. "Have you forgotten Leonine Marrable? I say she's angry and looking for her missing jewels."

A look of shock touched Cissy's features. "You mustn't say such things," she reproached, then dropped her voice. "You know Adrian blames himself for their loss."

Vanessa quickly glanced to where the viscount still stood, his gaze fixed on the portrait. A muscle flexed along his jaw, his look darkening.

Nigel Pendergast cleared his throat, snaring her attention. "Perhaps it is a more recent ghost."

His suggestion drew more horrified looks, including that of Majel. Though none would voice it, Vanessa realized their thoughts were of Lord Marrable's two deceased wives.

"Well, if Lady Gwen has taken up residence, we can all be assured she will prove a gentle ghost," she offered lightly, trying to relieve the moment.

Lord Marrable slowly turned to the others, his midnight eyes moving to one, then another. He smiled darkly.

"Do not fear. I'll not explode in a temper. In truth, it would not surprise me if Clairissa did damn me from the grave. But if there *is* a specter haunting the gallery, I hope to God it is Olivia's. At least then, I could be certain she is truly dead."

Astonishment washed over the faces of all as Lord Marrable left the fireplace and strode from the room.

Majel turned huge eyes on Lawrence. "Whatever does he mean?"

Lawrence stared after his brother. "Adrian has entertained some rather bizarre notions of late. If you'll excuse me, I best speak with him."

Vanessa's heart raced. She was as astounded as any at Lord Marrable's comments, but at a loss to understand the full scope of his meaning. Certainly, she should not be privy to such personal matters.

She glanced to Lawrence as he started toward the door. Outwardly, his aspect reflected his obvious worry and deep filial concern. Yet, as Lawrence tossed

her a parting glance, she beheld something else in his
eyes, something shuttered, impossible to read.

Vanessa returned her gaze to the other family members and found them collecting in a small circle, murmuring their astonishment at the scene that had just
passed. Feeling wholly awkward and out of place,
Vanessa withdrew and headed for her bedchamber.

She climbed the great staircase, its steps softly illuminated by the light of the immense chandelier suspended in the stairwell. All else, however, remained
swallowed in deepest shadow.

Adrian Marrable's words continued to weigh on
Vanessa's thoughts. For what possible reason would
his first wife, Clairissa, wish to damn him from the
grave? And why would he question if his second wife
was truly dead? Was not the last viscountess entombed in the Marrable mausoleum, as she'd been
told?

Vanessa could not say whether spirits dwelled at
Sherringham, or even if she believed in ghostly apparitions. But, as to the defect on the photograph, she
maintained her belief—it was caused by an excess exposure to light.

One thing was certain, she decided. In the morning,
she would visit the Tudor gallery and inspect it for
herself.

Chapter 8

Arriving soon after dawn, Vanessa found the gallery rinsed with the morning's bright, crystalline light.

In contrast, flat, musty odors layered the air, clinging to the immense faded tapestries and lime-washed walls and rising from the dark, oaken planking underfoot—odors that bespoke of ages long past.

Vanessa shifted the camera and tripod off her right shoulder and set it on the floor. Since Geoffrey had another engagement today—picnicking with his parents, siblings, and puppy at one of the estate's follies—she traveled lightly, with the camera already affixed to the tripod, and with only one case containing the negative plate holders and accessories.

Setting down the case, she gave her attention to the tripod and stabilized it, expanding its legs. Satisfied, Vanessa next began a calculated survey of the gallery's interior. Calculated because she wished to—no, she *needed* to—know whether anything here could account for the luminous flaw in the photograph she'd taken from the lawn outside.

As she considered the gallery and its sparse furnishings, the likeliness of that dwindled. There were no mirrors to reflect sunlight, or additional windows on adjacent walls, no lanterns, lamps, or sconces present of any kind.

Vanessa moved to the great expanse of diamond-paned windows and looked out onto the terrace below. She visualized the others there at tea, two days before. Lifting her hand to the cool, nubbly glass, she continued to gaze out. It occurred to her she now stood precisely where Lady Jane once did, and countless others, watching for their loved ones' return.

Thoughts also arose of the fatal sword fight that purportedly had taken place here, and she could not help but wonder if the Cavalier's specter frequented the gallery, seeking his head. But more significantly, she reminded herself, she occupied the very place from whence the source of light had emanated the day before yesterday. The thought set her pulses thumping in her veins.

Vanessa stepped from the window and crossed swiftly to her camera and equipment, intent on photographing the space. Whether she ever resolved the puzzle of the glowing light or not, the gallery, with its long and intriguing history, would make a fascinating addition to her book.

Vanessa started to remove the camera's lens cap, then paused to rub the dull ache pulsing in her temples. She'd slept fitfully last night, the tales and events of the evening churning endlessly through her mind. They continued still.

What plagued her most were Lord Marrable's parting words concerning his last viscountess. Vanessa had assumed he'd loved her profoundly. After all, had he not designed and built the exquisite Orangery expressly in her honor? Yet, last evening, he'd stated his desire to be assured his late wife, Olivia, was "truly dead."

Vanessa deemed the comment bizarre at best, macabre at worst. Then, too, there was his remark regarding his first wife, Clairissa, who'd evidently died despising him.

Such dark sentiments to harbor, Vanessa reflected, releasing a long breath. She knew none of the particulars of the two women's deaths, excepting that the last viscountess's had been accidental. Perhaps, it was best she remained unaware of the details, Vanessa told herself. In all honesty, she did not wish for shadows to blight her growing esteem of Adrian Marrable.

Vanessa pushed the troubling thoughts to the back of her mind, and concentrated once more on the gallery.

Several angles would offer an agreeable composition, she observed. What most interested her was capturing the contrasts of textures and shapes—the coarse-grained flooring, the busy patterns enlivening the tapestries, the spare furnishings, particularly one knobbly-legged chair of ebony, positioned against the wall. The main center of interest, of course, would be the double-high row of multipaned windows on the exterior wall.

As Vanessa decided on the placement of her camera, she mused that, for the gallery supposedly being the most haunted part of Sherringham, it was neither extravagant nor remarkable in the least, certainly not when compared to the rest of the castle complex. And yet, time seemed to cling to this place somehow. At least, she sensed it to be so.

Vanessa shook away her thoughts. She finished positioning the camera then retrieved her notebook and pencil from her case. Noting the differing intensities of light throughout the gallery, she made the appropriate notations and consulted her tables in the back of her book.

The gallery proved substantially larger than she'd anticipated. In addition to the main, windowed area, two corridors led off from it, stretching out of sight in opposing directions. She presumed any sword fights that might have raged here did so along the adjoining wings as well. She resisted the temptation to search for mysterious, non-disappearing bloodstains, the sort described in popular Gothic tales.

Instead, she concentrated on capturing the image before her, freezing it in time, on glass. She decided to overexpose the negative slightly, which was usually a safe guide to follow. A camera's "eye" possessed a limited response to the range of light, and she wished to lose none of the setting's detail, which, when photographed and printed, would be transposed to tones of gray.

Vanessa studied the composition in the viewing glass. When inverted, the wonderful paned windows would appear left of center, with a portion of tapestry visible on the right. The dark floor led the eye from the bottom of the frame into the picture and, overhead, there was even a glimpse of the simple but elegant plasterwork on the ceiling.

As Vanessa made her final adjustments and stopped down the lens, her thoughts strayed to what the gallery must have been like in times past. She could easily imagine the bustle of human activity that once filled it—the rustle of cloth and solid bootfalls, the hum of voices, all so real. Even now, their buzz seemed to faintly fill her ears . . . and grow steadily louder . . . As she listened, she could almost distinguish the words . . .

Vanessa massaged her temples. The phantom sounds subsided at once. Yet, in the next instant, she questioned whether she'd heard anything at all. A prickly feeling crept over her skin. Vanessa thought to lay the sensation to a sprightly imagination, then realized a chill was spreading along her arms. The air had turned wintry cold.

She cast a hasty glance around, her senses sharpening. "There's no one else here," she assured herself aloud. "There's no Lady Jane, or Leonine Marrable, or anyone else. You're completely alone."

She didn't feel alone. She felt watched. Yet, all in the gallery was utterly still, "silent as the crypt," as the saying went, offering little solace.

Vanessa gave her full attention to the camera and replaced the viewing glass with the negative plate in its holder. As she worked, she noted the temperature had little improved. If anything, the gallery was growing colder.

She blew warmth into her palms, then briskly rubbed her arms, thinking she best make the exposure and depart before she contracted her death of cold.

"I'll have to bring my woolen wrap next time," she muttered, then pulled the slide from the negative.

As her fingers closed over the string and released the shutter, a noise leaped out from the silence, directly behind her. Vanessa whirled in place, gasping sharply as she met two eyes, peering back at her.

"Hello, Mrs. Wynters." Nanny Pringle greeted, her round eyes crinkling. They contained a bright smile, reflecting the one upon her small, narrow lips.

"Nanny!" Vanessa heaved for air, pressing her hand to her breast. "You gave me such a fright."

"Oh, I am sorry for that, dear. You probably didn't expect to meet a soul at this hour, at least not in the gallery."

"N-no, I didn't." Vanessa hadn't expected to meet any soul, embodied or otherwise. She prayed, in another moment or two, her heart would dislodge itself from her throat and return to its proper place.

Nanny continued to smile. "I was just on my way to my rooms. Would you care to join me for a morning spot of tea, Mrs. Wynters? It's just around the corner."

"Thank you, that would be lovely. And please, call me Vanessa. If you will just allow me a moment to finish here."

"Do what you must, dear. And do not hurry yourself overly. I'm content to wait."

As Nanny bided the moments, Vanessa quickly replaced the slide and removed the negative, returning it to the case. Repacking her accessories, she capped the lens and took up the camera, tripod and all, and caught hold of the case.

"I'm ready." She smiled.

Vanessa started to follow Nanny, but took no more than two steps, then halted. It suddenly struck her the temperature in the gallery had warmed, its frigid edge now gone.

"Around the corner" proved to be a fifteen-minute walk which took them into a newer part of the complex.

Nanny preceded Vanessa through a tall, cream-and-gilt door, motioning her to follow, then gave a tug to the bellpull on the wall.

"Mary Ethel will be up presently," Nanny said, a smile wreathing her plump face. "She brings a pot of boiled water each morning at this time. Dear girl, she would bring the tea already steeping, but she knows I much prefer to make my own."

Nanny sallied across the room to a tall, mahogany sideboard and brought out a tea caddy and varied pieces of a green-and-white porcelain service.

"Would you prefer Earl Grey or something more robust? A Ceylon tea, or Russian, perhaps?"

"Earl Grey would be quite agreeable," Vanessa assured as she placed her camera and case beside the door. It struck her that Nanny seemed unusually energetic and clear of mind this morning, not at all distracted and confused as she'd been the day of the funeral.

Turning, Vanessa found herself standing in what could only be described as a front sitting room. It possessed a snug informality, the furnishings being of no particular style, all cozily cluttered with mementos and bric-a-brac.

Two upholstered chairs, one striped, one floral, flanked a tiled fireplace, over which hung a large, photographic portrait of an elegant couple. A dozen more smaller, framed photographs crowded the mantel ledge. Right of the chairs, in front of the sideboard and several feet apart, stood a round table draped with a fringed scarf and cheered with a vase of slightly drooping wildflowers.

As Nanny continued to putter, laying the table with cups and saucers and a round-bellied teapot, Vanessa moved toward the fireplace, her gaze fixed on the double portrait there. A moment later, Nanny joined her, her hands folded, one over the other.

"Those are the late Viscount Lionel Marrable and his wife, Alyce," Nanny supplied.

"Lord Adrian's parents?"

Nanny nodded. Vanessa could see a likeness between Lord Lionel and Lawrence in the fair hair, but none to Adrian in any feature. Lady Alyce's coloring appeared most similar to Majel's. Certainly, both girls favored their mother facially.

"I first came to Royal Sherringham when the twins

were but three months old." Nanny lifted down one of the pictures from the mantel and handed it to Vanessa.

Vanessa's eyes widened at the sight of Nanny, years younger, standing proudly beside a double-wide pram containing two bonneted babies.

"How very splendid," she exclaimed. "The picture, I mean. How wonderful to have it as a remembrance of that time."

A light twinkled in Nanny's eyes. "We were quite fortunate that Lady Gwen was so talented with a camera. She was ever posing and photographing the children, though I daresay, they found it a trial to sit still at times."

Touching her tongue to her upper lip, she chuckled to herself as if remembering something from those occasions.

"Lady Gwen was kind enough to print copies for me. They are my dearest treasures now," Nanny added with a wistful sigh.

"I should have guessed Lady Gwen photographed these." Vanessa smiled, returning the picture to the older woman.

Nanny replaced it on the mantel and took down another.

"This one was taken the summer before Master Adrian and Master Lawrence left Sherringham for boarding school at Harrow." She tapped the frame lightly, as if in thought, then fell to silence.

The photograph showed all four children sitting on the entrance steps with several mongrel dogs and a cage filled with tiny finches. The boys, Vanessa noted, appeared to be roughly six years of age. She could not help but think Adrian was conspicuously handsome even then.

"How difficult it must have been for them to leave Sherringham."

Nanny nodded pensively, her smile fading somewhat as she traced a finger over the boys' small images.

Vanessa could not help but feel a pang of sadness for boys so young, barely out of the nursery and into breeches, being shuttled off from their homes, into starchy institutions.

That was the way of things among aristocrats, she knew. If she'd understood Lawrence correctly, Lord and Lady Marrable had never been enormously present in their children's lives, residing more often in London. Still, Nanny, Lady Gwen, and the staff of Sherringham would have composed the very heart of what the children would have known as "family."

Vanessa glanced to one of the larger pictures on the mantel. Surprise rippled through her as she thought to recognize the attractive blond woman shown mounted on a snowy horse, the twins perched in front of her.

"Is that Lady Gwen?" she asked, wholly amazed.

"Yes, dear. She would have been twenty-three or -four at the time. She is exceptionally handsome, is she not?"

Vanessa found herself nodding, at a loss for words. Truly, it was a wonder Lady Gwen had chosen to remain in virtual seclusion at Sherringham, never to marry.

Leaning closer, she noted there was a certain quality about the photograph, soft and slightly out of focus. It seemed vaguely familiar somehow.

"Do you know who actually took this picture?" Vanessa transferred her gaze to Nanny.

"Oh, yes, Julia Cameron."

"Julia Cameron, the photographer?" Vanessa tried to conceal her astonishment. Mrs. Cameron was renowned for her allegorical groupings and romantic portraits, many of them of celebrated individuals such as Tennyson, Longfellow, and Browning. The out-of-focus quality was her hallmark.

"Oh, yes, the same Mrs. Cameron. Lady Gwendolyn and she were good friends, despite the family's rivalry. They'd visit back and forth when Mrs. Cameron and her husband were in residence at Eastnor Castle. The Third Earl Somers was her brother-in-law, you know," Nanny confided the choice tidbit.

"No, I didn't know. You say there was a rivalry?"

Nanny placed the photograph of the children she still held back with the others. "Indeed, it was a cordial but serious competition between the Lords of Eastnor and Royal Sherringham. Each strove to outdo the other, ever increasing and improving to their estates. That is the period Sherringham acquired so many new follies."

Nanny returned to the table and busily completed the settings, adding spoons and napkins. As she worked, she picked up her tale.

"The rivalry began with the first Earl of Somers, who built Eastnor Castle, and Viscount Talbot Marrable, Lord Adrian's grandfather. The competition continued with their sons. Lord Lionel used to say Eastnor could never best Royal Sherringham, no matter how large it grew, for Sherringham possessed what Eastnor did not—authentic thirteenth-century remains. Eastnor Castle was begun only recently, in the year 1812, I believe."

Vanessa better understood Lord Adrian's reaction when, the day of the funeral in the Grand Saloon, she'd witlessly remarked that some considered Sherringham a rival to Eastnor. Lord Adrian's clipped response should have alerted her she'd just made a huge faux pas. Eastnor was but a mock castle after all, though a castle it was architecturally. Truly, she'd done no worse had she simply put her proverbial foot in her mouth and chewed most vigorously.

Reflecting back on that moment in the saloon, she smiled inwardly. The pride of the Marrable lords in their ancestral home continued to flow strong in its current viscount. Lord Adrian's long absence from Sherringham had not lessened that in any way.

As Vanessa looked again to the photograph, she noted the soft expression in Lady Gwen's eyes—a loving, maternal look as she gazed on the children. Such a pity she never had children of her own.

A rap at the door signaled Mary Ethel's arrival with a pot of steaming water. Nanny promptly allowed the maid in, then gave her full attention to warming the teapot and spooning in the appropriate measure of tea. She scarcely took notice when Mary Ethel quietly withdrew.

While the beverage steeped, Vanessa continued to peruse the other photographs on the mantel, most showing the four Marrable children at various ages and at special times in their lives. There were photographs of the brothers, grown to manhood, enjoying their "grand tour," and others of their sisters, gowned for their debuts. Two additional photographs showed Majel and Cissy on their wedding days, each posed with their bridal parties on the steps of Hereford's cathedral. Vanessa observed, even on that grand day, Majel's mouth appeared no more than a slit.

Oddly, for all the plentiful pictures, tracing significant moments in the lives of the Marrables, two were noticeably missing.

"Come, dear, the tea is ready," Nanny chimed.

"Lady Pendergast's and Lady Norland's wedding pictures are quite marvelous," Vanessa offered conversationally as she seated herself at the table. "But tell me, are there no photographs of Viscount Marrable on the occasions of his marriages?"

Vanessa hoped she did not sound overly curious about Lord Adrian and his late wives. In all honesty, she did wonder about the ladies he'd chosen to make his viscountesses. Were both marriages arranged, or was there something about each lady that had particularly attracted him and won his heart? Were the women average in looks, or extraordinarily beautiful?

"Photographs of Lord Adrian's weddings? No, I don't keep any," Nanny replied matter-of-factly. "Sugar?"

"What? Oh, yes, one lump, thank you. No, no cream."

Vanessa assumed Nanny must have removed any such pictures after the viscountesses' deaths.

"Never did—keep any that is." Nanny chatted pleasantly as she poured hot tea into the cups then, set the teapot on its decorative trivet. "I'm not one for gossip, mind you, but, truth to tell, I never cared much for either of them—Lady Clairissa or Lady Olivia."

Vanessa coughed, mis-swallowing her tea. Nanny, meanwhile, stirred her drink thoughtfully.

"They were each quite different, you know. Had Lord Adrian consulted me—not that he should have, mind you—but had he done so, I would have warned him away from both young women. Likely, my advice would have gone unheeded. Lord Adrian can be a stubborn, impassioned man, God bless him." She sighed heavily and wagged her head. "In the end, his wives, each in their own way, brought Lord Adrian bitter pain."

"Whatever do you mean?" Vanessa lowered her cup to her saucer, stunned by Nanny's words.

Nanny stilled, a look of alarm rounding her eyes, that she might have spoken something she shouldn't have.

"I shouldn't say. I'm not one for gossip, you know. It's most improper to bear tales of the dead. Most improper, indeed."

Pinching her thumb and forefinger together, Nanny made a gesture as if buttoning her lips tight. She then released another weighty sigh as if a deep fatigue was creeping over her.

Vanessa felt a mild disappointment. She longed to make sense of Lord Adrian's comments of last evening, and to that end, learn something of his former wives, so she might better understand him. As it was, Nanny preferred to dwell on other topics, in particular the four Marrables in their youths. Vanessa gave into that course and asked Nanny how she first came to Sherringham.

"The twins were born abroad, in a villa in the south of France. Or was it Italy?"

Nanny's brows drew together as she quested the memory. Failing to pinpoint it, she gave a little shrug and took a sip of tea.

"Lucklessly for Lord and Lady Marrable, their nanny left their employ upon their return to Britain. Or, perhaps it became necessary to dismiss her? One does not inquire of such details, of course."

"Of course," Vanessa offered softly, not wishing to disrupt Nanny's flow of thoughts.

"The infants were positively beautiful. Not at all alike, and each quite a separate handful, I can assure you." Nanny chuckled as she thought back to those times. "Lord Lionel assigned extra nursery maids, and Lady Gwendolyn, herself, helped, even changing diaper cloths at times! She was never too proud to do so."

Nanny took several more sips of tea, then squinted into the distance, her thoughts piercing time. "Of course, as the boys grew, Lady Majel and Lady Cissy arrived.

Those were happy, busy times. The children thrived at Sherringham. They were all so bright, and the boys, being twins, were particularly close."

Nanny's brow dipped downward, as if a dark cloud drifted through her memories.

"When the boys were small, they were inseparable, though not so much so as they grew older. Of course, Master Adrian and Master Lawrence had such markedly differing temperaments even then. The one sunny and charming, much more easygoing than his brother. The other was more grave, and brooding, totally inflexible at times. Then, there were flashes of a dark, hidden streak that would emerge from time to time. At others, it seemed he carried a large block on his shoulder."

Vanessa could scarce follow the path of Nanny's thoughts, or to whom she referred. "Sunny" and "charming" might easily describe Lawrence, and "grave" and "brooding," Lord Adrian, or at least one's first impressions of them nowadays. It was far more difficult to guess which brother harbored a "dark" streak, and she was surprised Nanny confessed as much, not being "one for gossip." But as Nanny's energies continued to visibly subside, her comments were becoming increasingly less guarded and somewhat rambling.

"Would you care to move to the chairs by the fireplace?" Vanessa suggested, mindful it was not her place to do so, but certain Nanny would be more comfortable in one of the plushy, winged-back chairs. "The fire looks most warm and inviting. If you'll allow me, I'll freshen your cup and bring it over."

"I didn't realize you were chilled, my dear. Forgive me. These great places always seem to have a draft, do they not?"

Vanessa found she couldn't agree more. Once Nanny was installed by the fire with a restoring cup of tea, Vanessa joined her. Nanny stared into the fire, watching the dance of the flames, then began to reminisce once more.

"At times, I wonder if the Marrable line will continue through Lord Adrian," she commented reflectively. Her eyes shifted to Vanessa. "Not that he does not wish to have children. He's most affectionate with them and would make a fine father—an exceptional one for an aristocrat."

Vanessa smiled. "Yes, I believe so as well. I've seen how he is with his nephew, Geoffrey."

Lord Marrable did indeed require an heir if the family line was to carry on through him. And, to that end, he required a wife who could bear him children, Vanessa reflected with a twinge of despondency.

Her own deficiencies loomed in sharp contrast to Lord Adrian's needs. She could not be certain beyond doubt she was barren. Still, despite Reginald's numerous absences, they'd been married sufficiently long to have conceived a child. Dispiritingly, she'd never experienced even a moment's false hope she had.

Vanessa cleared her throat, banishing her plaguing thoughts. "Lord Adrian is far from old. Is it so unlikely he will remarry and produce an heir?"

"He may not wish to," Nanny volunteered cryptically. A troubled look suddenly congested her eyes. "Neither of his marriages were easy ones and both ended in shocking tragedy. Lady Clairissa died in childbirth, God rest her. Some may not consider that unusual or startling, but the circumstances . . . Oh my, they were quite beyond the pale."

Nanny gulped down several mouths full of tea as if it

were a potent drink, bracing her against some galling memory.

"Then, there was Lady Olivia." Nanny shook her head. "Tragic, tragic."

She set aside her cup and saucer on the little table beside her chair and folded her plump hands. Complex emotions filled her face as her eyes drew to Vanessa.

"After his first wife's death, Lord Adrian became a joyless soul. Morose, actually. He seemed disinclined to remarry at first, but while in London, he met Olivia Chase. She utterly bewitched him."

Nanny returned her gaze to the fire, sadness tingeing her expression.

"Lord Adrian had been so wounded, he could not easily see what was obvious to others. Perhaps, it was because Miss Chase was so different from his first wife. Lady Clairissa had been a pale, fragile creature, as delicate in build as she was in temper. Oh, she enjoyed being viscountess and having a husband so handsome as Lord Adrian. But, if I may say so, she apparently never accepted certain aspects of married life."

Nanny leaned forward. "What lies between a man and a woman," she divulged in a part-whisper then sat back again. "Lady Clairissa's pregnancy came as quite a shock to her. She deemed her state utterly appalling, and blamed Lord Adrian regularly for her 'sufferings.' She did so even in front of the staff."

"How distressing for Lord Adrian." Vanessa felt great sympathy for the man. "And then she died in childbirth."

Again a look of pain pierced Nanny's eyes at the mention of Lady Clairissa's manner of death.

"As I was saying before, Miss Chase was dramatically different from Lord Adrian's first viscountess. She was a fiery beauty, as fiery as her red hair, and with an immense appetite and passion for life. She was not shy in the least and spoke her mind openly to all. And yet, she seemed somehow disingenuous. I once overheard Lady Cissy say as much. The marriage seemed happy at first, but it soon became turbulent. Leastwise, while at Sherringham, the couple quarreled openly and often. Their last words to one another were spoken in argument. Lord Marrable feels responsible for Lady Olivia's death too."

Vanessa found this astonishing. "But didn't she die in an accident? How could he blame himself for that?"

"It was possible she left to pursue him. Or that is one thought often expressed among Sherringham's staff." Her look grew clouded. "It doesn't explain everything, of course."

Vanessa inclined her head. "What do you mean? What happened?"

Nanny released a soft sigh, resting her head back on the chair. "I really know nothing of the accident firsthand. I went to sleep early that evening, and it wasn't until the next morning I discovered the night had turned tragic."

Nanny continued, revealing, in a meandering and sometimes incoherent way, how Lady Olivia had arrived at Sherringham several days before the accident, without her husband. On the fateful night, however, Lord Adrian evidently arrived after dark and left several hours later. A violent argument had ensued between the viscount and viscountess, Nanny learned the next morning. After Lord Adrian's departure, Lady Olivia left also, accompanied by her lady's maid.

"I like to think the viscountess was pursuing Lord Adrian to mend matters between them. But, oh dear—"

Nanny's hand flew to her mouth, covering it, and tears sprang to her eyes. "The axle on the carriage broke, just as Lady Olivia reached the sharp turn in the road—Devil's Hairpin. The carriage plunged into the ravine and burst into flames from the lanterns. Poor Master Lawrence, he was in residence, too, and tried to save her. He bears a permanent scar on his palm. Have you seen it?"

Vanessa realized immediately he'd always been careful to keep it from sight. "No, I haven't."

Nanny plucked a handkerchief from inside her sleeve and dabbed at her eyes. "Lady Olivia was burned so severely she could only be identified by the ring on her finger. That very night, the Marrable jewels disappeared. Presumably, the viscountess carried them with her and after the accident the maid, Bonnie Beckford, absconded with them. She hasn't been seen since that night."

Understanding flashed through Vanessa, understanding of why the family ever shielded their references to that horrifying night and deemed the subject forbidden in Lord Adrian's presence. Understanding as to what could have compelled Lord Adrian to leave Royal Sherringham for so very long a time.

"The viscount has been searching for the jewels and that wretched woman ever since," Nanny's voice drew her attention back. "He tells me he is working with Scotland Yard on the matter." She tucked her handkerchief back in her sleeve. "I can tell you it's a relief he's not involving himself with the Constable of Hereford. Dreadful man. Dreadful."

Nanny did not elaborate on her low opinion of the constable. Instead, she rested her head back once more and closed her eyes, falling silent.

Vanessa considered the many things Nanny had re-

vealed, but nothing in it explained what she'd seen of
people's reactions to Lord Adrian. From the moment he
arrived at the funeral, he had been greeted with looks of
fear mixed with aversion.

Was there something she'd missed? Some piece of information evading her? She couldn't begin to imagine
what it might be.

How had Lady Gwen's Final Testament read? She
mentioned the Marrable jewels as being lost, but also advised Lord Adrian directly, writing something to the effect that he should "Let go the pains of the past," and
that "Courage grows strong at a wound." Surely, Lady
Gwen held his tumultuous marriages in mind when she
wrote those words.

Vanessa glanced over to Nanny and found she was
napping off, her head nodding softly forward. Rising,
she retrieved Nanny's cup and saucer and carried them
with her own to the parlor table. Quietly, then, she
crossed the room, gathered her camera and case, and
slipped out the door.

Troubling images crowded Vanessa's mind as she retraced her steps along the corridor. Restless, she decided
to return to the Photo House and develop the plate she'd
taken earlier in the Tudor gallery. Surely, the familiar
repetition of the process would prove soothing. However, she doubted Adrian Marrable would soon leave
her thoughts.

Vanessa turned up the flame of the ruby lamp. Withdrawing the negative from the final wash, she drained
the plate of liquid and moved closer to the light.

As she scanned the gallery's reverse image, her heart
stilled in her chest. In front of the windowed wall, dark-

ened silver crystals collected in a curious pattern, revealing a distinctly human form.

The shape, when printed, would be ethereal at best, the portion from the shoulders upward gauzy and the features obscure. Still, there could be little mistake. The image frozen upon the glass belonged to that of a woman.

Unlike the previous photograph, the figure did not gaze out the windows onto the terrace and lawn. Instead, the apparition faced the camera directly, one diaphanous hand extended forward, as if beckoning to the viewer. But not to just any viewer, Vanessa realized with a jolt.

She swallowed deeply, recalling the frigid cold that had invaded the gallery, recognizing it signaled the specter's arrival and continued presence in the gallery—if she was to believe such things. The figure, captured on the plate, gestured specifically toward *her,* as it had done at the precise moment she'd stood behind the camera and released the shutter.

But to what purpose? Vanessa wondered. What did the specter wish her to see? Or to know?

Chapter 9

Acquiring a horse at the stable, Vanessa set out along the main road. Her mind roiled with thoughts of the beckoning phantom. Roiled, too, with Nanny's tales of the Marrable family and the deaths of Lord Adrian's ill-starred viscountesses.

Vanessa pressed the mare to a swift pace, giving it rein and allowing it to stretch out and lengthen its stride. Tendrils of hair tossed about her face as the breeze streamed over her. She savored the feel of the horse moving under her, its power and vigor matching her own restless energies and need for release.

Galloping on, she soon came upon the remembered path that led to the follies and mausoleum and turned the mare onto it.

Perhaps she'd not made a wise decision in remaining at Sherringham, an inner voice murmured.

Yet how was she to know of its unusual activities when none forewarned her, reason argued back.

Still, the night she and the family gathered in the drawing room, the Marrables had made no secret of Sherringham's history and visitants. It was she who'd clung to the belief that the luminous figure in the terrace photograph was an accident of light.

What did she propose to do now? the voice continued

to needle. The figure had manifested itself for a second time and could no longer be dismissed.

Vanessa felt tempted to flee altogether, rather than brave any unearthly presences biding here. Truly, the estate would be more aptly named "*Haunted* Sherringham" than "Royal."

She tightened her jaw. Despite her unnerving discovery, she knew she could not easily leave this place. It was as if a great, invisible lodestone drew her to Sherringham and to all who belonged there. Or, at least, to one in particular. What was it about the man that arrested her so?

Her blood began to thrum in her veins as Lord Adrian's handsome features filled her mind's eye. He was like fire, and she the moth, unable to resist.

Familiar cautioning bells knelled deep in her heart. Dare she venture too close, that flame had the power to consume her and scorch her to cinders.

The blackest of thoughts suddenly loomed. The other women in Adrian Marrable's life had not fared well at all, leastwise not his wives, each perishing well before their time.

Anger shot through Vanessa that such thoughts should even arise in her mind. She quelled them at once, along with that nettlesome inner voice.

Willfully, she concentrated on the Tudor gallery and its mysterious occupant, revealed only during development of the exposed negative plate. The possibility of the image being proof of an authentic apparition was sufficient to cool the heat in her veins, as well as any fantasies she entertained concerning Viscount Marrable.

Ghosts. Spirits returned from the dead. Was she to believe in such after all? If she accepted their existence, she must then question why this particular wraith should attempt to communicate with her.

Vanessa pressed her lips to a line. Most likely, the answer lay with her camera rather than herself. Somehow, the ghost had been able to record its form on the sensitized glass. Or could it be the photographic solution, itself, that had been inadvertently responsible for registering the ghostly manifestation? Or a bit of both?

Vanessa didn't confess to understand how such a thing could be accomplished, only that it had—twice now, and without any conscious effort on her own part.

As she continued to wrestle her thoughts, she urged the mare over the grassy road. In short time, the first of the follies appeared—the Abbey Ruin.

Slowing the mare to a walk, Vanessa gazed on the skeletal arches, outlined against the day's dull sky. She remembered Geoffrey saying parts of the folly were authentic and others quite new, but she found herself unable to differentiate between them. Each portion appeared as ancient as the next—the whole of it standing as a massive relic and testament to ages past.

As Vanessa contemplated the weathered remains, an uneasy sensation wrapped itself about her, impossible to describe, yet unnatural, eerie. She was about to dismiss the feeling as sheer imagination when the horse grew restive, stepping sideways and tossing her head, communicating her sentiments about tarrying here.

"You too, Delilah?" Vanessa patted the mare's neck, addressing her by name.

Vanessa prodded the horse on, suddenly eager to depart this place herself.

Continuing along the path at an even pace, Vanessa struggled once more with exactly what to believe regarding the revelations on the photographs. Since the

specter—if that was what it truly was—had materialized both times in the gallery, Vanessa reasoned whatever it wished to show her lay there.

On the other hand, the equally pressing question remained as to whether or not she should reveal her latest discovery to anyone else. For the moment, she
thought not. First, she wished to return to the gallery
and explore it further.

Vanessa's mood lifted as the Orangery came into
sight. Even with overcast skies, it shone brightly like a
diamond in the glade. As she closed on the pavilion, her
impulse was to dismount and remain awhile. The architecture was pure delight. But as she started to bring
Delilah to a halt, she spied a dabble-gray horse tied at
the building's far side and recognized it to be
Lawrence's.

Vanessa refused to be alone with the man, especially
in so secluded a place. And they would be alone, she
noted as she scanned the grounds for signs of others
and found none.

Setting her heels to the mare's flanks, she headed in
the direction of the mausoleum. She knew no other
paths to follow except to turn around and return to the
manse. Not wishing to do so, she deemed it an excellent
time to make a visit of sorts to the family crypt and pay
her respects to Lady Gwen.

Long minutes later, she crested the rise in the road
then began the descent to the wooded dell and temple-
like mausoleum. Vanessa released a breath of relief
when she'd covered half the distance and found herself
still alone. She feared Lawrence might have caught
sight of her leaving the pavilion and followed. Blessedly, it would seem he had not.

Slowing the mare to a walk, she approached the

grand marble edifice. Its classical design and elegant proportions pleasured the eyes. Such love Charles II must have possessed for Leonine to have commissioned it—"his last gift," Lord Marrable had said. Gazing on it now, Vanessa could easily imagine Leonine's spirit growing restless and rising to seek her lost jewels. They would be irreplaceable for sentiment alone, not to mention their worth—priceless favors of her royal beloved.

The twitter of birds invaded Vanessa's thoughts. As she glanced to the grayed and distant skies, a light breeze arose, stirring fine strands of her honeyed hair to dance about her face. Brushing them from her eyes, Vanessa returned her gaze to the mausoleum, thinking back to the day of Lady Gwen's funeral.

Abruptly, she stilled. Memories assailed her like bolts from the sky. Memories of Knights Chapel and the Marrable banner rippling to life. Memories of icy airs bedeviling her, and of an invisible hand upon her shoulder in the banqueting hall, forcing her back into her chair when she voiced her intention to leave Sherringham.

After she'd decided to remain at the estate, the incidents continued, if not intensified. There were the bone-chilling episodes inside the Photo House and the courtyard without, then again in the drawing room last night and the Tudor Gallery this morning.

She'd been thinking too narrowly, Vanessa realized with a start. On discovering the misted figure on the negatives, she'd thought of it as solely inhabiting the gallery. But if spectral presences could be detected by cold spots and severe drops in temperature, as many believed, then obviously this spirit was not limited to any single location.

Vanessa's throat went dry as another disturbing

thought presented itself. Either she'd encountered a single, exceedingly mobile ghost, or there was more than one shadowing her.

Quickly, she scoured her memories of the past weeks, seeking anything she might have overlooked. As she rummaged through her mind, she became aware of the uncommon silence that had fallen around her. The twitter of birds had ceased. Even the breeze had died. Nature seemed to have inhaled and now held its breath.

Vanessa's gaze drew to the horse. Delilah's ears flickered, swiveling this way and that, as if picking up minute sounds, or seeking to find some. The mare snorted and stepped sideways, her eyes opened wide and her tail swishing rapidly.

"Easy, girl," Vanessa soothed, as Delilah grew increasingly skittish. "We'll leave if you're unhappy here."

Vanessa turned the horse and began to set her heels to the mare's flanks when something brown and furry sprinted across the open ground, directly before them. As the animal disappeared into the shrubbery, Delilah bolted, white showing in her huge eyes as she broke into a gallop and left the path.

Vanessa screamed as her hands slipped on the reins and she came off the saddle, nearly plunging to the ground. Miraculously, she regained her seat and gripped tight the reins and a handful of mane. The panicked mare raced on, carrying her across the green toward the dell's forested rim.

Vanessa clung to the pommel, trying vainly to recover control of the reins and slow the horse's maddening pace. Her eyes teared fiercely in the face of the wind, and her hair whipped about her face.

A shout rang out from somewhere behind. Vanessa

chanced a swift glance back and beheld a dark figure on a coal-black stallion, emerging from the far side of the mausoleum and thundering after her. He looked like the devil himself with his black cape billowing, anger slashing what little she could see of his features beneath the brim of his tall hat.

Vanessa dared not hazard a second glance back to determine who the rider might be. Instead, she concentrated on staying mounted as Delilah drove on and entered the greenwood.

Branches clawed at Vanessa and caught at her dress as the mare bore her deeper into the forest. Suddenly, she cared not at all who rode behind her, only that he hasten and help her bring the frightened mare to a halt.

Ahead, Vanessa spied what appeared to be the mouth of a road, opening a way through the sylvan thicket. Hoping it led back to the main road, Vanessa used the reins and pressure of her legs to direct the mare onto the track.

Vanessa's hopes continued to rise as the road proved wide and free of entangling vines and brush. Lucklessly, within several hundred yards, it began to quickly diminish.

Just then, Vanessa felt Delilah tense beneath her and resist her efforts to guide her on. Scanning the road shrinking before them, she spied a fallen tree, blocking their passage.

Dread washed through Vanessa. There was no time to stop and little distance left to make a clean jump.

Adrian leaned into the great black, pressing the stallion for speed as they left the shadow of the mausoleum and crossed the open expanse.

Thank God he'd been near. He'd ridden out this

morning to revisit the scene of the accident, then decided to exercise Samson over Sherringham's many acres. After a good run, he'd found himself, unintentionally, at the mausoleum. There, he rested his steed, remaining mounted as he gazed out over the River Wye, coursing far below. A woman's scream drew his attention. Rounding the building within moments, he sighted the panicked horse and rider racing away. Fear ripped through his insides when he'd realized the woman was Vanessa.

Adrian bore down on Samson, striving to close the distance between them and the mare, Delilah, a skittish horse if ever there was one. The lather on her neck and flanks told him she was more than startled or frightened. She was wholly terrified.

"Damn!" he swore as Delilah entered the wood, Vanessa clinging to her. Adrian drove Samson on, easing back only when they verged on the forest, then urging the stallion into the woodland no faster than he dare.

Adrian's insides wrenched a second time as he caught sight of Vanessa reining Delilah toward an old, abandoned path, one that led toward a precipice screened with trees and plunging to the River Wye.

Adrian shouted but to no avail as Vanessa and the mare disappeared from sight. Seconds later, they came into view again. His heart nearly stopped as he saw Delilah's hooves leave the ground. She scarcely cleared the fallen tree, having jumped late and her form poor. She landed hard, stumbling at first and hurling Vanessa from the saddle, onto the forest floor. Regaining her footing, Delilah rushed on, deserting the choked path for the woods.

Adrian hard-reined Samson to a halt before the tree

and flung himself down to the ground. Vaulting over the barrier, he hastened to where Vanessa lay sprawled on the ground, unmoving.

Everything felt sore. *Very* sore. Vanessa told herself to be grateful. If she could feel pain, she was still alive.

She lay on her back, motionless, trying to catch her breath. Still, it hurt even to breathe. Lord, but she felt filthy. She remembered rolling several times over in the layers of leaves and debris carpeting the forest so richly. At least they had cushioned her fall. Somewhat, she added, feeling fresh pain shoot along her hip. Surely, she was bruised from head to toe.

As the pain passed, Vanessa remained perfectly still, content to stare up at the leafy canopy overhead, and the patches of sky peering through. A dark figure came suddenly into view, blotting out the delicate tracery of leaves and light. As he leaned toward her, his features collected into familiar lines belonging to Lord Adrian. Vanessa's heart began to thump madly at his nearness and at the mixture of fury and fear etching his face.

He enveloped her all at once. Desperate concern charged his voice as he fired a barrage of questions, his hands moving rapidly over her, seeking whatever might be broken. Vanessa forgot the pain, aware only of Lord Adrian's closeness and the scent of his bay rum cologne. Despite her harrowing ride, she decided the moment had turned rather agreeable after all.

"Don't move!" he ordered, worry sharpening his tone. "Are you all right? Does anything hurt or feel broken? You scared five lives out of me."

"Then, let us hope the Marrable panther enjoys as many lifetimes as his smaller cousins." Her lips drew into a smile. It was the only part of her she could move without smarting.

Lord Adrian halted his inspection and stared at her, blinking several times as he absorbed her words. The corner of his mouth twitched upward. "At least your tongue is in fine shape," he quipped, then smiled fully.

Vanessa chuckled too, sharing the humor, then winced. "Please, you mustn't make me laugh."

His look sobered. "What hurts? Perhaps you've broken a rib. Can't tell with this cursed corset." His fingers began to feel between the stays, moving from her waist upward.

Vanessa's hand flew to cover his, then flinched at the soreness her movements wrought. "Sir! I'm only bruised, truly. Probably from the whalebones. Likely, I'll have blue stripes all along my midsection."

His hand remained resting over her rib cage, just below her left breast. She made no effort to remove her hand either. As it continued to lay atop his, she felt the heat increase between their flesh. His dark eyes lifted from their joined hands and coupled with hers, holding her captive.

Vanessa's breath left her once more as she drank in his expression—an intense, consuming look.

"My dear Vanessa, I'd much prefer you with stripes than the alternative. Had you ridden much farther, in all likelihood, you would now lay broken upon the rocks at the bottom of the ravine."

"Ravine?" Her eyes widened, then she remembered the River Wye. "I didn't know the path led there. Oh, no. Delilah . . ."

"Will be fine," he assured. "She left the path and headed into the woods. She'll probably find her way back to the stable before we do."

Vanessa quirked a smile. "I didn't know she was so smart."

"Smart enough, though she's a bit of a skittish lady. What frightened her?"

"I'm not completely sure." Vanessa decided not to share her suspicions of what really alarmed the horse. "Something darted across our path. A rabbit, I think."

He looked disbelieving. "Only a rabbit? She seemed genuinely terrified."

Vanessa refrained from offering anything further, lest she reveal her own thoughts on the ghosts of Sherringham.

"I believe I can sit up now," she suggested, hoping to distract him.

Lord Adrian's gaze drifted over her face and disheveled hair then returned to fasten on her eyes.

"All right," he agreed, his tone filled with caution. "But slowly."

With great care, he eased her upward to a sitting position, his arms encircling and supporting her.

Vanessa grimaced, unable to cloak her discomfort.

"Maybe you shouldn't—"

"I'm just sore, as might be expected when thrown from a horse. You've probably experienced the same. Please, help me to stand."

His tight expression told her what he thought of the idea, but he helped her nonetheless. She winced again, a small moan escaping her this time. She was right. She was bruised completely from head to toe. At least, she felt she must be.

"This won't do, Vanessa."

Before she could object, Lord Adrian swept her up in his arms, bringing her face close to his. Whatever complaints her body made, she took no notice, discovering her lips mere inches from his.

Vanessa lost herself in his midnight eyes, aware only of the solid beating of his heart beneath her palm as it lay pressed against his chest. Their gazes mingled a long moment, as neither she nor he could find their voice.

Lord Adrian pressed his lashes shut then and seemed to fight some emotion. Opening his eyes once more, he said nothing but began to pick a path around the fallen tree, bearing Vanessa toward the waiting stallion.

"Are you quite sure Delilah will be all right?" She broke the silence at last as he came to stop before the horse.

"Samson will never forgive me if she's not. Have no fear, I'll send a lad out to find her after we get you back to the manse."

"Samson?" Vanessa raised a brow as he lifted her onto the stallion's back. She recalled Lawrence's mention of the steed over dinner, and how he made the horse sound like a devil-incarnate. "This is *Samson* and the mare is *Delilah*?"

Lord Adrian grinned at the observation, causing her heart to leap. "I liked the story as a lad. Besides, like the biblical tale, the mare has this brute totally beguiled and submissive to her will."

"Delilah? I thought you said she was skittish by nature."

"Not where Samson is concerned." Lord Adrian climbed into the saddle behind her then shifted, gently lifting her into his lap. "I suspect Delilah's as enamored as he. It's difficult to fight nature after all."

Slipping a protective arm around her waist, he held her against the hard length of his torso and turned the stallion back along the path. As they gained the open green, Lord Adrian set the stallion to an easy pace.

"Samson is a spirited fellow but, I promise, he has the smoothest gait of any horse I've ever ridden. Hopefully, you'll not find yourself in too great of pain."

Samson did not embarrass his master. The stallion's gentle, collected gait surprised Vanessa. Indeed, the experience was akin to being rocked, with the added bonus of the viscount's warm strength safeguarding her.

Adrian knew Vanessa's body ached from her fall, but his own throbbed from her very nearness. Truly, it had been far too long since he'd held a woman in his arms, and Vanessa filled them perfectly.

He wanted her. But he dare not follow his impulses. He'd convinced himself some time ago, he was a man cursed in matters of the heart.

How had she slipped past his defenses? Perhaps the acute desire and protectiveness he felt now was a momentary illusion—an understandable reaction after the assault of emotions he'd just endured.

His initial shock of seeing her imperiled, turned quickly to alarm and dread and, yes, raw fear for her very life. He'd next nearly gone mad at the sight of her flying from the horse and then lying pale and unmoving upon the ground. When he realized she was alive and reasonably sound, he wanted to kiss and scold her all at once. Now, as he held her in his arms, a part of him did not wish to ever let her go.

Bridling his emotions, he held Samson to an easy gait. Within minutes, the Orangery appeared. It surprised him only mildly to discover Lawrence standing outside. His brother spent many hours at the pavilion of late, overseeing the installation of the upper-level fireplace. What surprised Adrian more, however, was his brother's glowering look as he beheld Vanessa seated on the stallion before him, encompassed by Adrian's arms.

Adrian could not ignore the prickly patch of jealousy sprouting in his own chest as he recognized Lawrence's interest in Vanessa.

Did he intrude on his brother's territory where Vanessa was concerned? Or had he been correct last night, when he'd sensed she'd been avoiding Lawrence in the drawing room? Perhaps they'd quarreled, that and no more. Perhaps Vanessa did hold affection for his brother after all.

The thought set ill as he acknowledged Lawrence with a nod of his head and urged Samson on.

Vanessa felt Adrian's arm tighten about her as they rode past the Orangery, having given Lawrence only a cursory greeting. If she wasn't so sore, she'd turn to see what look Lord Adrian wore on his face.

"I apologize for not stopping," he said in a tight voice. "It's important we get you to the manse and send for a physician. I'll speak with my brother later so he doesn't misinterpret anything."

"Misinterpret? Whatever do you mean?"

Again his arm tensed about her as if he feared she would slip from his grasp.

"Our riding together like this. Our relationship. I mean, it is apparent that you . . . he . . ."

Vanessa stiffened, bringing a small amount of pain. "Lord Marrable! I believe you are the one who has misinterpreted matters. There is no attachment between your brother and myself. He came to my aid in Paris, and for that I am most grateful. But aside from friendship, there is nothing more between us. As to '*our* relationship,' as you call it—"

"Adrian."

"Pardon?"

"I'd like you to call me by my given name—Adrian."

The man sounded like he was smiling, if it was possible to hear a smile.

"Would that I had been the one to rush to your aid, Vanessa. I'd certainly have done so, and overseen Aunt Gwen's return to Sherringham, had I been informed in a timely manner."

"But, Lawrence wired—"

"He wired Scotland where I had been fishing, but I had already gone on to London. His telegram bearing news of our aunt's death didn't reach me until it was nearly too late."

"I didn't know," Vanessa said softly, thinking back on the disparaging remarks Majel had said of him in Knights Chapel. Thinking, too, of her own low opinion of his absence. An arrow of guilt traveled a straight line, piercing the center of her heart.

She cleared her throat. "Lawrence didn't know of your departure from Scotland?"

"It would seem my own telegram informing my brother of my movements missed him as well. Lawrence had left the country estate where he'd been staying to come early to Sherringham. He is overseeing some work in the Orangery and needed to approve a shipment of Italian tiles for the fireplace."

Lord Adrian fell silent on the subject as they continued toward the manse. His only comments were ones insisting his private physician be called. Vanessa equally insisted a doctor was unnecessary.

As they arrived at Sherringham and approached the stables, one of the hands, whom she recognized as Timothy, raced out. As he captured Samson's reins, Adrian informed him Delilah had bolted and was still straying about.

"Actually, she came back about five minutes ago, your lordship. She's being rubbed down now. William and I were about to ride out and search for Mrs. Wynters. We were sore worried when Delilah came back riderless." The young man shifted his gaze to her. "I warned the mare was spooky, mum. But, I see you are in good hands after all."

"Yes, you did, and I am." Vanessa sent him a smile.

Adrian said nothing but dismounted and lifted Vanessa down into his arms. He gave Timothy instructions regarding Samson, then proceeded to carry her toward the mansion.

"Lord Marrable—"

"Adrian."

"Adrian, I'm quite able to walk."

"Nonsense. Enjoy my services while they are yours."

Once inside the mansion's entrance hall, Adrian bore her the entire distance up the grand staircase to the Upper Cloister and her bedchamber. All the while, maids trailed them and then scurried to help, opening the door and turning back the bed. Adrian proved a master of authority as he called for hot water, beverages, food, and his personal physician, Dr. Hambley.

"The good doctor need not tax himself with a long journey merely to examine my bruises." Vanessa tried to reason with Adrian as he lay her on the wide soft mattress. It felt heavenly.

He braced his arms on either side of her. "Are you afraid of what he might find beneath your stays?"

She sent him a quizzical look.

"Blue stripes—all along your midsection."

Vanessa's brows winged upward. Slipping a glance to the maids, she found their eyes darting away. Obviously, they'd heard more than an earful. Quickly, she shifted her glance back to Adrian.

"I propose a compromise."

Now it was his turn for his brows to shoot upward. The sight caused her to smile.

"I'll see your physician, but only if you agree to sit for your portrait tomorrow—for the mourning album in your aunt's honor. Cissy is eager to assemble it. She is already personalizing the borders for the different pages."

Vanessa boldly held Adrian's gaze as she awaited his answer.

"Very well then." Adrian vented a breath. "But after Dr. Hambley departs, I expect you to rest for the remainder of the day."

He lifted a hand and outlined the contours of her face with his finger. "You were so pale, lying there in the forest. I'd like to see some color return to your cheeks."

He started to withdraw, then hesitated. Vanessa suddenly realized the maids had quit the chamber and they were quite alone. A certain look appeared in his eyes, a look that set her heart to beating madly. He spoke not a word, but smoothed back her hair, then dropped a light kiss on her forehead.

For hours to come, her skin burned with the remembrance of his lips.

Chapter 10

Vanessa touched a hand to the large, coiled chignon at the back of her head, then smoothed the black-and-teal striped skirt of her gown. Unabashedly, she'd chosen the dress knowing its color and graceful design to be especially flattering.

For a dozenth time, she checked her watch, anticipating Adrian's arrival. The piece showed it to now be five minutes beyond the agreed time.

Vanessa returned her attention to the drawing room and to the double doors that opened onto a small, light-filled conservatory. She'd taken scant notice of the room when the family gathered here two nights before. With its walls of clear glass and its sun-washed space, the conservatory provided an excellent source of light for the portrait, strong yet indirect.

Vanessa moved to adjust the carved oak chair she'd chosen for Adrian's sitting, repositioning it closer to the open doors. Her every muscle issued a complaint, being yet sore and stiff from yesterday's misadventure. Dr. Hambley had assured she would continue to be so for days to come, but confirmed she'd suffered no breaks or fractures.

Vanessa's thoughts ran to the hours ahead. Geoffrey would not be assisting her until much later as he'd joined his father for a dawn fishing expedition to the River Wye. Before their return, Vanessa hoped to print out her latest photograph, taken in the gallery.

When she'd stopped by the Photo House this morning to collect her equipment, she made a quick examination of the negative which she was keeping stored out of sight. The detail on the plate showed no signs of change or deterioration. The figure recorded there remained distinctly visible, beckoning with its glowing, transparent hand.

Sooner or later, Vanessa knew, she must disclose her discovery to the family. For the present, however, she was inclined to keep her secret until she could learn more. The shade seemed benign enough, and its interest apparently centered on her alone. Besides, were not the Marrables accustomed to sharing the manse with otherworldly entities? Presumably, this particular spirit was a long-haunting resident already.

Again, Vanessa consulted her watch and wondered if Adrian had changed his mind. The possibility pricked unpleasantly at her heart. Just then, as if he'd heard her concern, Adrian entered the drawing room.

Her spirits rose as he moved briskly toward her, obviously aware of his belatedness. But in the next instance, she perceived a marked tenseness in his body and observed how he held his broad shoulders in a straight, rigid line.

Apprehension purled through Vanessa. There was a hard shine to his midnight eyes, and an equally hard set to his jaw. Adrian was not simply in a rush, he was wholly agitated.

Self-consciously, Vanessa fingered the frill of pleated satin surrounding the square neckline of her bodice. The small movement drew Adrian's attention to the exposed column of her neck. His gaze slid downward then, skimming over her breasts and figure-conforming basque. Unaccountably, his countenance darkened further.

Vanessa tensed. Had she done something wrong? She gestured toward the chair, at a loss to understand his mood.

"Please, be seated and we'll begin."

Adrian complied and moved to the carved, Gothic-style chair. Lowering himself onto the seat, he planted his feet solidly on the floor and faced the camera straight on.

Vanessa caught her lip between her teeth. He looked like a block of granite. This would never do.

"Could you turn a trifle toward the conservatory door, please—so you are sitting at an angle to the camera? Yes, that is better." She sent him a quick smile. "No, look toward me—not just your eyes—yes, turn your entire head."

Vanessa stood silent, studying the fall of light and shadows on his features. She grew warmly aware that Adrian stared back with equal intensity. Heat blossomed in her cheeks when his gaze left her face to travel downward over her bodice and skirts once more. Still, he wore a black look.

Disconcerted by his grim perusal, she took refuge under the focusing cloth and checked the viewing screen. Even upside down, Adrian's scowl dominated the image. Vanessa reemerged a moment later, wondering what she might do or say to lighten his expression, how she might dispel the sullen mood that seemed to possess him.

Mulling her thoughts, Vanessa took up her notebook and consulted her table for exposure times. Stepping to the front of the camera, she made the appropriate settings and stopped down the shutter. As she finished, she stole a sideways glance to Adrian. He'd turned his head and now sat staring out the conservatory doors, through the glass wall to the landscape beyond. Vanessa could not help but notice that a muscle jumped along his jaw.

She cleared her throat purposely to draw his attention. "If you would look over this way again, I'll check your pose a final time in the viewing glass and then we'll be ready to make the exposure."

Adrian's eyes swept toward her, but he scarcely moved his head. A shudder passed through Vanessa as those eyes penetrated her, for they burned with an inner fire. When, still, he did not assume his former pose, Vanessa traversed the space that lay between them, coming to a hesitant stop directly before him.

"I need you to look directly at the camera, more like so. . . ," she said softly.

Vanessa reached forth a trembling hand and placed it along the side of his jaw, urging him to turn and lift his head ever so slightly. She thought his gaze would melt her as his eyes continued to burn into hers. Beneath her fingers, she felt the muscle leap in his jaw. Vanessa withdrew her hand. Truly the man could scorch her very soul with his look alone. She was too close to the fire.

"Please, do not move now." She quickly returned to the camera and checked the viewing glass, her heart thumping in her ears.

Adrian's eyes remained riveted on her, his gloomy look unimproved. What had Nanny said of the twins' temperaments—one possessed a dark, hidden streak that would emerge from time to time? She'd hoped the reference was not to Adrian. Presumably, she was wrong.

Vanessa felt her heart dip down to her toes as she remained at a loss. Yesterday, she'd felt a special closeness unfold between them. At least, she thought it had. Today, she couldn't fathom Adrian Marrable at all.

Vanessa closed the shutter and removed the glass viewing screen, inserting a negative plate in its place.

Perhaps, Adrian simply felt awkward and unnatural posing before a camera, she told herself. He'd not be the first intelligent, well-educated person to freeze when confronted by the camera's cold eye.

Taking hope camera nerves were the source of Adrian's moodiness, Vanessa flashed him a smile of encouragement.

"You can relax. I promise, this won't hurt."

Hurt? He was in sheer torture. It helped matters not at all that, whatever Vanessa had done with her appearance, the sight of her positively ravished his senses.

Adrian expelled a breath. He was a man severely conflicted, at war with his inner self. Yesterday, he'd dropped his guard when he'd raced to Vanessa's rescue. Fear had ravaged him at the sight of her endangered. In those moments, he'd allowed her past his defenses and dangerously near his heart.

Later, after he'd departed her bedchamber and downed several bracing drinks, he'd been able to reassert his self-control and regain his perspective.

Regardless, however much he might find himself physically, mentally, or soulfully attracted to Vanessa Wynters, he must resist his impulses and the temptation to become involved with her, or any other woman. To do so would require too great a risk, too great a vulnerability. His heart could not survive another calamitous relationship.

Adrian watched Vanessa, his gaze skimming her shapely figure as she disappeared under the focusing cloth and materialized a moment later to make some adjustment. His blood began to pound heavily in his veins and his soul twisted in pain. Could anyone even begin to understand the scope of what he'd suffered? Could he ever trust again?

He did not deny that a small blossom of hope flowered in the shadows of his heart. Indeed, he'd made a multitude of arguments in Vanessa's behalf, reminding himself she was unlike either of his former wives, and quite possibly capable of a true and lasting love.

Yet, he'd misjudged twice before—disastrously so.

Admittedly, Clairissa was to be more pitied than despised. Fragile and unsuspecting, she'd learned of the carnal expectations of marriage only hours before standing beside him at the altar. She never recovered from the shock. During their brief and bitter marriage, she'd made him feel like the most vile of men—a beast, or worse, a leper, becoming hysterical if he attempted to touch her, taking weeks to recover if he did. Certainly, it was nothing short of miraculous he'd gotten her with child. She nearly plagued his heart out after that, distraught with the changes of her body. Still, she did not deserve the horror of the death she suffered. No one did.

Adrian closed off the thought. As he watched Vanessa's graceful movements, he reminded himself she'd been previously married and was experienced in—or at least, acquainted with—the ways of men and women and lovemaking. He deemed this a most desirable attribute, given his history with Clairissa.

His mind turned to his second wife, Olivia. She'd been a fiery, lusty creature. Though she'd restored his self-confidence as a man and a lover, she betrayed their marriage bed without qualms. It came as a double shock to discover her to be a thief as well. Quite obviously, he'd underestimated Olivia's lust for riches, as he'd underestimated her in so many other ways. Even then, she too, did not deserve the excruciating death with which she met, perishing by fire.

If it was she who died that night, he amended.

Adrian's grip tensed on his knees as he brooded over that possibility. Only the silken swish of Vanessa's skirts drew him back to the present again.

What was Vanessa Wynters's heart truly like? he wondered. He could not claim to know her well in so short a passage of time. On the other hand, he could trust his aunt's judgment. She'd known Vanessa over the course of two-and-a-half years and esteemed her greatly.

Still, given his wretched history with women, what if he misjudged Vanessa or overlooked something vital? His heart could not withstand another bludgeoning. Then, too, would she despise him should she learn of the accusations leveled against him? Would he become a leper in her eyes, as well?

It hadn't improved his mood last night when he'd skimmed through the clippings of the accident which he'd saved from Hereford's local paper. They'd baldly intimated that neither of the recent Viscountesses Marrable had died naturally. In short, that he was a murderer. The constable had done nothing to alter that misconception. In fact, he'd done everything in his official capacity to find evidence to convict him.

Such massive pain he'd endured these past few years. It served only to sharpen his resolve to forswear all women. Adrian gazed on Vanessa with desire burning a hole through his soul. He had to ask himself, what sane woman would accept a man with his shadowed past, knowing she might possibly be keeping company with a murderer? Could she ever fully give him her heart, or would she always harbor the hidden fear she might become his next victim?

Adrian bolted shut the door to his heart. It was best he remain behind the walls of his own making. He would be a fool to allow anyone entrance and risk his own destruction.

Vanessa could not still the tremble in her hand. Adrian's look had turned morose. She was suddenly unsure whether she should attempt to inject even a small dram of levity into their session. He held his pose perfectly, but sat stiff as a plank. It would have to do, she decided.

As she prepared to release the shutter, she stayed her hand, changing her mind and stepping apart of the camera. There must be something she could say to coax a lighter expression to his face.

She pursed her lips, then offered him a smile. "You realize, if you insist on glowering at my camera, you are like to crack the lens."

"I should think a sober countenance is appropriate," he replied, his tone terse with annoyance. "This is a mourning portrait after all."

"A *sober* countenance, yes. But you look ready to murder someone."

Adrian shot to his feet, overturning the chair and, with a lunging step, seized her by the arms. His fingers pressed into her flesh as he hauled her against his chest, a ferocious look sweeping his features.

"Never so much as breathe such a thing in my presence," he thundered. "Not ever again, do you understand?"

Not waiting a reply, he released her and staggered back several steps. He shoved his fingers through his hair.

"It's not true what they say. None of it."

Turning on his heel, he stalked from the room, his anger still towering about him.

Vanessa stumbled toward the nearest chair and grabbed hold of it, bracing herself. She heaved for breath, devastated by Adrian's outburst.

What had she said? she wondered desperately, her heart nearly pounding from her chest. God in heaven, what had she done to enrage him so?

Chapter 11

The image of Adrian's features, slashed with fury, tormented Vanessa throughout the remainder of the day. Scarce could she thread two thoughts together, let alone hold them there for any significant amount of time.

Later, unable to trust her emotions, she decided against appearing at dinner or joining the others afterward. Instead, she relayed her excuses and regrets and kept to her chamber, facing what promised to be a night devoid of sleep.

Later still, just before turning down her lamp, Mary Ethel appeared, delivering a note from Cissy—an invitation to join her and her husband the next morning for a "happy escape to Hereford." Vanessa gladly accepted. The diversion was just the tonic she needed while her shattered nerves healed.

Vanessa rose with the dawn and prepared for the outing, taking a modified breakfast of tea and toast in her chamber. At the specified time, she slipped down the grand staircase and into the entrance hall to meet her traveling companions, the Norlands. She found Cissy, standing before the hall's soaring mirror, giving a final check to her bonnet and skirts. Lord Norland, however, appeared nowhere in sight.

"Henry's taken a dreadful chill, poor darling," Cissy said as she came away from the mirror and tugged on her gloves. "It was that fishing jaunt he made yesterday—all that wading about, knee-high in icy waters. Young Geoffrey escaped without so much as a sniffle, but I fear Henry fared the worse and won't be able to leave his bed today."

Cissy stopped before Vanessa and smiled, giving a tilt to her head.

"There's no need to cancel our outing, however." Looping her arm through Vanessa's, Cissy swept her along with her through the front door and onto the portico. "My brother has agreed to accompany us."

Vanessa's heart lurched at the thought of Adrian serving as their chaperon. Cissy took no notice of her distress—which surely shone like a beacon upon her face—but chattered on as she scanned the drive for their carriage.

"Henry insisted I keep my appointment with Madame Chaston. She's cleared her entire morning to fit me for my winter wardrobe. Well, not an entire wardrobe exactly, only four or five dresses. Maybe a sixth."

Vanessa barely followed Cissy's words, her dread mounting by the second at the prospect of facing Adrian. What could she possibly say to the man? She still didn't understand how she'd offended him.

She watched as a carriage approached from the direction of the stables and drew before the portico. In the same moment, she heard a man's swift bootfalls, leaving the portal of the manse and coming to a halt directly behind her.

Vanessa's blood pulsed solidly in her veins, her thoughts scattering in a hundred different directions, as she slowly turned to confront Adrian. As she lifted her eyes to meet his, she discovered Lawrence's spreading smile instead.

"Good morning, ladies." He tipped his hat and sketched a charming bow. "I understand you are in need of an escort to our fair city of Hereford."

Cissy sent Vanessa a wide-eyed glance, appearing as stunned as she. "That would be most kind of you, Lawrence," she replied politely, though with a touch of hesitance. "Forgive me, but I thought Henry sent word to—"

"Adrian? He did indeed, but it seems our brother rode out earlier. Timmons came to me with your request and explained the circumstance. Now, ladies, if you will allow me to assist you, we'll be on our way. Let it never be said chivalry does not flourish at Sherringham."

Full of sunny good cheer, Lawrence aided Cissy and Vanessa into the carriage, then followed, bidding the coachman to drive on.

Vanessa wondered to herself which would be more stressful—the day spent with Adrian or with Lawrence. At least she shared the bench seat with Cissy and would not be plagued with wandering hands. Of course, that meant Lawrence sat directly opposite, in a prime position to stare at her all the way to the city.

Knowing she could not escape the circumstance without being embarrassingly obvious, Vanessa accepted the turn of events and glanced out the window to the passing landscape. She'd not abandon Cissy simply to avoid her brother. Lawrence best behave himself, however, especially in public. She released a sigh. If only she'd had the foresight to carry along her umbrella!

Vanessa continued to ride in silence, admiring the pastoral beauty of the countryside gently rolling past. Her nerves remained bunched in a thousand, jumbled knots. Still, as strange as it seemed, her heart harbored a sting of disappointment that Adrian wasn't escorting them after all.

As Cissy and Lawrence engaged in a pleasant exchange, Vanessa kept her focus on the changing views, noticing how nature had swept her autumnal paintbrush over the woods and hills and fields, washing everything in shades of terra-cotta. She surveyed the scene only superficially, however, her thoughts far removed.

What had Adrian meant yesterday by his parting remark? "It's not true what they say," he'd thundered. "None of it." None of what? And who were "they"?

"Majel is furious, of course." Cissy's comment netted Vanessa's attention. She shifted her gaze from a herd of contentedly grazing sheep and sent Cissy a quizzical look, having missed the first of her comment.

"Adrian has assigned Nanny and Mr. Timmons's wife, Jane, to oversee preparations for the sale of Aunt Gwen's clothing—for the widows and orphans fund, as her will required," Cissy explained. "Majel is incensed he did so and caused a bit of a row when she found out."

"Has Adrian taken leave of his senses?" Lawrence's brows drew together, his tone tinged with ridicule. "Or is our brother completely oblivious to Nanny's declining mental state?"

Vanessa's gaze sheered to Lawrence, an unexpected fierceness springing to her breast. Oddly, she found herself prepared to take up shield and sword in Adrian's behalf, and Nanny's too. A retort poised upon her tongue, but Cissy spoke before she could give voice to it.

"Adrian is well aware of what he is doing," she insisted. "Nanny has long been concerned for those less fortunate. He believes the benefit is an excellent project for her to busy herself with and that it will give her a renewed sense of purpose. Frankly, Nanny is thrilled at the opportunity and is positively bustling with energy. I do believe the excitement has even quickened her mind."

"As if that were possible," Lawrence muttered with a roll of his eyes.

Again, Vanessa simmered at his cutting ridicule. At the same time, she remembered Nanny's bright cheer and amazing clarity of mind when they'd taken tea together, several days earlier. She seemed a changed person then. Not changed, she corrected, *revitalized.*

"Lawrence, don't be cruel," Cissy scolded. "Nanny is the dearest soul, and don't forget Mrs. Timmons. She's long been Sherringham's head housekeeper, and a more efficient and well-organized soul you'll be hard pressed to find. Adrian is confident she can handle any difficulties that arise. He's not so unaware of circumstances at Sherringham as you might believe."

A curious look entered Lawrence's eyes, one Vanessa could not read.

"On the other hand, dear sister, Adrian might not be fully aware of *all* circumstances, either."

Vanessa bit her inner lip, considering the comment odd at best. She chose not to pursue that course. "What of Majel?" she asked instead. "Will she interfere in your brother's decision, do you think?"

This brought chuckles from both Cissy and Lawrence.

"When doesn't she interfere?" Lawrence commented, smiling wide once more.

Cissy smiled too. "Actually, Majel and her family were prepared to leave Sherringham in the coming days, but she has decided they will remain."

A gleam came to life, sparkling in Cissy's eyes. "I was present when she threw down the gauntlet to Adrian. Majel challenged him directly, saying he couldn't possibly object to her remaining to inspect Auntie's clothing as she had a mind to offer on some of them herself as the solicitor suggested. You should have seen Adrian's face. His look turned black as night."

Vanessa need not imagine it. She knew the look first-hand.

Lawrence leaned forward, giving Cissy a teasing wink. "Sister, dear, you are turning into an incorrigible gossip."

As the threesome fell to a companionable silence, Vanessa's thoughts turned once more to Adrian. His thoughtfulness and sensitivity toward Nanny, his generosity and many kindnesses to others including Lady Gwen, formed an image that didn't square with a dark, forbidding side to his nature. What was the truth about Adrian Marrable? Did she really know him at all?

The narrow road wound through the countryside, following the River Wye and bringing them eventually to the ancient market town of Hereford. As they approached an aged stone bridge spanning the river, Vanessa caught sight of the red sandstone cathedral rising in the distance, on the Wye's northern bank.

Crossing over, they progressed in the cathedral's direction, following a series of streets that ended one into another, leaving them directly opposite the sandstone mass with its great square tower and bristling spires.

"Madame Chaston's shop is just a little farther," Cissy said to Vanessa as the carriage turned to the left and trundled along Broad Street. "The shopping district surrounds the cathedral. Though the layout of the city is literally medieval, it's difficult to become lost if you keep the tower in sight."

As the last words left Cissy's lips, the carriage pulled to a halt before a narrow, Georgian-style house. Lawrence preceded the ladies out and handed them down, then followed behind as they entered the House of Chaston.

Vanessa found it to be a wonderful shop, airy and bright with shelves brimming with fabrics and trimmings and a tall, triple mirror filling one corner of the room. Through open doors, she glimpsed busy seamstresses bent to their work, their needles flying over yards of cloth.

From a separate door, a tiny round figure with a thick braid of black hair crowning her head, bustled forth. Cissy stepped forward to greet Madame Chaston then, in turn, introduced her to Lawrence and Vanessa.

"*Eh bien*, Mrs. Wynters also wishes to be fitted for a gown today?" Madame Chaston took Vanessa by the hands and turned her about, assessing her figure and coloring. "*Alors*, something for the day in green cashmere? Or for the evening—a gown in pale blue satin *merveilleux* and duchesse lace?"

"Perhaps another day, thank you." Vanessa declined

as graciously as possible, knowing she needed to save all her funds for her fledgling profession. At the same time, she wondered how she would look in a creation of pale satin and lace and what Adrian might think.

Did it matter? she asked herself in the next instant. She didn't wish it to. And yet, somehow it did.

"Actually, while Cissy is being fitted, I am hoping to locate a photographer's studio," Vanessa disclosed. "That is, if there is one in the city."

"You are in luck, Mrs. Wynters." The woman's eyes brightened, her smile plumping her cheeks. "There are two studios—one on Commercial Street and the other on St. Owens."

"I know just the ones," Lawrence volunteered, then he checked his watch. "We'll return in, shall we say, two hours?"

"Three." Madame Chaston slipped a smile to Cissy. "I'm sure Lady Norland will appreciate the extra time to decide upon her wardrobe."

"Three then," Lawrence confirmed, catching Cissy's gaze. "We can lunch afterward at the inn on Castle Green."

After leaving the House of Chaston, Lawrence gave the coachman directions to the nearest photographic studio on Commercial Street. Fortune smiled on Vanessa when she inquired within and found the owner possessed the specialized paper she sought. After a brief negotiation, and at a slightly inflated price, he agreed to part with several sheets of Platinotype.

Last night, during her many awake hours, Vanessa decided if she was to pursue the ghost in earnest she needed the costly printing-out paper which was sensitized with chloride-of-platinum, rather than silver. The platinum process offered a superior range of tonal values, far greater than any other. She hoped it would render the ghost's features with better definition and thus reveal her identity.

With several hours left to spare, Lawrence suggested they visit St. Ethelbert's Cathedral and its gardens.

"It's quite fascinating really," he asserted. "Hereford's bishopric claims to be the oldest in England and the cathedral, itself, houses many marvelous treasures."

Vanessa agreed. Thus far, Lawrence had conducted himself faultlessly. She trusted he'd continue to do so in the house of God. She also trusted they wouldn't be alone.

Arriving on the cathedral's west side, they alighted from the carriage and entered by way of a well-tended close. Inside, it took several moments for their eyes to adjust to the reduced level of light. Hushed murmurings drew Vanessa's attention to small clusters of other visitors, drifting about the nave and side aisles. There also appeared to be a number of long-robed clerics tending to varied tasks, and a few scattered parishioners praying in the pews.

Lawrence proved a perfect guide, pointing out various details and recounting the tragic tale of Ethelbert, the young East Anglian king who, on a visit to his promised bride, was beheaded by her father, Offa, the famed Mercian king. Ethelbert's ghost demanded burial on this ground, guiding those bearing his remains by a pillar of light.

"The present church is a mixture of architectural styles," Lawrence continued. "It has been destroyed and rebuilt many times. In fact, the original Norman tower collapsed altogether a little less than a hundred years ago."

They moved beneath elaborate vaulting, supported on massive piers and viewed the bishop's throne. From there, they made their way to the ornate shrine of St. Thomas de Cantelupe, once bishop of Hereford but also, purportedly, England's Grand Master of the Order of Knights Templar.

"The cult of St. Thomas and his shrine were once as famous and well-visited as that of Becket's at Canterbury," Lawrence apprised. Turning to Vanessa, he tucked her hand in his arm. "Come. You cannot leave without seeing the Chained Library. I promise, you'll find nothing comparable anywhere."

Lawrence's solicitousness continued to surprise Vanessa. His charm had grown so thick and polished throughout the day, she wondered whether he was endeavoring to mend her image of him or possibly be wooing her.

He brought her to an exceedingly narrow staircase, spiraling upward in a cramped turret. As they began to mount the stone steps, her concerns multiplied. Despite the cathedral's overall size, it seemed Lawrence now led her to a sequestered corner, away from others.

The stairway, itself, was so confining two people could not pass. One was forced to keep moving toward their destination without stop in order to clear it for those kept waiting. But Vanessa perceived there was no one caught in that dilemma, though she'd seen another group precede them. She found herself grateful to know of their presence. Otherwise, she'd suspect Lawrence meant to trap her alone at the top.

As they finished the long climb, however, she was immediately struck by a most fascinating sight—at least a thousand books, stored row upon row, their leather bindings secured to the shelves with long chains.

"There are over fifteen hundred volumes in the collection," Lawrence informed, his hand lifting casually to her waist as they came to a stop. "Some date back as early as the eighth century."

A tremor of unease passed through Vanessa at his lingering touch. Seeing the other visitors departing, and trying not to appear overly anxious, Vanessa stepped from his side and suggested they descend. He appeared surprised she did not wish to linger among the ancient texts.

"There is still much to take in before meeting Cissy," she asserted, her words rushing out, though her throat felt constricted. "You mentioned there being tombs with colored effigies. I'd very much like to see them now."

Vanessa moved quickly to the top of the stairs, but as she began to step from the landing, her toe caught in the hem of her skirt, puling her off-balance and pitching her forward. Lawrence instantly lunged, seizing her by the arms and jerking her back and away from the treacherous staircase.

"You little fool!" he shouted, whirling her around to face him, his fingers digging into her flesh. "Are you so desperate to flee me? You could have broken your neck!"

Vanessa stared at him, aghast. His eyes burned a brilliant, fevered blue in a face that had gone stark white.

"It's Adrian isn't it?" He barked, giving her a firm shake, his fingers pressing deeper.

"Lawrence, stop . . . You're hurting me."

The look in his eyes changed from one of fury to shock. He instantly released her and stepped back, his features transforming themselves into a cast of repentance.

"Vanessa, I—I'm sorry. Forgive me. I don't know what came over me. You started to fall and I . . . God, I feared you were going to kill yourself."

Vanessa's heart hammered against her ribs. Were all the Marrable men given to such gross overreaction?

As she glanced up at Lawrence, she could not deny the alarm imprinted on his face. How could she doubt the sincerity of his words, even if not all of them made perfect sense?

What was it mothers so often said? Something about their children frightening them so badly that, once they knew their child was safe, they tasted only a white-hot fury for having been so scared. Fear and anger were two emotions that often ran together, entwined.

As Vanessa's nerves calmed, a twinge of guilt rose inside her at the troubled look still creasing Lawrence's eyes. She laid a hand to his arm and gave it a gentle squeeze.

"Lawrence, there is nothing to forgive. I owe you my thanks. You did save me, after all."

He dropped his gaze to her hand and, covering it with his, nodded. "Let's get down from here, Vanessa. The library can wait till another time."

Lawrence insisted on preceding Vanessa down the twisting staircase lest she misstep again. That way, he explained, he would break her fall.

With the time left to them, they made their way among the tombs, some mere slabs, others fascinating for their reposing, full-size sculptures of the occupants within. There were noble lords, and noble ladies, and worldly-looking clergymen. Vanessa's particular favorite was that of a knight in full armor with a serpent-headed dog curled at his feet.

Entering a side chapel dedicated to St. Ethelbert, Vanessa paused at the tomb of a couple, bearing their colored effigies. The woman appeared very young and an infant lay swaddled by her side. Chrism marked the babe's tiny forehead, confirmation of the child's baptism before its death.

Vanessa touched a hand to the sculpture, feeling a great sadness here.

"This is the tomb of Alexander Denton and his wife—his first wife. She was an heiress and only seventeen when she died in childbirth." Lawrence released a long breath. "Whenever I see it, it reminds me of Clairissa."

Vanessa glanced to him at the mention of Adrian's first wife. "And was she buried with hers and Adrian's child?"

Lawrence nodded. "Yes, a son. I didn't realize you knew how she died."

Vanessa drew away her hand from the sculpture. "I know little more, except that she died in great pain. Her suffering was beyond the pale, I was told."

"That is true. Quite true." A grave look entered his face.

Vanessa gripped her hands together, unsure she should venture her next question. Yet it refused to remain locked inside.

"I upset Adrian horribly yesterday. I have no idea why he reacted as he did, but I suspect it is linked somehow to his past—my guess is, to his wives. Everyone at Sherringham tiptoes around that subject, yet I believe it is the source of his moods. Though, I am aware of the circumstances of Olivia's death, I cannot help but wonder if there is something I am missing about Clairissa's—or something about Adrian himself."

"'Adrian' is it?" An odd gleam appeared, then disappeared, in Lawrence's eyes. He drew his brows together in the semblance of a frown. "What precisely did you say to him?"

Vanessa stepped away from the tomb and moved toward the chapel's entrance, Lawrence following at her side.

"He agreed to sit for his portrait for the mourning album. When he arrived, he was already in the blackest of moods and scowling. I tried to encourage him to improve his expression—not to smile, just to appear moderately pleasant . . ."

"Yes, but what did you say?"

She fidgeted with the button at the waist of her jacket. "That if he continued to look at the camera as he was, he'd crack the lens."

"Is that all?"

"No. I said he looked ready to murder someone."

Lawrence halted in place, his jaw dropping open. He took a step to even himself with her, then cleared his throat.

"My dear Vanessa. That was possibly the very worst thing you could have said to him. I don't quite know how to tell you this about my brother, but he was—*is*—under suspicion of having murdered both his wives."

Vanessa's breath left her, the shock of his words jolting her to her core. "That cannot be! It's a lie! Surely, it's a lie."

Her cry drew the attention of a nearby workman and a half-dozen of the faithful scattered in pews, praying before the nave's central altar. Vanessa crossed her arms over her stomach. For a moment she thought she might become ill. Lawrence quickly led her down the side aisle to a bench at the back, away from others.

"We all wish to believe Adrian is innocent. Things have a way of working themselves out."

"You speak as if you have doubts."

Lawrence's silence was damning. "There are things you do not understand," he said at last.

Vanessa began to tremble, anger and frustration overtaking her.

"I *understand* his first wife died of natural causes in childbirth. I *understand* his second wife died in a carriage accident. Neither of those are uncommon in any way. They happen every day. If there is something I don't understand, then pray enlighten me, but do not leave me in the dark to have my head snapped off by your brother!"

Lawrence held her gaze a long moment. Finally, lacing his fingers together, he braced one arm on the back of the bench and nodded.

"Very well. It's not fair to leave you uninformed, vulnerable to Adrian's shifting moods and temper. Let me begin with Clairissa."

He rolled his eyes to the vaulting overhead and back again as he chose his next words.

"Clairissa was a small, delicate thing— pctite, fragile, like a doll. She stood just under five feet." He sighed heavily. "Need I expound of the difficulties such women have in childbirth, their hips so narrow, they are unable to deliver the babe?

"She labored three days. You would have had to

have known Clairissa to understand how much she loathed the least physical pain. You can imagine her screeching—and shall I add cursing—that the pain of her labor wrought. Her screams could be heard throughout Sherringham.

"I stayed with Adrian much of the time, outside her bedchamber. The doctor attending Clairissa was not her regular physician. He had been drawn out of town on personal matters. The doctor who arrived—a Dr. Anderson—was visiting from Edinburgh.

"Deep in the hours of the third night, he came to Adrian with grim news. Clairissa and their child would be dead by morning unless something drastic was done or a miracle intervened. She was exhausted and weakening by the minute. To be blunt, she could not pass the babe. Dr. Anderson suggested a radical procedure, which he claimed to have seen used on occasion. He proposed breaking the mother's pelvic bones to deliver the babe. With luck, he could save both his patients."

"He broke her pelvic bones?" Vanessa's blood ran cold. "How ghastly. Did Adrian agree?"

"He had no choice. He was about to lose them both either way."

Vanessa closed her lashes against the image, her hand moving to her throat. "Poor Clairissa."

"As you can well imagine, Adrian was utterly destroyed by events. To his credit, after he gave the doctor his approval to go forward with the procedure, Adrian never left the corridor outside her room." Lawrence shifted, and glanced toward the altar. "I confess I was far less noble and could not bear to stay. I can still hear Clairissa's screams. I'm sure Adrian can, too."

Vanessa fell silent beside Lawrence. She understood now what Adrian had meant when he said Clairissa cursed him still.

"And so the procedure failed and mother and child were both lost," she commented softly, stating the obvious.

Lawrence released another, deep-held breath. "Yes. Only later was it discovered that the doctor had been drinking heavily at Clairissa's bedside. Neither Adrian nor I guessed it. He didn't appear inebriated nor did we notice the smell of alcohol. But hell, we'd been drinking ourselves."

Vanessa digested this, careful to form no judgments. "I imagine Adrian blames himself for Clairissa's death, not only for getting her with child, but for approving the doctor's plan and not knowing he was drunk."

"Yes, very much so."

She wet her lips. "That still doesn't explain how anyone could accuse him of murdering Clairissa."

Lawrence looked at her squarely, holding her gaze. "The suspicions arose after Olivia's death. That is when the first accusations began to surface about Clairissa. It was no secret their marriage was troubled. Clairissa made sure of that."

"I'm not sure I understand."

"You would have to have known her. Clairissa was raised like a princess of royalty and used to having her perfect world and everything in it perfectly her own way. She thought Adrian perfect, too, which is why she pursued him with such zeal. But no one told her about the realities of marriage until the morning she was deposited on the church steps."

Lawrence studied his fingertips a moment before looking back.

"Pardon me for being blunt, but she did not cope well with that particular reality. She discovered that one thing she could not change was nature itself. Nor could she totally deny her husband his marital rights, though it is my impression she tried mightily. Her hysterics were real enough, and I'm sure she deemed herself misused. What I cannot forgive her for was trying to convince others that Adrian was brutalizing her. Most saw through her complaints. They were as transparent as air and had just as much substance."

Lawrence wiped a hand over his face, as if wishing to forget it all. "Sorry, I suppose I'm the one becoming the gossip now, but you wished to understand. The short of it is, Clairissa made the most wretched of wives. Some even thought her unbalanced. And later, others believed Adrian took the chance offered him, knowing full well the doctor was drunk and incompetent and that the procedure would fail."

"That is reprehensible," Vanessa protested. "Did they also believe he meant to kill his own child?"

"No. Never that. At the very least, the procedure should have saved the infant. Those who accept the theory, believe he only sought to rid himself of Clairissa and that his means were unconscionable."

A lump rose in Vanessa's throat and lodged there. What more did she not know? "You said these accusations arose at the time of Olivia's death. But that was an accident, was it not?"

Lawrence rose from the bench and offered her his hand. "Let us take a turn outside, shall we? The fresh air will do us both good."

Minutes later they paced the expansive grounds of the close where the shrubbery was just beginning to blush with autumn colors.

"The investigation revealed Olivia's carriage had been tampered with—the axle weakened so that it would break," Lawrence disclosed as they walked arm in arm. "Just hours before, Adrian and Olivia had become embroiled in a ferocious argument. Most everyone in residence at the time must have heard it. Excepting myself. I was going over some papers in the west tower.

"Adrian left Sherringham directly after the quarrel and headed for London. That is where the news finally reached him two days after the accident. Hereford's constable is convinced Adrian sabotaged Olivia's personal carriage before he departed, being well aware of the deadly stretch of road at Devil's Hairpin. Since then, the constable has done everything in his power to ruin Adrian."

It all seemed so unfair to Vanessa that Adrian should be so vilified.

"But it doesn't make sense that Adrian would sabotage the carriage and send it into a ravine if Olivia was carrying a fortune in jewels."

Lawrence shook his head. "He didn't know she had them. No one knew. Personally, the family believes she was leaving Adrian for good and assuring her future by taking the jewels. Of course, when she stepped into the carriage that night, her fate was already sealed."

"Nanny believes Olivia was racing after Adrian to mend their rift."

A smile touched his lips. "Nanny would. She is a kindly soul, no matter how befuddled she becomes."

"You indicated that Adrian is still under suspicion. Were you speaking of Hereford's constable?"

"Yes. He's convinced of Adrian's guilt and longs for the day he can lock my brother away. He'd have done so already had he solid evidence. But nothing could be proven. It all got very ugly, of course. Adrian was ostracized from all polite society for a time. Even now, many doors remain closed to him."

Lawrence brought Vanessa to a halt and turned toward her. He dropped his gaze away for a moment, as if debating whether to say something, then looked again to her face.

"It was at the time of the investigation that Aunt Gwen chose to leave. It was all so stressful. I hate to admit it, but I believe Auntie left Sherringham because she believed in Adrian's guilt. And for the same reason, she did not return."

Vanessa couldn't find her voice for a moment as his words sank in fully.

"I think that unlikely," she commented with no real basis for doing so. "Lady Gwen didn't speak of the tragedy."

"No, I wouldn't imagine she did. The entire affair pained her deeply."

"And what of you? What do you believe?"

Lawrence shuttered his look. "I have to stand by my brother, of course. Especially since he is my twin."

"That is no answer, Lawrence, and well you know it." Vanessa felt her temper rise at his lack of conviction in Adrian's behalf. "Certainly you do not believe he is capable of murder?"

"And are you so certain he is not?"

"Yes, I am and so should you be," she returned with more force than necessary.

Lawrence loomed over her, a shimmer of light passing through his eyes. "Adrian has a fierce protectress, does he? I would be jealous if I didn't already know my brother has forsworn all women. I'm sorry, I see that surprises you. I thought it was rather obvious."

Vanessa found herself at a complete loss for words. Nanny had implied as much when she questioned whether the Marrable line would continue through Adrian, saying he might not desire to wed again given the unhappy experiences and tragedies of his previous marriages. But to hear Lawrence say it so concretely, well, he might just as well have slipped a blade into her heart.

Vanessa watched numbly as Lawrence checked his timepiece.

"We should be on our way to meet Cissy. Shall we walk?" Lawrence asked, his tone almost cheery.

At her nod, he signaled to their waiting carriage to go on ahead, then offered her his arm.

The walk helped refresh Vanessa as she and Lawrence proceeded in silence along Broad Street. At first she simply drank in the overall scenery, finding it soothing to do so. Soon, she turned her attention to the colorful shop windows and their crowded displays, welcoming their distraction.

Coming upon an antiquarian shop, she discovered a watch in the corner of the window. The case appeared to be of pewter, and the numerals upon the face, bold and easily readable. She could also see that the second hand was functioning, and, happily, the little card laying before it stated a most reasonable price.

"See something you like?" Lawrence inquired, standing close beside her.

Vanessa smiled, never taking her eyes from the watch. "Yes, something quite perfect. Perfect for a budding photographer."

Vanessa stepped swiftly through the shop door with

Lawrence following on her heels. Ten minutes later she emerged with a small bundle in her hand. Lawrence tarried inside, considering a cherrywood pipe.

Smiling to herself, Vanessa tucked the package into her drawstring purse and imagined how surprised and delighted Geoffrey would be. As she lifted her gaze, her smile faded from her lips. Directly across the street, Adrian Marrable stood framed in the portal of the Herefordshire News and Telegraph Office.

He did not detect her presence, since he was engrossed in reading a small missive, presumably a wire. Finishing, he creased the paper in two and stepped onto the walkway, at the same time glancing up. Adrian's eyes collided with Vanessa's, and like her, he stood stock-still.

Vanessa had no idea how to react, or what she could possibly say if he crossed the street to approach her. More than his angry, parting words separated them, more than the fresh knowledge of his past and the accusations that stood against him. What truly separated them was the wall he'd erected around himself, barring any from drawing too close.

And yet, the wall was not impenetrable. She'd peered through the cracks and caught a glimpse of his heart. In no way could she believe his was the heart of a murderer.

"Well, well, speak of the devil," Lawrence's voice floated to her ears as he came out of the shop and joined her.

Vanessa bristled, recognizing his tone to be identical to the one he'd used at the funeral, when Adrian arrived unexpectedly. She bristled again when he laced his arm around her shoulders.

She glanced back to Adrian as his eyes traveled to Lawrence then returned to her. A shadow fell over his features. Touching his hand to the brim of his hat, in a polite but stiff gesture, he turned on his heel and strode swiftly away in the opposite direction.

A heaviness suffused Vanessa's heart as he disappeared down the street.

Adrian lengthened his stride, the image of the two firing his mind. He had only himself to blame for driving Vanessa to Lawrence's arms. He was a fool. A damnable fool whose jealousy was feasting on his insides.

Vanessa, Vanessa. Her name echoed through his mind as did her face. What was it he'd seen in her eyes just now? He'd expected to find anger, pain, even fear perhaps. But there was something else. A look of awareness, comprehension . . . of something. But of what?

He quickened his pace, a vile thought entering. Had she questioned his brother? Had Lawrence disclosed the details of his past?

Adrian squeezed his hand to a fist, then heard the crumple of paper. He glanced down to Cameron's telegram then stuffed it in his coat pocket.

His friend at the Yard had reviewed his theory that Olivia might still be alive and supporting herself with the sale of the Marrable jewels. Cameron dismissed his speculations outright but offered encouraging news.

"Another jewel has come to light. Have full description of woman. Strong lead. Unless Lady Olivia possessed sizable mole on right jaw, woman described is someone else. Bonnie Beckford?" The message ended:

"Accept your wife is dead, friend. Get on with the matter of living."

Adrian unclenched his fist. It would seem he was free of Olivia after all, unless she could reach him from beyond the grave. Still, would he ever be free of the past? Of the rumormongering, the suspicions, the outright accusations of blood staining his hands?

Thoughts of Vanessa flooded his mind and once more his heart warred against better judgment. He should distance himself from her, an inner voice argued. Besides, if she knew the truth already, she surely must despise him now.

Better she not be touched by the curse that followed him, another voice spoke up, lest that evil destroy her as well.

But his heart battled back, undaunted, its armor bright and strong. There was no curse, only choices poorly made. A far worse choice would be to abandon Vanessa to another. Then Olivia would have truly won, and he would be left to tilt against shadows, alone and isolated behind his wall of pain.

Chapter 12

After a long session of developing and printing out the negatives for the mourning album, Vanessa and Geoffrey set the Photo House to rights—washing the pans and implements, scrubbing down the tables, and storing the solutions in their proper places.

While Geoffrey refilled the buckets with fresh water, Vanessa unpinned the photographs from the edges of shelves, checking each one before placing it into a deep drawer. She was pleased with the results of the portraits—those of the Norland and Pendergast families, Lawrence, Nanny Pringle, and the many household servants who knew Lady Gwendolyn while she lived.

Adrian's photograph, of course, was not among the others. The way things were progressing, Vanessa doubted it ever would be.

Vanessa's emotions coursed restlessly through her as she thought back to yesterday and to Adrian. She'd watched him walk briskly away down Broad Street and would have continued to watch till he disappeared from sight had Lawrence not insisted they hasten on to meet Cissy. Vanessa hadn't seen Adrian since.

Her spirits flagged at that thought. Directing her attention back to the shelf, she unfastened the last of the pictures and glanced down at it. There, beneath her fingers, was the image of Lady Gwendolyn lying in her coffin in Knights Chapel, her hands folded one atop the other. A familiar pain splintered through Vanessa's heart. She steeled herself, choosing to feel gratitude instead of grief—gratitude to have known so exceptional a lady and to have been touched by her light and joy and kindness.

Vanessa began to place the picture in the drawer with the others then drew back her hand. Though the quality of the photograph was without fault, there was something about it that struck her as not quite right.

As she puzzled over the picture, Rascal, who had been lying patiently outside the open door, lifted his head from his paws. A low growl rumbled in his throat.

"What's the matter, boy?" Geoffrey called as he replaced the last of the buckets.

The pup continued to growl at something in the courtyard, out of sight. An instant later he sprang to his feet, the fur along his neck and back bristling as he began yapping excitedly.

Vanessa deposited the picture in the drawer and closed it, then started across the room to see what agitated the animal so. She halted, seeing Geoffrey reach the door before her and step outside. He glanced right and left then looked back to Vanessa and gave a shrug. Squatting down beside the puppy, Geoffrey ruffled his fur and gave him a thorough petting.

"Quiet, boy. There's nothing out here."

Unconvinced, the pup maintained its stiff-legged stance and continued to bark noisily.

"Calm down, boy. Rascal, *no!* Stop!" Geoffrey commanded.

Rascal pinned back his ears and sat down on his haunches. But as the boy rose and left his side, the pup began to whine. No sooner had Geoffrey reentered the Photo House and taken several steps, than Rascal bounced to all fours again and launched into a fresh fit of barking.

"We're almost finished here, Geoffrey. Why don't you go on ahead and take Rascal for a run? He's a high-spirited pup and the exercise will do him good."

"Are you sure, Mrs. Wynters?"

"Quite sure." She cast him a smile.

Geoffrey started for the door, then stopped on the threshold and turned back. Digging into his pocket, he produced the pewter watch and held it up. His face mirrored his delight.

"Thank you again, Mrs. Wynters. It's capital! I'll treasure it always, I promise."

His words drew another smile from Vanessa. "Tomorrow, we'll photograph one of the follies—your choice, Geoffrey—and you can time the exposures."

"Can I really?" His face brightened further.

"Really." Vanessa chuckled at his enthusiasm.

At that moment, Rascal bounded out of sight, barking wildly.

"Probably a squirrel." Geoffrey shrugged, then dashed after the ungovernable pup.

Vanessa stacked the porcelain trays at the end of the long worktable then crossed the room and closed the doors on the cupboard. As she started to step away, the temperature plunged around her, turning a sharp, bitter cold.

Wrapping her arms about her, Vanessa took a long, deep swallow. "I know you're here," she called out to the empty room. "What do you want?"

Unsurprisingly, there was no detectable response. Nor was there a change in the frigid air. Wary, Vanessa reached out her hand and felt the space directly before her. "Polar" was a term that came to mind. As her arm remained stretched forth, the air's iciness abruptly dissolved, the room returning in an instant to its former temperature.

Vanessa snatched back her hand, her heart pounding fiercely. Was the specter gone or still present, watching? What did it want? Why did it come here, to the Photo House?

Vanessa assumed her unseen visitor to be the same entity that had appeared in the gallery photographs— the misted lady, beckoning with a vaporous hand. If it—or rather, if *she*—wished to reveal something, where had she evanesced to now?

Vanessa paced the room, searching for chilly areas but found none. Her hands shook and her heart thumped madly yet, curiously, never for a moment did she feel threatened. Vanessa waited a quarter-of-an-hour longer, timing the passage on her watch. The minutes stretched out for a seeming eternity. Still, the phenomenon did not recur. Deciding she couldn't wait the remainder of the day on a ghostly whim, Vanessa prepared to leave.

"Let me know when you're ready to have your picture taken," she addressed the empty room with a dash of humor, though her nerves and patience were stretched thin.

All remained silent, unchanging. Perhaps, the specter had departed after all. Or perhaps she was going a touch mad, Vanessa told herself. She had, after all, just attempted to communicate with a disembodied spirit.

Slipping her shawl and keys off the peg by the door, Vanessa stepped through the door, quitting the Photo House. As she fitted the key to the door's lock, the temperature plummeted dramatically around her once more.

Vanessa whirled in place. She swept on her shawl then, composing herself, reached forth her hand and felt the characteristic frigidness in the air. She sensed it to be the same as before, the degree and quality of the cold almost like an icy fingerprint. Certainly, the specter was the same one she'd experienced moments before and, she believed, the one that had inhabited the gallery as well.

As Vanessa continued to explore the chilly expanse of air, she discovered it possessed a definite form, like a huge icy sphere. She could extend her hand deep into its center as well as move around its perimeter.

Suddenly, the ball of cold drew away from Vanessa, but she easily located it several feet from where it had hovered moments before. Again, the sphere of wintry air moved off and, again, she located it.

Vanessa's pulses quickened. "You wish for me to follow you, is that it? All right. Stay here a moment. Don't leave. I need to get my camera."

Vanessa raced back inside the Photo House and retrieved her equipment from the far corner. Thankfully, the tripod was already attached to the camera. It took her another minute to affix a lens. She then grabbed the oak box containing a small cache of sensitized dry plates and her brass stops and started back outside. She knew she'd have to depend on her experience and guess at the proper settings. Yet, even should the exposures print out poorly, at least she would learn where the specter wished to lead her and hopefully what it wanted.

With camera and case in hand, Vanessa rushed into the courtyard. When she didn't immediately locate the frigid mass of air, she worried she'd taken overlong, and that the specter had withdrawn. But seconds later, the glacial cold engulfed her once more.

"Good"—she panted for breath—"you're here." She shouldered the tripod and camera on her shoulder and gripped the handle on the oak box. "I'm ready. If there's something you wish to show me then, please, lead on."

Vanessa followed the moving sphere of chill air. It led her in a steady line to the far end of the courtyard, coming to a stop before the entrance to the west tower.

Vanessa gazed up at it, remembering the night she'd thought to have seen a figure there in the topmost window. Realizing the specter continued to hover before the entry, Vanessa assumed it wished her to enter.

"Let me make an exposure before we go inside. I'll be quick about it, I promise."

Vanessa worked hastily, hoping the entity would remain patient. After stabilizing the tripod, she swiftly brought the tower's arched door into focus on the glass viewing screen, wasting no time for artistic considerations. She estimated the settings, stopped down the lens, and adjusted the shutter, judging everything by instinct.

"If you are there, stay there. Uh, look toward the camera." This was insanity, sheer insanity. Not only was she talking to a ghost, now she was posing it for its picture.

Removing the glass screen, Vanessa inserted the negative plate holder, pulled the slide, and released the shutter. Immediately, the ball of bitter-cold air moved off.

Hurriedly, Vanessa replaced the slide to protect the negative. Gathering up her equipment, she followed the frigid mist inside the tower, pausing only long enough to open the door, unlike her "companion" who'd just passed straight through!

Vanessa found herself standing in a stone stairwell, confronted by a long flight of stairs. It turned back on itself many times, reaching upward and out of sight. The sphere of cold hovered before the staircase, then began to ascend, skimming upward over the steps, leading Vanessa high into the tower.

The temperature within the stairwell quickly fell, the stone reflecting the spectral cold. Vanessa trembled and her teeth chattered, but she climbed steadily onward. At one point, she passed a door that opened onto the connecting wing, but the specter did not divert or tarry there. Instead, it continued its ascent, bringing Vanessa at last to the spacious landing at the top and to a substantial, multi-paneled oak door.

The sphere of cold centered before the door then passed through the wood. Obviously, it expected her to follow.

Testing the brass S-curved door handle, Vanessa found it gave under the pressure of her hand, allowing her entrance as the door swept easily open.

Stepping inside, she found herself standing in what she assumed—by its masculine decor and antiquarian curiosities—to be a private study. The furnishings offered solid comfort while, additionally, there were glass cases containing varied collections and even an entire suit of armor for both man and horse displayed to one side. Books lined the walls all around, both on the entrance level and in the gallery above. There, tall, arched windows interrupted the bookcases periodically, each window containing an ancient seal in its apex.

Vanessa recalled being advised on several occasions that hers and Lady Gwen's photographs were stored in the west study. Surely this must be the place, she reasoned, being that this was the west tower.

Her interest drew to the beautiful wrought-iron spiral staircase in the corner which led to the gallery above. Its narrowness reminded her of the staircase she'd encountered, and almost toppled down, yesterday in St. Ethelbert's Cathedral.

The spectral cold flowed over her, catching back her attention before moving off again. Once more, Vanessa followed and was mildly surprised when it led her to the bottom of the twisting stairs. Almost at once, the sphere of cold began spinning rapidly, as if greatly agitated, and creating a distinct gust of wind.

Vanessa fumbled with her equipment, swiftly setting up her camera. For whatever reason, the steps held significance and she knew she must capture its image now, while the specter was communicating, well, whatever it was communicating.

Removing the exposed negative, still lodged in the camera, she quickly judged the distance and light, estimated the shutter setting for an indoor exposure, and inserted a fresh negative. As experience could only guide her so far, Vanessa decided to make two exposures with two different settings, lest one guess was wrong.

Again, barely had she finished than the sphere of cold began to move off, ceasing its spinning as it advanced up the twisting iron stairs.

Vanessa left her camera where it stood, sensing she no longer needed it. Catching up the skirt of her gown, she mounted with care, thankful the climb was far shorter than yesterday's. Still it was not insignificant.

As Vanessa gained the top, she discovered the icy sphere waiting. Immediately, it led her along the gallery to a series of shelves containing rows of deep cardboard boxes. Each was marked and dated in a neat hand. Lady Gwen's hand, Vanessa realized, recognizing the script at once. Presumably, the boxes contained family photographs. But what, precisely, did the ghost want her to do now?

"Is there something here you wish me to see? A photograph? Which box should I look in? Show me."

Vanessa touched her hand to the boxes, one by one. As her fingers grazed the one labeled "May 15, 1878," the air surrounding her hand turned icy. She caught her hand back, stung by the cold.

"All right, I understand. This is the one."

Pulling the box from the shelf, Vanessa sank with it to the floor. As she lifted off the lid, she hoped the specter wouldn't decide to watch over her shoulder. She thought she was already turning blue.

To her delight, the box contained a thick stack of stereographs, all neatly tied with a creamy satin ribbon and a spray of artificial orange blossoms. Beside it was a handsome, Holmes-Bates stereoscope by which to view them, the condition new. With a start, Vanessa recalled the double-lensed stereoscopic camera she'd inherited from Lady Gwen. These, then, must be some of the pictures Lady Gwen had taken with it.

As she lifted out the bundle of ribbon-wrapped stereographs, she discovered a note at the bottom of the box. Thinking the note might be somehow significant, she slipped it from its envelope and scanned its contents.

Again, she recognized Lady Gwen's neat script. The missive was one of congratulations to Adrian and Olivia on the occasion of their marriage. The stereoscope and stereo cards, with their unique double images, were Lady Gwen's wedding gift to them. As Vanessa loosed the ribbon and sifted through the collection of stereographs, she saw the pictures they bore were of the couple's wedding itself.

Taking up the viewer, Vanessa fitted the first of the cards onto the holder and peered through the shielded lens. The figures leaped to life, appearing startlingly solid and three-dimensional. They could be present in the room, standing on the other side of the stereoscope, they looked so real.

Of course, she knew how this magic was technically accomplished—two pictures were taken at the same distance from the subject but at slightly different angles. The idea was to approximate the distance between a person's eyes so that, when the two near-identical photographs were then mounted side-by-side, they rendered an illusion of depth.

Even with that knowledge, Vanessa found it did not detract from the results as she gazed on the two people before her eyes, both smiling and obviously in love—Adrian and a strikingly beautiful woman, Olivia.

Changing the stereo card for another, and then another, Vanessa began to slowly make her way through the many images and memories of that day. She recognized the cathedral steps upon which the wedding party posed, and then a stretch of the south lawn where tents were raised for an out-of-doors reception.

From time to time, she felt the air turn chill at her side, reminding her of the entity's presence.

As Vanessa studied the pictures, she couldn't deny Olivia was indeed beautiful. She stood taller than most women, her figure an enviable hourglass, with ample endowments to say the least. Her red hair translated to a medium tone of gray, though Nanny had called the color "fiery."

Vanessa felt like a secretive spectator—a trespasser, really—as she examined the last of the pictures. The particular stereograph she gazed on now showed the couple filling each others' arms, dancing. Lady Gwen must have posed them, of course. The movement would have been far too rapid for the camera's lens and would have printed out as a blur.

Vanessa affixed the last of the cards, a particularly charming scene of Adrian and Olivia as they left the festivities and entered Sherringham. A sharp pang of jealousy flashed through Vanessa's heart as she imagined the couple proceeding to the wedding night ahead.

She closed her eyes and rubbed them, silently upbraiding herself. She had no right to be jealous, especially knowing this happy day soon lost its luster and ended in such tragedy. It was just difficult to see Adrian and Olivia like this, so astonishingly realistic that if either took a breath or smiled a little wider, she'd not be surprised.

Vanessa retied the stack of stereo cards and placed them and the stereoscope back in the box. Unsure of what she'd been expected to find, she'd discovered no shattering revelations. They were solely wedding photographs. Perhaps the entity had something more to show her.

Rising, she stretched her legs, since they were feeling slightly numb, then replaced the box on the shelf. As she straightened, she realized the air had lost its frigid edge.

"Is there anything more you wish to show me?" she addressed the seemingly empty study.

When the temperature remained constant, Vanessa assumed she'd been abandoned by her ghostly escort and moved toward the stairs. She was unsure why the specter wished for her to see the photographs. On the other hand, the newly exposed plates might contain important clues or information. There was still time for her to return to the Photo House and develop the negatives, and print them out, before dinner.

Just as Vanessa reached the top of the staircase, the door to the study suddenly opened wide and a man entered. Her heart picked up its beat as Adrian looked up and caught sight of her.

He slowed his step but did not halt until he came to the bottom of the stairs, his eyes never leaving her. The surprise that first touched his features altered to an unreadable look. And yet there was heat smoldering in the depths of his midnight eyes as they continued to hold her.

"Adrian . . ." His name slipped softly from her lips. She must talk with him. She must clear the air of any misunderstandings that lay between them, apologize for any pain she'd caused by her unwitting words.

Vanessa started to descend, her foot leaving the topmost step. In the same instant, an ice-cold air swept over her and she felt a solid push from behind, sending her toppling down the spiraling staircase and over the side into a well of darkness.

Chapter 13

Muted voices surrounded Vanessa. She strained to catch the words, recognizing Adrian's deep, rich tones. He spoke with another man, Dr. Hambley she thought, and with Cissy . . .

A heavy weight pulled Vanessa downward into the darkness once more. She sank deeper and deeper then floated a time before climbing once more toward consciousness.

Vanessa dragged open one eye, then the other. The room swam in her vision then slowed to a stop as she came fully awake. To her left, a lamp glowed on the stand beside the bed, creating a soft halo of light in the otherwise pitch-dark room.

Silence layered the chamber, the voices now gone, everything utterly still. For a moment she lay wondering how she'd gotten here in her bedchamber, then remembered falling, headfirst, down the twisting stairs.

Something shifted in the shadows just beyond the lamp, causing Vanessa's breath to catch in her lungs. A figure leaned forward into the light—a man seated, bracing his elbows on his knees and dragging his fingers through his dark rumpled hair. Adrian.

Her heart quickened at the sight of him then slowed. He looked terrible. Deep lines sharpened his face, lines of concern making him appear years older. He wore no jacket or tie, and his shirt gaped open at the neck, revealing crisp black hair on his chest. He clasped his hands together and rested his head against them, looking for all the world dismantled by his thoughts.

Lord in heaven. Was she the cause of his distress? Just two days before, she'd stung him with her thoughtless words. Now, had she somehow afflicted him further?

"Adrian," she called softly.

He lifted his head, surprise skipping through his eyes as he discovered her own eyes open and gazing upon him. He rose instantly and came to her side. Easing himself onto the edge of the mattress, he caught up her fingers in his, pressing his lips to the back of her hand then her palm, wholly astounding her.

"Vanessa, thank God, thank God!" He leaned forward, half covering her with his torso as he buried his head against the curve of her neck. "You've been unconscious for hours. I feared you might never awaken."

Vanessa couldn't find her voice, overcome as much by his words as by his actions and display of emotion. Just as she began to lift her hand to his rich head of hair, he shifted, raising himself above her. A smile touched his lips.

"You scared several more lives out of me, you know. I'm not sure I have any left."

Vanessa smiled back, relishing the feel of his arms surrounding her. It felt so right, so very right. If this was a dream, she didn't wish to wake.

Her gaze drifted over his handsome features and wonderfully long lashes, then settled on his cheek and the side of his eye. Even in the dim light, she could make out a bruise spreading there.

"Adrian, you are hurt! What happened?" Reaching

up, she feathered her fingers over his jaw, below the discoloration. "Who did this to you?"

"You did, my darling. Your elbow caught me when I broke your fall. You do remember falling, do you not?"

"Falling?" she stumbled over the word, her mind veering back to fixate on two previous words out of his mouth—"my darling."

"Your head struck the railing," he continued in a rush. "You flipped over the staircase entirely and knocked yourself unconscious in the bargain."

Sitting up fully, Adrian turned to the bedside stand and began to pour her a glass of water from a small decanter there.

"How are you feeling?" he asked with a forced brightness that did little to veil his concern. "Dr. Hambley had to leave for another emergency, but he'll return as soon as he is able in the morning. Meanwhile, he's instructed Cissy and myself thoroughly in your care."

Vanessa smiled at the thought of Adrian caring for her and noted that Cissy had obviously been dismissed for the night.

"I feel as well as can be expected, I suppose. Whatever aches and pains I've gained will just be added to those from my spill off Delilah."

Adrian set the glass and decanter down and braced his hands on his knees. He bent his head as some disturbing thought crowded in, weighing heavily upon him.

"This is my fault," he said at last, then shoved to his feet and began to pace. "Vanessa, you might have been killed, and I am to blame."

Vanessa lifted herself onto her elbow and stared at him, stunned. "Adrian, what are you talking about?"

He turned back to her, his eyes like onyx in the faint light, his expression troubled once more.

"Twice, within the short space of four days, you have been injured seriously—at the mausoleum and now on those damnable stairs."

Vanessa sat upright, aware the covers had fallen to her lap, exposing her nightgown to his view. "You cannot blame yourself for my mishaps, Adrian."

"Mishaps?" he vented a short laugh. "If only they were that and no more. At least then I could better protect you." He raked a hand through his hair then turned and faced her, his eyes coupling with her. "Do you not see? I am a man cursed. I didn't wish to believe so, but I can no longer deny it."

Adrian crossed to the bed and lowered himself beside her once more. Reaching out, he threaded his fingers through her thick fall of hair, sweeping it back from her shoulders.

"My lovely Vanessa, when I saw you fall and then held you, pale and seemingly lifeless in my arms, I realized how greatly I've come to love you. So greatly in fact, that for your own sake, I must now leave. Whatever curse plagues my existence, it has claimed two wives from me already. I will not allow it to endanger you."

He encompassed her with his arms, a look of pain cleaving his eyes as he drew her against him. Vanessa felt her softness yield against his hard chest.

"I *must* leave you, my darling." His mouth poised over hers, scant inches apart. "It is the only way to keep this blight from harming you."

His mouth moved over hers, kissing her long and deep, drawing the very breath from her soul. He broke the kiss as abruptly as he began it. Pulling away, he rose to leave, his face a tortured mask once more.

"I'll send Cissy to sit with you until Dr. Hambley returns."

Vanessa panted for breath, her mind sprinting through her disordered thoughts and all he'd just said. Adrian loved her. But deemed himself cursed. Quite nobly, he intended to leave her, in order to save her from himself. Or the curse.

Panic seized her as Adrian stopped before the door and reached for the handle. Swinging her feet from beneath the covers and onto the floor, she stood, took two wobbly steps, and grabbed for the bedpost.

"Adrian, don't leave! You are *not* cursed. Nothing that has befallen me is in any way your fault. It was the ghost that pushed me. The same ghost that caused Delilah to bolt."

Adrian pivoted slowly in place, his look incredulous.

"*Ghost?* Sweet Vanessa, you hit your head far harder than I thought."

Vanessa realized her explanation sounded more senseless than his. Perhaps they were both a bit crazed, but she wasn't about to let him walk out of her life so easily. She loved him. Loved him most profoundly. All the while she'd resisted her feelings, she knew the truth in her heart. And now, if she must throw herself into the flames of that love to keep him from leaving, then so be it.

Vanessa released her hold on the bedpost and started toward him, disregarding her state of undress. He quickly moved to meet her, catching her by the arms and steadying her against him. Worry filled his eyes.

"Darling, you should rest."

"Adrian, listen to me. What I am saying is true. There

is a ghost. I have proof of it—a photograph, showing the specter in the Tudor gallery."

"The photograph you took at tea?" Adrian's brows pulled together. "I thought you said the form in the window was an aberration of light."

Vanessa shook her head. "There is another picture. I took it the following day inside the gallery itself. The image is quite distinct. It shows the luminous figure of a woman. Her hand is held toward the camera and she's beckoning. Adrian, at the moment I released the camera's shutter, she was beckoning to *me*."

Adrian's eyes widened at that, but he continued to wear a look of disbelief. Vanessa lay her hands on his chest and smoothed them over his shirt.

"I thought the Marrables acknowledge Sherringham is haunted. Surely you believe so. You've witnessed apparitions yourself." She tipped her head to one side, angling her gaze at him. "Or were you and your family leading me on the other night?"

Adrian brought up one of his hands, covering both of Vanessa's and arresting their straying movements.

"I have seen ghostly apparitions, it is true. But that was long ago. In any case, what does the photograph have to do with your fall in the study?"

"Nothing. And everything. Please, come sit a moment. There's more I must tell you."

Vanessa drew Adrian back to the bed and began recounting for him how the entity first manifested itself on the day of Lady Gwen's funeral, and how a spectral cold had subsequently followed her about the mansion and grounds.

"It was the ghost that spooked Delilah. I had just developed the second exposure of the gallery and decided to ride out. I was quite disturbed with this new finding and still struggling with accepting it. Delilah and I both sensed an unnatural presence at the Abbey Ruin and again at the mausoleum. You were right when you said Delilah was terrified. She was panicked, but not from the rabbit that darted across our path."

"You're serious," Adrian said in an amazed tone, his words more comment than question.

"Go to the Photo House and see the photograph for yourself. It is in the long worktable, left of the door as you enter. Look in the rightmost drawer."

Adrian held her gaze a long moment. "I do not doubt your honesty, my darling, and I will look at it later. But tell me about today. What happened exactly? And how did you come to be in the gallery?"

Vanessa glanced down at her hands and back. If he didn't deem her balmy already, surely he would after this.

"The entity manifested itself at the Photo House. I believed it wanted me to follow it, so I did."

"You followed it? How?"

"By the cold. It has a form of sorts—like a sphere of bitter-cold air. It led me to the West library and to the upper gallery there. Adrian, it directed me specifically to the box containing the stereoscope and stereo cards. For some reason, it wanted me to see the pictures of—"

"My wedding? To Olivia?"

"Yes." Heat rose to her cheeks. "You'll think it terribly rude of me, but I confess, I viewed all of them."

"Darling, you don't possess a rude bone in your body. Many filled with curiosity, perhaps, but none rude." Adrian flashed her a smile, then dragged a thumb over his bottom lip as he turned his thoughts. "Have you any idea why this 'entity' you followed wished for you to see the stereo cards of the wedding?"

"Either for me to discover something specific in the pictures themselves, or"—she paused and moistened her lips—"Adrian, it's possible the specter was identifying itself—herself—as Olivia."

A shocked horror washed over Adrian's face. Vanessa immediately regretted her words and lay her hand on his arm.

"That is only one possibility. There are others. Many, I should imagine, given Sherringham's long history of hauntings."

Adrian stood to his feet and began to pace once more. "I'd begun to wonder of late if Olivia might have survived the carriage accident and yet lives. Cameron wired me, insisting she was dead and to get on with my life."

"Cameron?"

"Cameron Kincaid. He's a detective with Scotland Yard." Adrian stopped his pacing and halted before her. "You've heard mention that the Marrable jewels are missing?"

Vanessa nodded. "I understand Olivia had them in her possession the night she died. The maid accompanying her somehow escaped the accident and disappeared with them."

A look of surprise registered in his face. She'd forgotten that Adrian would assume her to be uninformed on the matter. What information she'd gained came mainly from Nanny and Lawrence. Gratefully, Adrian chose not to question her about her knowledge.

"What you may not know, darling, is that some of the Marrable jewels have reappeared—four to be exact. Cameron contends the maid, Bonnie Beckford, is selling them off. I could not help but wonder whether there could have been a switch of identities, and that it is

Olivia who is selling the jewels. However, the Yard now has a description of the woman. She is quite obviously not Olivia."

Vanessa pondered this. "If your wife possibly is alive, might she have sent someone else to sell the jewels?"

Adrian shook his head. "Not Olivia. She knew their value and would want to be assured she received their full worth." He vented a breath. "I find I must agree with Cameron after all, not that that disappoints me. You said the entity pushed you on the stairs. That occurred moments after I entered the room. Perhaps, the ghost *is* Olivia. She always was the jealous type."

Vanessa took hold of his hand and rose. "Adrian, I'm really not sure it was her. I can't quite explain it, but I sensed no malice. I truly think the ghost was trying to tell me something."

"Even when it pushed you?"

"Especially then. Perhaps I'll know more when I develop the plates I exposed today." Concern lanced through her. "The camera and box of plates weren't damaged, were they?"

"No, not at all."

"Good. There may be something of significance recorded there."

Memories of the entity's agitation at the foot of the staircase swarmed back. She set aside those thoughts and gave Adrian her brightest smile.

"So you see, my dearest. No curse caused my accidents. There is no reason for you to leave."

He stroked his thumb over the back of her hand. "Perhaps you should reconsider remaining here at Sherringham, if you are the object of otherworldly interest. Though we've long accepted ghostly presences, they've never been so active or brought harm to anyone."

She smiled softly. "I'm not afraid, especially with you near to save me."

Freeing one of her hands, she touched his arm, giving him a warm, reassuring squeeze. But in the next moment, she felt his muscles tense beneath her fingers. At the same time, Adrian's expression grew grave once more and he averted his gaze.

"Vanessa, there are things about me you do not know. Even if I am not cursed, a darkness follows me. I would not have that poison touch you. It is still best that I go."

Vanessa gazed on Adrian, his words taking her aback at first, then giving way to a deep feeling of sadness for him. Adrian remained chained to his past, to its overriding sorrows and injustices. Did he not see it was within his power to release himself from those bonds?

"I know your burden," she offered gently, cautiously, fearing to say the wrong thing but unwilling to say nothing. "I know you have been falsely accused of murdering both your wives."

Adrian's gaze swept to hers, his brows colliding over onyx eyes that flashed with anger. "Did Lawrence tell you this?"

"Do not blame him. I questioned your brother yesterday in Hereford and pressed him for the truth. I'd bungled things so badly during your portrait sitting, I insisted on knowing how I'd hurt you."

A muscle flexed in his jaw, but the look of anger disappeared from his eyes. "You say I was accused 'falsely,' but do you not fear the accusations are true?"

Vanessa held his gaze, sensitive to the challenge contained in his voice, sensitive to the raw emotions underlining its tone.

"I know you are no murderer, Adrian."

"Do you? How could you possibly know with any

certainty one way or another?" He grasped her by the
shoulders as he loomed above her. "I am engulfed in
shadows, Vanessa. Shadows of which I will never be
fully free. I won't have them consume you too."

Vanessa gasped at the look of unrelieved pain knifing
his eyes. His anguish cut at her heart as if it were her
own. Before she could speak, he loosed his hold of her
and started for the door.

"Adrian!" she choked out, realizing his intentions.
"You claim to love me. Can you turn from me so easily?"

Adrian clenched his hands to fists at his sides, staying
his steps. "It's not easy. God, nothing has been easy
these past years."

Vanessa crossed the distance that stood between
them, coming to stand directly behind him. She reached
out to touch him, then pulled back her hand. Tears
began to trickle from the corners of her eyes.

"Adrian, you can leave this room if you wish. You can
leave Sherringham and England itself and escape to the
ends of the earth. But you cannot escape your heart.
And neither can I escape mine."

Adrian remained motionless—for three solid heart-
beats—then spun around. He pulled Vanessa into his
arms, holding her fast against him. His mein had taken
on a fearsome cast, and she could see the conflict in his
eyes, his emotions running high as he warred within
himself. She braced herself as she faced the storm of
those emotions, refusing to be shaken or dissuaded
from drawing Adrian out of his darkness and opening
his heart.

"You do not know what you ask," he declared gruffly,
his arms tightening about her, unaware of his strength.

Vanessa locked her gaze with his. "I am asking for

nothing, and I'm saying only that I love you, Adrian. For too long you have walled yourself behind a fortress, enshrouded in shadows. But, my dearest, I see the light that yet shines in your heart. You cannot hide it, and I would see it burn brighter still."

Vanessa raised her hands to his chest, spreading open his shirt at the neck and downward, forcing the buttons to pull free of their moorings. She pushed aside the cloth, her heart drumming in her chest. Then boldly, unabashedly, she pressed her lips to his heated skin, placing a kiss directly over his heart.

Adrian groaned, a tortured groan that issued from his soul. His arms encompassed her and he sank his fingers into her hair.

"Vanessa, Vanessa," he called out, his voice taut and strained.

She glanced upward as he clamped shut his eyes and struggled against the bonds that had held him so long. Suddenly, she felt the tension flow out of him, his muscles easing, though his hold on her remained secure.

Opening his eyes, his gaze drew to Vanessa and melded with hers. She watched spellbound as the light in his eyes transformed, and the barriers seemingly tumbled down from around him. Where pain had congested his eyes only moments before, now they blazed bright with fiery passion.

Adrian's lips descended, his mouth coming together with hers in a hungry, urgent kiss. Impatience possessed them both as they eagerly tasted one another, their hands clasping, exploring, holding each other tight.

Without breaking their kiss, Adrian swept Vanessa off her feet and into his arms. He carried her swiftly to the bed and, in one movement, lay her upon the wide mattress and followed, covering her body with his.

Her heart racing, Vanessa tugged Adrian's shirt free from his trousers then splayed her hands over the hard planes of his chest. She reveled in the texture of his hair-roughened skin and brushed her fingers over the tight nubs of his nipples.

Adrian lifted himself long enough to rid himself of his shirt altogether, then covered Vanessa once more, raining kisses over her throat and beneath her jaw.

Desire consumed Adrian as much as need—a desire for this one woman alone, and a need to merge with her, to be one with her, in body as much as soul.

Claiming her mouth once more, he urged her lips apart then invaded the sweet recesses there. He felt her hesitate at first, but as his tongue stroked and tantalized hers, she came alive to his seductive invitation. They rolled together on the mattress several times over as their mouths mated in a frenzied, fevered dance.

Adrian fumbled at the ribbons fronting Vanessa's gown, tugging them free. As the fabric parted beneath his fingers, he strewed kisses to the hollow of her neck and along her collarbone, at the same time pulling the fabric from her shoulders, down to her waist.

Heat surged through Adrian's loins as he unveiled the naked beauty of Vanessa's full breasts. Cupping them in his hands, he worshipped one, then the other, taking their sweet, waiting crests into his mouth. He laved them with his tongue then suckled them erect. Swirling his tongue over their globes, he continued to love them, exulting as they beaded in his mouth.

Vanessa squirmed beneath his attentions, her fingers pressing into his back. He smiled as she arched toward him, a soft groan escaping her lips as he feasted upon the ambrosial sweetness of her breasts.

As his own need sharpened, Adrian spread kisses lower over her stomach and abdomen as he dragged her gown past her hips. Pressing a kiss to her feminine mound and the promised treasure that awaited him, he yanked the fabric free of her knees, then her legs, and tossed it to the floor. He rose only long enough to strip away the remainder of his clothes then quickly rejoined Vanessa amid the rumpled sheets and pillows. Immediately, their bodies entwined, flesh searing flesh as they devoured one another with mouths and lips and tongues.

Adrian felt Vanessa wrap her legs about his and press against him, urging him to fill her. He gripped her tight, more than ready and eager to bury himself in her heat. But instead, he slipped his hand between them, sliding his fingers into her feminine folds and sought the core of her desire. Vanessa gasped, bolting against him as he began to caress her. He found her to be already swollen and sensitive, hot to receive him. First, however, he was determined to pleasure her thoroughly.

Vanessa gasped again as Adrian rolled with her and brought her atop him, causing her legs to straddle his hips and remain opened wide to him. He continued to stroke her most secret place, at the same time drawing her forward and capturing her nipples in his mouth, suckling and laving them once more.

Wildly erotic sensations coursed through Vanessa as a molten fire built between her legs. Adrian possessed her completely, bringing her to the brink of a delicious, torrid delirium, unlike anything she'd ever experienced. But as her passion and need continued to rapidly multiply, she could no longer bear to remain separated from him in any way.

"A-d-rian, please. . . ," Vanessa's voice broke, her fingers digging into his shoulders as she rocked against his hand.

He shifted at once, poising his silken steel at the entrance of her womanhood, prepared to claim her as his. Capturing her hips with his hands, Adrian guided her back, sheathing himself in her with a long, deep thrust. Vanessa's breath first caught in her throat, then she gloried in the feel of him, filling her so completely.

Adrian stilled, his muscles tensing. "My God, Vanessa, I'm likely to burn to cinders in your fire," he grit out.

With that he began to move against her, thrusting into her with deep, rhythmic movements. The contact was exquisite, startling, spawning a sharp need in Vanessa. Her desire burgeoned to a staggering craving that she scarce understood. It radiated like a pulsing fire from the very center of her femininity.

Vanessa panted for breath. Having once been married, she thought she understood the act of lovemaking and the urgent, carnal needs of a man who quickly must find his release. Nothing had prepared her for Adrian's ardor or his ability to prolong and heighten their enjoyment. Indeed, he'd wrought more pleasure in her than she ever knew to be possible.

As they moved together as one, an urgency continued to build in Vanessa. Whatever Adrian sought from her, he could have, she thought hazily. She'd never known such wondrous, unfettered passion.

Vanessa gave into that passion as Adrian rolled her beneath him, his mouth and tongue seemingly everywhere and all at once, the brand of his love moving inside her, carrying her higher and higher to some unknown plane. Her hands grasped him, then swept downward over the muscles flexing in his back and buttocks, as he drove into her.

Vanessa matched his pace, moving against him, savoring the exquisite torment he wrought as he feasted upon her breasts, her craving intensifying, almost painfully so. Still, she met his thrusts and tightened her legs around him. Suddenly, it seemed she hurtled toward some precipice, catapulting out beyond its rim.

"A-d-rian!" she cried out as she convulsed against him, a thousand needles of pleasure and pain exploding in her feminine core.

Waves upon waves of passion overwhelmed her as she strained against Adrian, her hips rocking against his, faster and faster. Suddenly, a roar ripped from his throat, and he surged against her as well. Joining Vanessa in that vibrant ecstasy, he thrust deep inside her, filling her with the gift of himself.

Together Adrian and Vanessa strove as one, a fierce, primal coupling that shook the very heavens around them. On and on they rode their passions until, at length, they were fully spent.

Exhausted, they drifted back to earth—two made one in love's fiery inferno.

Chapter 14

Vanessa lay contentedly in the circle of Adrian's arms, her naked length draped about his, her head resting upon his shoulder. Together, they gazed out the chamber's graceful, six-lobed window and watched as the first blush of dawn pinkened the skies.

Supremely happy, she turned and pressed a kiss to Adrian's bare chest. He gently squeezed her arm in response, conveying his own contentment.

They'd slept little during the last hours, their initial coupling but a prelude to a night filled with ecstasy and love. Once Adrian and she had recovered from their first, cataclysmic joining, they'd made love again, this time slowly, leisurely, two lovers exploring and cherishing one another, leaving no secrets between them.

Vanessa had been astounded when, once again, Adrian swept her to rapturous heights where they'd strained and burned together in exquisite torment. She'd not known such an experience was possible. Truly, though she'd not come to Adrian a virgin, it was in his arms and beneath his touch she'd fully become a woman.

After their second impassioned coupling, they'd drifted into a light slumber. Shortly before dawn, they'd awakened, craving each other anew, this time with an urgent need to assure all they'd shared was real and not merely a dream that would vanish with the coming dawn. Now they lay entwined in the afterglow of their latest lovemaking, sated and spent, their hearts beating in perfect unison with one another.

As the sky continued to lighten, Adrian dropped a kiss to Vanessa's temple. "I must go, love, before we are found out and your reputation is hopelessly ruined."

Smiling, Vanessa raised herself and leaned partially atop him, her breasts pillowing against his chest.

"I suppose you could use a shave, or I'll soon have no skin left on me at all," she teased, drawing her hand across his beard-roughened jaw. "I shall probably shock the good doctor as it is when he examines me and discovers red blotches covering my face and neck."

"And many other places as well." Adrian chuckled, flashing her a thoroughly wicked and unrepentant smile.

Vanessa returned his smile with her own, silently rejoicing in his transformation. Free of the pain shackling him to the darkness of his past, he was now like a man resurrected and brought into the light. His very soul glowed, she thought to herself. Even his countenance had changed, the lines of his face relaxed and softened, making him more handsome than before—if that was possible.

Adrian rolled Vanessa onto her back, the covers dropping away from them. He gazed on her lovingly, then reaching out swept her hair from her shoulders, baring her to his view.

"Are you all right, my love? You've had an exceptionally vigorous night for one recovering from a fall."

"More than all right." She smiled up at him. "Though,

I intend to lay blame for all my new aches and pains entirely to you."

"For that, I will most gladly plead guilty," he avowed, then bent his head to her breasts and flicked his tongue teasingly over her nipples before taking them into the heat of his mouth.

A pulsing throb sprang to life between Vanessa's legs as he gently sucked her, but he abandoned that pleasure as quickly as he'd begun it. Dropping a quick kiss to the end of her nose, he rose from the bed and stood before her, unabashed by his nakedness as he reached for his clothes.

Vanessa shifted onto her side, drinking in the sight of his tall, well-muscled body as he donned his trousers and shirt and began to work the buttons. Finishing, he sat beside her on the edge of the bed and pulled on his boots. He then turned and brushed a kiss over her lips, love shining in his eyes.

"No man on God's earth could be as happy as I, my darling. I want you always by my side. I am an honorable man, Vanessa, and I intend to keep you an honorable woman. Have no fear of that."

Vanessa laid her fingers to Adrian's lips, realizing where his heart and words led, but not wishing to face the question of their future yet. He knew nothing of her inadequacies. Indeed, she'd forgotten them herself, or suppressed them at the very least, allowing her heart to rule her head. In all probability, she could give Adrian no children, no heir. Thus, she could hope to be no more than his paramour.

"Kiss me, my dearest," she said quickly, unwilling to confess her shortcomings to him just now, and ruin his happiness.

His mouth moved over hers in a firm but gentle kiss,

then he pressed his lips between her breasts before rising and crossing to the door.

"Rest now, love, and regain your strength. I promise you will need it before the day is through." With a sparkling wink and a grin, he departed, closing the door behind him.

Vanessa lay back on the pillows, visualizing Adrian even after he'd gone. He'd walked several feet off the floor, his demeanor infinitely more relaxed than yesterday. Everyone in Sherringham would notice. They'd have to be blind not to.

She drew up the sheets, covering her nakedness. Perhaps there was no reason to hide their feelings for one another, only their nocturnal rompings. On the other hand, with one look at Adrian anyone could guess he'd released his tensions and taken his pleasures in the most physical of ways. One look at her, they'd know exactly the playground upon which he spent his passions.

Vanessa sank farther into the bed, pulling the covers to her chin. Perhaps, she would take Adrian's advice and rest in her chamber today after all, safely away from curious, prying eyes.

By mid-morning, Dr. Hambley arrived to poke, prod, and question his patient. He pronounced Vanessa well but encouraged her to remain abed for as long as she need and to take particular care when exerting herself. She could only wonder if he'd encountered Adrian upon his arrival, and if the two were in collusion together.

To Vanessa's surprise, shortly before noon, a steady trickle of visitors began to arrive at her chamber, all bearing well wishes and outwardly elated by her recovery. She felt like royalty holding court, though she was keenly aware of the inquisitiveness that lay behind their smiling eyes.

Only Nanny, with her clutch of wildflowers, and young Geoffrey, who arrived with his parents, were unaware of the speculations thickly layering the air. Nanny chattered on about the upcoming benefit for the orphans and widows over which she and Jane Timmons had charge. Geoffrey, on the other hand, assured Vanessa that he'd retrieved her camera and box of negatives from the tower study and returned them safely to the Photo House.

"Thank you, Geoffrey." She smiled at the boy. "I'm sorry we must postpone our outing for another day or so. You were going to choose the location and time the exposures."

"That's all right, Mrs. Wynters. Besides, I'm teaching Rascal new tricks. Maybe we can photograph him instead," he said cheerfully, then scratched his nose. "If I can get him to sit still long enough, that is."

Vanessa chuckled. "Keep practicing the pup then. He'll make a captivating subject and be worth all your efforts, I'm sure."

Geoffrey took leave of Vanessa and his mother, who chose to remain behind, and together with his father, led Nanny out, promising to escort her back to her rooms. Once the door closed behind them, Cissy settled herself in the chair beside Vanessa's bed and smiled, her eyes twinkling.

"I'm not sure the news reached you, but Adrian was heard singing in the corridors when he came down to breakfast. He proceeded to regale us all with an array of witty stories over our meal, as he was once given to do."

Cissy sat forward to the edge of the chair, her eyes wide and intent as she drew close to Vanessa.

"My brother is obviously overjoyed and relieved that you have recovered from your accident and without serious harm. I do not know what might have happened between the two of you, nor do I wish to. But something transformed Adrian. He is not the same tormented man who insisted he alone keep vigil over you last night, barring even myself from your side."

Cissy swept her gaze over the chamber then returned it to Vanessa, tears glossing her eyes. "Whatever took place here, thank you. Thank you for restoring our brother to us—the brother we've always known until these last horrid years stole him from us."

Cissy's words took Vanessa aback, touching her deeply. "But, I really didn't do anything—"

"Of course you did." Cissy reached out and squeezed Vanessa's hand. "You opened Adrian's heart and helped him to feel again, to love again. I feared he never would. Now I know those fears were misplaced. A special angel brought you to us, Vanessa. Perhaps that credit belongs to Aunt Gwen. You know, in a way, you've already been part of the Marrables for several years now. I hope that won't change."

Rising from the chair, Cissy bent to Vanessa and kissed her on both cheeks.

"I really must go now and help Henry and Geoffrey with Nanny." She smiled, swiping away a tear. "Majel has a way of popping up unannounced. She's been giving Nanny a bit of difficulty over Aunt Gwen's clothes and the pricing. But oh, Jane Timmons is a marvel with them both. Adrian really does know what he is doing there. Still, I like to look in on them and do what I can."

Smiling, Cissy withdrew, passing Mary Ethel as she departed the room.

The maid entered with a porcelain tea service on a

tray and carried it to the table standing right of the fireplace. She turned and started to speak when Lawrence appeared at the door and strode across the room.

Vanessa straightened at once and pulled the covers high, despite the fact she wore a concealing bed jacket.

Mary Ethel's timing was impeccable, she thought to herself. Thoughtfully, Adrian had assigned the maid to attend her needs and requests. As Vanessa had few, Mary Ethel had spent much of her time embroidering by the window, leaving only long enough to bring the pot of tea. Now Vanessa was especially grateful that she'd returned in time to serve as her chaperon.

Lawrence's smile seemed somewhat strained to Vanessa as he came to stand before her and held forth a bouquet of crimson roses, arranged in a crystal vase. Vanessa felt a twinge of guilt, as well as embarrassment, as she accepted them. Lawrence had made his interest in her quite clear on more than one occasion—the last just two days ago in fact. Meanwhile, she'd not only fallen in love with his brother, Adrian, but given herself to him entirely.

"What lovely roses," she commented self-consciously, avoiding his gaze but feeling his eyes burn into her nonetheless. "I'm amazed there are any in bloom this time of year."

"They are from the Orangery," he said stiffly. "I've already begun to cultivate certain plants there. I had hoped to present them to you on a much different occasion."

Vanessa glanced to the maid and held forth the flowers. "Could you place these by the window, Mary Ethel?" Giving the vase over, she watched as the maid placed them on the sill.

"You appear well," Lawrence declared, his tone carefully leashed. "Positively glowing, I would say, for one who's taken so frightening a fall."

Vanessa turned and met Lawrence's gaze squarely, trying to bridle her nerves and not tremble before his judgmental assessment.

"Yes, I'm very fortunate. I should have listened to you more closely in the cathedral when I tripped on the staircase. I suppose it was an omen."

"Yes, you should have listened to *all* I said. I tried to warn you."

"Of the stairs?"

"That too." He shifted his stance, blocking her view of the maid at the window. "Obviously, there is something between yourself and my esteemed brother. I'm not oblivious to his moods, Vanessa."

She lifted her chin defiantly, sensitive to the angry undercurrents in his tone. "If you must know, we care deeply for one another. Are you not happy for your brother, that he could again find love?"

A hard glitter shone in Lawrence's eyes. "Boundlessly. But are you so sure it is love?" The side of his mouth slid upward into a hard smile, then faded.

"Take care, Vanessa. I fear for your choice. The women in Adrian's life have not fared well in the past."

A chill passed through Vanessa. "I don't believe in curses, Lawrence," she shot back, her ire rising.

"Neither do I, sweet Vanessa. Neither do I."

At that, Lawrence turned on his heel and quit the room.

Vanessa scrambled from the bed, rushing to take hold of the vase of roses and hurl it across the room. She restrained herself, of course, though she was sure it would bring great satisfaction. If Lawrence did not believe in curses, then what did he suggest—that Adrian was a murderer after all? He deserved the roses crashing at his back.

Vanessa turned to Mary Ethel whose eyes at this moment were great, round discs. "Please leave me for a little while, and take these. I don't want them in my sight."

After the maid had gone, Vanessa proceeded to pace the room till her anger was largely spent then returned to the bed to rest again and warm her feet.

Her spirits lifted when Adrian entered a short time later, bearing a tray of cold meat pies, cheeses, and wine. She resolved to mention nothing to him of her conversation with Lawrence and set the episode from her mind. Giving her attention fully to Adrian, she smiled in greeting, happy to see him.

He returned her smile but she immediately detected something amiss, his mood somehow changed. Her stomach clenched to a tight knot. Had Lawrence said something to him? Did Adrian regret last night? She quickly slid from the bed and went to where he stood by the table, slipping her arms about him.

"What is it, darling? Is something wrong?"

He placed a kiss to her forehead, encircling her with his arms. "Nothing is 'wrong,' exactly. I went to the Photo House as you suggested and retrieved the photograph of the gallery from the drawer."

He released her long enough to remove the picture from his pocket. Together, they gazed on the misted figure.

"I never doubted you for a minute, my love. I just find it startling . . . and disturbing . . . to see proof of the ghost for myself, that's all."

"It was difficult for me at first, too." She gave a squeeze to his waist. "That is why I rode out on Delilah—to clear my head."

"You say you took more pictures yesterday?"

Vanessa nodded. "Yes, one outside the tower itself and a second inside, in front of the spiral stairs. The specter seemed particularly agitated there."

Adrian rubbed her arms, his interest piqued. "Why don't we take our lunch here, love? Then, if you feel up to it, we can go to the Photo House and develop the negatives."

"As you wish, darling, but I really have little appetite. Why don't we bring the food with us?"

"Ten, nine, eight . . ."

Vanessa counted off the remaining seconds then transferred the negative plate from the fixer to the wash and lit the ruby lamp.

As Adrian moved off the stool to join her, she quickly washed her hands then began gently agitating the pan to remove the last traces of the solution from the negative. In the lamp's ruddy glow, they stared at the image on the plate through the wavering water.

"Adrian, there's something here."

Lifting the plate from the water, Vanessa drained off the liquid then examined it more carefully.

"There is definitely a misted form standing before the tower entrance. Can you see it—these dark crystals here? This is a reverse image, of course, and the dark areas will print out light and the light ones dark. Unfortunately, the negative is underexposed. Much of the detail in the shadows will be lost when the image is printed out."

"Is there anything you can do to recover it?" Adrian gazed intently at the plate, seemingly enthralled.

"The detail in the shadows? No. But, this misted form which appears to be a woman is more important. I intend to use the platinum-treated paper that I acquired in Hereford for printing out the photographs. With its long tonal scale, hopefully it will reveal sufficient detail to identify our spectral lady here."

"Then perhaps we should begin."

"We can't. It's not a chemical process. We'll need to expose the negative onto the Platinotype in strong sunlight. However, we still have another plate to develop." She smiled.

Dousing the light again, Vanessa proceeded to remove the second negative plate from its holder and take it through the development process, step-by-step. Submersing the plate in metol for the prescribed time, she next shifted it to the chemical bath, then to the basin of fixer to remove the silver salts, and finally to the wash.

Adrian waited on the stool, out of the way of the chemicals, as Vanessa requested.

"No one can deny Sherringham's being haunted now," he observed to her dryly in the dark, though she discerned a smile in his voice. "Who would have guessed, love, that you have a special gift for spirit photographs?"

"Very amusing, Adrian, but you know we must not let others know of the haunting just yet. The specter hasn't finished telling what it wants yet."

After relighting the lamp and washing the traces of solution from her hands, Vanessa gave her attention to the new plate in the wash bath and lifted it out.

"Adrian"—she swallowed deeply—"I think you better see this."

Without hesitation, he came to her side.

"Is that a figure on the stairs?" he wondered aloud.

"Yes. It appears to be a woman, lying head downward on the bottom steps."

"Look at the angle of her head." Adrian pointed to its awkward position.

Vanessa's stomach slowly rolled over. "Adrian, I have a terrible feeling about this. What if the ghost wants us to know that she—or some other woman—died on these steps?"

She set the negative plate on the table and quickly turned to face Adrian.

"Don't you see? I felt no malice when the specter pushed me on the steps. Perhaps, it simply didn't know its own strength and was only trying to convey how it— she—died. Now that we know, hopefully, the specter can rest."

Adrian considered her words, then shook his head.

"I confess, I'm mystified. I know Sherringham's history thoroughly—or so I thought. There are no accounts of anyone dying in the west wing. On the other hand, if some woman did meet her death there, that would preclude Olivia. She died in the carriage accident at Devil's Hairpin. Lawrence witnessed it from the tower."

"Then who is the woman in the picture with the broken neck? And who is the specter that has been leading me all about?"

No sooner did the words leave her lips than the temperature dropped around them. Adrian pulled Vanessa into the protection of his arms.

"My God, Vanessa, what's happening? It's frigid in here."

She wrapped her arms tight around him and felt him shudder against her.

"Adrian, it's her—the phantom in the photograph."

Chapter 15

At Vanessa's urging, Adrian stretched forth his hands and explored the frosty air surrounding them.

Initially, it seemed the entire room had turned to an icy cell. But he quickly discerned a limit to the chilly expanse—a bitter-cold rim and, beyond that, the room's warmer temperature. The phenomenon possessed a spherical form, as Vanessa had described. At the moment, however, it held them at its center, no matter where they moved.

As intriguing as Adrian found the phenomenon, he distrusted it completely. The phantasm had wrought harm on Vanessa only yesterday. Perhaps its intent now was simply to freeze them to death.

Vanessa shivered with cold beside him, but she did not appear in the least frightened or intimidated by the anomaly. In truth, her composure amazed him. As for himself, a shot of good Scotch whiskey would be most welcome right now—for warmth as well as nerves.

Adrian reached for Vanessa, intending to enclose her in the heat of his arms. But she stepped from his side before he could stop her.

"I found what you were trying to show me." Vanessa addressed the entity as she turned in a slow circle. "The exposure I made of the staircase shows a woman sprawled over the bottom steps, her neck apparently broken. That is what you wish to be known, is it not? A woman died in the tower study. You, perhaps?"

Vanessa exchanged a glance with Adrian. They perceived no response, excepting for the room's temperature, which felt increasingly bitter.

Adrian started to speak but Vanessa raised her hand, staying his words, as she appealed to the specter once more.

"I don't believe you meant to push me from the stairs. I think you were only trying to demonstrate what happened to *you*. Someone shoved you down the spiral staircase, didn't they, and as a result, you broke your neck?"

The frigid air continued to envelop them a moment longer, then suddenly withdrew. Incredulously, the room warmed in an instant. Adrian reached out his hands and tested the encompassing air.

"I think she's gone."

"Or only moved off."

Vanessa likewise searched for evidence of the entity's continued presence. Halting before the room's only door, she slid her hands over and around an illusionary spherical shape.

"She's over here, Adrian."

He started toward Vanessa, watching her hands follow the movement of the invisible ball of cold as it rose upward, no less than a foot. Suddenly, she pitched forward, her palms flattening against the wood of the door as she caught herself. Vanessa cast a wide-eyed glance over her shoulder at Adrian as he hurried to join her.

"She's gone through the door," Vanessa gasped. "I think she wants us to follow her outside!"

Adrian started to caution Vanessa, but just as he reached her, she snatched her shawl from the wall peg, flung open the door, and hurried out.

Pivoting in place she darted back into the Photo House. "Wait! I'll need my camera."

Adrian was uncertain whether she directed the comment to himself or the specter. Glancing out the door, he noted the late afternoon light was already falling toward sunset.

"Are you sure there is enough light to make your exposures?"

Vanessa halted her movements and followed his gaze. "No, you're right. It will soon be dark." Looping her arm through his, she pulled him with her, back out the door. "Come, we must hurry."

Astonishingly, Vanessa was able to follow the movements of their ghostly companion, tracking its chilly mass of air. When they reached the end of the courtyard, Adrian feared the entity meant to lure them into the tower once again. This time, thankfully, he was present to protect Vanessa.

Unexpectedly, the icy sphere moved off again, leading them through a series of arched portals and adjoining courtyards, bringing them at last outside the complex itself and onto Sherringham's main drive. From there, it directed them across the open fields in the direction of the mausoleum. Adrian didn't wish to speculate on what the entity intended to show them in the house of the dead. Again he gave thanks that he accompanied Vanessa on this uncertain venture.

"We could be in for a long walk, darling. Are you up to it?"

She nodded, smiling though she was already somewhat breathless as she continued to locate and attempt to keep up with the specter's movements. With Vanessa's guidance, Adrian took over the task and, together, they hastened over the grassy and uneven field, moving in a straight line.

Two-thirds of the way across, the sphere of cold veered sharply westward. Adrian guessed the entity now led them on a course that would bring them out somewhere between the follies and to the narrow road that lay beyond.

The sun hung low in the sky when the Abbey Ruin came into sight. They had not journeyed as far as he'd supposed, Adrian realized. To both his and Vanessa's amazement, the spectral cold led them directly toward the folly itself, rather than around it to the road that lay on the other side.

The ruin jabbed at the fiery sky, its ancient ribs like a graveyard of so many forgotten bones left to molder through time.

As the entity continued to lead them among the stones, Vanessa reached out and touched Adrian's arm.

"Is it safe to be here?"

Adrian raised a brow at the sudden concern in her voice. "Of course, darling. Unless you have some notion about climbing the stones."

Vanessa blinked at his jest, then dismissed it with a shake of her head. "I understood the folly is in disrepair, crumbling, and that the children are not allowed to play here."

"That was long ago, when I myself was young." When Vanessa continued to give him a questioning look, he reconsidered. "I have been away awhile. It could need new repairs, I suppose, but I would think someone would have mentioned it to me."

Vanessa did not respond as the sphere of cold moved rapidly ahead of them and they were forced to hasten on, in order to keep pace with it.

Passing beneath soaring Gothic arches, eroded by time, they came to stand in the heart of the abbey. What existed of the structure stood roofless to a blood-red sky. The windows, empty of their glass, stared like hollow eyes, and the floor was a coarse carpet, strangled with knee-deep weeds.

The light continued to fail as the sphere of cold led them to the rear of the ruin—to a sheltered portion which once would have formed the back of the sanctuary. Two of the walls were largely intact, the third half tumbled down.

The entity brought them to a halt before the half-fallen wall which, Adrian noted, still stood taller than he. Suddenly, the sphere of icy air began spinning, picking up speed and generating a furious wind.

Adrian sheltered Vanessa in his arms as he squinted through the dust and debris caught up in the specter's wake. As they watched, the gusting wind began to glow before the rough-hewn wall.

"D-do you see that?" Vanessa pointed then grasped hold of his arm, her fingers digging in.

Adrian hugged her close as the luminous whirling mist hovered high above the ground, its shape transformed, assuming a funnel-like form, much like a whirlwind. Abruptly as it began, it swirled into the face of the wall and disappeared.

Adrian stood stunned, his hold loosening on Vanessa. She broke from his arms and ran to the wall, placing her hands on its stony surface.

"She's gone inside! Feel for yourself, Adrian. The stones are like boulders of ice. Surely, she's trying to tell us something, but what? I mean, she can't expect us to follow her through solid rock."

Adrian joined Vanessa, placing a hand to the stone, then drew it back. The flesh of his palm stung with cold.

"She doesn't expect us to go through solid rock. This particular section is a mock wall. It's no more than wire and plaster and cement, all cleverly painted up and made to look real. My guess is, the specter wants us to open the wall itself."

Vanessa turned huge eyes on Adrian. "I'm not sure I want to know what is behind the wall, not after what we discovered about the tower study."

She turned and touched the wall's stony surface again.

"You say it is a mock wall but it feels so solid."

"It's not exactly fragile. It will take a pickax to break through the facade."

Adrian tested the stonework to see if anything might be loose or easily give way beneath his fingers. As he continued to pry at the wall's surface, horses' hooves sounded on the road nearby. Vanessa and Adrian looked up in unison to discover Lawrence reining his horse to a halt.

"Ho, brother!" he called out, remaining mounted. "I saw you both cross the field on foot, and it struck me as odd given that Vanessa is still recovering. When you didn't return, I decided to ride out and assure all is well."

Adrian strode toward Lawrence, glad to be able to draw on his help. "I need pickaxes, brother, and some strong arms. I intend to open this wall tonight."

Anger flashed across Lawrence's face. "Are you mad, Adrian? You propose to destroy this . . . this *monument* to our grandfather? It was he who had it moved here stone by stone and later improved it. Why, Adrian? Why would you purposely destroy it? And to what end?"

Adrian clenched his jaw. "You will have to trust me in this for now, brother. I will explain later. *After* we open the wall."

"No, Adrian! I'll not let you ruin the crowning work of our grandfather's efforts at Sherringham." Lawrence defied him.

Adrian's anger boiled over. "Ever since I returned here, my authority has been ever challenged. I shall remind you, brother, *I* am Viscount Marrable and Master of Sherringham, and I shall do as I will with *my* follies. Now I intend to open this wall, and I shall repair it too at my own cost. Do you understand?"

"Perfectly," Lawrence grit out, his nostrils flaring. "Being only a second son—though second only by minutes—I have no say over a brother destroying the Marrable legacy."

As Adrian and Lawrence continued to glare at one another, the hooves of horses and wheels of a carriage clamored over the road.

Vanessa came swiftly to Adrian's side. "It's Henry. Cissy must have sent him out."

"Good." Adrian clipped out, his eyes still locked with his brother's. "Maybe Henry will be more willing to lend his aid here."

"Do as you wish, brother. Sometimes I fear what these past years have truly done to you." Kicking into his horse, Lawrence rode off, back in the direction of the mansion.

A half-hour later, pickaxes in hand, Adrian and Henry struck into the wall, breaching the stonelike surface and opening the facade. Vanessa and Cissy held up lanterns for the men, while Majel and Nigel observed from a safe distance in their carriages.

The iciness continued to dwell in the wall, confirming the specter's presence and guiding the men where to work. Adrian pulled away thick chunks of plaster and cement, glad for the heavy work gloves his sister had thoughtfully provided.

"There's something here," Henry called, working at a height in the wall chest-high to Adrian.

Adrian assisted him as they broke away another large chunk of wall and pried back the base of cooping wire inside.

"Vanessa, the lantern."

As she raised the light for him to better see, he started to reach into the hole then jumped back as a skeletal face gaped out at him—hollow-eyed, with high, bony cheekbones and a grotesque grin that made his blood run cold.

Adrian swallowed long and hard then turned to Vanessa and took the lantern from her.

"Darling, you and Cissy should join Majel in the carriage. You won't want to see this, believe me."

Vanessa stood her ground. "Adrian Marrable, I appreciate your protecting my sensibilities." She walked toward him and dropped her voice. "But, it's my ghost too!"

"Very well, but stand back."

Cissy joined Vanessa as Adrian and Henry worked apace, breaking open the wall fully. As they freed the last large block of cement, the skeleton spilled from the wall and onto the ground.

Adrian held the lantern close, bile rising in his throat as he spied the fiery red hair and familiar brocade gown with its stained and tattered lace. A band of gold glinted on its bony finger.

Adrian's breath congealed in his chest as he gazed on the wedding ring he'd wondered about so long. It took him many long minutes before he could find his voice. Even then, only a single word rose in his throat—"Olivia."

Chapter 16

Vanessa could barely contain her emotions as she paced the floor of the Photo House. She'd not slept during the whole of the night. Few at Sherringham had.

At present, Adrian and Lawrence closeted themselves with Hereford's constable, Miles Grealey. Cissy, Majel, and their husbands waited in the Grand Saloon for the men to emerge. Meanwhile, Vanessa rushed against time to print out the negatives from the tower, as Adrian requested she do.

Eyeing her watch, Vanessa moved to the table at the back of the room. There, beneath the unshuttered window, she'd positioned the glass plates on the platinum-coated paper and exposed them to the full light of the sun. Viewing them now, she estimated six minutes remained before the process would be complete. She took up her pacing anew.

Part of her wished Adrian had not been so quick to inform the authorities of their startling, late-night discovery. Another part knew he had little choice. Finding a skeleton walled up on the property was not something that could long be kept quiet—particularly when the victim was thought to have died elsewhere and in far different circumstances.

Adrian was right—best they reveal their find at once.

To hide it even briefly would give the appearance of guilt. Adrian had no desire to draw fresh suspicions or accusations on himself. Seizing the initiative, he'd dispatched Timmons to Hereford before dawn with instructions both to inform the constable and to wire Cameron Kincaid at Scotland Yard.

Vanessa skimmed a glance to her watch as she came to stand by the open door. Four minutes. Gazing out into the courtyard, her thoughts shifted to Constable Grealey.

She hadn't cared for the look of the man from the moment he'd arrived at Sherringham. It wasn't his brevity of height or the fleecy muttonchops covering his jowls that she so disliked. It was the gleam in his hard, marble-like eyes and the gloating smile barely visible beneath his drooping mustache. He looked every inch the cat ready to feast on its prey. Lawrence had warned of the constable's eagerness to charge Adrian in his wives' deaths and to lock him away. From the look of the hairy little man, she believed Lawrence hadn't understated the matter in the least.

Vanessa massaged her forehead then dragged her hand over her face. Dr. Hambley had arrived with the constable to inspect the skeletal remains. He then conveyed them to Hereford for further examination. Before he left, he confirmed to all—Olivia had died from a broken neck.

Vanessa turned from the door and crossed to the back table once more, her watch showing only three minutes' time remaining.

The constable continued to bedevil her thoughts. Despite his apparent zeal to find fault with Adrian, certainly Lawrence's account of events two-and-a-half years past must now be called into question.

Last night, when she and Adrian returned to the manse, they'd encountered his brother and informed him of their grisly discovery. Lawrence appeared genuinely shocked. Still, he stood by his original description of Olivia's flight with her maid and the subsequent misfortune at Devil's Hairpin. He found it inexplicable that Olivia should now be found sealed in a wall in the Abbey Ruin. He asked again and again of the identifying details, proving the remains to be hers.

Since Lawrence appeared distraught, Adrian chose not to question him about his presence in the tower study late that fateful night. Nor did he mention the photograph Vanessa had taken of the spiral staircase there or their ghostly companion who guided them to the ruin wall.

Later, Adrian explained his intentions to her in private. After the authorities had arrived and departed Sherringham, he would convene the family and disclose all to them including the revelations contained in the photographs. He did not plan to share this information with the constable or his men, however. It would only complicate matters and likely be regarded a hoax.

Vanessa sensed the dark concerns crowding in on Adrian as they spoke into the early hours. Yet, she understood his worries. Officially, Olivia's death had been recorded as an accident—despite the faulty axle on her carriage. But the discovery of her remains, walled into the ruin, could only point to one thing—murder.

It also brought with it a thousand questions.

Vanessa sighed tiredly as she gazed on the second hand, sweeping over the markings on the face of her watch. Hopefully, the photographs would resolve some of the questions. But they wouldn't answer all of them.

Even if a plausible explanation could be found for

how Olivia either departed the carriage early or survived the crash and returned to the manse, what of the Marrable jewels that disappeared that night? And why did the body found in the wreckage wear Olivia's ring?

Vanessa directed her attention to the prints, the processing time finally complete.

Removing the glass negative from the square of Platinotype, she gazed on the developed photograph. And smiled. Quickly, she removed the second plate from the adjacent paper. She'd judged the timing correctly and, thanks to the paper's superior quality and tonal range, the details in the prints were truly remarkable. She and Adrian might have their answers after all—leastwise some of them.

Vanessa reached for the photograph showing the interior view of the tower study. Her interest drew immediately to the spiral staircase and the distinct but transparent figure sprawled over the bottom steps.

The woman's head angled awkwardly, facing away from the viewer, her features not clearly visible. Still, the tonal values of her hair and dress were consistent with the shade of Olivia's red tresses and the yellow-gold gown in which she'd been found. Then, too, there was the figured design of the gown's fabric and the lavish lace, spilling from elbow-length sleeves—identical to that which clothed Olivia's remains.

There could be no doubt. Olivia had died, not at the bottom of the ravine consumed by fire, but in the tower study, from a fall she'd suffered on the staircase.

The event must have happened that same night, Vanessa concluded. Olivia had disappeared at the time of the accident and never been seen again. But was her death an accident, or had she been deliberately pushed? And who shut her into the wall?

Remembering the other photograph waiting on the table, Vanessa took it up and glanced on the ethereal figure standing before the tower door. The facial features appeared clear and distinctive enough for Vanessa to identify the woman as Olivia, appearing much as she had in her wedding photographs.

Everything became plain to Vanessa now. Olivia had led her to the box of stereographs so that, when Vanessa printed out the tower exposures, she could easily recognize Olivia, not only as the entity accompanying her, but also as the figure on the staircase.

Vanessa carried the photographs to the long worktable where she added them to the prints taken at the Tudor gallery.

Lady Gwen had always claimed spirits could communicate across dimensions if an urgent need existed. The thought struck Vanessa that there had been no further contact from Olivia since Adrian opened the wall at the ruin.

Perhaps, she felt she'd fulfilled her restless mission and returned from whence she came. On the other hand, her remains had yet to be properly laid to rest and, in fact, had been removed to town.

The fine hairs lifted on the back of Vanessa's neck. Wary, she drew her gaze over the room. If Olivia's spirit hadn't followed the good doctor into Hereford, quite possibly she yet lingered somewhere nearby.

"I *told* you, Constable, I left Sherringham that night at approximately ten in the evening and rode straight for London."

Constable Grealey crossed his arms over his thick, barrel chest and pulled thoughtfully on the whiskers covering his cheek.

"Let me see if I have the right of it, your lordship. You arrived mid-afternoon by train—bringing no luggage—and after a disagreement with your wife, rode horseback—in the dark of the night—all the way back to London. Is that correct?"

"Yes," Adrian snapped, his temper flaring at the note of ridicule in the man's voice. "That is why I could not be reached for several days. The wire informing me of Lady Marrable's death awaited me on my arrival."

The constable's hand fell away from his woolly jowl and he began to pace a short path in front of Adrian while staring at the tips of his boots.

"As I see matters, you arrived in Herefordshire with no intention of staying beyond that day. Elsewise, you would have brought a trunk or two of luggage."

"I don't deny it."

"Then you will also acknowledge you did not obtain a return ticket to London by rail and, thus, were bound by no set schedule. Thus, relying upon your own means of transportation, you could depart Sherringham anytime you chose."

"Your point being?"

The constable stopped his pacing and pivoted to face Adrian. "My point being, you had ample time to tarry about the grounds unseen, even after others believed you to be gone. You had not only time, but opportunity, to do away with your wife and conceal her body in the folly wall."

"Damn it, Grealey, I did away with no one!" Adrian blazed, his voice rebounding off the walls as he clenched his hands to fists. "I would never have killed my wife, no matter how angry I became with her."

Grealey's brows rose as did the right side of his mustache, his mouth quirking into a half-smile beneath.

"And you were angry, were you not? According to reports, it was no small disagreement in which you and Lady Olivia engaged, but a raging fight—a fierce shouting match that could be heard for hours and at differing locations within the manse."

He paused long enough to withdraw a small, battered notebook from his vest pocket, then began thumbing through the pages.

"You'll remember, I interviewed Sherringham's servants at the time and procured their statements. I have descriptions of some rather costly vases and marble busts being smashed. And, yes, here it is—one servant overheard you threaten Lady Olivia with divorce."

"That is none of your business," Adrian growled, turning away from the odious little man and glaring out a nearby window.

"It *is* my business when threats turn to crime. You see, by another account, I know Lady Olivia made her own threats. She vowed to fight you publicly and steep you in scandal, didn't she? She claimed you would *never* be free of her. That left you with a knotty problem, did it not, your lordship—ridding yourself of an unwanted wife? But then, it's a problem you've solved before."

"I didn't kill my wives—either one of them!" Adrian shouted, swinging around, and lunged for the man.

Lawrence lunged too, rapidly interposing himself between the two and restraining Adrian. "He's baiting you, brother. Lay a finger on him and he'll give you a personal tour of Hereford's cell block."

The constable shifted his beaded eyes to Lawrence. "Ah, the faithful brother who clings to a story increasingly difficult, if not impossible, to reconcile with emerging facts. Are you so certain you saw the viscountess fleeing with her maid the night of the accident, and not someone else?"

"It *was* Olivia, I tell you!" Lawrence barked back, his face reddening with anger. "The two women rushed to the stables and drove out minutes later in Lady Olivia's personal carriage. I recognized the viscountess by her clothing."

"But you didn't actually *see* her face?" the constable pressed.

"I've explained before, she wore a long, hooded mantle—of ivory satin and trimmed with marten. I'd seen her wear it on a dozen occasions."

"And yet, the mantle wasn't discovered with her remains. Or am I wrong?"

Adrian exchanged a glance with Lawrence, then shook his head.

The constable pulled at the end of his wilting mustache and began to pace a slow circle around the two men.

"Refresh my memory, Mr. Marrable. Are you absolutely sure the carriage did not slow before reaching Devil's Hairpin—say, long enough for Lord Marrable to intercept his wife and force her from the carriage?" He gave a shrug. "After all, she was in the course of carrying off the renowned Marrable jewels."

"I did nothing of the kind!" Adrian snarled, unable to remain silent any longer. "No one knew the jewels were missing until the following day. It was Timmons who made the discovery."

"Your manservant? How convenient," Grealey said dryly.

Lawrence stepped toward the man. "In answer to your question, for once and for all, the carriage did not slow or stop at any time, nor did I observe Viscount

Marrable riding about anywhere on that black beast of his."

"Black? No, I imagine you couldn't see him at such a distance, at night, on a black horse."

The constable slipped his watch from his waist pocket then gave his attention to Adrian.

"You are fortunate indeed, your lordship, to have such a *supportive* brother. And yet, despite what you've told me, I must wonder what prompted you to open the wall at all, or precisely where you did."

"Call it a sixth sense," Adrian returned in an even tone. "But you might better ask, if I was guilty of my wife's murder, why I would risk opening the wall and suffer the insinuations and charges sure to be leveled at me—as you do now?"

The constable nodded as if to concur. "True. A guilty man would not be expected to reveal his crime. It would lend an aura of innocence, if he did—and did it cleverly enough. You will find, your lordship, I am not easily misled. I intend to sift the finest details of this investigation. We are not done yet, I promise you. Hopefully, you brought extra trunks with you this time and intended to remain a while longer at your estate. It would be unwise to leave Herefordshire just yet."

With a curt bow, Constable Grealey turned and quit the room. Adrian ground his back teeth as he watched the stocky little man depart, then turned his gaze to Lawrence.

He expelled a long breath. "I don't know whether to thank you, brother, or challenge your account as the constable did."

"What is that supposed to mean?" Lawrence barked, obviously stung.

"I know where Olivia died, at least I believe I do. Unfortunately, it complicates your account even further."

"Have you been consulting tea leaves or crystal balls?" Lawrence scoffed, his tone incredulous. "First—despite Sherringham's extensive grounds, buildings, and follies—you go directly to the place she's entombed and rip open the wall. Now, you tell me you are able to reveal where she died? Perhaps, you have reason to know firsthand after all."

"Or proof."

Lawrence snorted. "What proof could you possibly have?"

At that moment, Vanessa appeared at the door, a thin stack of photos in her hand. She gave him a nod, confirming their suspicions, then withdrew.

Adrian returned his attention to Lawrence. "You shall see for yourself in a moment, brother, when we join the others in the Saloon. But I will give you this much. Olivia died in the tower study, near the time of the accident, I assume."

Lawrence's eyes widened. "What?" he choked out. "How?"

"She fell down the spiral stairs—accidentally or otherwise—breaking her neck."

"My God, you think I did it?"

"I am accusing you of nothing, but by your own admittance you were in the study that night."

"*Late* that night. I didn't arrive there until well after you departed Sherringham. I went looking for you to play billiards, which is how I came to learn you'd rode back to London. In the end, I took on old Jennings, the gameskeeper. If he were still alive, he could vouch for the hours we played at billiards. In any case, Olivia wasn't in the study when I arrived there, nor was her body lingering upon the stairs. I didn't return to the study after I witnessed the accident from the window and fled to the scene. Or have you forgotten my own efforts to save your wife that night?"

Lawrence held up his hand.

Adrian winced at the sight of the ugly, patterned scar branded into his brother's palm and felt instantly repentant. He thrust a hand through his hair.

"Forgive me. After last night, I guess I've been grasping at everything to reconstruct events that led to Olivia's death. Just when I thought I was free of the past, it has come back full blown to haunt me."

"*Haunt* you?"

The corners of Adrian's mouth lifted in a grim smile as he met Lawrence's gaze directly.

"Come, let's join the others, and I'll explain everything. There's much more happening around this grand old pile than you could possibly imagine."

Vanessa rested her head against Adrian's bare shoulder as she gazed out the bedroom window at the stars.

It had been a thoroughly exhausting day, especially for her beloved. After spending several taxing hours with the constable, he'd met at length with his brother, sisters, and in-laws in the Grand Saloon. Vanessa joined them as well, the topic of the late viscountess consuming the entirety of their time and energies.

Vanessa recalled the pained look reflected in Adrian's eyes, the protective walls rising about him, as he vowed his innocence in his wife's death once more. She interpreted his look as one of concern that, with the discovery of Olivia's body and the host of questions and suspicions it raised, his family might believe him guilty in the matter after all. But, by his family's warm and supportive response, Vanessa knew his concerns to be unfounded. Inwardly, she smiled and wept for joy all at once.

Together, Vanessa and Adrian then disclosed the extraordinary, otherworldly events which had been transpiring at Sherringham.

The family's reactions were strong, though predictably mixed. While Lawrence, Majel, and Cissy found the tales of supernatural happenings amazing, they did not doubt their occurrence. Nigel and Henry proved less accepting—until they viewed the newest spirit photographs for themselves. Their disbelief turned quickly to worry that Olivia's disembodied presence might yet bide in or about the manse.

After additional hours of discussion, the family agreed with Adrian's position—under no circumstances should the photographs be revealed to Constable Grealey. Lawrence made the particular observation that since Adrian and Olivia were known to have argued in the west wing near the tower itself, the pictures of Olivia's lifeless, if somewhat transparent, body on the staircase would be much too damning if exposed.

After the family dispersed, Vanessa and Adrian had walked for a time in the darkening gardens. The day's tension still held him in their grip, the old wounds ripped open afresh while multitudes of new questions continued to devour his thoughts.

Many of these, Adrian voiced aloud. Why had the Abbey Ruin been considered too dangerous to go near these past years, and when were its walls last known to have been mended? What drew Olivia to the tower study after he'd departed that night, and what was the truth of her death? Above all, who had entombed her body in the wall?

Much later, wishing to abandon the topic altogether, they took a light supper in a small, private dining room. When Adrian's mood remained heavy, Vanessa had gently pressed him, sensing there was something more that remained unsaid. Something that gnawed at him deep inside.

Adrian closed his eyes and fell silent a moment as he struggled with whether or not to give it voice. She gazed on the long sweep of black lashes shadowing his cheeks, and the muscle that jumped fitfully in his wonderfully square jaw. Another moment passed before he again opened his midnight eyes and settled them upon her. It was then she'd beheld the pain slicing their depths, sharp and bright. Her heart thudded solidly against her ribs as she realized his fear—that she believed him a killer after all.

Vanessa rose instantly from her chair and went to his side. Lacing her arms about his neck and shoulders, she smiled softly into his eyes.

"Do not ever doubt my love, dearest. Not ever. My heart harbors no uncertainties of you, but only the greatest admiration and passion."

Her smile spread as the look of pain disappeared from his eyes, replaced by a kindling fire. She bent toward him, her mouth caressing his, then parting, inviting his entrance, teasing him to do so with the tip of her tongue. Drawing her down onto his lap, Adrian complied fully, invading and coupling his tongue with hers in an erotically quickening dance.

Their breathing grew rapid, their needs heightening, as they kissed on and on. Adrian encircled her within his strong embrace, his lips leaving her mouth to move hotly downward. Vanessa sank her fingers into his dense hair as he spread kisses over the swell of her breasts, where they rose above her gown. At the same time, he cupped her fullness in his hand and caressed her nipple through the fabric with his thumb. Vanessa felt herself tighten as he continued to stroke her, then gasped when he took her in his mouth, cloth and all. Desire traveled through her like liquid fire, settling between her legs and setting her whole being aflame.

Somewhere between their ensuing heady kisses and eager, searching hands, they'd made their way to Adrian's bedchamber which lay surprisingly nearby. She vaguely remembered reaching it by way of a servants' passage which proved blessedly quick and direct—as well as deserted.

Entering, they hurriedly rid themselves of their encumbering clothes, leaving an unsubtle trail from the door to the wide, canopied bed. There, wrapped in Adrian's love, Vanessa withheld nothing from him, nor did he from her. Together their bodies and hearts fused as one, burning to cinders in passion's fire.

Now, having awakened to the early morning light, pleasantly fatigued but wondrously sated, Vanessa gazed upon Adrian's fine profile. She knew she should leave and slip away to her own chamber, yet she could not bring herself to leave him just yet.

Leaning forward, she placed a light kiss on Adrian's cheek then raised up again, smiling.

Adrian stirred, then opened one eye. A grin broke over his face and he opened the other. "I could wake every morn to find you smiling upon me as you do now, and never grow weary of that beautiful sight."

Drawing the sheet from her, he raised himself up and sought her waiting breasts with his mouth. As he did, he rolled her beneath him and covered her with his length. Vanessa felt the firmness of his arousal, pressing against her stomach. But her thoughts strayed as he possessed her breast thoroughly, bathing her nipple with his tongue then fanning it with the warmth of his breath.

"Marry me, Vanessa," he murmured, trailing a path of kisses between her breasts. "Marry me today so I'll not wake alone in bed without you ever again." He circled her nipple and flicked its beaded tip with his tongue. "Say you will consent to be mine, and remain with me forevermore. Let me cherish you to the end of my days."

Vanessa felt the muscles move in his shoulders beneath her fingers as he lavished kisses downward, loving and tasting her with lips and tongue. Her body cried "yes" to his proposal, as did her heart ten times louder. But her head warned it could not be.

Adrian's hands framed the curves of her hips as he continued to spread hot kisses lower over her abdomen, evoking a throbbing response between her legs.

"Say you will be my wife, darling, or I shall be forced to torment you to a fine madness until you agree."

When Vanessa did not immediately reply, Adrian paused. "Forgive me, my love. I am rushing you and as a bride you will wish to choose the date and arrange for your gown. Do not keep me waiting long. We could marry in a small, private ceremony, then repeat our vows later in a much larger one—as grand as you desire."

Adrian moved upward again, returning his attention to her breasts and nibbling at their undersides.

Pain rifted Vanessa's heart as she lay surrounded by the great love of this man, knowing she must deny him—deny them both—their most cherished desire.

"Adrian, I can't—"

"When we are past the present madness, then," he cut short her words, undeterred to set a wedding date. "After the official paperwork is finalized with the constable's office—"

"No, Adrian, you don't understand. I cannot marry you. Ever."

Adrian went cold in her arms, a black look slashing his face as he lifted himself up and stared at her.

"Can't, or won't? Do you fear I am guilty after all? Or just cursed with the touch of death for any woman who bears my name?"

Thrusting upright, Adrian moved to abandon the bed, but Vanessa quickly reached out and seized his arm with both her hands, staying him.

"No, it's not you, Adrian, or your name."

He swung back toward her, his brows colliding together. "What then?" he thundered. "You refuse to marry me *'ever,'* you say. For what possible reason, if not because of me?"

"I am barren, Adrian," she blurted, hot tears welling in her eyes. "I can give you no heirs."

Adrian froze, excepting his jaw which dropped open, a look of surprise registering in his eyes.

Vanessa swiped at her tears as they began spilling in earnest over her cheeks.

"At least, I think I am. My marriage was brief but still long enough that I should have conceived. Yet I did not." She reached toward him and touched Adrian's face with her hand. "Do you not see? I cannot marry you—not because I don't love you most desperately, but because as Viscount Marrable you must have heirs—heirs I cannot give you, though with all my heart I wish I could."

She looked aside, palming away more of her tears, utterly miserable.

"The truth is, I am inadequate to be your viscountess."

For a moment, Adrian sat utterly wordless, looking at her as if dumbfounded. His brows drew together once more and he almost appeared angry again. But in the next instant, he drew her into his arms and hugged her close.

"My God, what a selfish boor I am, thinking only of myself and my own wounded pride. But, darling, even if what you say is true, do you really think I would cast you aside because of it? You are my heart, Vanessa. My lifeblood. I will take no other to wife save you."

"But your heir . . ."

Adrian pressed a kiss behind her ear as he eased her back onto the mattress. "There are other Marrable males to carry on the family name and titles."

He kissed her lids, one by one, causing her to close her eyes.

"Sherringham will continue on, long after I am gone—whether through a son, or a brother, or a nephew . . ."

He brushed his lips over hers and then smiled on her in earnest.

"Do you not understand, dearest? True, it would make me the happiest of men to fill the entire manse with our babes—provided the effort brought you no harm, that is. But I have no wish to live the remainder of my days without you."

He smoothed back several long strands of hair from her cheek.

"Perhaps, it is fated I shall have no heir. That I am willing to accept. And if it is to be so, my only real concern will be to arrange provisions for you in the event of my demise. That and no more. As a man wealthy in my own right, I do not consider that an issue."

Vanessa's throat clogged with emotions. For a moment she could not speak at all. How was it she deserved such a man, willing to sacrifice so much for her, to risk never having a child of his own? But then, his heart led him now, in this moment. A heart long chained in pain, now pulsing with life and love.

Gazing on him, beholding the consuming look in his eyes, she did not doubt his love one moment. Nor could she deny him hers. Yet in time to come, she feared Adrian would sorely regret his choice in her—a choice that left him without a direct heir.

A jarring realization suddenly struck her. Should anything happen to Adrian, Lawrence would be the one to assume his place. Her stomach twisted tight at that thought. Truly, Adrian *must* have an heir, for the future sake of the House of Marrable.

"Marry me, Vanessa." Adrian dropped kisses to her brow and temple. "Marry me soon."

"If only I could," Vanessa whispered, her voice breaking with unshed tears, her heart splintering anew.

"You can," he insisted then claimed her lips, silencing any further objections. He kissed her long and thoroughly, communicating his great love for her with a most eloquent use of mouth and tongue.

Lacing his fingers with hers, he pressed her hands against the pillow to either side of her head. Several more minutes passed before he broke their kiss, his lips traveling slowly over her. When he savored her breasts, she arched against him, her nipples surging in his mouth, afire with the sensations he aroused and commanded. All thought deserted her. She wriggled, wishing to free her hands and explore him, but he held her captive to his passion, as he continued his intimate journey.

Leaving her breasts, he kissed her lower and lower, pausing to moisten her navel with his tongue and trace patterns over her abdomen. Every inch of Vanessa's skin came alive to his touch. She craved he not cease his masterful seduction, her body aching to meld once more with his.

Adrian released her hands and shifted to trail kisses along her inner thighs. He continued downward over her calves and ankles, then retraced his path upward, moving higher toward her hidden desire.

"A-Adrian, what are you . . . No, you mustn't . . . ah-h-h-h!"

Not heeding her objections, he continued to love her. Vanessa's fingers dug into his back, then her bones melted as she became a throbbing mass. As she neared her release, Adrian shifted upward, entering her and moving against her swollen core.

Vanessa met his passion, burning with the same intensity of ardor and need as he. She blanketed his chest and shoulders with her kisses, her hands straying feverishly over his muscled back and along his spine and hips. Adrian continued thrusting into her with a steady rhythm and Vanessa matched his pace, relishing the feel of his silken steel against her.

Scaling the heights of passion with a frantic, pulsing speed, they quickly gained that precipice and hurtled from its summit. Vanessa imploded and exploded against Adrian, causing him to erupt. Together they spiraled out of time and place, two made one, blazing brightly among the stars.

Long minutes later, they smoldered in each other's

arms, their seal of love upon each other as they lay gasping for breath amid a tangle of sheets.

Basking in the afterglow of their lovemaking, they shared smiles of joy and tender kisses. A sudden rapping at the door shattered the bliss of the moment.

"What the devil?" Adrian lifted his head from the pillow and glared at the door. He shifted his glance to Vanessa. "Quiet, love. Perhaps if we don't answer, whoever it is will go away."

Again, the quick series of knocks came. "Your lordship?" Timmons called out, his voice strained and thready as if overcome by some urgency.

"Lord Marrable?" he called again, this time his voice cracking. "Forgive the intrusion at so abhorrent an hour, but Constable Grealey and a number of his officers have arrived from Hereford. The constable is adamant he speak with you. By the look of him, whatever his purpose is in coming, I would venture it does not bode well."

Chapter 17

Tears stung Vanessa's eyes, blurring her vision as a fresh wave of emotion engulfed her. Scarcely had she and Adrian descended to the entrance hall this morning when Constable Grealey and his officers arrested Adrian, cuffing him and leading him away—the charge, murder.

Lawrence arrived within minutes of their departure, Timmons having had the foresight to awaken him. Learning of events, Lawrence rode after the authorities, vowing to do whatever he humanly could to secure Adrian's release.

For innumerable hours now, Vanessa and the family had closeted themselves in the "Gothic" drawing room, awaiting news from Hereford. At their request, Timmons and she recounted, many times over, what had taken place earlier—the constable's arrival, his shocking accusations, and his officers' subsequent seizure of Adrian.

Cissy, Majel, and their husbands continued to dissect and debate the matter now—in particular what should be done, if anything, before Lawrence's return. Fatigued by their endless discussions, Vanessa stepped toward the double doors adjoining the conservatory and opened the right-most one. She paused

at the portal and glanced across the space to the transparent, paned walls. Beyond the barrier of glass, the
landscape's autumn colors glowed dully beneath
leaden skies.

Vanessa's emotions plummeted, the sight of nature's encroaching gloom tapping into her mood. Her
feelings remained raw, susceptible to such moments,
the early morning events still vividly emblazoned in
her mind's eye.

Vanessa's throat knotted up as she recalled the initial shock on Adrian's face at the vile accusations
hurled against him. Recalled, too, how his look had
next turned to one of blistering anger. Again it transformed as his gaze leaped to hers in that final moment
when the officers forced him out the door.

Tears welled as she remembered that look with perfect clarity—a great shaft of pain piercing his eyes, and
in turn piercing her heart clear through. Adrian's
nightmare had returned full force, a thousand times
worse than before.

Vanessa dashed her tears away, her own anger
mounting, her determination solidifying. Adrian had
been falsely and outrageously accused. She must help
him. Though she knew not how precisely, if it required
she move heaven and earth, then move them she
would and more.

Her thoughts skipped to Grealey. Little insect of a
man, she fumed. He'd been quick to produce a creased
and soiled letter this morning, claiming it proof of
Adrian's motives and all the evidence he required to
make an arrest.

"Your wife had taken a lover," the constable pro-
claimed almost gleefully, holding up the mysterious
folded paper for them to see. "That was the cause of

your last argument, was it not, your lordship—a detai
you carefully omitted two-and-a-half years ago?"

Grealey began to pace a circle around Adrian and
Vanessa as they stood together in the center of the en
trance hall. Protectively, Adrian stepped before her
keeping himself between Vanessa and the constable
But she'd never been the object of Grealey's interest
and like a hawk prepared for the kill, the constable's
eyes never left his noble prey.

"I will be direct, Lord Marrable. When you discov
ered the truth of Lady Olivia's infidelity, you hastened
from London, taking with you not even a single item
of luggage. You acquired a ticket on the first train
bound for Hereford, your intention being to confron
your wife and have it out with her." Grealey's smile
spread. "And have it out, you certainly did. There is
no shortage of witnesses to the fierceness or duration
of yours and Lady Olivia's quarrel that night. Most
everyone residing at Sherringham at the time was
privy to it."

"I don't deny what you say," Adrian growled. "Bu
you cannot arrest a man for engaging in a shouting
match with his wife when he learns of her betrayal."

"Ah, but the true mystery has ever been—what happened *after* the shouting ceased?"

The constable stopped his pacing and held up the
square of paper once more, smiling in earnest now.

"Behold, a vital piece to the puzzle, come to us directly from Lady Olivia's unfortunate grave. From her
very person in fact, tucked into a hidden pocket in her
gown. I daresay, even you did not know that after your
explosive argument with your wife, she returned to
her chamber and penned a quick letter to her lover. A

most telling letter, I would add, even after these many years past."

Adrian stiffened. "I doubt there is anything of import Olivia could have written which isn't known to me already—excepting the actual name of her lover."

"No, no name." The constable lifted his brows, shaking his head as he began to unfold the letter. "She addresses him only as 'beloved,' that and no more. Her opening lines read: 'Adrian has found us out. He is in such a rage, I fear he could kill us both.'"

"That is rather overly dramatic, even for Olivia," Adrian remarked, his voice tight.

Grealey pulled on his whiskered cheeks, his eyes fixed on Adrian.

"Some may not see it that way, in view of your argument preceding the letter. She goes on to write you swore to divorce her, then shut yourself into your private study, stating you purposed to erase her memory 'with a bottle of brandy.'"

The constable glanced to the letter once more.

"Lady Olivia continued, beseeching her lover to flee with her. She writes, 'Let us escape across the border tonight, or to the coast to catch a packet to the Continent. I've ordered Bonnie to pack my trunk, just one, so we might be away with all haste. Do not worry as to how we shall manage. I am still Viscountess Marrable, after all, and have access to means that will secure our comfort for the rest of our years. You know of that which I speak and, though I can hear your disapproval already, I believe your objections will give way to reason. Do you not see, beloved, if Adrian ever found out—'"

Grealey stopped, lifting his beaded eyes to Adrian.

"There the letter ends, the ink smudged as if Lady

Olivia had been interrupted. Perhaps she knew who her visitor was, perhaps she only heard his approach."

"You cannot be sure it was a man," Adrian argued.

Grealey shrugged. "For whatever reason, Lady Olivia ceased her writing and hid the letter. It was intended for her lover and ultimate proof of an affair, after all."

He took up his pacing once again.

"It is my supposition, she hastily folded the missive and slipped it into the pocket of her gown. My men nearly missed finding it altogether. The pocket is of the sort that is cleverly concealed, its opening being positioned in the gown's seam, itself, so there appears to be no pocket at all."

Adrian clenched and unclenched his hands at his sides. "The letter may be morbidly fascinating to someone like you, Grealey, but it proves nothing."

"Circumstantially, it is enough, especially when added to what else we know. Admit it, Viscount. Drunk and enraged, you went to your wife's bedchamber and during yet another heated argument, you killed her."

"That's not true!" Adrian vented angrily, taking a step toward the man.

Vanessa quickly placed her hand to Adrian's arm, cautioning him to hold his temper as Grealey continued to spew his venomous charges.

"It's easy to imagine the spirited Lady Olivia matching your furious words with ones of her own. Easy to imagine your craving her to be silent, going so far as to place your hands about her throat to stop her flow of words."

Grealey mimicked the gesture in the air with his thick hands. Infuriated, Adrian started forward once more, but Vanessa tightened her hold on his arm, reminding that any show of aggression would be a mistake. But the constable continued his badgering.

"You didn't know your own drunken strength, did you, your lordship? And as you began to squeeze off Lady Olivia's breath, in the process you snapped her neck."

"That's a lie! You've hatched your own twisted version of that night."

"Have I? Do you deny seeking solace in a bottle of brandy as your wife claimed?"

"Yes, I deny it!" Adrian retorted. "I did return to my study with the intent of drinking myself to oblivion. But I smashed the decanter against the wall instead and left Sherringham. You can ask the maid who cleaned the mess I left there."

"And just who is this person? Is she still employed at Sherringham?"

"I don't know," Adrian snapped. "You will have to ask Jane Timmons, our head housekeeper. I didn't return to Sherringham until these last weeks and then only for my aunt's funeral."

Grealey stroked his drooping mustache, taking a step apart of Adrian and Vanessa. "Curious that you chose to remain after absenting yourself for so long. Even more curious that you opened the wall in the Abbey Ruin, exposing your wife's remains. One must question why. Did you wish to play me for a fool a while longer? Or did you wish to clear away the debris of the past and exonerate yourself before you entrapped yet another woman in your deadly web?" His eyes shifted meaningfully to Vanessa.

The insult cut deep to its mark and Adrian broke from Vanessa's grasp, lunging toward the constable.

Instantly, Grealey's officers sprang forward, seizing Adrian and clamping steel cuffs onto his wrists.

"They are lies, all lies!" Adrian shouted out. "You have no proof and you have no case—and you know it." His eyes narrowed over the constable, glinting with fury. "But then you aren't a man to let the truth get in the way, are you? What's in this for you, Grealey? Why have you been dogging me these years? Will a sensationalized trial bring you fame, publicity, and promotion to a prominent position?"

Grealey gave an unctuous smile. "Something like that. You are quite a prize, being rich and powerful, a member of nobility. Scandal has a way of helping as many as it hurts."

Grealey started toward the door then turned back.

"Oh, and you are quite wrong about my need for further proof. This letter, the numerous witnesses' accounts, your knowledge of the precise location of your wife's body—it's all I need to establish my case. I believe the court will see your guilt as strongly as I. Besides, as you know, it is up to you to prove your innocence against this mountain of accruing evidence."

Grealey gave a curt nod to his men. "Escort his lordship out of here," he ordered.

After the officers had guided Adrian roughly out the door, the constable stepped toward Vanessa.

"One day you will thank me, Mrs. Wynters. Do not forget, Lord Marrable is not only suspected of killing his second wife, but he also must have arranged the carriage accident that took Bonnie Beckford's life and possibly another's—all to cover his initial crime. I won't even begin to enumerate my suspicions concerning the death of his first wife."

"You are monstrous!" Vanessa blazed, no longer able to contain herself. "Get out! Get out this instant!"

Grealey jumped back a step, startled by her outburst. But he quickly composed himself.

"You may have aspirations of becoming the next mistress of Sherringham, young woman, but I will remind you, you are not viscountess yet."

Vanessa took a menacing step toward the despicable little man. "Then fear the day I do bear that title. Fear it greatly. The Marrables embrace the motto displayed on their crest—'Fierce when roused.' Remember it. It is no accident the family espouses that particular sentiment, I assure you."

Coming back to the moment, Vanessa wrapped her arms about herself as she continued to stand in the portal, gazing into the conservatory. Her defiance of the constable had sapped her energies. It had been well worth the look on his hairy face, even if she'd misled him as to her future status as viscountess. Gratefully, he'd not been present to witness the ocean of tears she'd shed afterward.

Of two things Vanessa was quite certain. She'd never thank Grealey for anything, and once they'd all awakened from this nightmare, she would do everything possible to see him demoted out of the constabulary forever. Grealey was an evil, demented man who undoubtedly saw his star rise with Viscount Adrian Marrable's fall. How many other lives had he destroyed for his own gain?

Vanessa inhaled deeply and drew away from the door. Adrian was no killer. On the other hand, *someone* was guilty of Olivia's death. Someone who had been at Sherringham that dreadful night. Someone who, unlike Adrian, remained free.

Vanessa massaged her forehead, a dull ache pulsing between her brows. Constable Grealey was correct on one count. They needed proof of Adrian's innocence.

Glancing across the drawing room, she saw that Cissy and Majel were now seated on adjacent sofas. Meanwhile, Henry and Nigel stood before the fireplace where Leonine Marrable's dark eyes seemingly watched from her gilded frame. It took Vanessa several moments to realize Majel and Nigel were in the midst of some disagreement.

"Consider the children then!" Nigel threw up his hands in frustration, as if he were striving to reason with a brick wall. "What with ghosts and bodies and talk of murder in the family—let alone Adrian's arrest—it's best we leave for our London town house immediately."

Majel thrust to her feet, her fine brows colliding over her nose and her color rising. "Nigel Pendergast, you are more worried about your precious name being tainted with scandal than you are about our children, and well you know it."

"Majel, how can you—"

"I am not through!" She cut off his words, slicing her hand through the air. "If you wish to leave then do so. But as I *am* your wife, you are already connected to the Marrable name and any scandal that might become associated with it. Or had you forgotten that?"

"No, not at all—"

Majel's hand shot up again silencing him.

"You might look on my brother as *only* a viscount, his title lower than the one you will one day bear. But, I will remind you the house of Marrable is very old, far older than that of Pendergast, and therefore its title of greater prestige. It would be wise to act with a measure of honor as well as backbone by standing by the House of Marrable and your brother-in-law and seeing him absolved of this deplorable injustice."

Vanessa's eyes widened. Majel truly astounded her. She actually felt proud of Adrian's sister in that moment.

Majel took a step toward her husband, her chin upraised.

"Marrable blood is strong and constant, Nigel. It binds us together, just as Aunt Gwen wrote in her will. I intend to remain at Sherringham—along with the ghosts, bodies, scandals, and all—and do what I can. If you still wish to flee to London with the children, I shall help you pack and see you to the station. Afterward, I owe Constable Grealey a visit, along with a rather large piece of my mind. He'll think the sky itself has fallen on him by the time I am through! How dare he lay hands on a Marrable, let alone imprison the viscount himself!"

Majel stormed from the room, her back stiff and her bearing utterly regal.

"Majel? Er, Pet?" Nigel looked after her, then transferred his gaze to the others. "Isn't she magnificent?" He uttered the words with a note of awe in his voice. Striding from the room, he hastened to follow her.

Vanessa's brows raised high. The day was full of surprises. For a man who could be an intolerably arrogant bore, she believed there might be hope for Nigel after all.

Cissy rose from the sofa to share a word with Henry. She then crossed to where Vanessa stood.

"We will accompany Majel and her family into Hereford. I am sure you wish to see Adrian, but would you mind staying at Sherringham lest anything new

erupts, or some word arrives? We wish to ensure
Lawrence has contacted Mr. Whitmore, the family's
solicitor. We also have yet to see or speak with Adrian
ourselves today."

"Of course I don't mind." Vanessa smiled.

In all honesty, she felt a strong pull to remain at
Sherringham. She'd yet to reason everything out, still
she sensed she was overlooking something important,
right before her eyes.

"Give Adrian my love." Vanessa reached out and
squeezed Cissy's hand. "Hopefully, he will already be
free before I ride to Hereford to see him. Oh, yes.
Adrian urged me to contact Cameron Kincaid should
anything befall him. I know Adrian wired him immediately after discovering Olivia's body. But Mr. Kincaid should be apprised of what has taken place here
today."

"We will see to it," Henry said as he moved behind
Cissy. "You are sure you don't mind staying behind at
Sherringham?"

Vanessa shook her head. "Someone must look after
the 'ghosts and bodies and scandals and all.'" She
laughed, quoting Majel.

After Cissy and Henry withdrew, Vanessa climbed
the grand staircase to her chamber to fetch a heavy
shawl. She then left the mansion to walk in the gardens outside and collect her thoughts.

Despite what Constable Grealey believed, he did not
hold *all* the pieces to the puzzle of Olivia's death.
Vanessa knew she must find the ones missing and fit
them all together. Where was Olivia's specter now,
when she could be of great service and reveal who
caused her death? There was never a ghost to be found
when one was needed!

Methodically, Vanessa reexamined the known facts surrounding the carriage accident and Olivia's death. She then pondered the questions to which they gave rise. Just as the discovery of Olivia's remains at the Abbey Ruin altered all previous beliefs held of that tragic night, so did the spirit photographs, taken in the tower, and the final letter Olivia had penned to her lover.

Lawrence claimed to have seen the viscountess and her maid procure a carriage from the stable and ride out toward Devil's Hairpin. Yet Olivia did not die in the fire, but instead, in the tower study when she fell down the spiral staircase.

In Olivia's letter to her lover, she'd stated that Adrian had gone to his private study after they'd quarreled. Vanessa had glimpsed that room last night and again this morning. It was part of the suite that adjoined Adrian's bedchamber—not in the west wing at all, and certainly *not* in the tower. At least, there was that small acquittal for Adrian, Vanessa thought to herself.

On the other hand, Olivia had been interrupted while she wrote her letter in her bedchamber. Had she actually ever left Sherringham's confines? Or had something drawn her directly to the tower study? Possibly, Lawrence was mistaken as to the women's identities. Yet, Vanessa couldn't fathom how he could be so wrong.

In any event, it was clear from Olivia's letter that she intended to steal the Marrable jewels. Since only she and Adrian would have had access to them, Vanessa concluded Olivia had succeeded in obtaining them. She further concluded, whoever killed Olivia, thieved the jewels for himself or herself just after Olivia's death.

Might the viscountess been murdered for the jewels? Although doubtful, Vanessa did not dismiss the possibility entirely.

Massaging the stiffness in the back of her neck, she lifted her face to the breeze stirring through the garden. Vanessa was unsure where her ruminations led her, except perhaps in a very grand circle. None of the details she'd considered explained the carriage mishap. The axle had given way, she'd been told, but by accident or sabotage? And if the latter, why? It made little sense considering Olivia did not occupy the carriage—unless someone anticipated she would.

Vanessa expelled a breath, suddenly feeling like a dog chasing its tail. This vein of reasoning was leading her nowhere new. She turned on her heel, changing the direction of her pacing as well as her thoughts. Deciding on a different approach, she focused on the events that occurred after the viscountess's death.

Adrian had been quickly accused of murder, followed by Lady Gwen's departure from Sherringham, never to return.

Vanessa stayed her step, canting her head. Lady Gwen's self-imposed exile had always been an odd chapter in all of this. But to her mind, so had Lady Gwen's prior years at Sherringham.

The photographs in Nanny's quarters showed Gwendolyn Marrable to have been a beauty as a young woman. From what Vanessa knew, she'd never been shy, outgoing if anything. Yet, Lady Gwen chose to remain tucked away in Hereford's countryside, never marrying. According to her words of praise in her will, her father and brother were both generous men. Assuredly, either one would have provided her a fine dowry. Yet, Lady Gwen stayed at Sherringham, leaving only occasionally. Through the years, she'd been deeply involved in the lives of her nieces and nephews. Otherwise, her time and talents had been absorbed by her photography.

But then Olivia had died. Adrian was accused of murder, and Lady Gwen . . . Lady Gwen left for self-imposed exile, abandoning everything that had been central to her life until that time.

While Vanessa had been in her employ, Lady Gwen never spoke of these things. She knew Lady Gwen had written with some regularity to her nieces, alternating her letters between the two. But to Vanessa's knowledge, she'd made no attempt to communicate with her nephews. Perhaps, Lady Gwen expected Cissy and Majel to share her correspondence with their brothers. She was ever traveling about, after all, and never long in any one place.

Deep in her heart, Vanessa knew the truth—though Lady Gwen could have returned at any time to Sherringham, she'd expressly avoided it. But why? Had she truly believed the claims against Adrian?

Vanessa continued to ponder the matter, making her way around a fading flower bed for a hundredth time. A youthful voice rang out, shattering her concentration. Looking up, she spied Geoffrey, rushing toward her.

"Mrs. Wynters, Mrs. Wynters!" He came to a halt, huffing for breath. "Mama and Papa have left for Hereford. They want you to know. Aunt Majel and Uncle Nigel have gone with them also."

"And your little cousins? Did they ride out with your aunt and uncle, too?" Vanessa queried, wondering if Nigel was leaving with the children for the station after all.

"No, Mrs. Wynters." Geoffrey stopped a moment and scratched his nose, his brows crimping. "Why would they take the young ones to the constable's office?"

"Is that where they are going?"

Geoffrey nodded. "Aunt Majel said she has something to give Constable Grealey, and Uncle Nigel said he was going to help her. I didn't see them carrying anything with them when they joined Mama and Papa in the carriage though."

"I see." Vanessa hid her smile, secretly pleased with Nigel's evident change of heart.

"Mrs. Wynters, I hope you won't tell Mama, but yesterday I was supposed to ask you for the mourning photographs and I forgot." Geoffrey scratched his nose again, then screwed his mouth. "I couldn't find Rascal anywhere. He'd gotten into a pond and was sopping when I did find him and, well, I forgot. I think Mama's forgotten too, for the moment."

Vanessa placed a hand to his shoulder. "It's all right, Geoffrey. We can get the photographs now. Tell me, has your mother finished decorating the pages in the album?" she asked conversationally, as they began to walk toward the Photo House.

Minutes later they arrived at the door, and she worked the key in the lock. The mechanism gave way with a click, and she and Geoffrey entered. It almost seemed strange to be here, for she hadn't been in days.

Proceeding to the long table, left of the door, Vanessa pulled open the center drawer and withdrew the cache of photographs from its depth.

"Here you are, Geoffrey." She gave them over, but as

he thanked her and started to turn, she stopped him, touching his sleeve. "Just a moment."

Reaching for the top print, Vanessa lifted it off and studied the image. The photograph was the one she'd taken of Lady Gwen in Knights Chapel, laying peaceably in her open coffin, her hands folded one atop the other.

Heat rippled through Vanessa as she realized what had bothered her so about the picture. It wasn't what she saw in the print, but what was missing—Lady Gwen's Bible. Vanessa had placed it in her hands just before the funeral commenced.

"My God," she whispered, thunderstruck as everything came together in her mind in one extraordinary flash of insight. Suddenly, she was transported back to Lady Gwen's last hours when Vanessa had hurriedly brought the Bible at her insistence.

"Burn it! Burn it!" Lady Gwen had cried out frantically, imploring her to destroy the holy book.

Vanessa gripped the edge of the long table, her mind reeling. Lady Gwen knew Sherringham's darkest secret. That is why she'd left. Not because she was a sheltered, sensitive soul, distraught by the last viscountess's death and her nephew's implication. She'd left because she knew the truth of that night.

The pieces fit, Vanessa thought with crystal clarity as she envisioned that restless soul—traveling endlessly, surrounding herself with multitudes of entertaining friends and acquaintances. Lady Gwen had filled all the hours of her days, all the moments of silence, as if afraid to be alone with her thoughts. Even at night, Lady Gwen would pace the floor, sleep eluding her. Eluding her because she knew who had killed Olivia.

Vanessa's mind continued to race furiously, fixing on the Bible. Lady Gwen had been desperate for Vanessa to burn it. But why, unless it contained evidence she wished destroyed? What then? A written account of something witnessed? A confession encoded in the pages? God above, was it possible Lady Gwen had been party to Olivia's death, accidentally or otherwise?

"Mrs. Wynters are you all right?" Geoffrey touched her elbow, concern filling his voice. "Should I bring you the stool?"

"No, Geoffrey, it's not a stool I need."

Vanessa swallowed deeply. What she needed was Lady Gwen's Bible. She must go at once to the mausoleum and open her late employer's coffin. Lady Gwen had literally taken her secrets to the grave and now held Adrian's future in her cold, dead hands.

Vanessa tore herself from her thoughts and rounded on the boy, her words coming out in a rush.

"Geoffrey, you accompanied the family into the mausoleum the day of your great-aunt's funeral. Can you tell me exactly where her coffin is located—where I can find it?"

The boy's eyes popped open wide. "Are you going *there*, Mrs. Wynters—*inside*?"

Vanessa held his gaze steadily. "I realize my request seems strange, but there's something I must see—must *recover*, actually. If I am right, it will mean a great deal for your Uncle Adrian. The mausoleum is a sizable building, and I suspect there are a number of rooms inside. Can you sketch the layout for me?"

Geoffrey straightened, drawing himself up several inches, importantly. "I can do better than sketch it, Mrs. Wynters. I can show you."

"Geoffrey, I'll not ask you to—"

"Please, Mrs. Wynters. I know what has happened to Uncle Adrian, and I want to help him, no matter what the task or how small."

Tears sprang instantly to Vanessa's eyes. Was she ever to weep at the slightest inducement?

"My dear young man, you have no idea how enormously important this is. If we discover what I believe we shall, we will be able to prove your uncle's innocence and see him set free. We must hurry, however. Do you know whether the mausoleum is kept locked?"

"I think so." He nodded thoughtfully. "Mr. Manning, the groundskeeper, should have a key."

"Good. We need to persuade him to open the doors for us. Keep in mind, Geoffrey, it's best no one knows what we are truly about. They might object to our doing . . . well, what must be done. Fortunately, the family is away for the time being. I don't wish to involve Timmons or his wife, Jane, either. I'm sure they would deem it most improper for us to disturb the dead."

"Is that what we're going to do?" Geoffrey's voice rose several notes, his eyes widening even more.

"Not really." Vanessa smiled.

Relieving him of the photographs, she returned them to the drawer.

"I want you to find Mr. Manning and tell him we wish to visit Lady Gwendolyn's crypt. With all the excitement of late, I imagine no one has thought to remove the withered blossoms from her tomb. Convince Mr. Manning that is our purpose. I'll arrange for a gig or cart to be brought out and meet you both at the stables."

Geoffrey preceded her from the Photo House, and Vanessa delayed only long enough to secure the door. As she traveled the length of the courtyard, she noticed how the skies had further darkened. The wind blew stiffer now, carrying the heavy scent of damp earth.

Arriving at the stables, she made her request then waited as a conveyance was rolled out and a horse harnessed. Geoffrey soon appeared with an imposing, bearded man who wore rumpled work clothes and grasped a large ring of keys—Mr. Manning. To Vanessa's relief, the groundskeeper proved an obliging fellow who asked no questions. In short order, the threesome were on their way with Vanessa at the reins.

She set the horse to an easy pace, following the now familiar route. She reminisced how, on the day of the funeral, the distance from the manse to the mausoleum seemed long indeed. Now, time passed quickly. Already, the Abbey Ruin was coming into sight.

Vanessa shivered as she swept her gaze over the ancient-looking relic. The sanctuary area, with its damaged wall, became visible for the briefest of moments, reminding of their recent, horrid discovery there. Vanessa looked away and pressed on.

The Orangery came next into view, its pallid facade glowing ghostlike amid the dark grove of trees. The reflection pool that stretched before the building appeared black as it mirrored the threatening sky. The only hint of color to be detected was in the dry, curled leaves of autumn, drifting across the water's surface.

Vanessa took hold of herself. Her imagination was beginning to overcome her, seeing death at every turn, in every leaf. She knew what was required of her, if she was to save Adrian, and she was determined to see it through.

The road dipped as they entered the dell where the mausoleum sat in majestic isolation. Rounding the building to its far side, Vanessa reined the horse and cart to a halt. From the near distance, she could hear the rush of the River Wye coursing noisily below the cliff's edge.

Vanessa stepped from the small conveyance, the breeze tossing her hair about her face as she gazed up the long flight of steps to the mausoleum's bronze doors and the black mourning wreaths there. Mr. Manning began to climb as she remained rooted in place, unmoving.

"Mrs. Wynters?" Geoffrey came to her side, his voice carrying concern. "Are you all right?"

"Yes. Quite all right. But let's get this over."

Together they mounted the steps, Geoffrey carefully matching his pace to hers. When they gained the top, Vanessa found herself short of breath but couldn't say whether it was due to the climb itself or the prospect of opening Lady Gwen's coffin.

Mr. Manning worked a large key in the door's lock. After a solid clunk signaled his success, he applied his strength to one of the massive bronze panels and began to push it open. The door protested their intrusion with a deep, metallic groan, grating along Vanessa's already taut nerves. She gazed inside the shaded depths and after exchanging a glance with Geoffrey, crossed the threshold, her heart pounding.

The mausoleum's chill air enwrapped her as she moved inside. Geoffrey followed directly behind, while Mr. Manning remained respectfully outside the family crypt.

As they entered the central rotunda, Vanessa beheld an amazing sight—Leonine Marrable's elaborate sarcophagus, centered directly beneath the dome. The dome, itself, floated above a ring of windows which, on a brighter day, would bathe the interior with light. Today however, everything appeared shadowy, the pure white marble of Leonine's effigy cast in grays.

Numerous other sepulchres encircled the rotunda, alternating along the walls with soaring Ionic columns and deep niches, filled with statuary. One statue, bearing a striking resemblance to Charles II, watched over Leonine's resting place.

"This way, Mrs. Wynters. Great-aunt Gwen is in the room directly across, on the opposite side." Geoffrey led the way, hastening past tombs centuries old, and paused before the portal that opened onto the backmost chamber. "She's in here with her parents and my grandparents, her brother, Viscount Lionel, and his wife."

Geoffrey pointed to an unadorned tomb, its plain slab top spread with a host of shriveled flowers.

Vanessa moved deep into the chamber to stand before the vault, Geoffrey trailing her.

"What do we do now?" he asked in a breathless whisper.

"You don't have to be party to this, Geoffrey. I'm going to have to open the tomb. The coffin too."

"How will you remove the top, if I don't help you?"

Vanessa found his gaze resting intently upon her, followed by a shrug and a nervous smile.

"How indeed?" She smiled too. "Come then, let's get on with it."

Clearing away the dead flowers, they set them aside along with Vanessa's shawl. They then considered how to best slide and turn the marble slab to the end of the tomb and applied themselves to the task.

Vanessa and Geoffrey first used their shoulders, arms, and hands to push at the lid's weight. Vanessa had forgotten how cold marble could be until she touched it. Her fingers quickly turned to ice.

The lid budged slowly—an inch, then two, then several more—causing a fierce scraping noise that echoed off the walls. They continued to shove at the slab, moving it bit by bit and revealing the coffin within the vault.

Vanessa quickly realized the slab was too heavy for a woman and a boy to lift down. It would need to be removed altogether in order to raise the coffin lid. Undaunted, she shoved at the slab once more.

"Need assistance?" a familiar voice sounded from behind.

Geoffrey jerked upright and Vanessa whirled around, her heart thrashing against her ribs. Several yards away stood Lawrence, pinning them both with his pale blue eyes. Past his shoulder, she spied Mr. Manning waiting by the door.

A brittle smile angled across Lawrence's face. "I see my timing is impeccable. I'd just entered the gates of Sherringham when I saw you at a distance. I thought it supremely odd to see you headed in this direction with Manning here, so I followed. He tells me you came to tend to Auntie's crypt—remove the dead flowers, I believe he said. Or is there something else you came to remove?"

"I'm no grave robber, if that's what you are insinuating," Vanessa declared, realizing how condemning this all must look. "I'm not here to steal Lady Gwendolyn's jewelry off her."

Lawrence's eyes shifted to his nephew then back to Vanessa. "I didn't suggest you were—either of you—though for the life of me, I can't conceive a single reason as to why you would be opening her tomb."

Geoffrey stepped forward, moving protectively in front of Vanessa—a gesture that reminded her of Adrian.

"Mrs. Wynters is trying to help Uncle Adrian."

Lawrence arched a skeptical brow. "And how is that, young man?"

Vanessa pressed her lips together, reluctant to confess her purpose, yet having little choice but to do so. Stepping forward beside Geoffrey, she quickly related her theory that Lady Gwen had known the truth of Olivia's death and concealed a written account of it in her Bible.

"She was absolutely desperate for the book to be destroyed. Don't you see? It all makes perfect sense—the timing of her leaving Sherringham, why she stayed away these past years—"

Lawrence held up his hands, stopping her rush of words. "I believe you, Vanessa."

He dragged his hand over his golden head and paced a moment as he absorbed all she'd said. He glanced to her once more, his eyes holding an intense, penetrating look that, inexplicably, made Vanessa uncomfortable. But in the next instant, the corners of his lips curved upward.

"Vanessa, you're a wonder. It wouldn't surprise me if you've solved the entire mystery single-handedly. But opening the casket of the dead is no task for a lady. Manning and I will see to it. Besides, Aunt Gwen is *my* relative after all."

Lawrence removed his jacket and gestured Manning

forward. The groundskeeper paled, but did as he was asked. Together the two men took hold of the slab, sliding it to the end of the tomb before easing it off and down onto the floor.

Manning appeared increasingly distressed and backed away as Lawrence turned to open the coffin itself.

"No fear, I'll do this part myself," Lawrence nodded to the groundskeeper who swiftly withdrew from the chamber entirely.

Lawrence chuckled, shaking his head, then returned his attention to the vault. Reaching inside, he lifted the coffin lid straight up. Vanessa drew Geoffrey back, her breath sealing in her throat, but like her, the boy could not pull his eyes away. Though Lawrence blocked their view for the most part, Vanessa could still glimpse Lady Gwen's white hair.

"Forgive us," she whispered softly, as Lawrence leaned forward to take the Bible from his aunt's hands.

Closing the coffin, he straightened, holding up the cloth-covered Bible for all to see. But instead of giving it over to Vanessa, he began searching through its pages himself.

"What are you expecting to find exactly?"

Vanessa and Geoffrey moved closer, but Lawrence kept the volume closely guarded.

"A letter, perhaps," Vanessa replied. "Or writing on the book's pages—underlining, perhaps. I'm not sure."

Lawrence flipped through the pages, then fanned them once more. Finding nothing, he examined the leather ends and felt through the woolen covering. Finally he removed the cloth altogether.

"Hello," he muttered. "Look here, the stitching has

been removed from the binding. There's something inside, between the two layers of leather."

Vanessa and Geoffrey waited anxiously as Lawrence worked a sheaf of flattened paper out of the binding. Handing her the Bible at last, Lawrence opened out the pages and began to quickly scan them.

Vanessa grew frustrated as he continued to withhold the papers. But as he read the lines of Lady Gwen's spidery script, all color drained from his face.

He raised his eyes to her, shock registered in their depths. For a moment he could not seem to speak.

"My God," he voiced at last. "You were right, Vanessa. Aunt Gwen *did* witness Olivia's death, and she names her killer."

Relief flooded Vanessa. They would be able to clear Adrian once and for all. Thank God. Thank God.

"What does the letter say?" she pressed, more anxious than ever. "Who killed Olivia?"

Pain creased Lawrence's eyes as he looked to her. He seemed to choke on the words.

"Vanessa, I'm sorry . . . I know you didn't expect . . . It's Adrian. Adrian murdered Olivia."

Chapter 18

The rains began minutes after the small group de-parted the mausoleum—a light sprinkling mixed with the wind at first, then a heavier, pelting downfall. Vanessa spread one side of her shawl over Geoffrey, hugging him close, while Mr. Manning drove their cart. Lawrence rode just ahead, leading the way.

For the whole of their soaking journey, Vanessa sat in a wooden daze. She welcomed the sting of the rain in her face, wetting her cheeks in place of tears. She found she could no longer cry, not after the rest of what Lawrence had revealed of her aunt's letter.

"Given that her rooms were located in the west wing, Aunt Gwen had been privy to the full scope of Adrian's and Olivia's quarreling there. When all quieted at long last, she writes she emerged from her chamber and went in search of Adrian. She found him in the tower study."

The claim had struck Vanessa as peculiar, then as much as now. The note Olivia wrote that same night stated Adrian had gone elsewhere—to his own private study, which was in a different wing altogether. Vanessa had said nothing of this to Lawrence, allowing him to continue without interruption.

"Auntie started to enter the tower study but found

Olivia to already be there. Neither Adrian nor Olivia observed her, so she remained quietly at the door. Olivia, as Auntie tells it, was in the course of disputing something Adrian had said. He gave her his back and began to mount the staircase to the upper level. Olivia stormed after him, hurling threats and accusations, striking at his back with her fist as she accused him of carrying on an affair of his own—one with her personal maid, Bonnie Beckford."

Vanessa pressed her lashes closed against the very thought of that charge. Somehow, she couldn't conceive it, not of Adrian.

Lawrence had continued the story without pause, not once needing to consult Gwen's writings for the details.

"Olivia angered Adrian thoroughly. They'd only reached the top of the staircase when she grabbed at his arm. He spun around on her then, shoving her away from him and slapping her. Olivia fell backward, tumbling down those treacherous, twisting stairs and breaking her neck."

Vanessa's stomach knotted fiercely when she recalled Olivia's lifeless image in the tower photograph.

"Aunt Gwen was horrorstruck," Lawrence went on, looking to the pages. "She returned to her rooms and locked herself inside. She claims to remember little after that as she'd lain on her bed for hours and fell asleep.

"The following morning, when she learned of the carriage accident and Bonnie's and Olivia's fates, Auntie knew Adrian had lied, and that he must have killed Bonnie too. She kept her silence when the authorities arrived. Adrian was her nephew, after all—a close blood-relative whom she'd practically raised and the Viscount Marrable. She couldn't betray him. But neither could she stay at Sherringham."

A jolt of the cart snapped Vanessa's attention back to the present. In that same instant, the manse came into sight. The light in its windows glowed dimly through the blowing rain. Long minutes later, Mr. Manning brought the cart around to the entrance portico, where she and Geoffrey alighted with Lawrence's aid and followed him inside.

Not a soul greeted them in the great, vacant hall, the servants apparently preoccupied elsewhere and the family still in absence. The light of the chandelier created dancing pools of golden light in the hallway, though most of its dimensions remained swathed in shadows.

Lawrence paused in the center of the room, turning toward Vanessa. "I realize you wish to read Aunt Gwen's account for yourself. You'll understand, however, given its content, I need time to go over the pages alone for a while, digest them and all that, before the others return. I promise to make them available for all to see later."

At that, he withdrew, leaving Vanessa and Geoffrey standing dripping in the hallway. As they watched Lawrence's retreat down the corridor, right of the entry, the boy suddenly pulled away from her, his face red and his eyes filled with tears.

"I don't care what Great-aunt Gwen wrote in her letter. I won't believe it. Uncle Adrian isn't a murderer. He's *not*, he's *not*!"

At that, huge tears rolling over his cheeks, Geoffrey ran down the opposite corridor, back toward his family's suite of rooms.

Vanessa's every impulse urged her to go after him, but she knew what Geoffrey needed most was a good, hard cry. As did she. Still, her own tears would not come.

Dragging the sodden shawl from her shoulders, she folded it to a square, then moved to climb the grand staircase to the Upper Cloisters and her chamber.

Vanessa arrived at the room at what seemed an eternity later, her heart feeling heavy as iron. After changing from her sodden clothes into a dry, woolen gown, she let down her hair and began combing it out. As she did, she stared into the mirror at her pale reflection, seeing yet not seeing herself as she pondered the last hours and worried the facts.

Her emotions suddenly boiled up inside her once more. Vanessa slammed down her comb on the top of the dresser, her anger sharpening, her forbearance at an end. She wanted to *see* Lady Gwen's condemning words with her own eyes. *Read* each damning sentence as it appeared in Gwen's spidery script. Even then, no matter what dire tale the pages told, Vanessa wanted to speak with Adrian before accepting the charges against him. Like Geoffrey, she would remain skeptical, believing Adrian's innocence till proven otherwise, beyond doubt.

Quitting her chamber, Vanessa went in search of Lawrence. He'd not refuse her this request. Fifteen minutes passed, then thirty, and forty. She encountered few servants about the manse and was grateful when she came upon the maid who so often attended her, Mary Ethel.

"Do you know the whereabouts of Mr. Marrable?" Vanessa asked in a rush.

"I believe he's gone out again, madam."

Vanessa looked at the young woman blankly. "In this storm?"

"Oh, he's not gone far I imagine. He oftentimes works at the folly."

"You mean the Orangery?"

"That would be the likely choice."

Vanessa smiled at the maid, grateful for the information. "Mary Ethel, I'd like you to take Geoffrey some warm milk and stay with him until his parents return. He's quite distraught over his uncle, the viscount."

"Of course, Mrs. Wynters, and a saucer of warm milk for that pup of his too," she offered.

Vanessa started to part then quickly turned back again. "Can you tell me where I might find Timmons? I've yet to see him tonight."

"I believe he and his Mrs. are with Nanny Pringle. She was quite undone when she received word of his lordship."

"Yes, I imagine she was. Thank you, Mary Ethel."

Vanessa headed for Nanny's quarters, deciding against traveling the Tudor gallery. Fortunately, she knew a much quicker route, well illuminated the entire way.

Perhaps it was providential the three people who'd been at Sherringham the longest were presently gathered together. Not *everything* she'd learned thus far fit neatly together. There were still several important questions needing answers.

Lawrence downed the last of his brandy, then picked up the small faded photograph to examine it once more. He'd found it tucked deep in the leather binding of Aunt Gwen's Bible.

No, "Aunt" Gwen was incorrect. Her letter contained far more than the details of Olivia's death. It disclosed what, for him, was the most shocking revelation of all. Lady Gwendolyn Marrable was his mother.

Lawrence tossed the picture back onto the table where the multipaged epistle rested. He then rose to pace the confines of the Orangery's upper drawing room and grapple with his swirl of thoughts.

Jamming his fingers through his hair, he changed direction and came back to where the table stood before the tiled fireplace. Glancing down to the photograph, he studied the dashing young man smiling there—William Darnell, once Sherringham's Master-of-the-Horse, many years ago. Darnell's golden features reflected Lawrence's own, down to the dimple creasing his left cheek.

Lawrence filled his glass for a third time and resumed his seat. Leafing through the pages of Gwen's letter, he scanned their lines. There was much more to his kindly "maiden aunt" than anyone ever knew—excepting her brother and sister-in-law, the Viscount and Viscountess Marrable.

Scarcely nineteen, she'd fallen madly in love with Darnell and given herself recklessly to him. Their brief affair resulted in Gwen's conceiving a child. It meant absolute ruin for her and scandal for the family, something Lord Lionel's wife would not abide. She'd aspirations of her own among the upper elite, to point the Prince's inner set. But such a stigma meant social oblivion.

Gwen described in the pages how she and her lover were separated, Darnell being dispatched to a post in India at Lord Lionel's arrangement. Her brother, Lionel, whom she portrayed as an indulgent and a forgiving man, blamed himself for being oblivious to what was right before his nose.

When the viscountess learned of her own pregnancy, a plan was quickly hatched to send the women abroad to the south of France for the duration of the viscountess's confinement—Gwen, of course, accompanying her. Nine months later, Viscountess Marrable returned triumphantly with twin sons.

Lawrence rubbed his eyes, comprehending at last why the woman he'd always believed to be his mama had been cold and emotionless toward him all these years, though in fairness, she'd not been overly warm to Adrian either. But then, "children are such sticky creatures," she'd ofttimes say, allowing none of her children—the boys or girls—to touch her and risk messing her gowns and hair.

Lawrence suddenly threw back his head and expelled a shout of laughter, the irony of it all welling up inside him. All these years he thought he'd missed out on the grand Marrable inheritance by a matter of minutes—the firstborn inheriting all, the second, nothing. He laughed again. By the dates named in Gwen's letter, he was a full month older than his "brother." Being a small child—or was it that Adrian had always been the larger—no one had discerned any difference of age in the "twins."

Lawrence crushed the letter in his hand, his mood swinging sharply. He and Adrian were *not* twins. If the letter was ever made known, being bastard-born, he would not only lose his place as next in line of inheritance, but he would be removed from it altogether—a shameful blot on the family's most recent history.

But history *could* be changed. None knew the truth of his parentage. If Adrian should be found guilty of Olivia's and Bonnie Beckford's untimely deaths—and possibly implicated in that of Clairissa's—he would face certain execution.

Lawrence rubbed his chin then rose to pace, his pulse picking up. With Adrian dead, he, himself, would inherit the Marrable titles, lands, and properties, not to mention the lucrative family coal mines.

He snatched up Gwen's letter and shuffled through the pages. She'd mentioned only one other piece of evidence of his birth—sealed in an envelope and given to the keeping of the family's solicitor. Lord Lionel had arranged in the event of his and Adrian's premature demise, the truth would be verified. The inheritance would circumvent Lawrence and go to another. Gwen agreed to this, in exchange for the facade of legitimacy for her son and Sherringham as their home.

Lawrence set the pages down. The envelope held by the solicitor posed no great difficulty, Lawrence deemed. There were those who could be employed to secure it—by whatever means. Besides, should Adrian die, wouldn't the solicitor be obliged to turn the letter over to him? Not even the solicitor knew its contents.

Topping off his brandy, Lawrence held his glass high to toast to Adrian.

"Our fates are yet entwined, 'brother.' But one must find its end, so that the other might thrive. You've long had your turn. Now it is mine."

Lawrence chuckled to himself, then downed the fiery liquid.

"It was a dreadful time for all of us at Sherringham, what with yet another viscountess' death—so tragic." Timmons wagged his head with remembered sadness.

His wife, Jane, patted his hand, nodding in agreement. She turned her large, doe-soft eyes to Vanessa.

"Of course, there were the accusations brought against Lord Marrable."

Her words brought loud sniffles from Nanny who was seated before the parlor's fireplace in one of the deep, upholstered chairs. Jane went to lay a hand to the older woman's shoulder and soothe her.

"The Mrs. and I had never seen Lady Gwendolyn so greatly distressed," Timmons went on to explain. "At first she kept to her rooms like a hermit and refused to come out. Excepting for the funeral, of course."

"She didn't seem the same after that," Jane added from where she stood. "Not while she remained at Sherringham. Too much pain, or memories. Lady Gwendolyn had lived at Sherringham most all her life. Then she left."

Nanny's sniffles became a muffled sob. Jane attended to her at once and suggested a comforting cup of tea.

"How extraordinarily sad for everyone at Sherringham," Vanessa commented as Jane moved to the sideboard.

When she offered her tea, Vanessa declined, thinking it time she withdrew from Nanny's chambers. Her conversation with the Timmons had yielded little new, leastwise nothing to shed light on Lady Gwen's letter or to aid Adrian.

As Vanessa started to move toward the door and take leave of the others, Jane brought the pot of tea to the table.

"Well, Lady Gwendolyn is home at last, God rest her," Jane remarked, filling the cups for her husband and Nanny. "It was fortunate his lordship's brother was in residence at the time and able to leave immediately for Paris. How distressing for you to be stranded on for-

eign soil, alone, and under such sorrowful circumstances."

Vanessa watched her fill the last cup. "Yes, fortunate
indeed. I've often thought it amazing how little coinci-
dences play so great a part in our lives."

"Madam?" Timmons's brows rose at a questioning
slant.

Seeing that neither he nor Jane had followed her
thought, she elaborated.

"Such as the coincidence of Mr. Marrable's being at
Sherringham when my telegram arrived. He'd come
only on learning of the shipment of Italian tiles for the
fireplace in the Orangery. Had the tiles not been delivered at that time, he would have remained at the country estate where he'd been summering and not been
here to receive my wire."

Timmons clasped his hands in front of him. "Forgive
me, but Madam is mistaken. The tiles arrived *after* Mr.
Marrable had already departed for Paris."

Vanessa felt her heart jar in place. "I don't understand. Didn't he come to Sherringham to approve the
tiles and oversee their installation?"

"Mr. Marrable did spend time at the Orangery, but I
am certain it had nothing to do with the tiles as they
were still en route."

"Yes, of course. That is logical." Vanessa rubbed her
forehead, trying to put order to the numerous pieces
and bits of information she'd been told over the last
weeks. She moved back to the table and lowered herself
onto a chair.

"I am sorry to continue to press this—I am not ques-
tioning your word—but it was my understanding
Lawrence, Mr. Marrable, received a telegram at
Hadleigh Hall informing him of the tiles' arrival from

Florence. In hastening to Sherringham, he missed Lord Adrian's wire stating *he'd* left Scotland for London and that another of the Marrable jewels had been recovered."

A look of unease crossed Timmons's features. "Again, I fear Madam is mistaken. Mr. Marrable knew of his brother's journey to London. The telegram was forwarded from Hadleigh Hall to Sherringham and arrived the day before your own."

An icy chill of foreboding spiraled through Vanessa's veins.

"I remember it, too." Jane moved to her husband's side. "I commented to Mr. Timmons how odd it was to have so much activity at Sherringham after there being none for so very long."

"When the viscount's telegram arrived, I delivered it personally and placed it in Mr. Marrable's hands," Timmons finished.

Vanessa stared at the two, flabbergasted. She was glad to be already sitting. If what Timmons said was true, then Lawrence had purposely withheld information of Lady Gwen's death from Adrian. Why, if not to assure Adrian would be absent and lower everyone's opinion of him even further? Lawrence would also have been able to act in the viscount's place.

Remembering the brittle look on Lawrence's face and the snide tone of his remark when Adrian arrived at the funeral unexpectedly, Vanessa knew, with a sick heart, she was right.

Nanny, who'd been listening intently from her chair, huffed an audible breath. "Just like him, that one."

"Like who, Nanny?" Vanessa crossed the room to her chair.

"Master Lawrence, of course." She referred to him as

if still a child in her care. "I see what he was about, trying to get his brother in trouble as he always does."

Vanessa blinked. Had Nanny read her mind? Or, more likely, did she simply know Lawrence so well?

"Master Adrian visited me, you know. Right here, after Lady Gwen's funeral." She poked a finger at the other chair, indicating he'd sat there at the time. "He explained how his and his brother's wires had 'crossed,' thus causing him to arrive late. *Crossed,* indeed." She huffed again. "Master Lawrence knew. He knew."

Nanny stared into the flames in the fireplace, shaking her head softly. "So different they are, from even before they could walk. And Master Lawrence with such a temper! A dark streak, some would call it."

She suddenly rolled her eyes to gaze up at Vanessa, concern in their depths.

"You must beware, child. His dark side rules him at times. Leads him to do things he doesn't mean. He even hurt poor Nanny at times, long ago." She sighed heavily and returned her attention to the fire and lost herself to her thoughts.

Shocked, Vanessa withdrew, crossing the room with the intent to leave. Before doing so, she queried Timmons once more.

"You are quite sure of the wire's content—that Mr. Marrable knew his lordship was no longer in Scotland?"

"Yes, madam. In fact, Mr. Marrable commented aloud to me about it, saying Lord Adrian had abandoned the Highlands to chase after another of the Marrable jewels. He viewed it in a humorous light, or so I believed."

Dear God. What else had Lawrence lied about? Vanessa wondered. She held a final question, unsure she should pose it or whether she wished to know the answer.

"Timmons, on the day of the funeral, Geoffrey told me his uncle forbade anyone around the Abbey Ruin, that it was unsafe. Might you know to which uncle he referred?"

"Yes, madam. That would be his Uncle Lawrence. As you know, Lord Adrian departed Sherringham after Lady Olivia's death and took up residence in London. His brother, Lawrence, was the only one of the family to visit Sherringham, and he did so regularly."

Regularly—when everyone else stayed away? The thought struck Vanessa as odd. According to Cissy, it was Lady Gwen's funeral that had reunited the family at Sherringham after their prolonged absence from the estate.

Why had Lawrence visited with such regularity? When everyone else had seemingly fled, what continued to draw him back to Sherringham?

Lawrence worked the brick free from the chimney-piece and set it aside. Reaching into the recess, he drew out a large velvet pouch, then emptied its contents onto the table's top.

He smiled as the mass of jewels flashed and sparkled with the fire's light. Lifting a large emerald and diamond ring, Lawrence watched it glitter between his fingers.

As part of his plan, he now intended to hide the jewels in the wall of the Abbey Ruin, near to where Olivia had been found. He purposed—with a hint dropped into the constable's ear—that they would be discovered, making it appear Adrian had possessed them all the while, keeping ready access to them.

Of course, there was the matter of the jewels Lawrence had already sold that would require explanation. He pondered the problem and decided on a simple, plausible account that could be put forth—Adrian had sold the pieces to cast suspicion away from himself. Further, Adrian had cleverly engaged Scotland Yard, posturing as the wronged party in the crime. As each item of jewelry came to light, he bought it back, thus returning it to Marrable hands and preserving the family's legacy.

Lawrence smiled. It was a tidy explanation. Entirely believable. The beauty and truth of it all was, he, himself, had received significant sums when he'd sold the jewels to pay down his debts. Adrian, on the other hand, had doggedly located them and purchased them back at his own expense. Lawrence's smile widened. Once Adrian was removed as viscount, the Marrable jewels would be in his possession once more—to keep, or to sell, all over again. He was not as partial to them as the rest of the family. And now that he'd discovered he wasn't legitimately related to them, he cared even less.

A dull, blackened brooch drew Lawrence's eye and he plucked it from the rest. The design was the same as the one burned into his hand—a heron with its wings outspread—easily discernible to anyone who examined it closely. That he could never allow, for then the truth would be out. He'd not been trying to save anyone in the fiery carriage accident when he'd burned his hand. He was trying to retrieve the Marrable jewels from the flames—to take for himself. Foolishly, he'd snatched this one from the fire without protecting his hand and instantly seared its design into his palm.

Lawrence closed his fingers over the scar and the memory of the excruciating pain he'd suffered.

He'd no idea, of course, when he scrambled down the ravine that he would discover the treasured jewels. He'd known nothing of Olivia's intentions to abscond with them until the moment he found them spilled from the small, broken chest and scattered on the ground.

As to the note she'd written him that night, he learned of it only this morning, at the constable's office. Grealey had then displayed the letter importantly, claiming it to be grounds enough with the other known "facts" for holding and charging Adrian. Grealey had not the remotest notion that Olivia had actually meant her note for him.

Lawrence returned the charred piece to the niche in the chimneypiece, placing it deep inside. It mustn't be found to raise suspicions of any kind.

Lawrence turned his attention to the other jewels piling the table and began scooping them back into the velvet pouch. At the same time, he mulled over his plans.

The authorities and courts must be convinced of Adrian's guilt. To that end, Lawrence knew he must carefully prepare the evidence. He'd place the jewels in the wall and alter Auntie's account. Then he'd play the role of the distressed brother, doing all that he could for the family, while at the same time assuring all progressed to the desired conclusion.

It would be a long, messy affair, no doubt. Vanessa would require consoling, which he'd willingly provide. He'd seen the shattered look on her face when he'd named Adrian as Olivia's killer. The lad too. Lawrence hadn't wished to hurt his nephew, but there was no help for it. He couldn't very well reveal the truth of

Auntie's letter and name himself the killer. It was incredible enough he'd been able to think as rapidly and
coherently as he had, despite having just read the startling truth of his birth.

Instinctively, in disclosing what information he did,
Lawrence had held close to the actual facts, hoping to be
convincing. The only alteration was in substituting
Adrian's name for his own, claiming his noble brother
to be the one Gwen had seen cause Olivia's death. Truth
was, Adrian had long departed Sherringham before
Olivia even came to the tower study. Lawrence knew,
because it was he, himself, she'd sought concerning the
matter of Bonnie Beckford.

Laying the velvet pouch aside, Lawrence took up
Gwen's confession and examined it carefully. The lines
opened with an apology to Adrian, followed by the revelation of her love affair with Darnell, her confinement
in the south of France with her sister-in-law, and the
birth of her golden-haired son. Those pages he'd burn,
Lawrence decided. Fortunately for him, Gwen had chosen to begin her account of the scene she'd witnessed in
the tower on a fresh page.

Scanning those pages now, he quickly noted that
Gwen had written out his name in full only once. As
ladies often did in their endless correspondence, she
employed initials for all the following entries, referring
to him simply as "L."

Again fortune smiled on him. His full name only appeared on one page, and it was at the bottom edge of
the sheet—the sole word on the last line. That could easily be cropped off, he decided. Adrian's name could
then be added at the top of the following page, mis-
aligning the margin somewhat but not noticeably. "The
"L's" he'd convert to "A's," incorporating the lower

weep of the letter as a seeming flourish—all still in keeping with Gwen's flowing script.

Taking heart, he assured himself his plan was completely viable. He would need to practice Gwen's handwriting and check for other capital "A's" in the pages that could be compared to his altered "L's." Gratefully, he'd never abandoned using the purply-blue brand of ink favored at Sherringham. He'd need to dilute the new ink to make it appear faded, or at least not so fresh, upon the page. He'd also need a fine-nibbed pen, to match the one used by Gwen.

His course decided, Lawrence took up the pouch of jewels and returned it to the cavity in the chimneypiece. He next collected the papers and separated out those detailing his birth, intending them for the fire. The remainder he added to the niche along with the photograph. That he'd not burn—just yet.

After working the brick back into place, Lawrence carefully remounted the carved, stone plaque bearing the Marrable panther, further concealing the secret vault.

Lawrence suddenly noticed how the room had grown cold, the temperature icy. Though he'd begun a fire in the grate on first arriving, the fireplace proved sorely ineffective.

It had never been properly tested, of course, especially with the tiles being newly installed following Gwen's funeral. Tonight was a particularly unpleasant evening and a sure test. Lawrence could hear the wind rattling the shutters in their casings on the floor below. He'd see to any problems with the fireplace another time. For now, it was adequate to do the work he required.

Taking hold of the brass poker from beside the

hearth, Lawrence stirred the fire. Satisfied, he returned
the poker to its stand, tossed the pages from Gwen's
confession into the grate, and strode from the room.

Shutting the door solidly behind him, he concen
trated his thoughts on obtaining the needed writing
supplies from the manse. There would be no saving
Adrian after he was through. There couldn't be.

As the flames licked at the sheaves of paper, a volley
of wind burst down the chimney, extinguishing the fire
and blowing the pages out of the grate and onto the
hearth.

The wind continued to whistle around the room, re
bounding off the walls and smiting the chimneypiece
The plaque tilted then crashed to the floor.

On the wind blustered, seeking its escape. Finding
one sufficient, it slipped through the crack beneath the
door and shrilled throughout the Orangery.

Vanessa watched from a nearby cover of trees as
Lawrence emerged from the Orangery and mounted his
horse. She waited as he disappeared from sight, riding
in the direction of the manse.

Looking to the Orangery, she saw the lamplight still
glowed in the room above, indicating the likelihood
Lawrence would return. Still, she reasoned, he should
be gone long enough for her to make a quick search and
attempt to discover what drew him there.

Securing Delilah's reins to a branch, Vanessa left her
shelter and hastened toward the entrance door. She
pulled her cloak tight against the wind and rain, wish
ing now she'd taken time to put on her waterproof. But
then, she'd surely have missed this opportunity.

Entering the Orangery, Vanessa found she could see

little of the space by the flickering light. Wall sconces bracketed either side of the doors, and a freestanding candelabra stood at the base of the stairs. Still, the space swallowed their light.

The shutters rattled against the unglazed windows, unsettling her nerves further as she crossed to the steps, and climbed to the upper floor. There, she immediately came upon a room. By the light seeping from beneath the door, she knew it to be the place Lawrence had just occupied and, thus, the room she sought.

Vanessa reached for the doorknob then snatched her hand back in surprise. It was bitter cold to the touch. Determined, she grasped it once more and, giving it a firm turn, opened the door and entered in.

Vanessa noted a distinctive chill gripped the room, but before she could think on it further, the disorder on the floor distracted her attention. Papers scattered the area before the hearth and amid them lay a heavy, sculpted plaque, broken to pieces. The plaque appeared to have fallen from the face of the chimneypiece, leaving a square space of coarse brickwork exposed to view.

As Vanessa bent to collect the scattered papers, she immediately recognized Lady Gwen's handscript. The edges of the pages were singed as if Lawrence had tried to burn them. Vanessa wondered at that as she glanced to the cold ashes in the fireplace, then over the room.

Giving her attention to the pages, she assembled them into order without the benefit of numbers. With this done, she began to read, imagining Lady Gwen's voice in her mind's hearing.

"May God forgive my weak and wretched soul. And may you forgive me, Adrian, for I have wronged you greatly."

Vanessa lowered herself onto the chair beside the table, stunned as she read on.

"It is out of love that I act. And fear, too, I admit. But believe me, nephew, I would never allow matters to progress so far as to truly put you at the risk of conviction for your wife's death. I would come forward before then and testify. For now, however, I am compelled to remain silent in order to protect another—my son."

Vanessa read quickly, her heart pounding. "Twice have I sinned greatly," Lady Gwen's words continued. Yet as Vanessa skimmed the lines, she found but one sin mentioned, and it was not at all what she expected.

Lady Gwendolyn confessed to being the unmarried mother of Lawrence. As Vanessa read on, a great sadness filled her for the beautiful, young aristocrat who'd waited decades for her lover to return and take her and their son away. She'd remained faithfully at Sherringham, but in vain.

Still, Gwen's letter was filled with gratitude for the years she'd enjoyed with her son, taking part in raising him alongside her nephew and nieces, all in great comfort and privilege, owing to the benevolence of her brother.

Finishing the account, Vanessa wiped at the tears rimming her eyes. As she did, her gaze alighted on the chimneypiece. She stared at it for a moment before realizing the center brick appeared loose. She'd lost track of time and knew Lawrence would soon be returning. Still, the brick did not appear to be cemented in place— as if it could be extracted . . .

Vanessa rose and went directly to her mark. The brick sat out slightly, allowing her to grasp it about the edges. Pulling and wiggling it forward, she drew the brick out then peered into the hollow. There, she spied more of the cream-colored pages she recognized as Lady Gwen's. However, these did not appear to be scorched. As she removed them, she discovered a small photograph of a man, his looks strikingly similar to Lawrence's—obviously, Lady Gwen's great love, William Darnell.

Vanessa reached into the cavity again, this time bringing forth a weighty velvet bag. Opening its mouth, she glanced inside. And gasped aloud. Fingering out a bracelet of braided gold with a locket attached, she recognized it at once from the portrait of Leonine. Vanessa knew she held in her hands the missing Marrable jewels!

Again she returned to the fireplace niche and searched for anything she may have overlooked. Immediately, her fingers closed on something hard—another piece of jewelry. Withdrawing it, the piece proved to be a brooch with a heron motif. Vanessa's eyes widened at its charred condition. She didn't understand its significance but added it to the other jewels.

One thing was clear—the purpose behind Lawrence's frequent visits to Sherringham. He kept the jewels secreted in the Orangery. Vanessa guessed the reason he'd been visiting Sherringham at the time of Lady Gwen's death was to check on his hidden fortune, possibly choosing yet another jewel to market in London.

Vanessa returned to the table and began rapidly scanning the second set of papers. She worried Lawrence might soon return but needed to read for herself the details of Lady Gwen's letter.

While the previous pages dealt with scandal, she saw now these dealt with death and murder. Vanessa tensed as the tale that unfolded beneath her fingers matched with the one told by Lawrence in the mausoleum.

Lady Gwen had indeed heard the full of Adrian's and Olivia's arguing in the west wing. After all had quieted, she waited a while longer then went to learn what she could of the quarrel for she'd overheard fearsome words of divorce. On learning Adrian had quit Sherringham for London, she headed for the tower study, having a notion she might find Lawrence there.

Lawrence. Vanessa reread his name thrice over, enormous relief sweeping through her. Lawrence had been the one in the tower study, not Adrian.

On arriving there, Gwen found Olivia locked in a verbal battle with Lawrence. Olivia was enraged, charging him with being unfaithful to her by having an affair with her maid.

Vanessa shook her head at the irony of that—the unfaithful wife angered at having, herself, been betrayed.

From what Gwen overheard, it seemed the maid suffered a cold at the time. While packing the viscountess's trunk in her presence, she withdrew a handkerchief from the bodice of her gown and applied it to her nose. Perhaps the girl had forgotten—or perhaps not—but the cloth bore Lawrence's initials.

Vanessa imagined Olivia as she sat at her vanity, penning a note to her lover, telling how her husband had found them out, only to glance up and observe the girl withdrawing *her* lover's handkerchief from between her breasts. Imagined too, Olivia smudging the ink on the page as she rose to confront the girl.

Lady Gwen's letter went on to describe the scene in the tower, Olivia taking a ring from her finger and throwing it at Lawrence. She'd screamed she no longer wanted his gift, meant to celebrate their clandestine love.

Lady Gwen concluded her narration, stating she

didn't believe Lawrence meant to kill Olivia. Yet in his anger, he'd struck her sufficiently hard, and shoved her from him with enough force, to send her toppling backward down the staircase.

Vanessa swallowed, remembering her own fall down those same stairs, and before that, her slippage on the staircase in the cathedral. She recalled Lawrence's violent, inexplicable reaction at the time, better understanding now the source of his emotions. Perhaps, Lady Gwen was right. Lawrence hadn't meant to kill Olivia. But what of Bonnie Beckford?

Lady Gwen's words offered no insight there, only suspicions, doubts. Had the carriage been tampered with? Why had it set so easily afire as it plunged over the ravine? Was Bonnie being punished for her carelessness while at the same time covering Olivia's death with her own? And when was it exactly that Lawrence gained possession of the Marrable jewels?

As Vanessa finished reading the entire account, she was left to assume, at the time of her employer's death, Lady Gwen truly believed Adrian was beyond danger of being prosecuted for his wife's murder. Not wishing the truth to be revealed or Lawrence destroyed, she'd pleaded with Vanessa to burn her Bible, knowing the secrets it contained.

A sudden urgency seized Vanessa to be away and to deliver this newfound evidence into the hands of the authorities. She wouldn't trust Grealey, however. She needed to reach Cameron Kincaid.

Intent on freeing Adrian, Vanessa quickly folded the pages of the letter together—singed and unsinged—and slipped them into the deep, inner pocket of her cloak. She then returned Leonine's golden bracelet to the velvet pouch, adding the burned brooch and photo-

graph of Lawrence's father. As a final thought, she returned the brick to the chimneypiece giving the semblance all was as she'd found it.

Taking up the pouch, Vanessa hurried from the room
and descended the staircase to the floor below. As she
emerged from the Orangery, she noted instantly how
the storm had quieted and the rain ceased. Overhead,
the sky had lightened to a deep blue. Despite the still-
ness that reigned over the glade, she detected a distinctive sound—horses' hooves upon the road.

"God in Heaven," she muttered. "Lawrence!"

Vanessa ran toward Delilah. Freeing the reins, she
cast herself upward, into the saddle. Lawrence blocked
the way back toward the manse and Sherringham's
main road. She had no choice but to ride toward the
mausoleum. She calmed herself, remembering there to
be a path there too, leading toward Hereford. The
mourners from town had used it to arrive and depart on
the day of the funeral.

Steeling herself, Vanessa turned Delilah toward the
mausoleum and urged her on. Still, as they moved
along the road, the sound of horses' hooves continued
to fill her ears. She assumed it to be Delilah she heard,
but glanced back anyway.

Vanessa's heart nearly stopped. Lawrence held her in
his sight, closing the distance between them.

Chapter 19

Vanessa raced on, not daring to look back again, yet aware of Lawrence gaining.

Entering the dell, Delilah slowed beneath her as the road dipped downward. When it stretched out again, Vanessa pressed her heels to the mare's flanks and gave Delilah her lead.

Over the narrow lane they traveled with no choice but to follow its course. It led them directly toward the temple-like building, before looping around to the front and disappearing on the other side.

Hope surged in Vanessa's heart as she and the mare verged on the mausoleum and began to round its drive. But as they fronted the building, Lawrence closed upon them, pulling his steed alongside.

"Vanessa, stop! Have you gone mad?"

Delilah shied, stepping sideways as Lawrence's horse crowded her. Leaning out from his saddle, he seized the mare's reins.

"What in blazes is the matter, Vanessa?" he shouted, forcing her and her mount to halt. "I saw you leave the Orangery. Were you looking for me? Has something happened?"

Vanessa sent him a sharp look. Even now the man remained composed, guileful.

"Adrian is wrongfully imprisoned, and well you know it!" she retorted. "I intend to do whatever I must to see him freed. Now, let go the reins!"

"Freed? He *murdered* Olivia. Or have you forgotten that?"

"Why do you lie when we both know he did not?" she spat, amazed that he should continue to feign innocence.

"*Lie?* That is a rash accusation. You know what Auntie wrote in her letter, what she witnessed."

"Yes, I do. All of it! Adrian didn't push Olivia down the stairs. He wasn't even at Sherringham at the time of her death, let alone the tower study. But you were, Lawrence. *You* killed Olivia. And as you said, Lady Gwendolyn—your *mother*—witnessed it all."

Lawrence's features rearranged themselves, his countenance transforming before her, the lines hardening, his eyes growing cold and glinting oddly.

"Vanessa, listen to me . . ." Lawrence implored, the tone of his voice not matching the malignant look that had entered his face. At the same time, he heeled his horse, causing it to jump forward and collide with Delilah. Horseflesh thudded against horseflesh.

"Let go!" Vanessa demanded once more when he did not release her mare's reins.

Lawrence's gaze slipped across the greensward that lay before the mausoleum, to where the land ended abruptly. It was as if she could see his next thought register in his eyes. Far below the ground's edge coursed the River Wye.

As Lawrence shifted his gaze back to Vanessa, a chill rippled through her veins. She didn't care for his expression, one filled with scheming.

"Do you intend to kill me like Bonnie Beckford?" she asked boldly.

His eyes widened a moment then narrowed, his brows deepening over his nose. "Bonnie deserved her fate after exposing me—*us*—to Olivia."

"She deserved to die? To burn beyond recognition in a fire?"

Lawrence's cold-bloodedness astounded Vanessa. She gathered her senses and delayed for time. He still trapped her, clenching Delilah's reins.

"How did you manage it, Lawrence—the carriage mishap? I know about the tampering with the axle, but how did you guarantee the carriage would burst into flames when it went over the ravine?"

The side of his mouth dragged upward in a half-smile.

"Come now, you're a smart woman. You know how volatile certain odorless lighting fluids can be, especially when applied to an abundance of rags. They had to be strategically hidden, of course, but the carriage lamps did the rest."

The man seemed to actually be gloating, Vanessa thought with a renewed sense of dread. Did a demon possess him or was he unbalanced? Was this the "dark side" of which Nanny spoke?

"Why, Lawrence?" Her thoughts sprinted as she continued to play for time. "Why kill Bonnie when you could have placed Olivia's body in the carriage and sent it over the cliff alone?"

"Too untidy, my dear. Much better to have someone else at the reins and not be directly involved with the actual 'accident.' Then too, Bonnie wouldn't have taken kindly to riding with a corpse in the seat beside her. Even she did not know her mistress was dead."

"And so after the deed was done, you raced to the fiery scene, posing as the concerned bystander?" she guessed. "But there must be more. Bonnie wore Olivia's

ring, didn't she? You wanted her body to be mistaken for
Olivia's. Yet you claimed *two* women had left from the
stables. Was there another woman or was that, too, a
lie?"

"Clever girl, aren't you?" he sneered. "If you must
know, there was but one—Bonnie. I needed her to be
identified as Olivia, and I needed to account for the two
women's absence. I could have suggested Olivia was the
one to have fled the accident, believing her husband had
attempted to kill her. But others would have expected
her to return at some time or other and press charges
against him."

"And so you made it appear the maid was the one to
have run away?"

"Precisely. I already had in mind claiming some of
Olivia's costly belongings to be missing, that the maid
had stolen them from Olivia's trunks following the accident. But I didn't know Olivia had taken the Marrable
jewels and added them to her trunk. When I discovered
them near the burning carriage, scattered on the ground,
I realized they offered the perfect motive for the maid—
the temptation of a fortune in jewels."

"But you took the jewels for yourself," Vanessa
charged, growing uneasy, knowing once Lawrence finished his boasting, he would likely decide she knew too
much and must be dealt with. She tried to keep him talking, at the same time glancing around, wondering how
she might make an escape.

"The ring—how did you get Bonnie to wear it? I
mean, it was Olivia's. It was the only thing that could
identify the remains as the viscountess. My God!" she
gasped in sudden horror. "That is why you went down
the ravine—to be assured Bonnie's body—"

"Had burned beyond recognition," Lawrence finished. "You are far too clever for your own good, dear Vanessa."

His thin smile struck fresh fear into her heart.

"The matter of the ring you are not likely to guess. I truthfully told Bonnie her mistress had flung it at me in a fit of rage. Pointing out her employment with the viscountess was at an end—but pledging my own feelings for her—I convinced her to flee to London with the ring. It was heavy with gold and rare stones. She was to sell it and use the proceeds to prepare our love nest. Of course, I insisted she wear the ring to remind her of my devotion and that it might not become lost."

"You are vile!" Vanessa hissed.

"I regret you feel that way, my dear. If you held the same affection for me as you obviously do for my brother—that is, for my *cousin*—then perhaps we could come to an understanding, share a special relationship."

"Like the one you shared with Bonnie?" She yanked at Delilah's reins, trying to free them from Lawrence's grip.

"Vanessa, Vanessa. I can't let you go. You know that."

Vanessa reached for the heavy pouch concealed in her cloak. "Don't you want the Marrable jewels back before you kill me?"

As surprise spread across his face, she seized the pouch by its drawstrings and aimed for Lawrence's jaw, slogging him hard. He yelled out in pain but still did not release his hold on the reins.

Thinking quickly, Vanessa heaved the sack of jewels back toward the mausoleum with all her strength. As Lawrence followed its path, watching where it landed, she cast herself from her sidesaddle, flinging herself off Delilah's back. Breaking into a run, Vanessa headed toward the cliff, hoping it would offer her an escape, and that she'd be able to climb down its side.

From behind, she heard Lawrence's roar, heard the hooves of his steed closing upon her. But the sound doubled, and tripled. It seemed to be coming from a different direction. Looking up, she saw men mounted on horses, rounding the far side of the mausoleum. At their head rode Adrian!

Vanessa's heart leaped for joy, and she veered her steps toward him. But Lawrence kicked into his horse, forcing her back toward the cliff as he moved between them. Reaching inside his jacket, he produced a small gun and aimed it for Adrian's heart.

"You can stop there, *brother*." He spat the word with contempt.

Adrian hard-reined his mount to a halt as did those behind him—Henry, Nigel, Grealey and his officers, and another man whom Vanessa did not recognize.

"It's no use, Lawrence. Give yourself up," Adrian called out. "Your lady friend from the acting troupe has been arrested. She sang like a nightingale. We know the truth—that you possess the Marrable jewels, how you used her to sell them, the disguises she wore to make her look like Olivia, all of it. Damn you, Lawrence! The letter Olivia wrote the night she died—it was meant for you, wasn't it? *You* were her lover. And, as if that wasn't enough, she didn't seem to believe you'd object to fleeing with her or stealing the family jewels."

"I—I didn't know she intended to take them—not until—"

"Not until you scrambled down the ravine to confirm your handiwork. You wanted to be assured Bonnie Beckford was dead."

Lawrence's face contorted, his rage taking hold of him.

"Really, Lawrence"—Adrian went on—"you know better than to confide in your lover when you are drunk."

"That slut!" Lawrence barked. "I'll, I'll . . ."

"Kill her? Like you did the others?" Adrian speared him with his gaze.

Vanessa watched as the men continued their verbal sparring. Seemingly, Lawrence had forgotten her. At least for the moment. Step-by-step, she inched along the rim of the cliff, ever aware of the drop to the river below as she moved toward Adrian and his men. Coming into range of Lawrence's peripheral vision, she squatted down and pressed on.

"You always had everything—the privileged firstborn of the firstborn," Lawrence vented at Adrian. "Did you know, I met Olivia first? That I warmed her bed before you ever climbed between her sheets?"

Adrian's face darkened at that, Vanessa saw, his own temper rising.

"But then you accompanied me to the Drayton's ball that night," Lawrence continued, unrelenting. "Afterward, she had eyes for only you—you and your titles, and lands, and wealth . . . How could I, a mere second son, ever hope to compete?"

Vanessa continued her progress toward Adrian, crawling now. Looking to him, she feared he might do something rash as Lawrence persisted in goading him. A muscle worked along Adrian's jaw, and the muscles of his neck stood out. Though not once did he glance in her direction, she felt certain he knew she was there.

"It was a challenge to seduce Olivia after she became your wife, I'll admit," Lawrence conceded, taunting

Adrian. "But I have pride enough to have preferred she desired me, for myself alone. But now—" His voice broke unexpectedly. "Now I find, even that position I thought to hold as your brother—even that—is not mine."

Adrian's anger visibly wavered, Lawrence's words perplexing him. As the two men's gazes remained locked, Vanessa began to rise. She'd passed Lawrence's position, and prepared to dash the last of the distance to the safety of the others.

"Well, you'll not have it all!" Lawrence bellowed at Adrian. "We were raised as twins, remember? One twin shares the other's pain—so it has been for all time. And pain you shall have, brother. I promise you that. Like me, you will remain a man cursed in love."

Lawrence's gaze swung to Vanessa where she rose to her feet. Realizing his deadly intent, she ran headlong toward Adrian. But Lawrence turned his gun on her and took aim.

"No-o-o. . . ! " Adrian cried out, kicking his horse forward. Hurling himself off his steed, he placed himself between Vanessa and Lawrence's bullet—offirng himself as a human shield, ready to take the lead.

But as Lawrence began to squeeze the trigger, a rush of wind hurtled over the grounds and swirled about Lawrence, jerking his arm to one side and causing the gun to fire. Grealey screamed, toppling from his saddle, then lay lumpishly on the ground, groaning.

To everyone's shock, the wind whipped upward with a choleric wrath, spinning into a funnel-like shape as it continued its assault on Lawrence. As Vanessa and the others watched, the whirlwind began to glow as if from within!

Lawrence flailed madly at his luminous attacker, but

was no match for its seething force as it knocked him from his mount. Scrambling to his feet, he continued to fight as the glowing, swirling wind encompassed him entirely, lifting him off his feet and sweeping him to the cliff's edge.

"H-Help me-e-e . . ." Lawrence cried out, but the wind held him in its reeling grip, glowing even more strongly now as the form of a woman appeared.

"Deceiver . . . Murderer . . ." The words carried upon the wind in a whispery-dry voice. "To the grave . . . To the grave . . ."

The wind turned to a bright ball of light, carrying Lawrence over the edge then evanescing in the blink of an eye. Lawrence dropped from sight, his screams echoing against the night as he plummeted the great distance to the rocks below. Then all was silence, except the rushing of the swollen waters.

Adrian hugged Vanessa against his chest, not allowing her to look and nearly crushing her in his strength. Their lips met and kissed then, their tears mingling.

"Are you all right, my love? Did Lawrence hurt you?" Adrian asked anxiously, his hands moving along her arms and back, assuring she was unharmed.

"I'm all right now, but he would have killed me if you hadn't arrived, darling."

"I'm not so sure about that," Adrian said solemnly looking toward the cliff's edge. "There were other forces at work here tonight."

Motioning over one of the officers, Adrian arranged for several men to make their way down to the river's edge by means of the old path and recover Lawrence's body. It was impossible he'd survived the fall, not with Olivia's enraged spirit ensuring he didn't.

"What of Constable Grealey?" Adrian asked the officer as he began to turn away.

"The bullet caught him in the shoulder and he's lost a good bit of blood, but he should be right as rain in a few weeks."

The officer paused, looking somewhat pale to Vanessa's mind. But then, they'd all been shaken by events this night.

"Yer lordship, I'm more than willing to climb down to the riverbank and do what must be done for yer brother." He shifted from one foot to another and back again. "But, d'ye think it, she—the thing we saw—d'ye think it's down there?"

Adrian clamped a hand on the officer's shoulder. "No. I think she's at peace now."

As the officer withdrew, Adrian turned his gaze back to Vanessa. Sheltering her in his arms, they embraced and kissed once more, then realized they were not alone. As their lips parted, they discovered they had a small audience of three—Henry, Nigel, and the man Vanessa didn't recognize. He appeared in his late twenties, tall, with chestnut hair and a trim mustache that leant him a dashing air.

"Darling, may I present Detective Kincaid of Scotland Yard," Adrian introduced his friend proudly.

"*Cameron* Kincaid?"

"Yes, madam." The detective smiled, bowing politely over her hand. "At your service."

Vanessa smiled too and wildly. "You are just the man I needed to find this night."

The four men exchanged quick glances, Adrian's brows lifting high.

"I—I'm flattered, Mrs. Wynters." Mr. Kincaid darted a look to Adrian then brought his gaze back to Vanessa.

He inclined his head. "Was there something in particular you wished for me to attend to, madam?"

"Yes, but not for me. For Adrian." From the folds of her cloak, Vanessa brought forth Lady Gwendolyn's confession and entrusted it to his hands. "This will clear Adrian from any doubts that might linger concerning Olivia's death."

Vanessa looked to Adrian, her smile wavering somewhat. "It seems your aunt witnessed all that transpired in the tower. But her missive contains more than that. There are things that are surely to come as a shock to you. But she was a good woman, even when her judgment was not perhaps the best."

Now it was Adrian's turn to slant his head and send her a puzzled look.

"Later, darling." She gave a squeeze to his hand. "We'll need ample time to discuss it all and . . ." Her eyes flashed wide. "Oh, no, I forgot—" She spun on her heels and pointed toward the mausoleum.

"There is a large pouch over there by the drive where I tossed it. It contains the missing Marrable jewels! Lawrence had them hidden in the Orangery."

"You've been busy tonight without me, my love." Adrian smiled and kissed her forehead, obviously pleased. He circled his arm about her as Henry and Nigel went in search of the pouch. "Is there anything else you've been about that I should know of?"

Vanessa hesitated thoughtfully. "Well, I'm not sure the marble lid is back correctly on your aunt's tomb—"

She clamped her mouth shut, seeing the renewed look of surprise on Adrian's face.

"I have a feeling we have a long night of explanations ahead of us," he commented dryly, but couldn't conceal his smile.

Vanessa nodded her agreement then stilled, concern filling her. "Lawrence—is it possible he's—"

"No, madam." Cameron shook his head, having moved off momentarily to the cliff's edge and now returning. "It doesn't appear he survived."

He turned to Adrian.

"I'll oversee everything here. Why don't you escort your lady back to the manse and we'll speak later. Your brothers-in-law, Lord Norland and Lord Pendergast, offered their assistance and intend to remain. They said they will be pleased to represent the family in your stead."

"Very well, then. Until later."

Adrian guided Vanessa toward the horses. Locating Delilah, he helped her into the saddle, then surprised her when he climbed up behind her. Holding her against his chest, he let the horse set its pace as they followed the road from the dell and passed the first of the follies.

Vanessa rested against him. They rode in silence at first, but at last she could no longer contain her questions.

"Darling, do not misunderstand. I am thrilled you are free. But, how is it that Grealey released you? And that Mr. Kincaid is here? And why did you choose to approach Sherringham from the direction you did, and not by the main road?"

Adrian began to chuckle. "Do you want answers, or do you want to ask more questions?"

Vanessa shot him a look over her shoulder. "The answers will do."

"Good. The first two can be covered with the same explanation. Grealey had no choice but to release me once Cameron appeared in Hereford this morning. He'd solved the case of the Marrable jewels and arrived with his evidence in tow—a certain young actress of varied talents, among them selling priceless stolen jewels."

"Lawrence's lover?"

"The same. She's now occupying some rather uncomfortable quarters where I'd been previously held."

"But how did Mr. Kincaid find you?"

"He didn't. He encountered Cissy and Majel in town and recognized them from pictures I'd shown him. On learning of my plight, he quickened to my aid, explained matters, and demanded my release. Grealey was not pleased at first, but as I said, he had no choice.

"As to Lawrence, once his role was known, it was easy to guess where he kept the jewels. By coming into Sherringham on the road we did, we'd hoped to keep surprise on our side and, either find the jewels at the Orangery ourselves, or catch Lawrence with them in hand. I can tell you, it was a shock to find the two of you when we rounded the building—and you in imminent danger."

Reining Delilah to a halt before the mansion, Adrian dismounted, then gently lifted Vanessa to the ground. For a moment, they stood unmoving in the circle of each other's arms.

Vanessa gazed up at him, smiling. "I'm glad you recovered from your shock. I fear to think what would have happened to me without you."

"Fear no more, my lady, for there is nothing in this world or the next that can keep me apart from you."

He started to turn and usher her inside the manse, then paused.

"Vanessa, there is one question that remains unanswered between us."

Her eyes widened as his midnight eyes brushed hers, all seriousness returned to them. " 'Between *us*?' "

He nodded. "I offered you a proposal of marriage. Will you marry me?" He quickly placed his forefinger to her lips. "Understand, I have no intention of living without you, nor would I think to keep you as a mere mistress. I want you as my *wife*, Vanessa. I want you by my side always, to love as my viscountess."

"But, Adrian, your heir—"

"I am willing to chance whether we shall have children or none. And if that is God's will . . ."

His gaze dropped momentarily to her hands. Taking them in his, he paused a moment then released a breath.

"With my brother gone, Geoffrey is next in line to inherit." His gaze returned to hers. "Would that trouble you so?"

"Geoffrey?" A smiling warmth spread through her as she envisioned the lad, so like his noble uncle. "Why, no, not at all."

Adrian tipped her chin up with his forefinger. "Then do not torture me a moment longer, my heart. Say 'yes.' Say you will be my wife."

Tears filled Vanessa's eyes, her heart swelling near to bursting as the concerns she'd held and anguished over dissolved to nothingness. Incredibly, the path lay clear before her to claim the man she loved.

"Oh, Adrian, yes"—she flung her arms around his neck—"yes, I will marry you."

Enclosing her fully in his embrace, Adrian's mouth closed over hers and they kissed long and deep. Without breaking their kiss, he caught Vanessa up in his arms and carried her across the portico and over the threshold, into the heart of Sherringham.

Epilogue

"You don't have to look so grim. I'm only taking your photograph," Vanessa commented, rechecking the camera's viewing screen.

Adrian shifted in the chair where he sat posed before the drawing room fireplace, beneath his ancestress's portrait.

"I was striving to look dignified, as befits a married man." He drew himself up stiffly, looking akin to an oak plank, and turned his head considerably to one side.

"Adrian, you've changed the pose!"

Vanessa popped from beneath the focusing cloth and swiftly crossed the distance to him. As she reached out to grasp him by the shoulders and reposition him, he seized her by the waist. A huge grin broke over his face as he pulled her onto his lap.

"You're right, darling. As I've done nothing but smile like a Cheshire since the day of our wedding, I should continue to do so now."

He pressed a kiss to the base of her throat, at the same time sweeping his hand upward, over her breast. Deftly, his fingers began to free the buttons fronting the bodice of her gown.

"Leonine is watching," she warned teasingly as he parted the silken fabric.

"I can't imagine her being shocked. Envious, but not shocked." He dropped kisses to the swelling mounds of her breasts where they rose above her low-cut camisole. "You know, darling, I've been thinking how much I'd enjoy having a boudoir painting done of you, just like Leonine's."

"Adrian, I'm beginning to increase *everywhere*. I'll need more than a spaniel in my lap to hide my enlarging dimensions."

"I want you to hide nothing." His lips continued to warm her flesh. "The sight of you swelling with our child will always fill me with nothing but joy."

Tears sprang to Vanessa's eyes. The discovery of her pregnancy came as a wondrous surprise and particular blessing for both themselves and the extended Marrable family.

The shock of Lawrence's death and the exposure of his part in the deaths of Olivia and her maid—let alone his intentions for Adrian and Vanessa—had left a lingering pall over the family. Even after Lawrence's and Olivia's remains had been lain to rest in the mausoleum, and Bonnie Beckford's disinterred and returned to her relations, even then a heaviness continued to linger in everyone's hearts.

It was to be expected, of course. The Marrable siblings had ever been close and Adrian and Lawrence raised as twins. Nanny, too, was immensely saddened as were those at Sherringham who'd known him.

The pain continued to cut deep. But then, not long after hers and Adrian's wedding, their honeymoon travels were cut short by her recurrent "illness." It was

a doctor in Edinburgh who'd confirmed that, miraculously, Vanessa had conceived.

The prospect of a new little life entering the world—
a child for the House of Marrable—brought vast and
unexpected happiness into their lives and swept away
any shadows that remained.

As Vanessa felt a coolness wash over her nipple,
then felt the heat of Adrian's mouth, she realized he'd
somehow freed one of her breasts from the confines of
her undergarments. The corset was of a looser fit, designed for expectant ladies, and Adrian had insisted
she keep it loosened further. Little wonder, she
thought to herself now as he began to free her other
breast.

"Dearest, someone may enter at any time. It would
be most embarrassing," she protested.

"I've left strict orders with the servants to not enter
unless expressly bidden to do so. There's nothing to
fear, my love," he vowed, bending to her other breast.

"Hello!" a familiar feminine voice rang out from
across the room. "Oh! . . . Sorry. How unforgivably un-
thinking of me to barge in unannounced. I'll wait over
here. Don't rush."

"You're incorrigible, sister," Adrian tossed in a brisk
tone to Cissy as he helped Vanessa put order back to
her clothes.

"I know." Cissy laughed, taking a seat on the sofa
farthest away. "But you must be nice to me. I brought
you a gift."

Minutes later, her cheeks still burning, Vanessa and
Adrian joined the smiling young woman who appeared enormously pleased with herself. A large,
square package rested on her lap.

"All right, Cissy," Adrian said with obvious annoyance. "What is it you wish us to see?"

"Here. Open it for yourself." She held forth the bulky package.

At Adrian's nod, Vanessa accepted it, then lowered herself beside Cissy on the couch. As she pulled away the wrappings, she discovered a beautiful wedding album, covered in white watered taffeta and embellished with artificial orange blossoms and seed pearls.

"Oh, Cissy, it's positively exquisite!" Vanessa said breathlessly. "Adrian, look, your sister has assembled the photographs of our wedding into a special album." She stole a glance of Cissy, then carefully opened the cover. "So, this is why you insisted the prints be delivered to your London residence, even before we'd seen them."

"I couldn't let you see what I was about and spoil the surprise, now could I?" Cissy burst into a brilliant smile, unable to contain herself.

Adrian took a place beside Vanessa and they began to slowly turn one page, then another, finding each enhanced with delicate watercolors by Cissy's own hand.

The wedding itself had been a small, but glorious affair. Vanessa lingered now over the photograph of their wedding party on the cathedral steps. A second assemblage of the family and servants was taken at Sherringham—on the patio, outside the banqueting hall where the wedding luncheon was served.

Vanessa smiled as she looked over the faces—her cousins up from Hampshire, Cissy and Henry, Majel and Nigel, and of course, all of the Norland and Pendergast children. Rascal sat importantly at Geoffrey's side, and Pasha lazed on the low sash of the hall's soaring window. At the heart of the grouping stood

Vanessa and Adrian. They gazed, not at the camera's lens, but at each other, love filling their eyes.

Vanessa looked to Adrian and found him smiling too. But as she returned her attention to the photograph, her gaze alighted on an upper window in the left of the print.

"Oh, no!"

"Darling? What is it?" Adrian slipped his arm about her at once.

"There . . . Do you see?"

Her pulses quickening, she pointed to where a luminous light filled a portion of the window. There appeared to be a figure in the glowing mist—that of a man . . . or a woman perhaps . . . ?